76-101692
DN
11-5-84

Music
and the
Culture
of Man

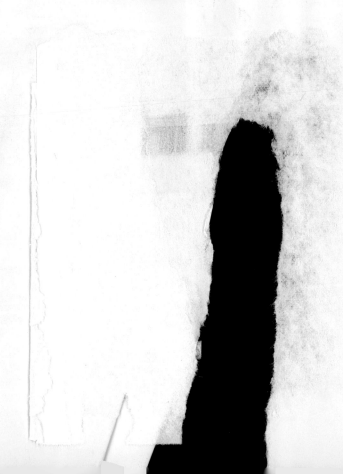

New York, Chicago, San Francisco, Atlanta, Dallas, Montreal, Toronto, London, Sydney

Music and the Culture of Man

Sharon Scholl and Sylvia White

HOLT, RINEHART AND WINSTON, INC.

Preface

The purpose of this book is to develop a comprehensive view of music as part of the cultural processes of the western world. Its historical nature is not dependent upon a strict chronology of events, but upon a developmental consideration of selected streams of thought that occur within the time span of each chapter. It is the intention of the authors to consider music as an integral part of the corporate life of man, rather than as the isolated activity of remarkable individuals. This book cannot replace the necessarily detailed account required for the music specialist, but it can enlarge upon this more technical viewpoint by presenting a history of music in its broad cultural context. It is intended for the non-specialist who wishes to understand some of the possible implications of music within the community of man.

Music and the Culture of Man not only takes the social history and ideology of each period into consideration, but it also structures the musical materials by reference to general cultural patterns. Music is thus considered within the context of the patronage system of the Baroque period, the composite imagery of ninteenth-century Romanticism, and the dominant cultural characteristics of the twentieth century. The practice of disregarding, to some extent, a sequential development in order to investigate the dominant imagery of an era has been found useful in literature and the visual arts, but has been used less frequently in music. It is therefore important that the reader note those sections in which music is not presented in an historical sequence but rather as one element within a specific ideology.

The book is necessarily selective; it does not pretend to be either a thorough or complete account. The choice of topics is not dependent upon

musical significance alone, but upon the importance of any individual movement within a total human context. Thus music of the Protestant Reformation is given a more detailed consideration here than would be appropriate
in a more specific musical history. Movements are chosen for consideration
with reference to those parallel developments in the visual arts and literature that would most likely be represented in a composite humanities
course. In addition, some musical forms that have previous or subsequent
manifestations are summarized in one particular section. The piano sonata,
for example, is presented in the chapter on Romanticism, although it has a
much more spacious temporal history.

The analyses of selected compositions are intended as an introduction
to methods of musical comprehension and verbalization. They are not
formulated in terms of structure and style elements alone, but also in relationship to human experiences and processes of visualization. They are
especially written for listeners who have little training in musical formal-
ities, but who are able to understand music in terms of a broader human
appeal. The usefulness of these analyses depends completely upon the
simultaneous hearing of the works themselves. Among the many representative works for each period suggested in the appendix are all the works
considered specifically in the text. Every effort should be made to collect
and listen to those compositions that serve as the focus of individual
streams of ideas.

Finally, this book suggests certain relationships between music, the
other arts, and society; these may be extended by many examples and
contradicted by others. The book as a whole should serve not so much as a
recounting of fact, but as a point of departure from which a broad spectrum
of musical experiences may originate.

The authors would like to thank Professor Barney Childs of Deep
Springs College, Professor Laurence MacDonald of Flint Community College, Professor W. F. Eifrig, Jr., of Valparaiso University, and Professor
Armin Watkins of the University of South Florida for their extremely valuable comments and criticisms, which fundamentally conditioned the style
and content of the present book.

Sharon Scholl
Jacksonville University

Sylvia White
Florida State University

Jacksonville, Florida
January 1970

Contents

Contents

List of Illustrations

Music
and the
Culture
of Man

1
The Ancient World

MUSIC AMONG PRIMITIVE SOCIETIES

The beginnings of music, like the origins of man, are shrouded in mystery. No single theory of musical evolution can be accepted as absolute because the earliest findings have not been preserved in sufficient quantity, and, therefore, we can draw no positive conclusions. Yet sources do agree that man's earliest awareness of music may have been born of his associating an emotional satisfaction with the phenomenal sound that accompanied his need for self-expression through body motion. Since movements such as hand-clapping and foot-stamping are audible, man's unique ability to coordinate such movements eventually may have produced a rhythmic consciousness. And there are some authorities who have traced the origin of music to the powers of vocalization, which are also common to speech. But whatever stimulated the need for self-expression, the sound that man heard and felt concerned him, whether its source stemmed naturally from within or mechanically from outside his own body.

From the first artistic records drawn across cave walls in a panorama of line and color, little musical significance is recognizable, with the exception of the innate desire to communicate. The basic naturalism—the freedom and spaciousness of early man's world concept in these cave drawings—led scholars to investigate the means by which such works

1

were produced. In the process, the very earth from which primitive man obtained paints and implements yielded the crudely preserved clues that document his life experiences. Digging in such places as cave tunnels and swamps, scientists have unearthed enough artifacts to piece together a concept of man's way of life during the waning centuries of the Ice Age. One piece of evidence of a primitive encounter with the art of music was found among such cave ruins and has been tentatively identified as a bone flute. The later Neolithic societies, with polished stone tools and more stable tribal organizations, offered a more fertile field for examining the status of music among the primitive groups of the prehistoric world. Dating from this period (8000–4000 B.C.), a pottery drum in the shape of two connected circles was uncovered in the southern part of the Soviet Union. Another clay drum shaped like a goblet was identified as a relic of the same primitive period, and bone whistles with five finger holes cut into the tubes were found in the vicinity of Hohenzollern, Germany.

Although enough evidence supports the fact that Neolithic man attempted to convert clay and stone into implements of sound, much of our knowledge about primitive life and art has been hypothesized from the study of contemporary primitive societies. This study, however, may not be entirely accurate, since it is difficult to distinguish those authentically primitive groups that have not been influenced by contemporary civilizations. The possibility of primitive adaptations of the songs and instruments of a more advanced culture is always recognized. But regardless of its form or function, music-making, is conceded to be universal among men to a degree matched by few other practices. Common musical attitudes that differ only in degrees of emphasis evolve out of the nature common to men everywhere.

Primitive cultures, in particular, weave music into the very fabric of existence in a manner unknown to higher civilizations. Music accompanies all activities—from the early morning hunt to the last lullaby crooned to a sleepy baby. Primitive man believed that through music he could control the elements, insure his survival, and revere unknown forces. Thus, songs consistently reflect human belief and experience. Because of their high regard for the mystical elements of music, the Yuman tribes of Arizona and California accept only those songs that originate in dreams as being true.

The traditional aspect of music making is so valued that tribal melodies change very little over the centuries. Like the repetitious use of visual motifs in guardian figures for the dead, the accepted musical motifs are never discarded as out of date. Innovations are made only by using the patterns of tone and rhythm in a slightly different arrangement. Songs are often personal creations in the sense that tribe members can recall who created each song. In many instances each person has his own songs —those he composes and those he buys; no member uses the songs of another member of the tribe. Some particularly expressive songs are adopted for the use of the whole group.

Unlike higher civilizations, primitive tribes do not primarily associate music with entertainment. However, even as significant spiritual truths are often translated into decorative objects, so many serious ceremonial songs may serve to entertain, as well as to educate. Only in highly organized tribes are professional musicians recognized. And when they are, they are often designated to sing the praises of the local chieftain.

In the tribal rituals of war and love, music is an indispensible ingredient. Men could hardly go off to battle without the shouting songs that are designed to raise their emotional level to the proper fighting pitch. In rituals of love, women are charmed by sincere songs sung in their honor or by a decorous melody played on the flute. People of all ages listen with rapt attention to tales told by the local storyteller, who punctuates his narrative with appropriate musical selections.

By far the most important use of music in both past and present primitive societies is its use in religious ritual. Civilized religions have preserved some of the most ancient customs in the rendition of their solemn liturgies. The role of the priest as a solo singer answered by responses from the congregation is of prehistoric origin. With the settled tribal life and its farming and cattle breeding came an awareness of man's vulnerability to the chance acts of nature and his fellow man. The concept of disembodied forces that could bring blessings or havoc was an early and universal recognition that necessitated the development of means for propitiating these forces. Idols, offerings, protective amulets, and musical charms became the essential ingredients of this religion of animism. Another important concept was the idea that people might also be inhabited by spirits which, at the demise of the body, might escape to do ill. Thus the placating of the spirits of ancestors became another common branch of religious consciousness. Music assumed the role of a magical power that could exorcise an evil spirit and relieve the fear of the unknown. The instruments used to produce this musical magic were sacred objects to be guarded jealously. To the violator, unauthorized handling could mean punishment by death.

The consciousness of unseen forces appears to have marked the beginning of a transition toward an art that was symbolic and abstract. Exaggeration of naturally observed forms was the primary artistic technique used as a magic wish device to bring about some envisioned result. The *Venus of Willendorf* (c. 10,000 B.C.)—a small pebble shaped in the form of a woman—was used in a magic fertility ritual. Music was often used as a hypnotic force; the very monotony of repeated tones could induce a state of trance. It could also induce an opposite reaction, particularly in connection with dance; a gradually increased pace of sound and movement could produce a high state of physical and emotional tension. Tunes as well as visual objects were used as magic charms. And the healing ceremony depended heavily on the curative powers of music and dance for its effect.

Through the ages, primitive man developed an astonishing array of tone-making devices; the percussion instruments, in particular, were variable and ingenious. Rattles made of strung deer hooves or turtle shells were common to North America. Log drums and trumpets made of conch shells were used by the ancient Indian cultures of Mexico. Whistles existed in all sizes and shapes, and were sometimes decorated with carved birds. A small bundle of bound reeds called the panpipes were common to most of Africa and Asia. Instruments shared the religious significance of much primitive music, although vocal music was the primary vehicle for the expression of religious ideas. As in the case of songs, individual instruments were often reserved for the exclusive use of one specific group of people. They were assigned not only specialized functions, but distinctive attributes as well. The flute gained a widespread symbolic connotation as representing the breath of life. Music was used traditionally to enhance with special grandeur those objects and actions that were part of the mysteries of life and death.

MUSIC IN EARLY CIVILIZATIONS

Civilization implies a number of important changes from the state of primitive tribal life. Such changes are marked by a great increase in the complexity of social organization with the rise of occupational specialists, an improved communication system, new tools and inventions, monetary and economic revolutions, and a gain in the rate of speed at which significant events occur. The early civilizations along the Tigris-Euphrates, Nile, Indus, and Yangtse rivers were made up of pioneers who had a life style that later generations would refine into complex patterns of human activity. Among their arts, music, in particular, transcended the level of primitive thinking and adopted the disciplining qualities of law and logic.

The oldest records of organized musical systems and practices (dating from about 3000 B.C.) have been found both in Sumeria and Egypt. One of the most ancient musical relics is a Sumerian eleven-stringed harp from 2600 B.C. The earliest known example of musical notation (800 B.C.) is a Sumerian hymn on the creation of man written in the familiar cuneiform symbols. The impossibility of deciphering the tune has led researchers to believe that each symbol represents a whole melodic fragment belonging to a large repertoire of traditional melodic formulas. Babylonian plaques and seals occasionally featured shepherds strumming on long, banjo-like instruments or blowing on simple flutes. Such relics attest to the existence of folk music as far back as the third millenium B.C. But it is the role of music in the ritual of church and state and as an intellectual discipline that has made its history.

Extant records tell of organized groups of singers performing in the temples under the direction of a training officer. The guilds of temple singers developed into a learned community devoted to codifying liturgical practices. These temple associations may well have been the world's first schools of advanced learning. Yet the Sumerian gods were deities of the earth, and their religious conception maintained important links with primitive tribal life. Ramman, the thunder-god, and Ea, the sea-god, had to be propitiated in their destructive power by an appropriate musical utterance. Even the symbolism of the reed-pipe as Ramman's breath and the drum as the roar of Ea form a continuity with earlier primitive thinking. A hymn ascribed to the great Sumerian king, King Gudea, attributed to music the power to fill the temple court with joy, to calm a troubled heart, and to chase away gloom. These benefits were provided for the gods by large ensembles of singers and instrumentalists. Excavations in the royal tombs at Ur unearthed a large temple harp with a golden bull and decorative shell inlays showing symbolic animals performing ritual acts. The harp was so closely related to the priestly utterances of holy laws that it was regarded as the instrument of the gods. The full temple orchestra was composed of a small seven-stringed harp, a two-stringed lute (ancestor of the modern guitar), and a number of reed instruments and flutes. In addition, a large choir of singers was part of the musical complement.

Religious ceremonies were daily observances that included instrumental music, traditional prayers, and spoken or sung hymns. Priests were the most prominent citizens in ancient Sumer because they knew how to contact the gods and insure their protective influences for the people. By the time of the rise of the Babylonian Akkad Dynasty, kings had assumed a dominant role, and the social function of music became strongly related to the kingly image. The private schools of the time taught writing, religion, history, mathematics, and music. Women, in particular, were encouraged to learn the art of music. In fact, some early pictorial records of musical ensembles show the participants to be women, eunuchs, or blind people—all coincidentally unfit for direct military or civil service to the king.

Assyrian musical practices can be reconstructed with some accuracy because of a series of well-preserved sculptural friezes showing processions of musicians playing on typical instruments of that time. On one section, the artist pictured an Assyrian king and his queen who are being entertained at dinner by a harpist and a drummer. Another segment reveals the prominent role of the royal animal hunts in the visual arts. The aftermath of one such hunt pictures the king pouring a solemn libation over the slain wild bull while two musicians pluck the strings of a zither. The Assyrian sculptor was meticulous in his representation of such events, recording such details as the varying number of strings on different types of harps and the distinct dress of the chief musician. Popular festivals were not neglected as a subject for the arts. One frieze pictures two mimes dressed in animal skins (reminiscent of primitive masked dancers) and accompanied in their movements by a man playing the lute. The most extensive of the musical reliefs shows a procession of eleven musicians plucking stringed instruments, blowing double pipes, and beating a drum with the flat of the hand (Figure 1.1). They are followed by a group of clapping, singing people going to welcome warriors returning from battle. The louder instruments of the brass family are conspicuously missing from military bands; rather, they are pictured as being used to

Figure 1.1 Court Orchestra of Elam. [British Museum].

give signals to warriors on the battlefield or to workmen at large construction projects.

When the Chaldeans inherited the cultural legacy of Babylon, the study of music became part of the intellectual tradition of the sciences. Devoted students of astrology and mathematics, they first sensed the relationship between the order of the cosmos and the ratio of string length that produced various pitches. The numbers four and seven, with their symbolic references to seasons and planets, were probably used as the number of pitches in their tonal system or scale. In turn, this ancient intellectual tradition provided the foundation for Greek musical thought.

In Old Kingdom Egypt, both royal and priestly functions were interlocked in the person of the king, whose dominance served to secure the character and continuity of that society. The necessities of a divine monarchy conditioned the status of the artist; he who could best serve the aims of the god-king was well rewarded. The architect, who insured immortality to the ruler by providing his spirit with a resting place, was given a high position and granted the privilege of sharing in the death cult. Small tombs of the architects huddled close to the great pyramids; memorial statues of the deceased showed them holding the measuring instruments of their profession.

Ancient Egypt maintained a strong literary orientation; honored scribes were often sons of pharoahs. The business and commerce of that bustling kingdom depended on written records. The contentment of the pharoah's spirit was secured through the rituals recorded in the *Book of the Dead*. In several written sources, artists were described as part of a lower social strata on a level with weavers and dyers. Undoubtedly both sculptors and painters achieved some artistic independence as members of a craft guild that must have been in demand for decorating the monumental buildings then being erected. However, the aim of their patrons was essentially static and dominated by tradition. The end result was a dedication to the preservation of existing patterns of life in stereotyped visual representations. High technical proficiency, rather than individualism of style, was encouraged. The course of the visual arts was deeply affected by the rise of Akhnaton and his cultivation of a more human image through a style of naturalism. However, within this whole eventful sequence of history, nothing in the musical sphere could match the legacy of the visual arts.

In Egypt, as in other ancient nations, the representations of musical practices in sculpture and painting constitute the most valuable record of musical life. One temple scene showed a priest offering incense to the accompaniment of a harpist, two flutists, and a player of the *tamboura* (a long-necked stringed instrument). The *sistrum* (a metal rattle) was especially characteristic of high priestesses and women members of the royal household. The harp was the central ceremonial instrument, and it was made in a variety of sizes and shapes. Small ones were carried on the shoulder, while the largest ones rested on the ground and loomed over the heads of the players. Harps provided instrumental interludes and aided the chanting of hymns. The Egyptian military band resembled a modern band in its inclusion of trumpets, drums, and cymbals. The artist who pictured a military band showed only five players, but they may have represented the instrumental distribution of an assumed larger group.

The Egyptians were particularly fond of music as home entertainment. A painting in a tomb at Thebes showed a group of girls playing the harp, *tamboura*, double pipes, and lyre for the entertainment of dinner guests (Figure 1.2). Dance was very popular and was performed by men and women from many stations in life. Descriptions by such Greeks as Herodotus and Plato indicate that the musical life of the ancient Egyptians was both abundant and of high quality. Plato admired their use of music within the educational system. Unfortunately, the art of music cannot persist without a codified system of notation to perpetuate its formal structure and performance practices. Thus, the melodic and rhythmic components and the emotional connotations that belonged to ancient Egyptian music must remain an enigma.

Figure 1.2 Egyptian Musicians, Dynasty XVIII. (From Thebes). [Courtesy, The Metropolitan Museum of Art].

The Swedish Egyptologist Säve-Söderbergh has given a colorful description of the celebration of the New Year's holiday with its various artistic accouterments. In the temples, the images of the gods were removed with great ceremony, carefully cleaned, and restored to their places in a joyful procession. The pharoah received his annual gifts and bestowed golden necklaces as tokens of his continuing good favor. Home festivities were central to the occasion, and in the upper-class homes no effort was spared to make the day a memorable one. Vases of sweet oil were often given as presents. The center of interest was the banquet, which was accompanied by music and dancing. It often featured the singing of a blind bard who accompanied himself on a lyre. All the delight of the senses and the beauty of the cool villa in its garden setting were reflected in this song for the New Year:

What a glorious day is this evening
   and tomorrow we shall say once again,
"Fresh is the hour of morning,
   lovlier still than yesterday's.
Because of its beauty,
   let us celebrate still another feast!"
Rejoice without worries,
   while singers exult and dance
   to make your day a festival.[1]

GREEK ROOTS OF WESTERN MUSIC

Any person who has been reared within the framework of western culture probably has some right to list Greece as his birthplace, for the fundamental attitudes that have since characterized western civilization were formed among the people of the ancient city-states. The Greeks were heirs of the past in almost every aspect of their culture. Yet, in many respects, their basic intuitions about the nature of man and his place in the world were strikingly different from those of their predecessors. Far behind the unfolding of Athenian culture in the fifth century B.C. lay a history marked with high civilizations and a tradition of dominance by war and seamanship. Mycenaean forebears left their imprint in the huge fortifications and circular tombs regarded by later Greeks as the work of mythical giants. The labyrinthine palaces of Crete left ample evidence of industrious, imaginative people who created a literate mercantile society. Classical Greeks inherited more than traditional gods from the Aegean kingdoms, as their life style was inherently marked by the pattern of the earlier merchant aristocracy and its independence of absolute gods or tyrannical kings.

During its archaic period, Greek artistic technique was greatly influenced by Egypt; the geometric vases reflected the stylization of their Egyptian models. The square blocks of Egyptian monumental sculpture with the predictable pose and wistful smile were the models for pre-classical Greek sculpture. Yet the direct stare of the large eyes and the implied movement of the figure uncontained by enclosing stone revealed

---

1 Torgny Säve-Söderberg, *Pharoahs and Mortals* (London: Robert Hale, Ltd., 1961; Indianapolis: Bobbs-Merrill Co., Inc., 1961); p. 124 (London), p. 218 (Indianapolis).

10   a typical Greek individualism. The Doric column may have followed the striated design of Mesopotamian reed-bundle columns and copied the stonecraft of Egyptian builders, but the resulting building, with its rhythmic proportions and inviting human scale, was a product of the Greek mentality. Like the visual arts, Greek music owed most of its original materials to previous cultures. The Greeks were known to boast of the eastern origin of their music and adhered with particular tenacity to the five-tone pentatonic scale common to eastern nations. They also used the very short tonal intervals (quarter tones) ordinarily employed in the music of those nations. All of their musical instruments had been known in some form both in Mesopotamia and in Egypt. Even the beloved *kithara* had been pictured on an Assyrian frieze as part of an army band. The same thoughtful, systematic self-awareness that pervaded the Greek visual arts endowed the Greek musical practices which became the mainspring for western musical development.

The subject of Greek music is at once tantalizing and forbidding. Judging from the attention given to it by ancient philosophers and theorists, not to mention enthusiastic accounts of the effects of music as described by other writers, Greek music must have reached a very high level of cultivation. However, the actual remains of that music are so few in number and so fragmentary in condition that to gain extensive knowledge of the nature and variety of Greek musical practices is all but impossible. Extant literature asserts that: Euclid (*c.* 300 B.C.) wrote on the acoustical theories of Pythagoras (*c.* 550–500 B.C.) as they relate to musical sound; Plato (427–347 B.C.) attributed ethic values to music; Aristotle (384–322 B.C.) commented on the uses of music in society; and Aristoxenus reformulated musical theory in the fourth century. The famous mathematician-astronomer Ptolemy (127–151 A.D.) wrote the *Harmonics,* which remains the most systematic account of the Greek theoretical scale system. Aside from such limited primary sources, other data have been extracted from miscellaneous writings which mention music. Many works of art show musical activity. Unlike other ancient civilizations, the Greeks did not rely totally on oral tradition, but deliberately sought means to record their musical ideas in some relatively permanent form. Even so, the ravages of time have left later generations with only the remains of the Greek musical legacy.

The origins of Greek music were couched in a mythological form bearing traces of historical truth. The Muses, who lived around Mount Olympus in northern Greece, were the guardians of study, memory, and song. They inspired the heroes Amphion and Orpheus to conquer life and death by the power of music. Such a myth supported the ritual magic aspects of music common to most primitive and ancient peoples. The Mycenaean settlers on the coast of Asia Minor preserved the ancient heritage of the Greek mainland and also incorporated into their culture the many philosophical, poetic, scientific, and musical systems that abounded east and west of the Aegean. But a total integration never occurred, so that certain differences in taste, character, and musical practices persisted in Greek life.

The lyre, a small harp-like instrument, was especially associated with the Dorian tribes of the mainland and with the cult of Apollo. The Greeks attributed an ethos or ethical character to music played on the lyre. The double reed instrument from Phrygia, the *aulos,* was the musical symbol of the god Dionysus and was associated with heightened emotion and un-restrained passion. To the Athenians of the Golden Age, the lyre connoted stability and moderation, while the *aulos* symbolized the excesses of the senses. These esthetic differences were illustrated by the story of Marsyas and Apollo. The mortal Marsyas discovered an *aulos* that had been dis-carded by Athena. Stirred by its sound, he challenged the immortal Apollo to a musical contest. As patron of the rational arts of reflection, the god chose to play the lyre, and in winning the contest proved the ascendence of mind over emotion. The fact that Apollo was the patron of both art and science revealed the Greek penchant for systematic art. This con-trolled intellectualism and restraint, which had grown out of a recognized social need for moderation, eventually flowered in the sculpture of Poly-clitus (450–420 B.C.) and in the philosophical systems of the Golden Age.

The dawn of a historical Greek musical tradition began with Homer (*c.* 800 B.C.). A half-legendary descendant of Orpheus, Homer was symbol-ically blind as an outward sign of his inner spiritual insight. Homer's *kithara* was derived from the lyre of Apollo, and his instruction came from the Muses. Homer's function was less that of the primitive musician-priest and more that of a bard for a feudal monarchy. He represented the tradi-tion of individualism and the glorification of the hero so apparent even in that archaic period. Homer's purpose was essentially that claimed by the later Roman poet Virgil—"to perpetuate the achievements of a people, the lords of the world." The Homeric style was a mixture of current and leg-endary history and myth within the framework of a ballad. His epics were a product of the Ionian environment, which was a composite of many national and ethnic qualities. As for their rendition, no unanimous under-standing prevails with regard to the relationship between the verbal epic and the music to which it was sung. Music and poetry were almost syn-onymous, and together exerted a considerable emotional and esthetic appeal. The melody may have resembled such ancient song forms as the Indian Raga in its use of independent melodic fragments subject to a variety of combinations. In like manner, Greek architecture was always predictable in content, but variable in arrangement. The simple *kithara* used by Homer evolved into a complicated instrument with as many as eleven strings. It may have been used merely to reinforce the melody, or it may have added short solo interludes.

Figure 1.3   Greek Vase painting (Alcaeus and Sappho). [Hirmer Fotoarchiv Munchen].

The rise of lyric poetry gave another dimension to the role of music. It expressed less formal and more personal views of love, war, politics, and related popular themes. The poetic form drew its name from the lyre by which it was accompanied, and it proved especially attractive to the aristocratic amateur. The Ionian Greeks were fond of the lyric movement, with its high individualism, whereas the Dorian centers on the mainland favored music that emphasized the communal spirit. The notable musical culture of the Greek islanders began with Terpander of Lesbos (*c.* 675 B.C.). His powers were reputedly so great that he was invited to Sparta to quell a riot. The lyric movement coincided with the rise of great urban centers such as Miletus, and the resulting cultivation of the artistic tastes of an aristocracy supported by commercial wealth. Poets such as Sappho (620–565 B.C.) and Anacreon (570–480 B.C.) revealed the same spirited elegance as the intricately decorated goddesses of the archaic *kore* statues. Born of Aeolian nobility, Sappho lived on the island of Lesbos, the cultural center of her people. She and her fellow poets were devoted to the color, vitality, and sensual pleasure of human experience to an extent not encountered again in western history until the troubadour movement in the Middle Ages. Aeolian women had much greater freedom than those confined either to the military discipline of Sparta or the oriental cloistering practiced in much of neighboring Ionia. The high regard in which women were held was evidenced by the fact that among the ancient islanders, the mother goddesses were the major cult images. Yet even with its sensual imagery, the rhythm and symmetry of lyric poetry reflected an Apollonian restraint. Sappho (Figure 1.3) wrote hymns, marriage songs, funeral songs, and a host of social testimonies for her young students to sing. Among the most famous of her poems is one beginning:

> O life divine! sit before
> Thee while thy liquid laughter flows
> Melodious, and to listen close
> To rippling notes from love's full score.
>
> O music of thy lovely speech!
> My rapid heart beats fast and high,
> My tongue-tied soul can only sigh,
> And strive for words it cannot reach.[2]

Part of the lasting charm of the lyric poems was their subtle sense of meter. Poetry was strongly oriented toward the quantitative accent, in which stress was interpreted as the length of time a syllable was held. Poetry conceived in such a way was already half music. The rhythmic modes described by later theorists were simply much-used poetic meters based on varying combinations of long and short syllables. Greek poetry was oriented toward music because the natural accents of the words were normally indicated through changes in vocal pitch. Thus the range of rhythmic and melodic resources was varied and flexible enough to have attracted master craftsmen to the form.

2 David M. Robinson, trans., *Sappho and Her Influence* (New York: Cooper Square Publishers, Inc., 1924), p. 56. By permission of Marshall Jones Company of Boston, Mass.

14   The Greeks used a multitude of musical instruments, most of which dated back to the earliest civilizations. The double pipe form of the *aulos* was common to both Assyrians and Egyptians. As the *kithara* added strings and grew larger, so the *aulos* added holes to produce a greater number of pitches. Like the bagpipe, the *aulos* was used to play a melody on one pipe and a constant drone on the other. A very simple version of a wind instrument was the pan-pipe or *syrinx*; it consisted of a group of hollow-reeds wrapped together. In the Orient, such bundles of reeds were attached to a gourd so that the player's breath could collect and enter many pipes at once. With an expansion in its size the ancient Greek organ developed into the *hydraulis,* which utilized water pressure to force air through the pipes. Rhythm instruments were plentiful, since the basis of both poetry and dance was rhythm. Much of the literature of Greek musical theory dealt with the interesting rhythmic problems provoked by their language and habits of accentuation. Castanets, cymbals, and tambourines were widely used and often pictured on vases as part of many festive occasions. No dinner party was quite complete without singers, dancers, or musicians. And some form of lyre was always popular for home entertainment.

      All the resources of the Greek arts were combined in the drama. The brilliant tone of the *aulos* was particularly suited to provide the accompaniment for the chorus. The *aulos* was capable of many nuances of performance, and its tone quality was highly suitable to express great passion and excited states of mind. Drama originated as a celebration of the birth of Dionysus, whose symbols were the *aulos* and the grapevine. It featured a circular chorus of men and boys who sang hymns and danced in praise of the god. The partially improvised cult song known as the *dithyramb* developed into an extended form that attracted such writers as Pindar (522-448 B.C.). The artistic level of his great choric hymns matched the heights established by the plays of the Greek dramatists. Even in its golden age, the drama still included the poetry, music, and the dance of the Dionysian chorus. Because they were rooted in this ancient tradition, the works of Aeschylus exerted their main appeal in their union of poetry and music. By the time of Sophocles, the requirements of plot, action, and characterization had begun to be more important.

      Because of its religious origin, the drama maintained a fundamental subject orientation toward such themes as man's relations to the gods. One reason for the organization of earlier religious celebrations into stable artistic forms lay in the wish of the governing authorities to control the more orgiastic aspects of the worship of Dionysus. Housewives, in particular, used certain annual religious celebrations as excuses for inordinately wild behavior.

      Even after the worship of Dionysus became a state-supported observance, many other cults maintained separate ceremonies, using music to accompany sacrifices and to induce the mystical exaltation necessary for their initiation rites. In the restrained cult of Apollo, the *paean* or hymn of praise was chanted by the whole company of worshipers in a choral dance. Holy baths of a baptismal nature were common to the cults of Artemis and Cybele, and were accompanied by the sound of flutes and drums. The Egyptian cults of Isis and Serapis, with their attendant chanted hymns and playing of wind instruments and rattles, also flourished in Greece. Music independent of a poetic text was gradually realized in drama, religious cults, and in the musical competition of the Olympic games.

Eastern Europe's emerging empires, transformed by the Hellenistic culture of Alexander the Great, kept the musical practices of Greece alive for many generations. However, the theory of music, as propounded by leading philosophers, formed the most significant legacy to the West. These writings described musical tradition as it had existed before the fall of Athens. The theory of music, one aspect of the scientific systems of the fourth century B.C., was regarded as an important reflection of the natural world. The earliest theoretical concepts can be traced to the discoveries of the mathematician Pythagoras, who measured the relationship between the length of a plucked string and its resultant pitch. Thus, Pythagoras provided one of the few demonstrable links between the world of abstract ideas and that of common experience. The scientific tradition initiated by the Pythagoreans reached its culmination in the writings of Aristotle. Mystical number symbolism, which related music to the cosmic forces of order, also began with Pythagoras and culminated in the writings of Plato.

Both Plato and Aristotle agreed that music was one of the requisites of the ideal state. Plato, in his *Republic*, and Aristotle, in his *Politics*, described the nature of music and its role in human affairs. As a mathematician, he regarded music as part of a universal force of numerical relationships, linking all phenomena and serving as a symbol of the suprasensible realm of ideas. Plato believed in music of the old tradition, inextricably linked with a text that taught the virtues every citizen was to possess. For this reason, music was the initial enterprise of his visionary educational system. Since his observations convinced him that not all music was equally good cultural propaganda, he developed a doctrine of *ethos*, which was an evaluation of the effects of music on the soul. *Ethos* reflected a markedly aristocratic concept of music, while perpetuating age-old beliefs in its magical healing powers. Music was said to spur men to action, to strengthen the whole being, or, conversely, to create mental instability, rendering the hearer irresponsible for his actions.

The interaction of musical elements that produced *ethos* is not sufficiently understood; however, the effect was certainly attributable to more than a simple scale arrangement of tones. The pitch level was significant in such an effect, the lower tones being calmer than high or shrill tones.

16   The same melody could sound slightly different in another tonal range. Plato preferred the Dorian mode or scale of tones because it lay directly in the middle of the Greek Greater Perfect System of available tones. The Dorian effect of moderation and good balance was associated with the *kithara* and the cult of Apollo. Classical sculpture of the Golden Age also claimed the same *ethos*. Each mode derived from the Greater Perfect System was organized around a tone situated in the middle of its pitch range; melodies composed in that mode gravitated to this tonal center. In addition to the nature of their scale structure, melodies were subject to other variables—such as the tempo of performance, the subject of the text, and the instrument used for accompaniment. The possible alterations of such variables could very well have been the basis for hearing qualitative differences between melodies.

Modern writers stress the theoretical nature of the Greater Perfect System and its derived repertoire of scales. Purely theoretical scale systems were probably constructed for speculative value alone, and were not meant to be understood as descriptions of actual musical practices. Since the Greeks, by nature, were fond of abstraction, they did not rely upon practical application as the measure of value. Aristoxenus, a fourth century theorist, was the son of a professional musician, and thus was probably aware of the discrepancy between theory and practice. Therefore, his description of the Greek musical system has been regarded as the most well-balanced interpretation available. Aristoxenus defined the exact or consonant intervals as the fourth, fifth, and octave. He felt that the ear could detect these tonal relationships with accuracy, whereas other intervals were not so obvious.

The interval of a fourth (a tetrachord) traditionally formed the basic unit of the Greek scale system; the eight tones of the longer octave scale were formed of connecting tetrachords. The two octaves that comprised the range of tones available in the Greater Perfect System were dominated by a pitch at the very center called the *mese*. The Dorian scale was composed of the seven tones immediately adjacent to this *mese*. Gradually, other patterns of two continuous tetrachords were selected from the entire system, but each probably used the same tonal relationships as the Dorian scale. One significant difference was that the *mese* occurred in a higher or lower position from scale to scale.

Each of the scales or modes was named for a dominant ethnic group within Greek culture. The Dorian mode represented the mainland Greeks; the Lydian and Phrygian represented colonies in Asia Minor. The versions of these scales that extended into a lower tonal range prefixed their name with the term "hypo." Thus some scales were known as Hypodorian or Hypophrygian. Even more flexibility was potentially available through certain traditionally practiced vocal inflections within each tetrachord. By the use of intermediate tones between the pitches of the mode, a singer could create certain delicate nuances of expression to enhance the meaning of the text. Yet also in this instance the relationship between theory and practice is exceedingly vague.

Participation in musical activities that molded the character was sufficient for the general populace in Plato's ideal state. But the rulers were to be introduced to the mathematical aspects of music as a science because it served as training for the comprehension of ultimate causes. In the *Timaeus,* Plato recorded his vision of the whole cosmos as regulated by the same proportions as the musical scale. The fixed stars, the movement of the planets, and the four elements of the universe were exemplified in the vibrational ratios between pitches. In Plato's system, music was a natural accouterment of many levels of thought. At its highest level of conception it was a metaphysical emanation of the archetypal Idea. At a more functional level it was a contemplative link between the physical and the abstract world. At the lowest level it was a pervasive element capable of forming the character of the young and the less intelligent.

Aristotle held a less mystical view of music, regarding it as one among many aspects of natural phenomena. The use of music in the attainment and exercise of virtue was his prime consideration. The key to a good society lay in the nature of man himself; the role of music was to support the virtuous elements of his nature. Aristotle revealed his own aristocratic temperament by his insistence that the practical study of music as an occupation was inferior to its use in the quest of virtue as part of the life style of a free man. The key to the role of music in the state was its ethical, moral character—its *ethos.* Although music might not exemplify the veritable harmony of the spheres, it could imitate moral states and the actions of man. To Aristotle, the basic principle of the universe was form realizing itself in matter. The musician was part of a divinely significant action when he imposed a formal arrangement upon tones and rhythms— the raw material of music. He imitated the highest state of the virtuous man in which the rational process realizes itself in good acts. Thus music could reveal the state of the soul in concrete form.

Although there are few remains of it, the Greeks did originate an adequate system of musical notation. Its source was probably the Near East and the symbols probably of Phoenician origin. Notation was first used to indicate placement of the fingers along the string of the lyre. Letters could be used upside down or reversed to indicate slight adjustments of the fingers necessary to produce intermediate tones. In its basic theory the system was rather like guitar tablature notation. Singers and *aulos*-players adapted this notation to indicate actual pitches, since they had no such finger placement problems. The understanding of Greek notation has been limited because of the lack of extant examples; the oldest is a fragment of the *Orestes* of Euripides that dates from 250 B.C. Another example was engraved on a tombstone to commemorate a lady

Figure 1.4 Skolion of Seikilos—a tomb stele at Tralles in Asia Minor. [American School of Classical Studies].

named Euterpe (Figure 1.4). It was probably carved during the second century B.C. at Tralles in Asia Minor, where it was discovered in 1883. The large letters constitute the text. The smaller letters above it are the alphabetic signs of vocal notation, and the scattered dashes serve as rhythmic symbols. The text is a drinking song, but its sentiments reflect appropriately upon the inevitable passage of life: "So long as you live, be radiant, and do not grieve at all. Life's span is short and time exacts the final reckoning."

THE ROMAN AMALGAMATION

Although the philosophical and theoretical speculations constituting the Greek musical heritage were largely forgotten, the art of music was destined to flourish in great abundance and variety within the sprawling Roman Empire. The Romans traced their ancestry to the Trojans and built their culture upon the Macedonian Hellenism of Alexander the Great. They were the offspring of stern, practical farming people who had a reverence for duty and an absolute devotion to the destiny of a state that they had forged through centuries of warfare. They possessed a genius for cultural absorption that transformed the qualities of other societies into elements of their own culture.

Greek gods took firm root in Rome, and the official seat of the cult of Apollo moved to Cumae, Italy. The Latin goddess Minerva assumed the duties of Athena as purveyor of wisdom and patroness of the arts. The Greek theater flourished and the entertainment aspects of all the arts achieved a new importance. Greek music teachers were well paid and highly valued. Instrumental forms of music evolved independently from poetry. Actors became distinguished from singers. The Latin farce was enacted to the accompaniment of cymbals, pipes, and castanets. In the very popular pantomime, a large musical ensemble was used to provide background music for the dramatic dance that illustrated the story.

The Romans were content to leave the theory and practice of music to the Greeks. They made few improvements in the mechanism of musical instruments, with the exception of those found to be useful in warfare. The Greek trumpet became the Roman tuba. Its long slender bronze tube curving upward at the end in a bell shape was graphically described as emitting a shriek. Among Roman soldiers a straight four-foot long trumpet of bronze sounded the call to attack. The repertoire of bugle calls familiar to modern armies began with the Romans.

Among Romans, music had a utilitarian function within politics and religion, and also provided entertainment for all classes of people. The concept of art as beauty, or art as a moral factor in the development of character, or even as a scientific force, did not attract the Romans as it had the Greeks. Whereas aristocratic Greeks viewed music as one measure of a man's intelligence, the socially ambitious Romans used music as a means to impress the privileged class with their dexterity at public performances. The sensate fancy of a Roman audience could be easily captured by a virtuoso with a reputation for being able to blow the loudest tone or hold the note for the longest time. They were ready for any kind of contest, including that of vocal chords and lungs. In a more positive sense, constant competition maintained high standards of performance and cultivated critical audiences.

Within Roman culture, music was found appropriate for a number of communal needs. Funerals were not complete without an *aulos* or a *tibia* to wail the lament for the dead. These reed instruments also contributed to the emotional intensity of a bacchanal or circus. Both the Greeks and Romans were well aware of the power of music to stimulate or calm a crowd. The Greeks believed the state should use this power to build desirable character. The Romans put this concept into practice in order to sway public opinion. As the empire drifted into perilous times, it depended more heavily on such entertainment as the public baths with harp and woodwind bands to distract attention from pressing economic concerns.

The wealthy could well afford the luxury of home entertainment by pipe and lyre players. The average man was content with the small bands of pipe, cymbal, and tambourine players who accompanied jugglers and acrobats at the nearest town square. On a typical evening in a small city such as Pompeii many musical events took place simultaneously. At a private banquet in a residential suburb a young woman provided background music by plucking a *kithara* with one hand and a small curved harp with the other. In the theater section of the town, the small roofed *Odeon* attracted a select audience for a program of serious music and poetry reading. In a distant street, late shoppers stopped at intervals to throw coins to itinerant musicians.

While music was more and more in demand as a cultural commodity, there was increasingly less public participation in music making. Music was reserved for the professional, for it was the professional elite who built Rome's institutions. The citizen-soldier was no longer dominant; even the cherished Roman law became too complex for an individual to understand without trained counsel. As long as music served the state as a popular distraction or as an element transcending the vast cultural differences within the empire, it was useful and, therefore, justified. The Roman philosophy of art did not hesitate to break the Greek architectural orders so as to accommodate the use of concrete. Innovations such as arches and vaults were employed to span vast spaces. Roads and bridges facilitated transportation; aqueducts harnassed distant water sources. The Roman emphasis on the practical aspects of life also influenced a development of naturalism in the visual arts that was a contrast to the restrained idealism of Greek classical sculpture. Landscapes, still life, and everyday scenes appeared as new subject matter in Roman painting. Because of their firm insistence upon the real world as seen and felt, Roman artists came close to portraying a convincing perspective of depth. Abstract philosophy was considered impractical by the average Roman who fell prey to the prophet wonder-workers and their respective cults. Philosophical and religious works were simplified for mass consumption by the varied ethnic groups living side by side in that sprawling empire. Consistent with such a practical outlook, the Roman public required a message that would appeal to more than the mind alone. Thus, in the best Roman minds, an admirable and entirely practical philosophy of the arts took shape. The purpose was to involve all man's senses without the loss of either self-discipline or the primacy of order.

THE EARLY CHRISTIAN TRANSITION

Rome and its dream of international law and peace died slowly, and beneath its collapse a new pattern of life, destined to bring eastern Europe to a new climax of cultural affluence was emerging. Swept into Rome with the influx of mystery religions, Christianity made its way from the underground secrecy of the catacombs, through houses of the rich, and into the palace itself. The razing of the Jewish homeland only served to scatter the followers of Jesus throughout Asia Minor, Egypt, Greece, and the Italian peninsula. Their teachings embodied strong elements of emotional symbolism and the didactic persuasiveness of parables. St. Paul, who had a talent for organization and administration comparable to that of a Roman general, found ways to absorb national differences and to establish the international quality that marked the new religion. Early Christianity was formed of a welter of Near Eastern ideologies, a secondary heritage of Greco-Roman culture, and a strong infusion of Jewish religious practices. Each of these derivative sources made fundamental contributions to the artistic development of the religion, but its musical history is particularly well related to the Jewish inheritance.

The Temple in Jerusalem (destroyed in 70 A.D.) with its sacrificial cult exerted an influence on the aspirations and imagination of early Jewish Christians that was comparable to the attitude that later Christians had toward St. Peter's in Rome and St. Sophia's in Constantinople. These sanctuaries were regarded as central spiritual strongholds where God was worshiped most perfectly. Such early church leaders as Jerome emphasized in their writings the parallels between the hierarchy and ritual of the ancient temple and the existent church. However, because Christianity grew up among relatively poor, rural people, the temple, with its urban sophistication, was somewhat resented. The more familiar practices of the local synagogue tended to be duplicated in the conduct of Christian worship and resulted in a simple liturgy drawn from the most universally shared sources. However, many of the traditional prayers of the temple were adapted to the needs of the synagogue form of worship, and possibly the more intricate administrative and ritual elements of the early church also had their origin in temple practices.

After the destruction of the temple the actual sacrifices that were performed there were replaced by the recitation of the statutes, verbal acceptance of the sacrificial offering, and prayer. Such scriptural passages as "the sacrifices of God are a pure heart . . ." were admirably suited to accommodate this substitution. The outright refusal of some officials with inherited rank to part with their ceremonial "secrets" obstructed the transference of some practices. Because the Levites, the temple musicians, were so jealous of their skills, they would pass them on by word of mouth only to their own descendants. Thus they left no written information by which to reconstruct their musical practices.

As the number of converts from outside Palestine increased, some allowance had to be made for those who had little background in the traditional observances of either temple or synagogue. Therefore, a translator, usually a member of the lower clergy, was appointed to translate the ritual into the language of the participants. Both Aramaic (a Hebrew dialect) and a vernacular Greek called *Koine* were used among the converts, and in the same manner the music of the Jewish ritual was translated into an international style of expression. In an effort to be heard in some common tongue, Christianity adopted vernacular Greek, Syriac-Armenian, and Latin as its chief languages.

The most similar element, shared by both Christian and Jewish liturgies, was the reading of the scriptural lesson. Rabbinic literature had long admonished the reader to chant the Scripture. "Whoso reads Scripture without chant and the Mishna without intonation, to him the word of Scripture is applicable; 'I gave them laws that were not beautiful.'" (Ezekiel 20:25). Whole cycles of these readings were arranged according to a calendar sequence that later evolved into the Roman and Greek Breviary.

The later Byzantine Church adopted the Jewish cycle of readings and followed the practice of naming each Sunday after the scriptural lesson for the day. The liturgical year of the eastern churches was formulated on the old Jewish calendar, and weekly observances were organized according to standardized scriptural readings. The major divisions of this old calendar, in turn, were based on the seven winds and seven seasons of Babylonian tradition. Certain musical practices arose through contact with other lands. King David owed the possession of his beloved harp to the Egyptian exile or to his Mesopotamian ancestors for their adoption of India's *kinnor-lyre*.

The chanting of Scriptures was not original with the Jewish liturgy. The practice can be traced to a singular heritage from a common Mesopotamian homeland. Three cuneiform scripts from that area (*c.* 2000 B.C.) have indications of semimusical renditions of sacred text that would seem to confirm such an assumption. In early Christianity the urge to sing must have been strong among those appointed to chant the Scripture. Documents of that period written by church authorities registered complaints against lectors who paid more attention to the sound of their voices than to the meaning of the text. The Council in Laodicea (*c.* 361 A.D.) limited the singing in each church to one official lector who was to be paid for his services.

A clear parallel between Christian and Jewish practices may be noted in their manner of chanting psalms. The style of chanting chosen for a particular psalm often depended upon its familiarity to the congregation. The lector might sing alone, except for occasional congregational responses of *amen, selah, hallelujah,* or *hosanna.* In congregations where the Jewish heritage was strong and the language of the psalm was their own vernacular tongue, a broad participation in the singing was likely to occur. In growing numbers, however, congregations left the singing of psalms to trained choirs, and limited themselves to simpler responses and hymns as their contributions to the liturgy. With the added resource of trained choirs, the psalms could be sung in more intricate ways. The lector might sing one verse and be answered by a choral response such as "Praise Him and magnify Him forever." Two choirs might alternate verses in antiphonal style for a particularly sumptuous effect.

Some survivals of the primitive magical influence accorded music surrounded the singing of psalms. One of the early church fathers, Diodore of Tarsus, attributed the calming of carnal desire, the banishment of demons, and the healing of wounds to the good influence of psalm singing. Babylonian documents on magic contained psalms and other elements of the Jewish liturgy that were believed to have magical powers. The Jewish attitude toward Christian adaptation of the ritual materials was somewhat ambivalent. On one hand, they condemned the appropriation of their own heritage and even reformulated portions of their liturgy to avoid duplication of either the spirit or the occasion for the parallel Christian use. On the other hand, such practices as that of singing psalms between Scripture lessons probably came into the Jewish ritual from Christian liturgy during the Middle Ages.

Opinion was divided as to what additional verbal expressions might be allowed, besides those found in the Scriptures. Both the synagogue and the eastern churches encouraged expansion of the basic texts by poetic allusion and allegory. The Roman Church remained unsympathetic to the cultivation of such a hymn literature as that sponsored by Ambrose of Milan (340–397 A.D.). Although Ambrose supported Latin as the popular language of the West, he was fond of Greek music and adopted

Greek musical practices for the structure of Christian hymns. He did not oppose the use of instruments, and was partial to the florid and exuberant melodies of eastern chant. Time seems to have proved Ambrose correct, as some of the most ancient elements of ritual still in modern use were hymnic prayers that embodied the essentials of the dogma. The Jewish *Yisrael* (Hear, O Israel) and the *Kaddish* (Great Doxology); the Roman *Gloria Patri* and *Credo*; and the Byzantine *Cherubic Hymn* are pertinent examples.

Early hymns reflected the internal strife engendered by theological disputes involving large segments of the Christian world. The gnostic viewpoint, which combined the teachings of Jesus with classical philosophy, was very popular among the Greeks. The apocryphal *Acts of John* revealed a gnostic viewpoint in its account of events in the upper room. In that document, Jesus poetically declared to his disciples:

> Grace danceth. I would pipe; dance ye all. Amen.
> I would morn; lament ye all. Amen.
> The Eight singeth praise with us. Amen.
> The Twelve danceth on high. Amen.
> The whole on high hath part in our dancing. Amen.
> Whoso danceth not, knoweth not what cometh to pass. Amen.[3]

The reference to the mystic numbers eight and twelve, and the expression "the whole" in reference to God reveal a Greek pattern of thought. The image of dancing is particularly significant, since dance was a basic element of most ancient religions. As a circle dance it symbolically reflected "the whole" or the essential unity of all things.

The oldest extant manuscript of early Christianity containing musical notation and text is the *Oxyrhynchos* hymn, which shows an excellent blend of Greek language and Jewish manner of expression. Its very grandeur of concept (". . . all splendid creations of God . . . all waves of thundering streams shall praise our Father . . .") is resonant with the language of the psalms. Ironically, the more heretical sects tended to have the most beautiful poetic literature until St. Ephraem Syrus, a sixth-century poet, created his mystical hymns for the eastern church. These hymns were simple compositions in which both the same number of accented syllables and the same melody were used for all succeeding verses. They originated from spontaneous outbursts of religious fervor and only gradually assumed a definite form under such writers as St. Ephraem. The eastern churches gradually absorbed these hymns into their worship service for use in conjunction with collective prayers. The Roman Church maintained a clearer separation between hymns and the other parts of the ritual, and allowed hymns only at certain seasons or for special observances.

3   M. R. James, *The Apocryphal New Testament* (Oxford: The Clarendon Press, 1924) pp. 253ff.

The idea of music as an agreeable sensation was foreign to music as related to religion. The Greek doctrine of *ethos* was akin to the attitude most early Christian writers had toward music. The concept of opposing qualities of beauty and ugliness was set into the context of holy and pro- fane. The exhortation of "Psalm 29" to "worship the Lord in the beauty of holiness" indicated an identification of beauty with moral or spiritual good, which dominated the Christian viewpoint. A purely esthetic evalu- ation of the arts was a Hellenistic idea that crept in under the suspicious eyes of the hierarchy. The appropriateness of music to express that which was good depended in part upon its performance at the proper time and place. The holiness aspect of *ethos* was combined with a strict regard for the order in which musical selections were sung and for their connection with certain times of the day.

One important aspect of the *ethos* of the early church was its steady rejection of instrumental music in religious observances. In actuality, instruments are mentioned so frequently in ecclesiastical writings that they must have been used continually, although the majority opinion was against such practices. Both church and synagogue probably held such an attitude in reaction to the widespread use of instruments in pagan rituals. Flutes, cymbals, drums, horns, bells, and harps were used in the mystery cults that had long recognized the cathartic power of such music. Clement of Alexandria condemned these "instruments of frenzy" and the supersti- tious men who played them. He urged Christians to banish such instru- ments, even from nonreligious activities.

The fact that the languages used in the early church were also the languages of pagan peoples was reason enough to restrict texts for wor- ship services to Biblical sources. Significant adaptations of pagan styles of expression did occur in time, however, and the Catholic scholar F. J. Doelger has traced the *Kyrie eleison* of the Latin Mass to its origin as a Helios-Mithra hymn. In order to justify their use, instruments had to be excused by an intricate web of allegorical interpretations. To the eminent theologian Origen (*c.* 185–254 A.D.), the trumpet represented the efficacy of the Word of God; the drum, the destruction of lust; and the cymbals, the longing of the soul for Christ. The church fathers were wary of them partly because instruments had been characteristic of ancient temple tra- ditions. Even as late as the thirteenth century, Thomas Aquinas opposed the use of the organ on the grounds that it might "Judaize" the church.

The role of women as musicians, or even as participants in the wor- ship of the early church, was a matter for some dissension. St. Paul had declared that women ought to keep silent in the churches. Nevertheless, choirs of women singers were not a rarity. Among the gnostics, in parti- cular, choirs of women flourished in a continuing tradition from the time of the Greek cult priestesses. In the churches of Asia Minor, women ordi- narily chanted a response to the psalm sung by the lector. However, in the western church the attitude was much against the inclusion of women in the ritual. Indeed, the strong monastic bent of that society precluded the encouragement of women's activities.

The same cultural amalgamation that produced a musical expression in the early Christian communities also stimulated creativity in the visual arts. In catacomb paintings there was a crudeness natural to artists who were humble craftsmen; however, the style in which subjects were portrayed was largely dependent upon Roman patterns. Popular statues from the ancient world, such as the *Calf Bearer*, were used among Christians in the guise of the Good Shepherd. By the time of Constantine, most of the characteristic features of early Christian art were fully apparent. The loss of classical naturalism and the tendency toward abstraction were represented in flat, bodiless forms without the impression of individuality. Divine images were presented in a solemn frontality; representation of the spirit, rather than the material form, was the dominant ideal in all forms of art.

Sculpture was regarded in much the same manner as instrumental music; both had been major vehicles for expressing the humanistic temper of the ancient world and were therefore suspect. The beginning of the transition from Greco-Roman patterns was apparent not only in Christian art but even in such secular monuments as the arch of Constantine. The medallions from the second century A.D. reflected the naturalism of the ancients with their strong sense of the human body and individualism. A rectangular frieze from the fourth century showed a distinct loss of these qualities. As a symbolic representation of Constantine's coronation, the frieze dealt with human bodies only as patterns to express a dependence upon the God-ordained emperor (Figure 1.5). Through such simplifications of worldly reality artists sought to endow the new cultural process with a primary spiritual significance.

Just as music was not considered as holy apart from its connection with sacred text, so reliefs, mosaics, and paintings existed, not for the visual interest they provided, but for their interpretation of Bible tales and legends of the saints. The artist's task was to give a clear presentation of the action or symbols; their actual appearance could be disregarded. If the artist included all the visual clues needed for a correct interpretation of the meaning, no particular advantage was to be gained by dealing further with physical reality. Just as ancient attitudes and practices merged in the music of the church, so the visual arts absorbed such familiar eastern elements as the use of size to indicate importance. The transformation within the arts was not totally due to the rise of Christianity, but to the atmosphere of impending disaster that hung over the whole civilization. When Rome and the Holy See were abandoned temporarily to the barbarian invaders late in the fifth century, the population had little recourse except to turn toward the supernatural for aid.

Intermittent but consistent renewals of the classical spirit occurred, particularly after such social changes as those brought about by the Edict of Milan issued by Constantine in 313 A.D. As the church became more wealthy and powerful, so its portrayal of Jesus changed from that of the humble shepherd to the young philosopher or the classical orator. The influx of such new converts as Junius Bassus, a Roman official with in-

Figure 1.5   Detail of the Arch of Constantine. (Medallions and Frieze). [Alinari].

grained classical preferences, conditioned a classical orientation for religious art. The mausoleum for Constantine's daughter Costanza, with its ceiling motif of a vinyard harvest, attested to a firm alliance with Pompeiian painting. Yet the figure of Jesus amid the curling vines and playful cupids symbolized the new meaning of wine as distinguished from its use in the Dionysian festivals. On the ornate silver plates which graced aristocratic homes Biblical stories such as the battle of David and Goliath were portrayed with all the trappings of a Roman campaign.

As in the case of music, all formative influences in art were not derived from Jewish or classical sources without reciprocation. Despite their traditional restrictions on visual portrayal, the Jews produced a large quantity of excellent mosaics under the influence of the cross-fertilization of religions during the fifth and sixth centuries. The result was a provincial art which did not attempt to assimilate complex classical techniques, but revealed a great flair for colorful decoration. The pavement of the Beth-Alpha Synagogue in Dura-Europos was particularly notable for its Biblical narratives interspersed with plant and animal designs. Thus the disparities of conflicting ideologies were reconciled by time, and the foundation was laid for a peak of cultural eminence reached by the Byzantine Empire.

THE BYZANTINE CULMINATION

The intricate history of nations comprising the Byzantine Empire began with the rise of the eastern federation under Constantine in the fourth century and lasted until the Turkish conquest in the fifteenth century. In the Golden Age of the sixth century, a new synthesis of both society and the arts was attained which reflected the Greco-Roman world and anticipated the modern history of Europe. During the reign of Justinian the basic quality and style of Byzantine arts became essentially defined. The period provides for the modern student an especially clear insight into the delicate balances of power upon which the social structure depended and the ways in which the arts were used to enhance their operation.

The story of the Byzantine Empire began with the decision of Constantine to move the capital of the Roman Empire to that "God-guarded city" named for him. The location was excellent for defense, communications, and control of shipping on the Black, Mediterranean, and Aegean Seas. This new beginning was devoid of the many historic associations surrounding Rome, and it was deeply influenced by eastern and Greek modes of thought and action. The power of the king rose partly because of his position as the major bulwark of the Roman Empire then under attack, and partly because of the traditional concept of a semidivine kingship native to the Near East. Although Justinian closed the Athenian schools which stood as the last outposts of classical learning, the university in Constantinople based much of its curriculum on Greek and Latin languages, philosophy, law, and classical literature. Justinian himself was a prominent legal scholar in the Roman tradition. Thus the emperor exemplified the international and historic forces which molded the sixth-century Byzantine Empire.

During that period Constantinople incorporated within its 600,000 inhabitants a vast diversity of people who called themselves Romans and spoke Greek. The only qualifications for citizenship were the ability to speak Greek and membership in the Orthodox Church. In its life style the city resembled a Greek metropolis with rich and poor living in close proximity and much of the business, legal, and educational enterprises being carried on in the open air. The general tenor of life was marked by extreme ceremonialism; the celebration of events of court and church symbolically unified the empire. Even the lavish apparel worn by members of the religious and secular hierarchy was not construed as a display of personal vanity; rather, it was accepted as evidence of the glory of the empire. The abundant and costly arts which flourished during that period all stood within this larger context.

Unlike western Europe, a strong nonecclesiastical element in education was consistently maintained; secular crafts, commerce, and the pagan amenities of life were never entirely discouraged. The Roman circuses and chariot races were still popular, and at least one revolution against Justinian came to a head there. Disgruntled Roman-style senators were a danger which could be minimized only by a conscious merging of the eastern concept of the divine ruler with the hero image prevalent in the West. With a slight adjustment to fit Christian concepts of the state, the king became the "elect of God" fulfilling his duty to lead the people to the Kingdom of God. This cult of the emperor became one important point of orientation for the arts; a regular iconography grew up around the image of the ruler and attracted a musical repertoire for acclaiming him. Since earth was a counterpart of heaven and God was absolute in heaven, His representative, the emperor, was absolute on earth. To remind the public of his status, Constantine initiated the practice of having the emperor's image engraved on coins with his eyes directed toward heaven as though receiving divine guidance. With God the true ruler, and the emperor His instrument, all duties of the imperial office assumed a sacred character.

Justinian supported this philosophical framework by declaring the church of St. Sophia (completed in 537 A.D.) as the spiritual center of the empire. He assumed that his divine responsibility was to name the senior bishop (or patriarch) to preside over the ecumenical council. Thus in the East as in the West the church developed an administrative structure matching that of the state. Religion played a central role in the daily life of the people, not because of an oppressive dogmatism issuing from the Orthodox Church, but most probably because of the varied religious viewpoints represented in that cosmopolitan city. Even a leading church official complained that it was impossible to purchase a loaf of bread without being examined by the shopkeeper on some subtle theological point. Appropriately then, one of the world's greatest church edifices arose in response to such a constant preoccupation with religion (Figure 1.6).

The architecture of St. Sophia represented a distillation of the primary qualities that were ever after to characterize Greek Christianity

wherever it penetrated. The impact of the centralized church plan lay in the hemispherical dome representing the heavens and symbolizing the unity of all worshippers within the larger unity of church and state. This symbolic unity was the most basic ideology underlying everything that transpired in the building, whether theological, artistic, or musical. The great altar often stood directly under the dome in centralized churches, giving an even greater impression of unity to the building and to its congregation. Lofty vaulted spaces imparted a feeling of grandeur, peace, and detachment. Some of the most notable ancient temples, such as the Parthenon, had been shrines to deities of wisdom; therefore, the dedication of St. Sophia to Christ as Holy Wisdom may have been planned to provide a purposeful continuity. In construction technique and mathematical intricacy it was a fitting culmination to the great buildings of ancient Rome. The geometric clarity and simplicity of the exterior delighted minds trained in Greek mathematical theories, just as the magnificence of the interior decoration delighted their senses. Multicolored stone had been gathered from the farthest reaches of the empire and carefully set into vast tapestries of light and color. Domes shimmered with gold mosaic; the altar was a slab of gold inlaid with precious stones; the holy vessels were of solid gold. At night thousands of oil lamps gave the same brilliant illumination as the sun by day. According to a legendary account, Justinian received the building at its dedication with the exclamation, "Solomon, I have surpassed thee."

Needless to say, the God worshiped in such an environment was not a familiar semimortal companion, but a figure of vast mystery. He was a God become flesh, not a man become God. His Deity was celebrated poetically by John Chrysostom as one "Whose power is inconceivable, glory incomprehensible, mercy unmeasurable, and tenderness to man, unspeakable." The grandeur of the liturgy was created not out of craving for sheer ostentation, but because it was symbolically adequate for celebrating the union of the King in heaven and the emperor on earth. Through the mediation of the senses was conveyed the great theme of the unity of all people—living, dead, and yet unborn. The Byzantine faith was characterized by a feeling for the continuity of life and the inevitability of the divinely ordained social structure. Not having experienced the centuries of disruption that marked life in the West, these people exhibited a life style that traced its origins to the early Mediterranean civilizations. This very consistency was, no doubt, one reason for the persistence and durability of their culture.

The Divine Liturgy was the central act of affirmation for the whole culture and its values. The eastern version of the service used at the time of Justinian has been credited to St. John Chrysostom (347–407). When Gregory assumed his duties as Pope of Rome in 590, his inclination was to organize a uniform liturgy to serve as a standard, universal observance for the West. Such uniformity was never thoroughly accomplished in the East. The diversity of peoples was too great, their nationalism too ingrained, and their ethnic habits too strong. Often in dissent politically, Syria and Egypt supported some theological viewpoints considered heretical in Constantinople. Characteristically, they also developed variant versions of the ritual. At St. Sophia the central act of the liturgy—the Holy Communion or Eucharist—was celebrated each Sunday in commemoration of the Resurrection. It was surrounded by a regularly repeated sequence of events designed to enhance the significance of the ritual. The splendor of the occasion was heightened by the attendance of the royal household at most major festivals. The service was very long, and much spoken and musical material was included. Typical of the many eloquent poetic statements used was the *Cherubic Hymn:*

> "We who mystically represent the Cherubim and sing the
> thrice-holy hymn to the lifegiving Trinity
> let us lay aside all worldly cares that we may receive
> the King of the Universe invisibly attended by the
> angelic orders. Alleluia, Alleluia, Alleluia."[4]

The importance of music was noted particularly in the retention of congregational responses inherited from the Jewish practice. The ancient blessing, "Peace be to you all," evoked from the worshipers the response, "And with thy spirit." The increase in the use of these formulas resulted in a continued musical dialogue between priest and people. In addition, many hymns were sung and were not considered extraliturgical as they were in the Roman liturgy. The fact that the Byzantine Mass was essentially dramatic in concept prevented the use of music not intrinsic to the ritual. As in the West, music was used extensively at such services as Matins and Vespers, which were celebrated by the monastic community.

The hymns of the Byzantine Church have had a significant effect upon subsequent eastern and western musical practices. They originated as additions between verses of psalms and developed in the time of Justinian into compositions of eighteen or twenty-four similarly constructed lines preceded by one or two introductory lines. Described as highly dramatic sermons, these *kontakia* were based upon Biblical passages. Justinian himself may be included among the poets who wrote in that form. Because the same person wrote both text and music, no professional distinction was made between poet and musician. The most famous hymn writer was Romanus, whom the eastern church recognizes on his feast day (October 1) as the father of hymnographers. Of Jewish extraction, Romanus arrived in Constantinople by way of residence in Syria. He reformulated existing hymns by restructuring them with rhyme into the *kontakia* form. Rhyme, a common element in Jewish hymns, had not been apparent in Byzantine

---

4   H. A. Daniel, trans. in *Codex Liturgicus,* iv (1853) p. 400.

practice. Romanus was an ardent spokesman for the western canons of orthodoxy supported by the Latin-oriented Justinian against the Monophysite doctrine, which denied the Incarnation. His antiheresy viewpoint is represented in his hymn on Pentecost:

> Why do the Greeks boast and puff themselves up?
> Why do they dream of Aratos the thrice accursed?
> Why do they err after Plato? . . .
> Let us praise, brethren, the voices of the
> disciples, because they captured all men
> by divine power, and not by fine words.[5]

Romanus spoke not as a rhetorician or theologian, but as a believer who sincerely preached the mysteries of his faith. His penchant for obscure poetic imagery is revealed in his hymn on the Nativity: "The Virgin today bears the Superessential and the earth brings the cave to the unapproachable."

The musical structure of the hymns and other Byzantine music has been made difficult to determine because of the destruction of art objects and illustrated manuscripts containing music that occurred during the Iconoclastic Controversy (the seventh and ninth centuries). However, a great deal of energetic modern scholarship has provided relevant information about melody as it was conceived in the Byzantine manner. Musical practice seemingly centered around, but was not limited to, the *octoechos*. They were probably a group of eight types of melodic constructions, rather than the individual pitches that comprise a modern scale. Either the origin or the dominant influence in the formation of the *octoechos* was Syrian. The universal qualities such as cold, warmth, dampness, and dryness, by which the melodies were characterized, were also notably Syrian. The selection of these eight elements implied the use of the melodies within an eight-week liturgical cycle. Each musical selection was chosen for its position in the cycle on the basis of its symbolic suitability. The number eight had long historic ramifications of mystical or magical numbers, culminated in the philosophy of the Christian gnostics. However, by the time of Justinian, the *octoechos* had lost their original mystical connotations and were regarded as a repertoire of melodic configurations out of which hymns could be formulated to provide a different tune for each Sunday of the liturgical cycle. Some melody types seem to be represented in the Syrian, Byzantine, Roman Catholic, and Jewish traditions. However, the passage of time produced more variance than concurrence of usage, and many chants have no obvious relationship to any central system. The early theory and history of the *octoechos* undoubtedly had some parallel

---

5 Egon Wellesz, *History of Byzantine Music and Hymnography*, 2d. ed. (Oxford: The Clarendon Press, 1961), pp. 188–190.

34   significance in the West, and their reflection of ancient cosmological speculations also had an effect upon the organization of the western liturgy.

By Justinian's time, the first stage in the notation of the chant had been attained (Figure 1.7). It was based upon the ancient grammatical signs of the Greeks, and its organization was attributed to Aristophanes of

Figure 1.7   Byzantine Ekphonetic Notation. [University Press, Oxford].

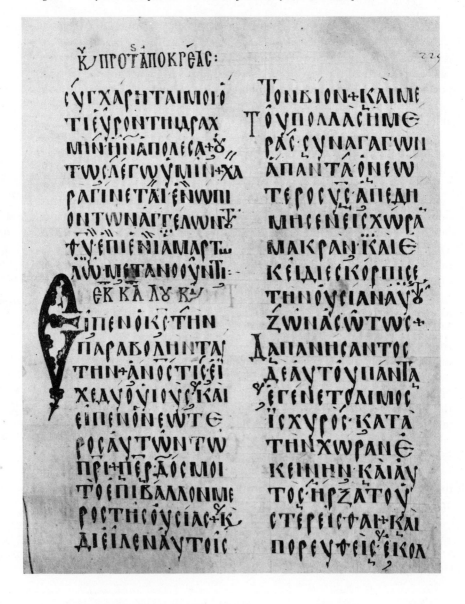

Byzantium (*c.* 180 B.C.). To the traditional lettering style used in the fifth and sixth centuries was added ecphonetic signs, indicating the manner of chanting to be used by the lector. Such signs served their purpose well—until their meaning became obscure by the end of the fifteenth century. Ecphonetic signs may be classified into groups of markings that provide different types of information. The familiar acute (/) grave (\) and circumflex (∧) accents regulated the actual pitch of vocal sound. Another group showed how long — or how short ⌣ the tone was to be held. Specific signs indicated the type of breathing used, either rough ⊢ or smooth ⊣. Additional signs were used to indicate the spirit of declamation. These marks were set at the beginning of the phrase so that the lector would be aware of the desired manner for rendering the ensuing text. The original ecphonetic signs did not remain long in this early stage, but evolved into composite flowing markings that could indicate rather subtle interpretations such as ✓ (to chant in a pleading manner) or  (a rise of the voice with slight accentuation).

The rhythm of the chant was without a definite division into equal accents. The chant was based on a single melody that could be sung with equal facility by either a choir or a soloist. The manner of performance in the eastern traditions varied with the locale. The Coptic Chant of Egypt was not preserved in notation because most of the singers were recruited from among the blind, the theory being that they had the serious unworldliness necessary for singing the liturgy. Ethiopia had a colorful ceremony in which priests sang themselves into ecstasy and exhaustion to the accompaniment of dancing, hand-clapping, and drumbeats.

Instrumental music was not accepted by church officials for use within religious ritual; however, it was an important aspect of most nonliturgical ceremonies. The organ was still vitally connected with the Roman games and other forms of mass entertainment. In the West the attitude was quite different. Organs given to Frankish kings on several occasions were accompanied by musicians to teach the use of the instrument. Since the only group of people with sufficient leisure and intellectual devotion to master its intricacies were monks, the organ was eventually developed as a church instrument. The western church organ far surpassed in size and flexibility the smaller Byzantine portable organ.

Despite the pervasive influence of the Orthodox Church, the climate of Constantinople was decidedly secular. The emperor was supported by a huge administrative staff of civil servants who were aware that their rise in rank depended upon outward conformity to the requirements of the official religion. Still their writings, their life style, and their objects of art all indicated an affinity for ancient gods and a humanistic orientation. They collected classical statuary and frequented the local theaters with a devotion akin to that of their pagan ancestors. The extensive floor mosaics in the Great Palace of Istanbul laid during Justinian's youth showed no loss of the Roman technical skill or observational power. Ivory carvings and silver dishes with portraits of ancient gods and heroes were typical of much of the commissioned art work of the period. Not only the subject matter, but also the beautifully draped, physically expressive bodies attested to the liveliness of the classical vision of the arts in Constantinople. Patronage came from such unexpected sources as the courtesans and women entertainers who had their portraits painted for purposes of advertising. Even Justinian was not above some artistic gayety. He commissioned a frieze of paintings to represent famous chariot races held during his reign. Even in the matter of copying and illuminating the Scriptures no evidence indicates that monks alone did this work, as was customary in the West. Large commercial art workshops most probably produced both secular and religious works for anyone with the money to purchase their wares.

In music, the classical styles survived brilliantly outside the church, particularly in the court of the emperor and in such public entertainment centers as the Hippodrome. Music for court use was as highly systematized and as rigidly regulated as that of the church. Leading church choirs accompanied by instruments customarily provided dinner music for the entertainment of foreign dignitaries. Important civic duties were performed by two choirs of court officials and laymen who were organized to sing acclamations to the king. These acclamations were speech–song expressions of good wishes which could be lengthened and decorated according to the occasion. For religious ceremonies Justinian had two choirs of clergymen who sang acclamations for him in the church. In addition, he could call upon the resources of the imperial band, which consisted of trumpets, horns, cymbals, and pipes. The royal family was surrounded by music even within the private precincts of the palace. On the third day after her marriage the empress was obliged to take a ceremonial bath, on which occasion she was acclaimed by the entire court (with the aid of three golden organs). Every birth, anniversary, or triumphant return was the occasion for an outburst of enthusiastic acclamations. As reported by visitors to the court, the result was one of grandeur, but also extreme theatricality.

Acclamations were not reserved entirely for the emperor. A well-developed repertoire of such greetings for high ranking members of the clergy was in evidence; even lower members of the nobility might be so saluted on important occasions. A bride was often conducted to the house of the bridegroom by choirs of the two leading political factions with their organs, tambourines, and cymbals. Foreign ambassadors were received by the combined noise of the emperor's golden organ and twenty pairs of cymbals.

Although the musical life of the ordinary citizen remains a matter of conjecture, some limited evidence indicates that the favorite gathering places of the citizenry had music in abundance. None of it was preserved because it was music for the moment, and because notation was reserved for the ceremonial music of church and state. The comedies of Aristophanes, the satyr plays in honor of Dionysus, and the dramas of Euripides, in addition to a host of other theatrical enterprises featuring music, were mentioned in writings of the time. Famous mimes elaborated upon the meaning of songs, and dancers flourished both in number and excellence. The Olympic games continued to feature an elaborate musical accompaniment. The rites of the mystery religions were celebrated to the hypnotic wail of horns, flutes, and the beat of cymbals. Church officials so feared the highly emotional effect of the music of these religions that they resorted to threats of excommunication to keep even the clergy away from such attractions.

The halcyon days of Justinian did not survive him. The delicate balance between church and state was shattered by the Iconoclastic Controversy. In that contest for power the clergy sought to strengthen its position through an alliance with Rome. The emperor, retaliating with an extensive program of religious and social reform, confiscated monastic property and sent monks to prison or into exile. The issue was settled only after much destruction of priceless art objects; but the whole society lost the war. Monks developed into feudal barons, and the spirit that formed the rich flowering of Byzantium vanished forever. A thousand years of distinguished culture died, and its artists and scholars eventually fled from the Turks, bringing to the West their ageless heritage of the human spirit.

SUMMARY OUTLINE

ANCIENT SOCIETIES

Paleolithic
Neolithic
Modern Primitives

GENERAL CULTURAL INFLUENCES

History: recession of the Ice Age; origin of tribal structure; early permanent villages.
Social Factors: tribal warfare; rites of love and hunting; rituals of maturation.
Religion: animism; ancestor worship; use of self-hypnosis and magic:
Applied Science: stone tool artifacts; animal husbandry; pottery; weaving; development of metal implements.

MUSICAL ATTRIBUTES

Theory: music as physical discovery; theories of origin.
Social Functions: magic charms; priestly incantations; ceremonial narratives; ritual dance accompaniment.
Instruments: bone flute, clay drum, turtle shell rattles, log drum, conch shell trumpet, and bound reed pipes.

ARTISTIC PARALLELS

Cave paintings; fertility figures: "Venus of Willendorf"; guardian figures; ritual dance as education and entertainment.

EARLY CIVILIZATIONS

Sumeria
Egypt
Babylonia
Chaldea
Assyria

GENERAL CULTURAL INFLUENCES

History; founding of city-states; rise of kings—Hammurabi, Akhnaton; familial dynastic traditions; written law codes.
Social Factors: division of labor and rise of social classes; invention of writing systems: cuneiform and hieroglyphic; craft guilds; educational systems.
Religion: deities symbolizing natural forces; myths of creation; religious epics: *Gilgamesh Epic.*
Applied Science: irrigation systems, mathematics of commerce, astronomy, construction engineering.

MUSICAL ATTRIBUTES

Theory: cosmic acoustical concepts; pentatonic scale; early notational systems.
Social Functions: temple orchestras and choirs: *Temple Harp at Ur;* instruments as god symbols; folk music; music in educational system; music for royal entertainment.
Instruments: harps, reed pipes, flutes, two-stringed lute, drum, zither, lyre, trumpet, cymbals, and Egyptian sistrum.

ARTISTIC PARALLELS

Sumerian plaques and seals; Assyrian sculptural friezes; Egyptian pyramids and tombs; Akhnaton style in art; mimes and masked dancers.
Literature: *Book of the Dead.*

GREEK CIVILIZATION

Archaic Period
Classical Golden Age
Hellenistic Period

GENERAL CULTURAL INFLUENCES

History: Aegean ancestors; mercantilism in Crete; Mycenalan heritage Dorian migration; mainland city-states; early dominance of Ionia; Persian Wars; rise of Athens under Pericles; Peloponnesian Wars; rise of Macedonia.
Social Factors: Spartan versus Athenian social ideals; Athenian Humanism; decline of reason into tyranny.
Religion and Philosophy: rationalism in the cult of Apollo; cult of Dionysus and founding of Greek drama; Platonic Idealism and Aristotelian Realism.

MUSICAL ATTRIBUTES

Theory: Pythagorean acoustical theories, musical scale related to cosmic harmony, Aristoxenus's Greater Perfect System, tablature notation.
Social Functions: Doctrine of Ethos as a social esthetic: *Timaeus,* music and the state in the *Republic, Dithyramb* and *Paean* as cult hymns, Dionysian chorus as used in drama.
Instruments: *Kithara* and *Aulos* as opposing esthetic principles.

ARTISTIC PARALLELS

Canons of proportion in sculpture and architecture: *Doryphorus* and *Parthenon.*

Homeric epic; geometric vases; *Kore* and *Kouros* figures; Sappho's lyric poetry; dramas of Aeschylus, Sophocles, and Euripides.

ROMAN CIVILIZATION
Italian Tribal Societies
Etruscan Golden Age
Republican Era
Empire Period

GENERAL CULTURAL INFLUENCES
History: Trojan migration; Macedonian Hellenism; Roman Law Codes established; founding of Republic; Empire initiated with Augustus.

Social Factors: professionalism in occupations; shift in Republican morality to individualism of Empire; mass cultural processes developed.

Philosophy and Religion: Stoicism and Epicureanism developed: Marcus Aurelius's *Thoughts;* influx of oriental mystery religions.

MUSICAL ATTRIBUTES
Theory: absorption of Near Eastern practices into Greek musical system.

Social Functions: utilitarian emphasis; music in religion and politics; exploitation of emotional affects; rise of the virtuoso performer.

Instruments: brasses for warfare; harps and woodwinds in public baths; *Tibia* for funerals and circuses; mixed bands for dance and home entertainment.

ARTISTIC PARALLELS
Use of concrete and vaulting systems for architecture; experiments in depth perception in painting.

Utilitarian art for mass entertainment; Roman theater with Latin farce; playwrights Plautus and Seneca; wall painting for homes featuring still life, landscape, and mythological scenes.

EARLY CHRISTIANITY

GENERAL CULTURAL INFLUENCES
History: Pax Romana; influence of Jewish heritage; Constantine's Edict of Milan.

Philosophy and Religion: absorption of Near Eastern ideologies; Gnosticism; Neoplatonism.

MUSICAL ATTRIBUTES

Theory: adaptation of Greek elements in *Oxyrynchos Hymn.*

Social Functions: Judeo-Christian parallels in ritual; adaptation of Greek ethical theories in music.

Forms and Styles: Psalmody; Gallican, Mozarabic, and Ambrosian chants; antiphonal and responsorial singing; Jewish *Kaddish,* Roman *Gloria,* and Byzantine *Cherubic Hymn.*

Instruments: Clement and his rejection of instruments; Origen and the symbolic justification of instruments.

ARTISTIC PARALLELS

Judeo-Christian arts in Beth-Alpha Synagogue mosaics; Christian adaptation of the Greek *Calf Bearer;* rituals adapted to vernacular languages; communal catacomb art.

Early church structure: *Sta. Costanza;* poetry of St. Ephraem; persistence of classical style; emergence of abstract, symbolic style.

BYZANTINE CIVILIZATION

The Age of Justinian

GENERAL CULTURAL INFLUENCES

History: persistence of Greco-Roman characteristics; fall of the western empire and rise of the eastern empire; Iconoclastic Controversy; economic and political rivalry of Islamic nations.

Social Factors: extreme ceremonialism; cult of the emperor; continuity of classical educational curriculum.

Religion: growth of monastic power; Monophysite heresy.

MUSICAL ATTRIBUTES

Theory: octoechos; ecphonetic notational system.

Social Functions: music featured in political ceremonials by royal bands and the singing of acclamations; musical entertainment in aristocratic homes; congregational responses and hymns in religious rites.

Composers and Forms: St. John Crysostom and the Eastern Orthodox ritual; Romanus as the leading hymnographer.

Instruments: religious uses uncertain in Orthodox Church; horns, flutes, and cymbals in mystery religions; portable organ, brass and woodwind bands for imperial ceremonies.

ARTISTIC PARALLELS

Olympic games and public entertainment; secular crafts flourish in commercial workshops; church of Hagia Sophia and its ritual.

Continued production of dramas of Euripides and comedies of Aristophanes.

2
The Middle Ages

THE PERIOD OF FORMULATION

Western civilization may have been born in Greece and nurtured in Rome, but it reached maturity only after a long and eventful development within the tribal kingdoms of Europe. This period of transition was called the Middle Ages by people of the later Renaissance. These people regarded the five centuries preceding their own era as a cultural chasm separating the classical world from their own newly enlightened society. Yet the accomplishments of those disparaged centuries were fundamental to the social, economic, political, and artistic environment of western man. The stark illiteracy of the Dark Ages (c. 500-800) gradually gave way to the blossoming of a fully international culture that witnessed the rise of vast cathedrals, bustling towns, and such famous universities as those founded in Oxford, Cambridge, Heidelberg, Paris, and Siena. Europe developed politically from little more than a collection of disparate, unruly peoples to a cluster of national states. Until the beginning of the ninth century, society itself was more migratory than permanent; it lacked the artistic and intellectual benefits of a settled community. Scandinavians moved through England and into France; the Magyars migrated to Hungary; the Burgundians, Angles, Saxons,

Figure 2.1   Litchfield Gospels—Cross Page. Litchfield Cathedral. [Courtauld Institute of Art].

and Jutes added to the constant surge of population. Their adoption of Christianity and a national identity was an extremely slow process that was finally achieved during the twelfth century. These tribal peoples left an indelible mark upon the arts of the West; their native animal style of decoration found its way into the Biblical illumination and church architecture of later eras (Figure 2.1). The gypsy music of Hungary and Spain celebrated an emotional intensity woven deep into the European heritage by the wanderers of a thousand years ago.

The beginning of this cultural epoch has been called the Dark Ages, and such it seemed to be in comparison with the glories of the classical past and other current rival civilizations. The Greco-Roman culture of the Byzantine Empire was enjoying a second golden age in the ninth century. Muslim culture was approaching the peak of its international influence. Maintaining a stronghold in southern Europe, one of its most powerful caliphates was established at Cordova, Spain. In this Spanish Muslim social climate marked by rare tolerance, the tradition of classical scholarship exerted a major influence upon the intellectual revival of western Europe. Although the Roman dream of peace within the rule of law was shattered, people clung for centuries to the remnants of that brilliant civilization through the power structure of the Roman Church. While the church itself was racked by struggles between East and West through such issues as the Iconoclastic Controversy, it retained the legacy of Roman law and Roman genius for administration within a stable succession of power. That the Middle Ages were styled an age of synthesis attests to a triumphant solution to social and intellectual diversity; that the era was labeled an age of faith attests to the triumph of the church in its impact upon human affairs.

Throughout the Dark Ages the church alone preserved the priceless gift of literacy. Scholarship was a tradition handed down from churchmen to other aspiring churchmen. Much of what was known about the thought of the ancients came into the West through the translations and commentaries of Boëthius (480-524). But the spirit of the classics soon died because classical literature was not valued for itself but as a means to promote and exploit literacy in the service of the Christian faith. The extent of the church's broad educational efforts was to familiarize the mass of mankind with the contents of the catechism. Only later, under the influence of chivalry and the courtly tradition, did education in the broadest sense become the recognized foundation for civilized living.

Textbooks used in the curriculum of monks were compiled by Boëthius, Cassiodorus, Bede, and Alcuin. However, standard works by pagan authors, such as the grammars of Priscian and Donatus, were also employed. With rare exceptions, medieval scholars were compilers rather than original thinkers. Their constant appeal to prior authorities dominated their reliance upon their own rational processes. The Venerable Bede (673-735) was a notable exception in that his *Ecclesiastical History of the English People* preserved the waning tradition of historical writing. He also instituted the practice of dating backwards and forwards from the birth of Christ rather than from an assumed date of creation.

The intellectual training of the time was largely based upon grammar and literature, which supported Latin as the international language of both church and state. Still couched in Roman numerals, arithmetic largely dealt with theories and allegories of ratio and proportion rather than with practical problems. Astronomy was highly involved with astrology; its one practical application was in the calculation of the church calendar. Natural sciences existed in the intellectual currency of the day only through fragments of such works as Pliny's *Natural History,* Hyginus' *Astronomica,* and the medical treatises of Hippocrates. A culmination of the scholarship of the Dark Ages was reached by Gerbert of Aurillac (*c.* 950-1003) who became Pope Sylvester II. A remarkable man for his time, Gerbert was particularly influential in the dissemination of Arabic learning in the West. Occasionally a few men such as John Scotus Erigena (810-877) became fluent in Greek. His translation of the fifth century Syrian document, *The Celestial Hierarchy,* had a decisive influence on the pictorial concept of heaven as portrayed by medieval artists.

In reference to music, two individuals in particular had a significant role in the development of that art in the West. The first was Pope Gregory the Great (*c.* 540-604) after whom the chant tradition of the Roman church was named. Although certainly not the actual composer of the many chants which formed the early Gregorian collection, he was one of the astute editors who selected from the many texts and melodies then in circulation those which were thought most proper to perpetuate musically in the central celebrations of the church. He not only helped organize the music of the liturgy but also was active in its wide dissemination as an international musical language. Pope Gregory was not the first to support worthy endeavors on behalf of church music. A *schola cantorum* for the training of professional church musicians had been established in Rome early in the fourth century; its graduates were subsequently sent as musical missionaries all over Europe to promulgate the official collection of chants and to teach the manner of their use. Also before Gregory's time, the great scholar and statesman Bishop Ambrose of Milan (340-397) formulated a collection of musical styles and practices that has continued to be associated with his name. Some of his texts and melodies were undoubtedly absorbed into the Gregorian tradition, but the fact that the earliest extant collection of Ambrosian chants is from the twelfth century makes it difficult to assess the relationship between the two repertoires of liturgical song. The texts *Aeterna Rerum Conditor* and *Te Deum,* and the tune to *Veni Creator Spiritus* are very likely survivals in the Gregorian practice of the earlier Ambrosian chants.

Pope Gregory is often found among lists of eminent theologians. He serves as the point of transition between the Roman patristic age of St.

Augustine and the intellectual outlook of the Dark Ages. Although his intolerance of secular learning dealt a bitter blow to the lingering pagan tradition of rational enlightenment, his praise of St. Benedict (480-543) elicited wide support for the scholarly labors of the Benedictine monks. As a typical man of his time, Gregory was absorbed by demonology, mysticism, miracles, and allegories. He was single-minded in pursuit of his vision of the world, which was defined in broad relief by the sin of man, the need for penance, and the terrifying nearness of a literal hell. Under his reign certain persistent hallmarks of western religious thought were perpetuated within the framework of this rather sombre spiritual outlook. Gregory gave much attention to the ritual that had grown up around the celebration of the Last Supper. The Mass, or coming together of the faithful to celebrate that supper, was the central rite of the church and its main point of contact with the populace at large. Gregory initiated an authoritative study and supportive rationale for both the theology and the art of that ritual which assumed its final form only after the elapse of many centuries. Thus the Gregorian chant evolved along with the Mass itself to become the very foundation of the musical culture of the Middle Ages.

The golden age of the chant was attained during the reign of a second significant figure, Charlemagne, who heralded the reestablishment of political and social stability. With his crowning on Christmas Day in the year 800, the dream of a successor to the ancient Roman emperors (under a Christian aegis) was first realized in the West. To insure such a dream required both the unification of the Frankish tribes and a recultivation of many cultural amenities of Roman life. Charlemagne's chapel at Aachen attested to his determination to revive Roman building techniques. He established royal schools and appointed as supervisor a brilliant educator named Alcuin. An accomplished linguist, educated in Latin, Greek, and a bit of Hebrew, Alcuin's writings dealt mainly with grammar and rhetoric. His most significant contribution may well have been made in his position as Charlemagne's advisor, for a well-educated consultant was of critical importance to the king's administrative reforms. Although Charlemagne was not functionally literate, he loved learning and actively encouraged the copying of books. His court boasted the presence of the poet-bishop Theodulfus and the scholar Einhard (Charlemagne's first biographer). An emphasis on the cultivation of a Latin language and literature resulted in the development of Carolingian miniscule script as the forerunner of modern cursive writing. Although Charlemagne's era did not boast an abundance of outstanding scholars, Charlemagne managed to secure the services of some of the most intelligent minds and to initiate a massive program of education for as many clergy and laymen as his schools could accommodate.

The traditional alliance between the Frankish rulers and the Roman Church had been initiated by Charlemagne's grandfather, Charles Martel. He won the good will of the church by leading his recently converted Franks against the Muslims and by preventing their further incursion into the heart of Europe.

Charlemagne's father, Pepin the Short, invited the Benedictine monks to settle in his kingdom to teach the people, to heal the sick, to practice animal husbandry, and to shelter travelers. Famous monastic centers at St. Gall, Metz, Mainz, and Reichenau developed under the protection of the Frankish king. Pepin was also convinced of the value of uniting his people through the bonds of a shared religious rite; but to achieve this end he had to suppress independent Christian traditions that had grown up outside the official Gregorian liturgy. Thus, the Benedictines were called upon to supplant the native Gallican liturgy and to teach those religious practices approved by Rome.

Figure 2.2   German 15th Century woodcut of singing monks. (Augsburg, 1479). [Courtesy, The Metropolitan Museum of Art, Harris Brisbane Dick Fund, 1926].

Much of the impetus for the musical development of the Carolingian era came from the monastery, where music was valued both as a means of religious expression and as a mathematical science in the classical tradition. The life of a monk was rigorous and included daily work in the fields, tasks of household management, and the study and copying of manuscripts. This very discipline of daily life may have stimulated the need for creative expression through the arts. Thus, among these people, the Gregorian chant reached its fullest development. The daily religious observances of the community became natural settings for the use of chant and the occasion for the evolution of the many subtle nuances characterizing the emotive significance of the music. The brothers came together to observe the eight services comprising the Divine Office of which the early services of Matins and Lauds and the evening service of Vespers were the most musically significant. Psalms were chanted; hymns and canticles were sung; and passages of Scripture, which served as the daily lesson, were intoned (Figure 2.2).

The style of the Gregorian chant was basically simple in both tonal and expressive elements. Yet it was subject to endless elaboration so that it eventually supported a vast accumulation of artistic practices. The music consisted of a single melody line sung without instrumental accompaniment; it had no recurrent rhythmic pulse or beat and used for tonal resources a system of scales adapted from the Greek modes. The chant was never intended to be judged upon musical merit alone, but upon the effectiveness with which it enhanced the words of the text. The general impression of the music was not focused upon either sensuous beauty or a personal emotional appeal. It was rather impersonal in effect and somewhat abstract and mystical in mood. The degree of complexity that characterized each chant was partly conditioned by the occasion for its use. Melodies used in the daily services of the Offices were generally shorter and simpler than those employed for more elevated occasions. High holy days naturally attracted more ornate and festive variations. The skill of the performers also determined the style of much of the liturgical music. Trained singers could negotiate florid melodies, while the lay congregation could aspire only to simple, syllabic melodies with a typical hymn tune sound.

Although the Offices were intrinsic to the life of the monastic community, the Mass gradually developed a more complex liturgy to become the principle service of the Roman Church. As the one occasion for the assembling of the faithful from all stations in life, the Mass has been the object of prolonged musical elaboration. The invariable portions of the service, which are repeated during each celebration of the ritual, assumed a great musical significance in later centuries, although they were less organically related to the rite than the Proper chants commemorating changing seasonal observances. Collectively called the Ordinary, the invariable sections are the Kyrie ("Lord, have mercy upon us. . .") Gloria ("Glory be to God on high. . .") Credo ("I believe in one God. . .") Sanctus ("Holy, Holy, Holy. . .") and Agnus Dei ("O Lamb of God. . ."). These selections were originally intended to be sung by the congregation; the Kyrie and Sanctus, in particular, retain a simple formal design using repeated phrases of text. The seasonal texts and their melodies, collectively called the Proper, were always intended to be sung by the choir; thus, they developed highly complex melody types. The Proper chants are the Introit, Gradual, Alleluia, Offertory, and Communion. The texts for the Propers are selected from the book of Psalms, while most texts of the Ordinary were not taken directly from the Bible.

Within both the Mass and the Offices, a wide variety of chants gradually developed. The most common type is the antiphon and psalm group used for chanting verses of Scripture of varying length. In its most simple form the psalm may be intoned on a fixed pitch or *lection* tone, with only a slight variation to produce the normal speech inflections and punctuation. Slightly more elaborate, the psalm tones begin with a formulated series of pitches rising to the level of the reciting tone. A slight fluctuation in pitch divides the psalm verse in half, and another formulated group of descending tones concludes the pattern. A priest often sings the first half of the psalm verse, while the second half is sung by the choir. Each succeeding verse is set to the same simple melody, which is well within the vocal capacity and tonal range of even untrained singers. Antiphons, the most numerous type of chant, are preface statements introducing and concluding the psalm verses. The Introit and Communion of the Mass consist of this typical alternation of antiphon and psalm. Such a chant form may have been intended originally for alternating choirs, but that practice has been largely superseded by the use of a soloist and one choir. Antiphons occupy a middle range of complexity between the speech-song intonations of the *lection* tone and the more intricate Tract, Gradual, Offertory, and Alleluia chants.

The Tract is a chant of great antiquity, which was used in place of the jubilant Alleluia for seasons of mourning. It seems to have been conceived originally for a soloist and is, therefore, very ornate and expressive. It is one of the few types of chant in which musical elements seem to dominate the needs of the text. The Tract consists of three or four psalm verses without an accompaning antiphon. The Gradual was probably first sung from the steps (*gradus*) of the altar after the reading of the Epistle. Its one verse with an antiphon or a response is divided between soloist and choir. Such responsorial chants exhibit a particularly clear formal design in their recurrent melody patterns of verse and response sung in alternation by soloist and choir.

The Offertory originated as a musical accompaniment to the offering of bread and wine; later it became associated with the presentation of the congregational gifts at the altar. When the latter practice ceased, the Offertory was shortened so that in modern use the verses of Scripture have been eliminated and only the antiphon remains. Such Offertory chants as the *Jubilate Deo* ("Make a joyful noise unto God") contain long sections of pure melody sung on one syllable. Such a style is unusual in its repetitious use of both melodic material and phrases of text. One hypothesis is that since the presentation of offering consumed unpredictable lengths of time, repetition was used to fit the music into the time-span of the liturgical action.

The Alleluia uses an elaborate melody that enhances only the single word "alleluia." It concludes with a long florid section using only the final syllable for a text. As in the case of the Offertory, the Alleluia features a distinct repetition of small sections of musical material which eventually developed into independent forms of musical expression.

The repertoire of tones that constitute the pitch resources of the chants may have been originally based upon short melodic composites reminiscent of the Byzantine *octoechos*. Scholars who later codified the official collection of chants for the West attempted to systematize their manner of melodic construction as well. Eight modes or patterns of whole and half-step intervals were established, and all existing melodies were related to these modes by some element of their configuration. Ideally, the beginning and ending tones of a chant should correspond to the lowest or basic tone of the mode it is written in. It should also confine itself to the normal range and relatively high or low pitch level of the mode. However, many Gregorian melodies show evidence of being in more than one mode.

Medieval mode names were borrowed from the Dorian, Phrygian, Lydian, and Mixolydian designates of the Greek modes. They differed greatly from the ancient modes in internal structure and in their arrangement in an ascending rather than a descending order. Although poorly understood, the classical ideology was adopted into the musical thought of the West and rationalized wherever possible in order to serve prevailing practical needs. Medieval modes were actually distinctive scale patterns with differing arrangements of whole and half steps. The Greek scale was most probably one single pattern that could be transferred to lower or higher pitch levels. Medieval modes did share some common elements. Some used the same final pitch; others shared a common middle tone. A relatively accurate impression of the sound of these modes may be obtained by playing from one pitch on the piano to its octave pitch eight tones lower or higher using only the white keys.

The development of the Gregorian chant was stimulated, rather than hindered, by the adoption of an authoritative, codified liturgical structure. Although church musicians were no longer free to include material with limited ethnic appeal or to experiment with the basic elements of the liturgy, the growing literacy and musical proficiency stemming from Charlemagne's educational enterprises demanded some means of expression within the established limitations. Thus, by the ninth century sections of newly composed text and music began to be interpolated between existing sections of chant. Known as a *trope,* this expansion of the liturgy allowed for individual artistic contributions which remained fully under the control of the authorized chant. The Kyrie was especially adaptable for troping simply by the insertion of such amplifications as "Omnipotent Father, Creator of all" between the words "Kyrie" and "eleison." Dramatic fervor and lyric intensity were the hallmarks of this musical development which stressed the virtues of originality within the dictates of an established form.

Another chant that attracted particularly elaborate extensions was the Alleluia. At first, the practice was to lengthen even more the flamboyant melodic passage occurring on the final syllable. Then, gradually throughout the ninth and tenth centuries, a series of paired verses evolved to produce a paired rhyme, syllabic hymn style. The famous Easter sequence *Victimae*

paschali laudes is one of the few surviving remnants of the widespread practice of troping the Alleluia. Most of the vast collection of medieval tropes
was suppressed by the Council of Trent (1545–1563) in its massive reorganization of liturgical practices. Only five of the products of this period remain
in modern use, among them the *Dies Irae* and the *Stabat Mater.* In the perspective of the Dark Ages, these tropes were legitimate interpretations of the
meaning of the liturgy. Indeed, much of the intellectual energy of that time
was devoted to explaining the implications of a vast range of ideas to the
mass of mankind. Exegesis and amplification were at the very heart of the
thought process of the era and served to symbolize the vital concerns of all
men within the spirit of the collective ritual.

THE GOTHIC CULMINATION

A Cultural Profile

The later Middle Ages was an extremely long era comprising a varied
series of human episodes. It was marked by such significant events as the
Crusades and the formation of European national states, and by such remarkable persons as Frederick Barbarossa, Richard the Lionhearted, and
Pope Innocent III. There took place a gradual evolution that altered the nature of society along with the arts and intellectual life. The eleventh and
twelfth centuries were characterized by an absence of firm international
boundaries or clearly defined modes of political, religious, and economic
behavior. But by the fourteenth century, Europe resembled a tightly structured network of commonly held attitudes growing ever less tolerant of
diverse opinion.

As late as the twelfth century Europe still had an open frontier on its
eastern border. Both Russia and the Byzantine Empire were firmly related
to European culture through commercial transactions and continuous intermarriage. Otto II married a Byzantine princess who brought to Germany a
preference for the compassionately human religious art then practiced in
her homeland. The fusion of that attitude with the native Germanic style
of art produced the poignant realism of the Gero Crucifix in its powerful
portrayal of the agony of death (Figure 2.3). Even though a serious rupture
of ecclesiastical relations between East and West occurred in 1054, some
interchange continued on a relatively amicable basis until the debacle of the
Fourth Crusade. The inhabitants of the eastern lands interpreted the unpro-
voked invasion of their territory as nothing short of war. After the relationship with the East was curtailed, an exchange of ideas along with commercial transactions continued with the flourishing Islamic communities in
Spain. Intellectuals in western Europe were eager to avail themselves of the
treasures of ancient civilization preserved by the Muslim people. Spain was
composed of a particularly tolerant mixture of peoples, and where these
ideological frontiers met, brilliant cultural enterprises, such as the Angevin

Figure 2.3 Gero Crucifix. Cologne Cathedral. [Hirmer Fotoarchiv Munchen].

Empire in southern France, arose. A blend of pagan and Christian influences were combined effectively without strictly defined limitations on form or content.

Only very gradually did national boundaries and other human separations begin to be recognized. Even so, many members of the aristocracy were related by land holdings and intermarriage to both sides of these nebulous frontiers. The structure of society also gradually became less amenable to the free movement of people through various ranks and stations in life. The aristocracy became a closed circle ruled by family succession. Europe itself became more isolated from other empires and actually provoked alienation by crusades against the Byzantine and Islamic peoples. Institutions became more clearly stratified, and the church and secular powers began a long struggle for domination. The intelligentsia, clergy, aristocracy, merchants, and peasants all developed separate identities and clung to their special privileges. Education was more specialized and narrower in relation to the general life of the community. Bureaucracy became dominant, and a growing intolerance for diversity was symbolized by the founding of the Inquisition. The final blow to the cultural consistency of the medieval world was the descent of the dreaded Black Plague, which demoralized and depopulated much of Europe in the fourteenth century. Before the last bitter agonies of the epoch heralded its cultural crisis, much of value evolved to sustain future life patterns of the West. Not the least of those values, was the concept of law as a binding obligation, and the formulation, through legal recourse, of the means to secure the lives and destinies of all levels of citizenry.

The primary institution that shaped the very process of society was the Roman Church. During the Middle Ages, its forms of worship and belief were gradually stabilized into an intricate rationale with an elaborate supportive bureaucracy. The clergy became organized into a graduated system of relationships governed by a regularly observed protocol. The influence of the Benedictine monastery at Cluny, France, was notable in reorganizing the administrative division of ecclesiastical authority. It eliminated secular control over the selection of priests and placed the election of the pope in the hands of the cardinals.

The various doctrines of the church would have availed little had it not been for the universal acceptance of the supernatural as the one vital force securing the very existence of the world. Such an unquestioned belief was the major cohesive factor that bound men together across all social and economic classifications. All earthly life was deliberately arranged in order to reflect a supposed reality only fully manifest in heaven. Society itself was organized along the lines of authority assumed to be observed by the heavenly host. Thus Charlemagne and his twelve peers symbolized the hierarchy of Christ and his twelve disciples. The arts were dedicated to reflect an ever-existent transcendent truth so that it could pervade the life of man. Trinitarian divisions of God into the attributes of Father, Son, and Holy Spirit were captured endlessly in the major structural divisions of Gothic architecture and music. Dante's *Divine Comedy*, in its cantos, rhyme scheme, and divisions of the universe, was a vast multiplication of this divine triad.

The church was the most highly organized structure of the entire epoch. Within its control were law courts, vast business and commercial enterprises, an effective penal system, and a whole system of laws founded on Roman ideals. The highest degree of criminal misbehavior recognized throughout medieval society was heresy. The most dreaded punishment was excommunication, for it meant certain loss of the means of salvation and immortality. Quarrels between the church and civil officials could result in the withholding of the services of the church from an entire principality until public pressure upon the offenders provoked a public apology. Such powerful medieval kings as Philip Augustus of France and John of England were thoroughly chastized by even more powerful popes. At the height of the medieval papacy, Innocent III possessed more political, economic, and spiritual power than any man since the emperor Hadrian.

The pervasive influence of the church had a decisive effect upon both the thought of the common man and the formal philosophical process. Philosophy was fundamentally conditioned by the acceptance of revelation as the basis of all knowledge. Medieval intellectual pursuits were collectively called scholasticism from the term *doctores scholastici* (meaning those who taught liberal arts or theology in the church schools). Such a broad application of the term indicated the influence the church exerted in all intellectual endeavors. In the specific sphere of philosophy, scholasticism characterized a mode of thought that drew from certain persistent, adaptable classical traditions and from the revelations of Christianity. Some stress was always apparent between faith and reason; the great achievement of St. Thomas Aquinas was to relate both elements in one comprehensive system. The very problems chosen for philosophical speculation were conditioned by religious motives. Proofs for the existence of God and rationale for His activity were among the primary topics considered by all thinkers of the period. Formal logic and other patterns of classical thought were used but were separated from their original content. Scholasticism was preoccupied with deductive logic, systematization, and syllogistic formulation. The main impetus to this thought process came through the twelfth-century influx of translations from the Arabic and Greek of the major works of Aristotle. Adequate philosophical tools were thus found to perfect in an elegant system the intellectual fervor of the entire era.

The medieval social structure was identified by John of Salisbury, a twelfth-century English monk, in a manner that has come to represent the political imagery of the age. He pictured the state as a human being for which the monarch furnished the head, financial officers the stomach, soldiers the hands, farmers the feet, and other classes of people the remaining vital parts. His explanation may have been overly picturesque, but his idea was that all people have some necessary position in life; all have a place and an individual dignity. All humans acted as agents, and any human (including the king) who abused his position could rightfully be removed. Medieval society was founded upon a systematic relationship to each man's superiors and inferiors in the social and economic scale. Such relations were initiated by an elaborate ceremony contracting their mutual obligation. Protection by the more powerful individuals was offered in exchange for service by the less powerful. However, what was in theory a clearly defined social network of relationships was snarled by conflicting obligations to conflicting authorities. Much of the turmoil of the time was occasioned by disputes over such contractual relationships.

The nature of this feudal relationship was personal rather than familial, political, or territorial; but gradually it became hereditary to the oldest male child. Inherited land and goods constituted the *fief* which an individual could place under the supervision and protection of a higher ranking person whom the *fief* owner would then serve as a vassal. Feudalism thus rested upon divisions of sovereignty in an era that had no monarchs powerful enough to secure the safety of most of their people against the quarrels of petty nobility. The feudal system broke down when such monarchical power was finally attained.

The main task of the feudal nobility was to protect those vassals upon whose goods and services they depended. A prime requisite was a large fortified castle surrounded by a moat in which the lord and his vassals could take shelter during a seige. These fortified dwellings grew from damp, drafty cells to gracious, well-appointed quarters decorated with many luxuries imported from the eastern empires. Tapestries insulated the walls and brightened the room; musicians occasionally performed at major festivities. The calendar painted for the Duke of Berry pictured the daily life of the various classes of people who belonged to such an establishment (Figure 2.4). Hunting and fighting were the primary interests of the male inhabitants. Women indulged in a great variety of activities from needlework to the management of the estate in the absence of the lord. As the power of the monarch rose, the life style of the court, especially in France, became more elegant and mannerly.

Admittance to the ranks of the nobility came through the conferring of knighthood, an honor that naturally went to almost every member of the hereditary aristocracy. Such a title could also be conferred upon commoners through their bravery in battle, but the possibility became less likely as society became more stratified. The position of the nobility was truly ironic in many respects. Their social attainment rested almost entirely upon skill at warfare; yet, with the exception of such supposedly noble causes as the crusades, the warfare was of the nature of petty bickering. They were the ruling class; yet they were so illiterate and unskilled at administration that a class of civil servants did the actual governing. Their life style gravitated constantly between the heroic ideals set forth in the epic *Song of Roland* and the demands of grim reality.

Figure 2.4   January page from Limbourg Brothers Calendar. [Courtesy, Musee Conde, Chantilly (Giraudon)].

The best statement of the social ideology of the aristocracy was contained in the concept of chivalry as a system of human relations. Chivalry was an ethical ideal, which exerted an element of control vital to medieval society. Individualism was emphasized within a powerful tradition of moral responsibility. Chivalry was an assertion of personal honor and personal emotional alliances which stimulated highly personal artistic expressions. Woman became the idealized symbol of spiritual veneration, eternal quest, and the summary of the noblest of human attributes. Love became the ideal human emotion and hardness of heart the greatest human flaw. In many ways chivalry was closely paralleled with Christianity. The cult of the Virgin Mary was a great stimulus to the cult of idealized womanhood in a secular context. The confession, penance, and loyal service traditionally given to Christ were placed in the service of human love. The quest for the Holy Grail also became identified with the quest for personal glory. As holy wars, the crusades were ideal combinations of religion and the life style of chivalry. Trial by combat was both excused and glorified by the assurance that the victor was chosen by God to win. Yet Christianity and chivalry were highly antagonistic in their basic orientation. Christianity taught selflessness and the ultimate sinfulness of pride. Chivalry stressed individualism and the ultimate importance of personal attainments.

At the opposite end of the social scale the common man was characterized by quite a different life style. There was no really powerful middle class of merchants, bankers, and craftsmen to hold the political balance against both mob rule and the excesses of monarchs. The masses of men retained primarily a rural mentality. Even the large cities were walled settlements surrounded by farmers' fields. Members of the urban mercantile community were often farmers as well. During much of the Middle Ages, a great deal of tolerance was exhibited by each social class for members of other classes. In his descriptions of the clergy, Chaucer reveals individuals prone to the sins besetting all kinds and conditions of men. They are presented without rancor, and almost in appreciation for qualities that show a common human frailty. Until the late Middle Ages, all classes of people were so closely related in physical proximity and in general outlook that there was none of the bitterly anticlerical spirit that dominated the eighteenth century.

The town was one of the early exceptions to the feudal relationships that bound both church and state. Each town was organized according to purely secular economic needs, and developed as a collective system of political power. A town could even enter into feudal relationships with surrounding farmers and thus regulate agricultural prices. Each medieval town had its own distinctive customs, costume, and systems of money and measures. As a self-sufficient unit, it maintained all the necessities of life within one walled enclave. The town heralded the appearance of a new way of life; it was the focus of the great universities, political innovation, social diversity, and such collective architectural enterprises as the Gothic cathedrals.

At the beginning of their existence, towns were usually subservient to a resident lord or bishop who provided most of the food and protection. However, craftsmen and merchants soon were able to acquire both food and goods and to take collective measures to assure their own defense. They were thus in a position to bargain with the feudal overlord and to make contractual agreements on duties owed and other economic issues. The city became an independent self-governing entity controlled by a council of merchants; it was the primary social innovation which stimulated a new international culture. As an institution, the town was organized to secure economic as well as political justice. Marketable goods were assigned a just price; nothing more or less could be asked for them. Guilds (associations of merchants) were established to fix that price and to assure the purchaser that goods met a proper standard of excellence. Such concepts as expansion of workshops, capital improvement, technological innovation, and competition were foreign to early mercantile thinking and would have been considered dangerously disruptive.

Despite the great variety of life styles and the inevitable changes occurring over a considerable time-span, the Middle Ages was dominated by a sense of unity, a shared world outlook, and a profound appreciation for order in the universe. The overwhelming feeling for the collective identity of Christendom transcended many differences of custom and nationality. Beside the ageless Latin of the church arose the vernacular languages of the European peoples. Within the international style of Gothic art, there existed notable regional differences in decorative detail. In a society that viewed all men as equal in the sight of God, marked differences existed between social classes. The clergy, with its intellectual tradition, and the nobility, with its cult of chivalry, were quite different from the common man. Yet all men seemed to feel a general and satisfying security within a cosmology that was in harmony with life as they knew it. Men could be sure not only of their earthly position, but also of their eternal destiny. God was utterly reliable in His regulation of both natural and human events, although it was not within the province of man to plumb the mystery of His decisions. Miracles were not emergency explanations to be adopted when scientific data failed, but widely held truths about the very nature of reality. The envisioned, heavenly world was equal in actuality and significance to that of daily experience. It was certainly superior to the precarious existence of most men who were subject to the ill humor of an overlord and the burdens of heavy taxation from both church and state. In an age of violent contrasts, chivalry often masked brutality; spiritual aspiration thrived amid material poverty; and scholasticism often excused a paucity of original thought. Medieval people were fully conscious of the stress between the ideal and the real; they glorified these extremes in gargoyles and madonnas. Yet they were not anguished by the discrepancies, as they were fully aware of the physical and moral limitations of mankind. They were assured that in the mind of God such failures and limitations were encompassed into a meaningful whole.

THE INTELLECTUAL TRADITION

The religious fervor that perpetuated the Crusades and inspired a sudden upsurge of church building produced one of the central musical innovations distinguishing western music from that of all other civilizations. That was the development of polyphony. The famous monastic centers of St. Gall, Switzerland, St. Martial and St. Victor in France, and Santiago de Compostela in Spain made early attempts to elaborate the basic chant by expanding the simple monophonic tune into two different melodic parts that were to be sung at the same time. The concept is a logical extension of the practice of troping. Instead of interpolating the newly invented material between sections of authorized chant, the chant and the newly composed melody were performed concurrently. This practice of singing more than one melody at a time was not without precedent, as secular vocal music among the Britons, Scandinavians, Celts, and Germans was known to have featured two voice parts that moved in the same rhythm at a pitch interval of a third apart. However, the interval preferred by the church was that of the fourth or fifth. The resulting sound was quite austere in comparison to the somewhat mellow sound of a chain of thirds.

Polyphony (simultaneous melody lines) was developed as a technique by musicians and theorists who gave an intellectual structure to the common practices of native European peoples. The traditional Gregorian chant melody provided the basic tune; then another melody line was added either above or below the chant. In the earliest stages of polyphonic practice, the two melodies moved along in close interval proximity and with very little independence. However, there was no consistent practice during this period; rather, it was a time of adventurous experimentation in which a number of variants were developed. As a term, polyphony implies not only the existence of more than one melody line, but also an independence of movement in which the melodies move toward and away from each other, sometimes intermingling. One prominent form practiced at the monastery of St. Martial used the Gregorian chant in very long sustained tones with a florid melody of more rapidly moving tones added above it.

The most significant evolution of polyphonic technique took place at the cathedral of Notre Dame in Paris. This same institution which supported the highest attainments of scholastic philosophy also endowed music with its most intricate intellectual development. The first landmark was the *Magnus Liber Organi*, a thirteenth-century collection of music in two voice parts for the liturgical services of the church year. The composers most associated with this collection were Leonin and his successor, Perotin. The school at Notre Dame initiated the development of the motet as the leading musical form of the Gothic period

The motet was an amazing structure that maintained a delicate balance of strict symmetry and freely entwined melodies. The fundamental organizing factor was the rhythm. Instead of using the Gregorian chant melody as a constant drone bass, or in evenly spaced tones without any particular sense of grouping, the motet composer reorganized the chant into a regularly repeated rhythmic pattern. The aural sensation obtained by such steady recurrence can be compared with a wallpaper design featuring many repetitions of the same small motif. This rhythmically conceived version of the chant tune, called the *cantus firmus,* gave the composition its formal cohesion. The *cantus firmus* was sung, and perhaps played on instruments, as the lowest sounding melody line in the music. Over this tonal foundation were placed two other melody lines, which seemed to move more rapidly because of the greater number of tones sung in the same time-span as that occupied by the more slowly progressing chant. The description of the form as a motet derived from the practice of adding words (French: *mot*) to these melody lines. The texts were sometimes derived from nonliturgical sources so that the motet gradually became a sophisticated, secular accouterment to the urbane culture of late Gothic society.

The diversification of the motet from its chaste, monastic origins into a motley assemblage of popular tunes, dance melodies, and love songs held together by a rigidly conceived intellectual structure has no better literary counterpart than Dante's *Divine Comedy.* Even the cohesion attained by *terza rima* and the omnipresent Trinitarian symbolism basic to the structure of the poem find a parallel in the standard three melody lines and three metric pulses fundamental to the motet. The intricate interplay of sound appealed to medieval minds in the same way literary visions fascinated them with an awesome delight. Gothic architectural style also bore a resemblance to the motet. Both had their origins in Paris; both combined the rational with the emotional, logic with mysticism. Both sound and stone defined the world beyond in a unified, emotionally appealing concept.

Musical theory was significantly related to the intellectual tradition because of its involvement with the general stream of philosophical development. Both flourished at the new university centers and particularly at the University of Paris. Theoretical thought drew extensively from St. Augustine's treatise *De Musica,* from the ancient Pythagorean traditions preserved in Neoplatonic philosophy, and from the newly revived writings of Aristotle on mathematics and astronomy. The process leading to the reconciliation of classical writings with Christian dogma also operated within the more limited scope of musical esthetics.

Certain philosophers were particularly notable for their analysis of the implications of tonal combinations. Boëthius's *De Institutione Musica* (sixth century) was the central source for all later treatises on music. The work represented a direct continuation of the theories of Ptolemy. Isidore, Cassiodorus, John Scotus Erigena, the Venerable Bede and Bishop Oldhelm left important works on music which document the development of polyphonic practices. From the practical point of view the pitch intervals employed in the early stages of polyphony could have reflected either the natural pitch ranges of baritone and tenor vocal registers, the pitch or tone quality changes occurring in antiphonal singing, or the order of intervals in the natural overtone series. However, once in practice, the chosen intervals were integrated into the thought process of the Middle Ages as though no other choices were possible. Thus the pitch distances or intervals of the octave, fifth, and fourth became "perfect" intervals reflecting the mathematical ratios that govern the movements of the planets and regulate cosmic forces.

As has been noted in the Greek and Byzantine cultures, most sophisticated musical systems arrive at an observance of some consistent repertoire of tones which comprise the scales or modes. The system devised by medieval theorists endured for hundreds of years before it was replaced by the major and minor scales. Because they accepted without question the classical tradition of eight modes, medieval theorists established eight scale configurations and gave them the names of the old Greek modes. They even assigned an ethical character to each mode in deference to the Greek practice.

In the case of rhythm, the necessities of compositional practice and the rationalizations of theorists were particularly complementary. Monophonic music could dispense with repetitive musical accents or beats because it adopted the normal emphasis of the text and because all participants sang the same melody at the same time. When the singers confronted two or more independent melodies at once, each perhaps with its own text, the problem of coordination became critical. The most logical solution was to observe some regularly recurring point of emphasis which was identical for each melody line. Shortly before 1200, the school of Notre Dame adopted a rhythmic principle of organization for polyphonic music as found in the motet. However, the theoretical rationalization of this innovation reflected the dominance of the classical tradition in Gothic culture. The rhythmic patterns employed were supposedly derived from the meters of classical poetry, although modern authorities admit difficulty in establishing a direct correspondence. As codified by the theorists, the patterns were formed into groupings of three beats that fused the ancient practice with Trinitarian symbolism. The rhythmic system upon which the notation of western music has been built thus seemingly arose in response to some pervasive craving for intricate and yet controlled design principles.

The complex growth of polyphonic music precipitated the development of a comprehensive system of notation, whereby the exact pitch and duration of a tone could be indicated. So long as there was only one melody line and the rhythm simply followed the natural inflection of the text, a very simple system of grammatical accents would suffice. For such music, notational marks, or *neumes,* derived from Greek accents were placed at varying heights directly above the Latin text (Figure 2.5). The addition

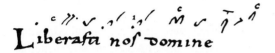

Figure 2.5   Late Ninth Century Neume notation.

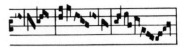

Figure 2.8   Late Thirteenth Century ligature notation.

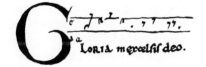

Figure 2.6   Twelfth Century two-line staff.

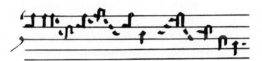

Figure 2.9   Sixteenth Century Gothic notation.

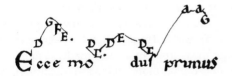

Figure 2.7   Late Eleventh Century letter notation.

Figure 2.10   Early Fifteenth Century French notation.

of small dots to indicate intermediate pitches provided most of the data necessary for deciphering the tune. A primary innovation was made by some anonymous scribe who drew a horizontal red line to represent the pitch "f" and grouped the *neumes* around it. Additional lines were subsequently added until the four-line staff became the standard form for the notation of the chant (Figure 2.6).

A great diversity of notational forms were used during this developmental period, many of which soon were discarded. One experimental system used letter names to indicate pitches (Figure 2.7). Several notational systems solved the problem of indicating pitch but failed to show how long the tones were to be held. The ligature system proved to be accurate in the designation of pitch and could also indicate a number of rhythmic specifications (Figure 2.8). The ligature form called Gothic notation was the style in which the chorales of the Lutheran Church were written (Figure 2.9). It lingered, along with Gothic architecture, until long after other more flexible systems were adopted in other parts of Europe. The elegant notation used by French composers resembled the delicate tracery of Paris court style in manuscript illumination and the slender proportions of sculpture (Figure 2.10). Richly decorated music manuscripts were among the most distinguished products of medieval art (Figure 2.11). Medieval contributions to the metric theory of music were equally significant. Modern meters were provided by mathematical theorists of the seventeenth century, but the fundamental system of western notation was perfected in the crucible of the medieval mind.

A modern listener is likely to regard the obstinately repeated rhythmic patterns of a Gothic motet as revealing a singular lack of creative imagination. Within a philosophical attitude controlled by tradition and a penchant for extreme systematization such styles could flourish satisfactorily; they did not survive the chaotic changes brought by the fourteenth century. Burgeoning social evils and waves of Black Plague undermined the cultural stability. The continuing schism in the church, the rise of heretical religious sects, the conflict among secular political states and an influx of classical humanism created an environment of agonizing transition.

The impact of Aristotelian Realism appeared in a new appraisal of music, not as a pure form revealing the harmony of the spheres, but as an element of motion and change measured by a man-made system. The sense of time as a humanly experienced phenomenon led to radical rhythmic innovations that departed from the strict repetitions of short patterns. The principle innovator was Philippe de Vitry (1290–1361) Bishop of Meaux, poet, musician, and theorist. His treatise, called *Ars Nova*, gave the name to this musical period of reformulation. The new system substituted for the old metrical units an almost infinite variety of rhythmic combinations subject only to a few standard divisions of temporal duration. The *Ars Nova* principles constituted the beginning of the modern mensural system with its familiar whole, half, quarter, and eighth note relationships. The Trinitarian attraction for rhythms grouped into three beats yielded to a complete acceptance of heretofore secular duple meters. The effect on the

Figure 2.11   Leaf from an illuminated Antiphonary. (Flemish 15th Century). [The Metropolitan Museum of Art. Gift of Louis L. Lorillard, 1896].

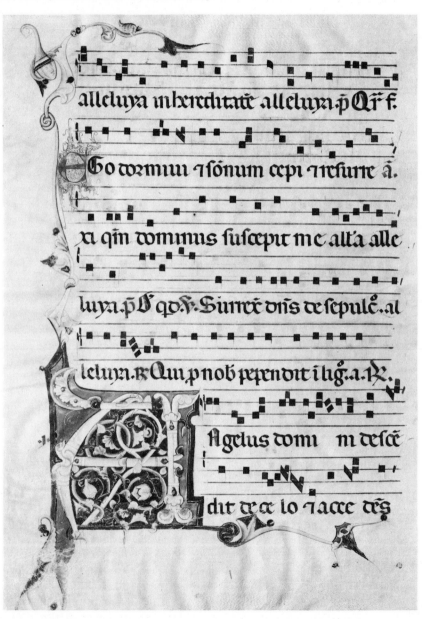

motet and other forms of polyphony was immediate and significant. The *cantus firmus* was still derived from Gregorian chant, but the tune was formed into longer, more flexible patterns invented by the composer instead of into short metrical formulas invented by the Greeks. The embellishing melodies were not limited to two; their texts often echoed the sentiments of courtly love. Composers felt little compunction to preserve the original character of the chant tune; it was simply raw material for new creative concepts. The *Ars Nova* movement was predominantly secular in orientation, and by its very name reflected the consciousness of a change in medieval culture.

Among the many famous artists, writers and musicians of the fourteenth century, three are particularly noteworthy. The leading composer was Guillaume de Machaut—a cleric, soldier, courtier, Canon of Reims, poet, and musician. He celebrated his love for a lady named Peronne in the best tradition of courtly expression. In his life style he revealed the same conservative and progressive tendencies as two other great men of the time. The humanist scholar Petrarch lived the same loosely clerical existence with his many official duties in the secular world. He established the form and style of the sonnet, by which he celebrated his own love for the lady Laura. The artist Giotto was a painter, sculptor, and an architect. He created in his frescoes a new dimension of emotional and spatial depth. His paintings established a visual position of orientation for the viewer and provided a dramatic formal focus. Yet, as innovative as they were, all three men were profoundly tied to the past in subtle but powerful ways. After climbing Mt. Ventoux, Petrarch first paused on the peak to glory in the sense of power and freedom he felt; then he read a selection from St. Augustine, chastising him for worldly ambitions. Giotto remained within the traditional subject matter prescribed by the church. His technical innovations served only to enhance the traditional beliefs he did not question. Machaut exhibited an increased skill in polyphonic writing, but his basic continuity with the medieval polyphonic tradition remained obvious.

Compositional freedom and the rule of whim were not rampant in fourteenth-century music. Indeed, Machaut imposed upon his flights of musical fancy the principle of isorhythm—one of the most complex sets of restrictions any composer has ever employed. He arranged the *cantus firmus* in a rhythmic pattern that operated independent of the melody. This rhythmic pattern was repeated a number of times, often at varying speeds, during the course of the entire chant melody. The problem of making the chant tune, the rhythmic pattern, and several embellishing melody lines relate well musically was most difficult. Machaut's masterpiece, the *Mass of Notre Dame* was the first polyphonic setting of the Ordinary to be composed by one individual. Within its four-part texture, all of the intellectual devices of the fourteenth century were amply illustrated. Yet Machaut maintained an allegiance to the perfect intervals—even when the philosophy surrounding their use was no longer valid. The strongest rhythmic points were still given the spare sound of the fourth, fifth, and octave. The most audible changes in his music included a more complex polyphonic texture and longer, more complete musical phrases. Each melody line featured tiny details that emerged first from one vocal part and then another like small wheels within an intricate balance of moving parts.

This century of transition came to accept many forms of medieval music having some religious content, but functioning also as pure entertainment. The popular Christmas carol originated as a dance tune to which a quasireligious text was adapted. Some carols were drinking songs that accompanied the more spirited aspects of Christmas merrymaking. Such mixed forms of expression occasionally approached the devotional piety of the humble St. Francis, whose philosophy of love and service to mankind provided a humanizing balance to the rationalistic focus of clerical intellectual life. His unbounded joy in the wonder of all creation was eloquently revealed in his "Canticle of the Sun":

> Praise be to Thee, my Lord, with all Thy creatures,
> Especially to my worshipful brother sun,
> Which lights up the day, and through him dost
> Thou brightness give;
> And beautiful is he and radiant with splendor great;
> Of Thee, most High, signification gives.[1]

The institutional church labeled the sacred folksong as religious, but regrettably secular as well. The church had opposed popular secular styles as far back as the time of the ninth century Celtic Lay. The song form of the lay used a series of improvised melodies sung to paired lines of text. It had very little in common with liturgical style; yet its form was eventually adopted to organize long tropes. Thus, while condemning certain types of music, the church managed to draw both inspiration and actual materials from secular sources. Rhythm, which became the main preoccupation of the intellectual tradition, was the veritable hallmark of secular music. The earliest form of polyphonic practice was most probably adapted from a similar technique used in secular singing. Knowledge of secular music is so limited that it is difficult for the modern student to draw more than general conclusions about its style or manner of performance. It survived for centuries by informal rote learning, as literate musicians who might have preserved it in notation lavished their attention on liturgical music.

At certain periods, church leaders became especially short-tempered with what they considered to be the demoralizing influence of popular song. Some went so far as to suppress popular expression in the arts. Charlemagne's son, Louis the Pious, shared the ecclesiastical opinion that

1 R. Robinson, *The Writings of Saint Francis of Assisi* (Philadelphia: Dolphin, 1906).

some popular arts were entirely too close to pagan rituals and must be legislated out of existence. After Louis' musical inequities, the next effort to impose artistic integrity upon secular forms of expression came through the Goliards—a group of vagrant students, uprooted clerics, and other social misfits. The Goliards did little more than roam about Europe composing and singing Latin songs of a decidedly nonclerical nature. As the self-appointed sponsors of the peoples' music they preserved much that would otherwise have been lost. They were conversant enough with the techniques of the intellectual tradition to achieve a surprising level of poetic excellence. Some of their poetry was included in collections commissioned by bishops and noblemen. In an outstanding collection called the *Carmina Burana,* one Goliard stated his philosophy of life:

> Watch the roast turn on the spit,
> And the wine that's clear and green,
> Orleans, Rochelle, Auxerre,
> That's the joy that's *unicum.*
> To drink and wench and play at dice
> Seem to me no such mighty sins. . . .[2]

In contrast with the pious Louis of France, Alfonso X of Spain sponsored one of the greatest collections of popular religious music, the *Cantigas.* These devotional songs in honor of the Virgin Mary were fundamental to the development of Spanish vernacular literature and music. They very possibly preserved the ethnic liturgy suppressed by the Roman Church and absorbed additional Arabic influences within their poetic style. Another important source of popular religious music was the flagellants—roving bands of penitent pilgrims who sang as they marched and beat themselves with whips. The flagellants were characteristic of the veritable penitential mania that swept Europe in the wake of the Black Plague. In Italy and Germany, songs called *laude* and *geisslerlieder* expressed the fervor of their devotions. This musical influence was persistent, and appeared later in the basic style of the Lutheran chorale. Popular secular music was all that liturgical music was not. It was highly personal in imagery and emphatically rhythmic. Its form was based upon a repeated refrain that seldom occurs within the structure of Gregorian chant.

Although the foregoing forms were important and enduring, the most significant blend of influences from the church and the world was medieval drama. Its history followed the course of the age in that the early drama was dominated by a pastoral monastic ideology, which eventually gave way to an urban, secular spirit. The drama was probably reborn during the Middle Ages, since ties with the theatrical tradition of

---

2 Helen Waddell, *The Wandering Scholar* (New York: Holt, Rinehart & Winston, 1932), p. 211.

Greece and Rome had long been broken. Its birthplace was the church, and its form was that of the liturgy. The essential elements of drama (impersonation, action, and dialogue) were present in embryonic form in the central celebrations of the church year. The earliest dramatic activity most probably centered about the dialogue between the two Marys and the angel of the Resurrection story. In its formative stages, the drama was not simply a Biblical dialogue, but rather a musical extension of the practice of troping. It was music-drama delivered in the same style of expression as the rest of the liturgical service, but containing elaborations of the events as recorded in the Scriptures. The costumes used were those employed in the normal priestly functions, and the properties were those used for church services.

Figure 2.12   PIETER BRUEGEL. *Peasant Theatre on the Market Place.* [The Bettman Archive].

The height of medieval drama was reached in the twelfth and thirteenth centuries when the writing and production of plays was still under the control of monasteries and cathedral schools. Like other masterworks of that period, the *Play of Herod* reflected the many social levels and cultural traditions of medieval society. It began with a processional to the folk hymn *Oriente Partibus,* which describes the journey of the donkey carrying Mary to Bethlehem. The body of the play consisted of dialogue between characters and was carried on in traditional Gregorian chant style. The scene was climaxed with the singing of a motet. The congregation was then invited to pay their respects at the manger to the accompaniment of a rollicking dance tune played by drum, string, and reed instruments.

Many secular elements were apparent in such a play; some portions were sung in the vernacular and were set to typical styles of folk music. However, a significant formal design and emotional restraint were placed upon such materials by writers and composers who represented the intellectual tradition. When these controlling elements were lost, the medieval drama became the mystery play with its rather obvious moralizing and open ribaldry. *Everyman* is the outstanding example of such a play, although the *Play of Noah* is much more typical of the genre. Drama lost its musical form and entered the period of the innyard theater with its wagon stages. The merchant guilds assumed responsibility for play production and created a genuinely popular theater (Figure 2.12). Thus techniques and traditions were gathering, which were to culminate in the works of Shakespeare and the golden age of Renaissance drama.

The Courtly Tradition

Slowly growing up beside the intellectual tradition was another tradition that annoyed, challenged, and finally broke the control of ecclesiastical authority over the content and style of the arts. The courts of the nobility provided a way of life basically antagonistic to the life style generated by religious institutions. Many influences combined to produce the cultural patterns of the medieval court; one was undoubtedly the example of eastern and Islamic rulers. Another came from the cathedral schools through which the literature of classical and Islamic civilization passed into European life. As centers of learning that served an increasing number of the nobility, the schools nourished a concept of life in which the enhancement of the arts was welcome. European nobles admired the opulence of the Spanish Moors and Near Eastern potentates, and an expanding economy was beginning to provide some modest luxuries. Castles, which began as barren fortifications, grew into elaborate stone dwellings. Even warfare became stylized into colorful tournament games. The major characteristics of medieval court life became apparent by the early twelfth century.

From the social milieu of the secular courts a literary and artistic tradition slowly took shape. The first notable creation was the *chanson de geste,* an epic tale based on legendary deeds. The *Song of Roland* was the most famous work in this form. Such tales had an important psychological effect in that they presented an idealized picture of the Christian hero and thus provided a cultural identity for the emerging nobility. The probable sources for the heroic epic were the Teutonic sagas and the pre-

Christian legends of the Celts. As an art form the *chanson de geste* contained the significant rudiments for a genuine secular tradition. Through them the Romance languages, which had become somewhat independent of Latin, acquired a means of expression above the merely functional. Epic poems were designed to be sung by itinerant musicians who served the daily occasions of the people much as the choir served the church. These *jongleurs* wandered from castle to village earning a precarious living as singers, dancers, acrobats, and animal trainers. The laws of the land abused them; they possessed no civil rights; and they were even denied the sacraments of the church. Yet, as epic singers, they perpetuated the ideals upon which courtly traditions were based. Because their music was not bound to the international style of liturgical practice it more readily absorbed regional traits. The *jongleurs* were only one segment of a great number of itinerant musicians whose counterparts were the scops and gleemen in England and the *gaukler* in Germany.

Jongleurs were neither poets nor composers; they sang and danced to the songs that more cultivated persons wrote. The nobility considered it beneath their dignity to perform their own music. *Jongleurs* who had the good fortune to become permanently attached to some noble household contributed their skill to the development of another form of secular literature, the courtly romance. The themes of the epic were heroism, sacrifice, idealism, and quest—all eternal patterns as styled by the Homeric tradition. The themes of the lyric poets of France and Spain were love, nature, and mysticism. Both poetic forms developed aspects of cultural psychology distinct from the monastic enterprise or the intellectual focus of the university.

Love, often in the guise of subjective mysticism, was an underlying element in the religious thought of the Middle Ages. Philosophers such as Bonaventura and Duns Scotus stressed the power of love over intellect and glorified the intuitive apprehension of God. Dante was conducted through Hades by Virgil in the guise of human reason; only Beatrice in the role of divine love could guide him to the heavenly realms. However, the love element of the lyric poets idealized the emotional relationship between an individual man and woman. The Grail quest was translated into a quest for a lady's favor. Heroism in a religious or political cause became self-cultivation in the code of chivalry. The lyric movement emphasized the conflicts growing within medieval society. Countering the monastic ideology of woman as an evil influence was the image of divine womanhood conceived by the French Provençal poets. The relationship of the knight and his adored lady became for many the only true measure of honor, justice, and morality.

If one person were chosen to represent the spirit of the lyric movement the honor would go to Eleanor of Aquitaine (1122–1204). With her husband, Henry II, of England, she helped create the Angevin Empire, encompassing areas of both France and Spain. Under her sponsorship, the poet-noblemen of her realm retold the exploits of Alexander, Caesar, and the Trojan heroes in terms of chivalrous ideals. Eleanor's grandfather was the first of the troubadours; he was greatly influenced by the poetry of Syria and Aragon. The modes of expression used by Moorish poets and the early forms of troubadour poems exhibited a great similarity.

The role of women in the Moorish courts was also influential in changing the status of women in Europe. In Spain, women often ruled in the absence of their husbands, and they were much respected for their individual personalities and accomplishments. After centuries of being regarded much as cattle to be traded for monetary or political advantage, Eleanor and her coterie were determined to change the status of women through poetic propaganda and other mannerly reformations. They succeeded unexpectedly well in presenting women as ideal images to be selflessly served by cultivated gentlemen. Their success was partly due to the fact that most men above the age of fourteen were away on Crusades; the women were free to mold younger minds without hindrance from male relatives. The results rather shocked the general public and directly undermined both the feudal and the clerical systems of authority. Ladies whose fortunes had increased through the death of crusaders in the family assumed great power to control the life style of the nobility. The famous "code of love" Eleanor had drawn up by her chaplain was a veritable symbol of women's rebellion against an overly oppressive masculine world.

The actual poetry and music of the troubadours in southern France and the *trouvères* in northern France was less revolutionary than the social change the movement itself represented. Despite all the assertions of individualism, most poems presented stereotyped situations. As represented in modern notation the tunes featured some regularly recurring rhythmic pattern. There was some instrumental accompaniment, although only to duplicate the melody line or add short monophonic interludes between verses. The repetition of phrases of the melody created a sense of form quite different from that of Gregorian chant. The popular *rondeau* and *ballade* forms exhibited typical patterns of repetition; both were eventually developed into polyphonic forms of great intellectual subtlety. Thus, the formative contributions of the lyric movement had an important influence for centuries to come.

A later generation of poet-musicians was represented by such outstanding figures as Bernart de Ventadorn, Bertran de Born, and Marcabru of Gascony. The movement flowered with great rapidity, but slowly dissolved amid the chaos of the Albigensian persecution. It was transported to courts all over Europe, where it blended Islamic and oriental mannerisms into medieval courtly tradition. The poets provided an additional impetus to the formation of a structure and style for the vernacular languages. Dante in his conception of Beatrice was deeply influenced by the courtly love tradition. He revealed his high regard for the French poets by having some appear

Figure 2.13   King David and Musicians from 12th Century Psalter. [Glasgow University Library, Haines].

as characters in the *Divine Comedy.* The world is richer for such expressions of the beauty of nature and love as those found in the writings of the lyric poets:

> At the gates of summer love stands to greet us
> The earth, to do him honor, burgeons beneath his feet.
> The flowers that attend him laugh at the golden prime,
> Should Venus not befriend them, they die before their time.
>
> Of all things the beginning was on an April morn;
> In spring the earth remembers the day when she was born.[3]

Dance music also served as the generative pattern for many songs and established standard instrumental practices to enhance the setting of the poem. The medieval musician had a variety of instruments from which to choose. In their medieval form, these instruments represented a midpoint in the evolution from ancient to modern forms. As a favorite instrument of the epic singers, the harp made its appearance first among the Irish bards. A native instrument of Syria, the harp was a typical instrument throughout ancient cultures and was represented in a variety of sizes and shapes. Along with physicians, scholars, and other learned men, the epic singer was subsidized by European royal courts. In manuscript paintings the harp was often pictured in the hands of King David, the fabled writer of many psalms of the Old Testament. An illustration from a twelfth-century psalter shows him surrounded by such typical medieval instruments as the *vielle, recorder,* chimes, and hurdy-gurdy (Figure 2.13).

The *vielle* was among the most prominent stringed instruments. A descendant of the Asiatic *fiedel,* it was made in several sizes. An early type was supported on the knee and played with what resembled an actual hunting bow. A later form of the instrument was held against the shoulder. Some *vielles* were plucked rather than bowed. The larger varieties were sometimes played as a hurdy-gurdy by inserting a wooden wheel with metallic projections that plucked the strings automatically when a crank was turned. A small stringed instrument, the *rebec,* was a descendant of the Arabian *rebâb* and resembled a mandolin more than a modern violin. It was pear-shaped and was held on the lap with the tuning pins resting against the shoulder.

Woodwind instruments were available in many shapes and tone qualities. The medieval flute, or *recorder,* was a simple wooden shaft with small bored finger holes; it was held downward in playing. The small flute could be played with one hand, leaving the other free to beat a small drum. The ancestor of the modern flute held transversely across the player's face was

3   Helen Waddell, *The Wandering Scholar* (New York: Holt, Rinehart & Winston, 1932), p. 222.

imported from the East and became popular in Germany. The *shawm,* an ancient type of oboe, was imported from the Sicilian Saracens in the twelfth century. It had a brilliant tone that was particularly effective for use out-doors. The bagpipe was a favorite instrument of the common people and became a national symbol of the Scotch. Like the Irish harp, it was associated with folk epics and the deeds of legendary ancestors.

Figure 2.14   HANS BURGKMAIR. *The Elder.* (Organ woodcut from *The Triumphal Procession of Emperor Maximilian 1.*) [The Metropolitan Museum of Art, Harris Brisbane Dick Fund, 1932.]

Medieval horns most probably developed independently from ancient Greek and Roman models. They were straight or slightly bent metal tubes of variable length. Small ones were used by shepherds and tower watchmen; larger forms were useful to give battle signals. A special form called the *oliphant* was prized as a symbol of knighthood. It was made of elephant tusk and imported from Byzantium in the tenth century. The *oliphant* was the famous horn in the *Song of Roland.*

The organ, in its early medieval form, resembled a huge bagpipe with a great bellows and hand-operated pump. Such instruments as the one at Winchester Cathedral in England attained an enormous size, but were not efficiently or easily played. The air flow into the pipes was controlled by means of levers that opened and closed to regulate the release of wind into individual pipes. The large board-like keys which operated the levers were difficult to depress; the resulting tone was extremely loud and variable in accuracy. Smaller forms of the organ could be moved about on wagons (Figure 2.14). The most musically effective organs were easily portable instruments played by one person who pumped the bellows with one hand and depressed the keys with the other.

In Germany, both vocal and instrumental forms of secular music were well adapted to the life style of the rising middle class and the collective interests of the city. Although the *touvère* style was transplanted in Germany through the marriage of Beatrix of Burgundy to Frederick Barbarossa (1123–1190), the German poet-musicians did not conform to the stock situations and characters of their French forebears. These *minnesingers* added an individual frame of reference and often wrote on such themes as their personal religious experience.

The aristocratically dominated feudal system, which had previously nourished secular artistic endeavors, fell before the rising importance of towns and the burgher mentality that sustained them. The old tournaments of song under royal patronage became the song contests between middle-class musicians. Music making became the function of a guild that was organized like any other craft guild; every song composer had to conform to specifications enforced by guild officials. The form, rhyme, and poetic meter had to conform to rule and not offend holy writ. Yet in Germany, as elsewhere, the art of the lyric poets often represented a rebellion against authoritarian systems. Poems might contain thinly veiled satires of either church or state, as found in Bertran de Born's comment: "My lords, I charge you, pawn castles and towns and cities before you renounce the joys of warfare." This rebellion stood at the heart of German mysticism; it was the spirit of St. Francis in a broader context. By the end of the Middle Ages, aristocrats were losing economic superiority, while middle-class merchants were gaining control through trade leagues. Even the new weaponry had the effect of making the commoner and knight equal in battle. With these events as a background, it is understandable why music which celebrated the feelings and aspirations of ordinary men was so popular.

The Middle Ages groped toward its end through years of turmoil, which often succeed long periods of stability. Yet the era left much of vast significance to the ongoing process of western culture. It had made a supreme effort to unify man in relation to the universe and to put him in contact with eternally existing forces. Much of the good in medieval culture was captured by Dante in his visionary description of paradise:

> To fix my eyes upon the Eternal Light
>
> .   .   .
>
> I saw that in its depths there are enclosed,
> Bound up with love in one eternal book,
> The scattered leaves of all the universe —
> Substance, and accidents, and their relations,
> As though together fused in such a way
> That what I speak of is a single light.[4]

4   Lawrence Grant White, trans., *The Divine Comedy* (New York: Random House, 1928), p. 188. Copyright 1948 by Pantheon Books, a division of Random House, Inc. Reprinted by permission.

SUMMARY OUTLINE

MEDIEVAL CIVILIZATION

Dark Ages
Carolingian Renaissance
Romanesque Period
Gothic Period
Late Gothic Transition

GENERAL CULTURAL INFLUENCES

History: international migrations; political dominance of the Roman Church; Muslim influence in Europe; Holy Roman Empire; foundations of nationalism.

Social Factors: feudalism; crusades; codes of chivalry; rise of towns; guilds and mercantile associations; founding of universities.

Philosophy and Religion: scholasticism; church schism; birth of humanism.

Science: Roger Bacon and beginning of scientific methodology.

MUSICAL ATTRIBUTES

Theory: St. Augustine's *De Musica;* Boëthius's *De Institutione Musica;* origins of polyphony; concepts of perfect and imperfect intervals; dominance of symbolic triple divisions; church modes; ligature notation; metrical rhythm.

Social Functions: development of Mass and Divine Offices as communal celebrations; rise of secular musical tradition through goliards, troubadours, and minnesingers.

Composers and Forms: Pope Gregory the Great and the western chant tradition; use of antiphons and psalms; tropes and sequences; Leonin and Perotin: *Magnus Liber Organi;* Philippe de Vitry and the *Ars Nova* movement; Guillaume de Machaut: *Mass of Notre Dame;* carol, folk epic, and ballade as popular forms.

Instruments: harp, vielle, rebec, recorder, shawm, bagpipes, horns, organ.

ARTISTIC PARALLELS

Latin as international scholarly language; influx of Arabic learning; translation of Aristotle's works; establishment of arts in education.

Medieval drama and mystery plays as education and celebration; rise of Romance languages and literature; Eleanor of Aquitaine and the lyric movement.

Monastic art production: *Lindisfarne Gospels;* Gothic cathedrals; naturalism in sculpture: "Gero Crucifix" frescoes of Giotto; Dante's *Divine Comedy;* sonnets of Petrarch.

3
*The*Renaissance

A CULTURAL PROFILE

In contrast with the Middle Ages, the Renaissance (*c.* 1400–1600) bears a limited but vital direct resemblance to the twentieth century. With a typical self-consciousness, the people of the fifteenth and sixteenth centuries pursued the concept of a renaissance or rebirth which identified their era. The same consciousness of departure from the past is a strong characteristic of the twentieth century. The historian Harry Elmer Barnes in his book, *Intellectual and Cultural History of the Western World,* places both periods at the initial stages of world revolutions which have transformed human history. Both eras exhibit a firm faith in the senses as the basic mode of knowing. Although transferred from the oceans to space flight, the romance of exploration is equally intense. Renaissance theories on the structure of the universe are represented in the twentieth century by even more elaborate theories concerning the origin of the universe. The religious rebellion that manifested itself in the Protestant Reformation is present in modern society as an individual quest for spiritual reality increasingly sought outside the institutional church. The attraction that the culture of ancient Greece and Rome held for the Renaissance has manifested itself in a twentieth century classical revival. The arts of the Renaissance seem closer to the cultural heritage of modern man because they are so well represented in museums and private collections and are venerated by the molders of public opinion. The limited feeling of kinship between the two eras has been enhanced not only by such shared attitudes but by certain common experiences as well.

During the Renaissance the pace of events seemed to quicken. Men were captivated, as well as disturbed, by innovations in society, technology, and intellectual concerns. The two centuries were characterized by events that influenced the social and political patterns of the modern world. Such memorable monarchs as England's Elizabeth I prefaced the absolutism of France's Louis XIV and Germany's Frederick the Great. While a medieval king was supported and sometimes controlled by the power of the church, and guided by his self-image as a Christian servant, a Renaissance monarch was proud that his individual efforts had gained him a kingdom and was determined to exploit his position to the best of his ability. Toward this end, Machiavelli (1469–1527) offered some astute advice on the use of political power. Jean Bodin (1530–1596) elaborated upon Machiavelli's basic assumptions to formulate the theory of unconditional sovereignty, which evolved into the divine right of kings. With this political philosophy, such rulers as Richard II, Henry V, Henry VII, Henry VIII, and Charles VII heralded the formation of the great national states of modern Europe.

The social and intellectual innovations of the era took shape within an atmosphere of continuing political tension. The Hundred Years' War between France and England (1337–1453) proved hazardous to the artistic and intellectual development of those nations. The War of the Roses in England and France's intermittent civil war between Burgundy and the House of Valois added to the turmoil. The fall of Constantinople to the Turks increased the influx of classical scholars, who further stimulated an interest in the culture of the ancient world. Although Italian arts continued to flourish until the middle of the sixteenth century, the invasion of a French army under Charles VII was regarded as the fateful event that closed the Italian golden age. Only Venice was temporarily spared the humiliating defeat that led Machiavelli to search for a remedy to Italy's political failure.

In economic life, the former manorial and limited urban economy of the Middle Ages had created little export surplus and had discouraged the accumulation and speculation of money and goods. The Renaissance brought an end to this older economic concept and substituted the introduction of the profit motive through a new mercantile social class that gravitated to the strategically situated Italian cities. A rising import and export trade between East and West made Venice one of the most prosperous cities of Europe; the golden age of Florentine art was partly supported by her traffic in woolens. Gold and silver coming from newly discovered lands for a time made Spain the most powerful nation in Europe. The search for profit motivated the development of many modern mercantile practices. Double-entry bookkeeping was described in a treatise by Luca Pacioli in 1494. Bills of exchange transferred money across national boundaries, and joint stock companies provided means for private investments. The famous *bourse* (or stock exchange) was opened in Antwerp in 1531 to enable mercantile representatives of many European nations to purchase goods not locally available. The Bank of Amsterdam arose as the first large public bank to facilitate such commercial enterprises.

The Renaissance was an exploratory, inquisitive age in endeavors other than politics and economics. The voyages of Spanish and Portuguese discoverers opened routes to unknown parts of the world and greatly improved the techniques of navigation. The exploits of such men as Columbus, Cortes, da Gama, Vespucci, Balboa, and Ponce de Leon extended not only the knowledge of the earth, but also the economic and political resources of their nations. The pure sciences began to flourish; studies in astronomy were particularly brilliant. Although more mathematician than observer, Copernicus (1474–1543) discovered discrepancies in the accounts of the universe held by Greek philosopher-scientists. These discrepancies led him to reject the traditional Ptolemaic explanations. Although hesitant in accepting Copernicus' theory of a heliocentric universe, Tycho Brahe (1546–1601) provided the necessary observational techniques and data. A growing interest in anatomy and biology led to the founding of modern medical practice under Andreas Vesalius of the famous school at the University of Padua. The notebooks of Leonardo da Vinci revealed a burning curiosity about the structure and operation of things both living and mechanical. Visionary designs for diving gear and flying devices shared space with optical theory, geological maps, calculations of planetary size, and detailed anatomical drawings. These vast innovations in science, economics, and politics occurred in response to a new spirit that generated the ideological climate of the age.

The word "humanism" is generally used to describe the essential spirit of the Renaissance with its commitment to the boundless creative capacity of man. Like Cicero's *humanitas*, humanism encompassed those mental and moral qualities that were felt to make for civilized living. The spirit of humanism rekindled a primary concern for the affairs of the world after the medieval fixation upon issues of salvation and eternal life. The quest of the Renaissance was for earthly fulfillment and intellectual satisfaction. Therefore, the humanistic attitude was supported by the profits of industry and trade and flourished in areas of great commercial activity. Although the descent of the Black Plague temporarily slowed the development of European culture into strongly humanistic patterns, the ideological power of the church and aristocracy was visibly broken by the end of the fourteenth century. The very conduct of society became increasingly complex and required more attention to business records, charters, financial statements, and other accouterments of the mercantile community. Revelations of the intricacies of human anatomy, discoveries in applied physics and mathematics, and the invention of the printing process redirected the thought patterns of the era toward the community of man.

Instead of proceeding in the medieval manner toward developing a rationale for the existence and activity of God, Renaissance philosophy was primarily devoted to developing a concept of man. The many eloquent portraits and biographies attested to the esteem in which individual men were held. Pico della Mirandola (1463–1494) stated decisively that there was nothing more wonderful than man, because he alone had the capacity to develop freely, unhindered by instinctual drives that control lower animals. Mirandola believed that man was relatively undefined and had the power to develop enlightened modes of existence. His view of man as the possessor of "the seeds of every possibility and every life" became a broadly shared, optimistic viewpoint. The tragic aspects of man's failure to formulate a stable and reasonable moral and social order were reflected in the more conservative view of man adopted by the Protestant reformers.

The Renaissance was not only a period of rebirth for the secular spirit and the philosophy of man, but also a rebirth of ancient aspirations. In Italy the longing for social peace and spiritual regeneration came to focus upon the ideals of ancient Rome. The requirements of a complex urban society were recognized earlier by Roman lawyers, philosophers, businessmen, and architects. The sense of immediate identification which men of the Renaissance felt for their ancient ancestors led to a revival and re-examination of existing documents relating to Roman life. The writings of many classical thinkers were continuously preserved by the Roman Church, although centuries of reinterpretation had obscured much in order to fit the requirements of Christian dogma. Renaissance scholars aimed to remove such interpretive accretions and to reveal exactly what ancient men had said. Thus, the fundamental resource that conditioned the humanistic view of man was the pattern of life revealed by documents from the classical past.

The Roman emphasis upon civic responsibility and intellectual competence made a notable impact on Renaissance government and education. Such scholars as Petrarch (1304–1374) and Erasmus (1466–1536) served as diplomats and teachers, rather than as medieval recluses. Practical resourcefulness was more valued than metaphysical speculation, and rich human associations were prized above saintly self-denial. A man's fate was thought to lie not in the mysterious action of God, but in his own prudence and skill in the management of events. The ideal of the age became the Aristotelian balance of an active life tempered by sober reflection. A growing esteem for individuality stimulated the recording of personal ideas and experiences. Petrarch wrote letters for a posterity which, he felt sure, would be interested in his particular manner of life.

At the same time, a genuine appreciation for qualities that form the common excellence of all men could be noted. When criticized for the lack of portrait likeness in his statues of Giuliano and Lorenzo de' Medici, Michelangelo (1475–1564) replied that in a thousand years nobody would care what the men actually looked like. Rather, their sculptured figures represented the ideals of nobility, intellect, and the physical perfection of youth. Thus, at its height, the Renaissance exalted the most positive and universal attributes of mankind.

The newly revealed glories of antiquity revitalized European education and heralded a burst of literary creativity. Because of the availability of the printing process, the writings of the Italian humanists spread rapidly. Also, such propagandists as Erasmus traveled the length and breadth of Europe teaching the new concepts of man and society. The many humanist schools that arose began to recast the literature of Greece and Rome into a mold of easy accessibility and wide social usefulness. These schools eventually developed into the modern public educational system; its original division of subject matter into grammar, rhetoric, history, and philosophy has continued to exist under the designation "the humanities." Although the highest degrees of learning were still largely the prerogative of the nobility, the increasing complexity of general social and business life made a higher level of education mandatory for most people.

The aristocratic enthusiasm for refinement in living was served by the Castiglione's famous commentary, *The Courtier*. More than just a book of good manners, the work attempted to turn Italian social and political life into more gracious patterns. The life of the mind was an important aspect of a full existence. The writings of Cicero became the guide for schoolboys, and large personal libraries became the joy of clerics and noblemen. Raphael's painting "The School of Athens" was an eloquent testimony to the glory of thought as it gathered ancient and modern philosophers and scientists into a peaceful community of intellectual endeavor.

Even the Roman Church was greatly influenced by the humanistic quality of society at large. Its involvement with commercial interests was one of the conditions which most rankled the Protestant reformers. Cardinal Bessarion was one of a number of leading churchmen who became devoted scholars and public servants. The focus of religious concern extended to the physical as well as the spiritual needs of men; hospitals, schools, and numerous charitable organizations were founded to alleviate mental and physical suffering. Such popes as Nicholas V and Pius II were outstanding humanists who even supported thinkers unsympathetic toward the institutional church.

Religion was a concern not only of the church, but of most intellectuals of the period; indeed, a resurgence of classical religious concepts necessitated a new interpretation of Christianity. The philosophy of Plato was admired by such men as Erasmus, Ficino, Mirandola, and More. These Neoplatonists represented a wide range of viewpoints from the sincere Christian Platonism of Sir Thomas More to an unrestricted mixture of Christian and pagan beliefs. Botticelli's "Birth of Venus" identified Venus with the Virgin

Mary surrounded by angels in the guise of winds. The craggy settings used by da Vinci in such works as "The Virgin of the Rocks" seemed to relate the maternal ideal more to the forces of nature than to the intervention of a supernatural Deity.

The forces of the past sometimes lay heavy upon the Renaissance despite monumental gains made in many spheres of human activity. The fashion for Latin temporarily eclipsed the further development of vernacular languages in the pattern established by Dante, Petrarch, and Boccaccio. The insatiable curiosity characteristic of intellectual life was often brought to bear upon the Roman past rather than the present. Reverence for the past was sometimes a handicap to basic discoveries in the sciences because projects might be abandoned if conflicts with ancient tradition appeared. The pervasive consciousness of self was not conducive to contentment; indeed, the Renaissance has been described as one of the most discontented periods in western history. Dürer's engraving, *Melancholia*, portrayed the state of man in the guise of a classically proportioned woman sitting disconsolately amid a heap of new inventions. A steady stream of domestic crises provided little hope for the alteration of an inadequate social structure to gain political security and international harmony.

Although the whole era was characterized by a great vitality, the arts in particular flourished in profusion and excellence. The social status of the artist was such that he had contact with the best minds of the day. No longer was he the humble craftsman destined to produce typographies of institutional forms and practices. He reveled in his individuality, and often regarded himself as one who lived by rules other than those governing ordinary mortals. The enthusiasm for antiquity provided superb models upon which to base a new art style. Sculptors from the time of Donatello to the later days of Michelangelo found inspiration in the heroic technique and humanistic attitude toward the body reflected by Roman artifacts. In painting, the symbolic, Biblical, supernatural figures celebrating the life of the spirit in an attitude of reverent contemplation became realistic and classically proportioned figures, participating in the activities of daily life. Thus visually, as well as intellectually and politically, the era may be regarded as a primary stage in the development of modern man.

LATE GOTHIC ROOTS OF RENAISSANCE ARTS

Renaissance culture manifested itself in several distinctive movements that were interrelated and yet somewhat contradictory. The Netherlands preserved a fundamental continuity with Gothic tradition, while making innovations that eventually transformed the older artistic style into a truly international technique. As leading proponents of this "Late Gothic" style in painting, Hubert and Jan van Eyck (*c.* 1390–1441) developed the use of oil paint to such a degree that the most minute details of color and textural variability closely paralleled perceived reality. The medieval penchant for sym-

Figure 3.1   Burgundian Chapel Singers (Philip the Good at High Mass in his Chapel). (Miniature). [Courtesy, Bibbliotheque Royale, Bruxelles].

bolic meaning was brought to a climax through the Renaissance devotion to the appearance of the natural world. The astonishing precision of the *Ghent Altarpiece* was exemplified in Christ's delicate golden crown and the intricate scenic detail of the "Adoration of the Mystic Lamb" panel. The range of subject matter extended beyond the usual medieval bounds, and genuine portraits were painted as major artistic projects. The wealth of the Flemish merchants supported a demand for art styles suitable to home or personal enjoyment as distinct from ecclesiastically inspired works. In music, the same social situation resulted in the perfecting of those modes of expression once regarded as conducive to the celebration of this life, rather than the contemplation of the next.

The high state of musical development reached at the cathedral of Notre Dame during the Gothic period dissipated with the advent of the Hundred Years' War. This war so exhausted France economically and artistically that by the turn of the fifteenth century musicians began to move to the more encouraging climate provided at the Burgundian court at Cambrai. The court chapel became the most celebrated music center of the century (Figure 3.1). King Philip the Good was succeeded by Charles the Bold (1461–1483), who ruled the province of Burgundy in the Netherlands. Charles was himself a musician who strongly supported the innovations in both sacred and secular music. Musicians nurtured in this stimulating environment eventually assumed positions as directors of music in royal courts all over Europe, thus spreading the techniques of the Burgundian school and facilitating the development of a genuine international Renaissance style.

The most prominent of the Burgundian masters was Guillaume Dufay (*c.* 1400–1474). In his development of new musical resources that both encompassed and modified Gothic practices, Dufay was the leading exponent of the late Gothic spirit that flourished in the van Eycks. After training as a choirboy in the cathedral of Cambrai, he spent ten years as a singer in the papal chapel in Rome. He became familiar with the ethnic musical styles of England, France, and Italy and absorbed all three into his own patterns of thought. He maintained a consistent continuity with the stream of polyphonic composition that had formed the intellectual foundation of medieval practice. Dufay could compose a strict isorhythmic motet in fourteenth-century style when the occasion and the patron demanded. But more often, he employed a free treatment of the borrowed plainsong melody, sometimes placing it in the highest voice instead of the traditional tenor. The greatest audible change was made by the predominant use of tones separated by intervals of a third or sixth. Such a tone combination had probably long been used by folk singers. Thus, within the compositions of Dufay, the theoretical system of perfect intervals with their assumed relation to the harmony of the cosmos was abandoned in favor of a harmony appealing to the ears of the rising burgher class.

In its organization, the music of Dufay maintained a strong resemblance to medieval forms, since one main melody sung almost continuously generally provided the framework over which other melody lines were entwined. Yet the dominant impression the music gave was that of high, light voices playing a delightful polyphonic game. The essential spirit of Dufay's music derived from the Italian *Ars Nova* movement and the ballatas of Landini. In response to a strong tendency of that time to blend elements of the sacred and secular realms, Dufay often used secular tunes as the *cantus firmus* of religious compositions. The popular melody to the text of *L'homme Armé* (the armed man) was employed by a number of composers in the same manner. Such tunes functioned only as an organizing framework stated in slow moving rhythmic values and woven skilfully into the middle of the tonal fabric. Whether listeners ever recognized the tune in actual performance can only be conjectured. The melody used for the *cantus firmus* was not always presented in its normal form as a secular tune. An elaborate array of technical devices was used to modify its original shape. The speed at which it was sung could be doubled or halved; it could be written backwards or even upside down. Thus, within the limitations of his form and style, Dufay expanded significantly the imaginative range of compositional resources and prepared the way for the musical giants of the succeeding century.

THE INTERNATIONAL SACRED POLYPHONIC STYLE

The need for a definitive system of musical organization, which became apparent in the works of Dufay, was met with particular adequacy in the works of Josquin des Prez (1450–1521). Like most of the migratory Flemish composers, Josquin worked for many years in Milan under the patronage of several cardinals; his artistic influence established the musical tradition of a later group of Roman composers sponsored by the pope. Josquin created music that sounded unpretentious on the surface, but proved, on closer examination, to be full of technical complexity. His use of imitation as the fundamental organizational principle was the basic difference between the music of later Renaissance composers and that of Dufay. Imitation was not a completely new device, since the medieval rondel used several voice parts beginning the same melody at different times. The practice is represented in a rather unsophisticated form in such rounds as "Three Blind Mice." However, when expanded by all the polyphonic techniques explored by Dufay, compositions of exceptional intellectual content could be produced.

The idea of imitation as an organizational principle was highly fruitful for nearly five hundred years. In practice, it is one of the most easily perceived musical devices. Typically, a composition begins with a single melody heard alone. Then another vocal line begins that same melody at a different pitch level, and the two sound patterns progress together. If the second part simply repeats the exact tones of the original melody at a later time interval, the result is a canon or round. In most instances, however, the melody conforms to the initial presentation only to a certain point, from which it digresses into small figures taken from the tune or its general style. The various voice parts (usually from three to five) repeat the original melody at regular intervals so that there is usually some part of it sounding at any given time. To construct a composition based upon imitative techniques requires excellent craftsmanship in order to maintain a pleasing balance among the parts and avoid tonal clashes.

Josquin stood at the apex of the development of the basic elements of Renaissance choral tradition. After him, composers developed and perfected the essential ingredients that were already present in his work. Through their efforts, the resulting style was disseminated throughout Europe as an international artistic movement. From the practices of Josquin and his contemporaries, there developed both the music sponsored by the church and the basic characteristics of secular song and instrumental music.

Until the papal exile in Avignon (1309–1377) and the Great Schism (1387–1417), the Roman Church was traditionally the most powerful and dependable sponsor of the arts. Because of the weakened power of the church, musicians began looking to the secular mercantile aristocracy of the Netherlands for inspiration and support. During the early Middle Ages, Italy provided the foundation for the development of art in the northern countries by fusing Greco-Roman culture with European tribal cultures. Italy itself only very gradually absorbed the resulting artistic practices that formed Gothic style. For example, the ancient Roman basilica was still favored by Italians, while much of northern Europe was developing a massive perpendicular architectural style. The popes at Avignon made some effort to maintain a certain conservative uniformity derived from Italian tradition, but the edicts that came from Avignon had less influence than those issued from Rome. A new sound structure, new forms, and new poetic modes of expression had evolved from the Italian *Ars Nova* and had been enriched by Flemish technical advancements. This ideological mixture exerted a greater appeal to church musicians. At the same time, secular composers began to adopt those stylistic devices previously belonging only to liturgical practice.

Experimental innovations of the radical "modern school" of the North and the Italian *Ars Nova* style had been opposed as early as the fourteenth century by Pope John XXII. But while the world he represented slowly collapsed, the new musical language became too persuasive for even the

Figure 3.2   *Palestrina hands Pope Marcellus his new Mass.* (Woodcut). [The Bettmann Archive].

most tradition-bound musician to ignore. The new techniques gradually lost their sacrilegious implications as the church began a long struggle to regain its pinnacle of influence once the Council of Constance (1414–1418) had settled the papal issue. Pope Martin V (1368–1431) re-established an artistic climate that encouraged the support of ecclesiastical music in the new Renaissance style. With the acceptance of the new means of expression and with increased security felt throughout the church, the way was open for the evolution of an international polyphonic tradition.

A significant ideological role for the new style was not long in coming, for the Roman Church was soon embroiled in a desperate struggle to win back its people after the initial shock of the Protestant Reformation. As a primary step, the Council of Trent (1545–1563) convened to eradicate long neglected ills, among which were certain musical practices considered unworthy of ecclesiastical propagation. There was a rather strong sentiment for abandoning the entire polyphonic concept and returning to Gregorian chant as the only music authorized by the church. Some of the new Flemish techniques were initially forbidden, in an attempt to simplify the whole liturgical structure. However, the influence of important musical patrons such as Duke Albert V of Bavaria, whose chapel master was Orlando di Lasso (1532–1594), prevented the council from taking drastic action. Emperor Ferdinand I of the Holy Roman Empire also sent a letter urging the retention of the polyphonic tradition. After some major skirmishes over the issue, the question was referred to lay deputies for study. Some of the finest composers of the era contributed polyphonic settings of the Mass for this investigating committee to study. A persistent and erroneous tale is that Palestrina's *Missa Papae Marcelli* so impressed the committee that they voted to preserve the polyphonic tradition. The work was dedicated to the memory of Pope Marcellus, who had been a key figure in the support of music reform (Figure 3.2).

The one significant new musical form that evolved from decisions of the council was the *missa brevis*—a short Mass written in a simpler polyphonic style consistent with the conservatism of the initial Counter Reformation spirit. If secular tunes were not eliminated as the *cantus firmus,* at least they were disguised under noncommittal titles such as "Mass without a name." Thus, in practice, a compromise was effected between the liturgical requirements of the council and the prevailing spirit of humanism that motivated much of Renaissance culture.

Giovanni Pierluigi (1525–1594), better known by the name of his birthplace at Palestrina, became the foremost representative of the conservative Roman Church tradition. The type of polyphonic composition that he brought to a peak of controlled perfection flourished for centuries after his death. As late as the eighteenth century, the famous English physician and traveler, Charles Burney, reported that the style of Palestrina was being used in churches along with the music of his own day. In fact, Burney confessed to preferring the Palestrina style for religious use. As a man, Palestrina was a rare combination of a sensitive musician and successful businessman (a furrier by trade) who gravitated between marriage and the priesthood. While his religious music exerted a sincere spiritual appeal, it frequently used a secular *cantus firmus*. The most numerous of the various

Figure 3.3 RAPHAEL. *The Alba Madonna*. [Courtesy, National Gallery of Art, Washington, D.C., Andrew Mellon Collection].

types of masses that he wrote was the *parody mass*, which employed long sections of a pre-existing and sometimes secular composition.

Because Palestrina represented the most conservative and universal practices of his day, he has since been used as a model for the study of Renaissance polyphonic style. His position in the history of music is much akin to that of Raphael in painting. Although Raphael contributed less than such artistic giants as Leonardo da Vinci and Michelangelo, he represented a synthesis of the prevailing innovations of his time. There is an affective similarity between the works of the two men in their preference for solidity of design and controlled means of expression. The gentle symmetry of a Raphael madonna (Figure 3.3) conveys something of the sense of monumental grandeur and gentle calm pervading much of the music of Palestrina. In each of the pieces in his enormous compositional repertoire, Palestrina particularly insisted that the music should follow the spirit of the text without hampering it by obscuring polyphonic figures of sound.

Renaissance polyphony was developed in a group of rather distinctive modes of expression so that no description could apply equally to religious and secular, or to vocal and instrumental music. However, some few basic characteristics are encountered frequently enough in the music of the period so that it is well to be aware of them. The traditional, conservative style of Palestrina is most often reproduced by unaccompanied choirs with voice parts that utilize bass through soprano registers. Quite often the meter is not easily isolated and seems to fit the words of the text more than any established system of beats. Melodies are most likely to be quite long and flexible without wide leaps; decoration is limited to a few simple turns or other embellishments. Although many scholars deny that Renaissance composers asserted a deliberate harmonic intention, there was obviously some harmonic content because of the use of concurrently sounding voice parts. This coincidence of tones tended to occur in rather simple patterns without extensive use of pitches lying outside the normal modal scale. Secular music particularly tended to use the major and minor scales adopted exclusively in succeeding centuries. With some notable exceptions, the voice parts were about equally balanced, each having a similar role to play within the texture of the polyphony.

The form was particularly predictable, both in sacred and in secular choral music. It was composed of a patchwork of many small motifs, each of which was given a particular phrase of text. When the text changed, a new motif was introduced. Thus there was no one main theme, but rather, many short, similar sounding melodies growing out of one another in elegantly smooth transitions. To provide contrast some phrases of text might be given chordal settings, while others would have strict imitative designs. Josquin was particularly fond of setting short sections in duet style using only two voice parts. Thus there is no actual prescription for Renaissance style; there is only a definable range of possibility.

As used by Palestrina and his colleagues of the Roman school, such elements were blended into a style that honored the initial Counter Reformation spirit in avoiding violent contrasts or deliberately theatrical effects.

The result was a serenely controlled musical texture with a timeless purity of expression. However, a later Counter Reformation movement frankly resorted to the emotional power of music and the other arts to create a new religious environment in which, contrary to much Protestant practice, the senses could be used to enrich the spirit.

The Jesuit Order, founded by Loyola in 1534, was the moving force

Figure 3.4   TINTORETTO. *The Origin of the Milkey Way.* [National Gallery Photograph].

of this second-phase movement. Serving as priests and teachers wherever they went, the Jesuits carried with them a powerful blend of Dutch-Italian style, which continued to be perfected at St. Mark's in Venice. During the time of the sixteenth-century religious wars in Germany, the Flemish composer Adrian Willaert (*d.* 1562) transmitted his native musical tradition to the Venetians and was himself captivated by the prevailing lyrical Italian

94   style. To fit the grandeur of the edifice of St. Mark's, Willaert wrote music
for several distinct choirs that answered each other across the vast architectural space in a musical dialogue. Willaert used less elaborate polyphony
and more purely harmonic or chordal effects; sectional contrasts were
provided mainly by changes in tone color or pitch range. Music based
upon such dramatic contrasts was propagated by the Jesuits and became
the initial framework for the Baroque style of the succeeding cultural era.

Venetian music reached its height in the works of Andrea Gabrieli
(1510–1586) and his nephew Giovanni (1557–1612). The Gabrielis were
organists who produced compositions not only for their instrument, but
also for many diverse vocal and instrumental combinations. Giovanni in
particular was fond of Willaert's practice of using multiple choirs (polychoral style). He achieved a great variety of tone color by blending small
sections from each choir with one another. Some of this same love of
opulent color was found in the creamy-skinned bodies and radiant landscapes painted by Titian and Giorgione. A nineteenth-century musicologist
commented that "Giovanni Gabrieli is the musical Titian of Venice, as
Palestrina is the musical Raphael of Rome." Venetian painting, like Venetian
music, represented a point of transition between the Renaissance and
Baroque eras. The style of painting called Mannerism, as practiced by
Tintoretto and later by El Greco, reflected the same penchant for glowing
color and vivid contrast as found in the music of the Gabrielis (Figure
3.4). The direct emotional appeal, the inner subjective focus, and the use
of pictorial illusion to connote the appearance of a mystical, spiritual realm
were decidedly removed from the original spirit of the High Renaissance.
In music, as in art, the Mannerist style attained an international status.
The polychoral music of Venice had such appeal that as far away as Essex,
England, Thomas Tallis (1505–1585) composed a motet using eight choruses
and forty voice parts in an eloquent blend of Dutch-Italian and English
characteristics. Mannerist artists were hired by such aristocratic patrons
as the Grand Duke of Tuscany and the King of France to paint portraits
of their families.

Despite the fact that the Venetian style in both music and art was
a powerful ally of the Jesuits, it also became highly popular with the
Germans of the Reformed Church. Hans Leo Hassler (1564–1612) was typical
of the many German composers who studied in Venice and helped to
develop a national musical tradition based upon Italian style patterns. In
the same manner, the German organist Froberger later transmitted the
techniques and compositional practices of the Italian organist Frescobaldi
to Germany, where they stimulated the instrumental innovations of a succeeding age. Thus the brilliant, flamboyant music of the Venetian masters
provided a contrasting interpretation of those central musical processes
that comprised Renaissance style.

MUSIC OF THE PROTESTANT REFORMATION

Germany

In 1510, a lowly priest from the lesser German town of Wittenberg visited Rome and witnessed the activities of that superlative politician and art patron Pope Julius II. After seven years of reflection and intensive study of the Bible, this same priest summarized for debate his objections to the sale of indulgences in ninety-five theses, which he posted on the door of the chapel of the local monarch. The vast difference in viewpoint between Rome and the priest Martin Luther was the product of much more than a theological disagreement. The conflict involved the very conditions of life that differentiated men in Wittenberg from men in Rome. Society in northern Europe was still largely agrarian; people were continuously subject to the onslaughts of nature and pestilence.

In such an environment of fear righteousness was successfully inculcated by threats of everlasting punishment. Life was brutal for people on the level of farmers and servants. An infinite range of tortures for criminals and burning at the stake for heretics resolved all problems of social deviation. Entering such a harsh environment, the new wave of humanistic thought and the rapid rise of the merchant class led to a revival of the basic spirit of society and initiated a tradition of social criticism. Trade, banking, and limited manufacturing radically altered the agrarian mentality of large segments of the population and awakened them to new social and spiritual vistas.

Such innovations as printing were not destined to produce a more serene existence. For the first time, people became aware of the political intrigues and wordliness of the church in Rome. Doctrine became less clearly defensible because of many conflicting viewpoints made available in printed form. The old simple answers no longer sufficed, and even the examples of churchmen disproved in practice their stated principles of Christian conduct. The condition of the peasant was largely unaffected by advantages available to the middle class. They were under crushing economic obligations to the local lord for the rent of lands and to the church for a tithe of grain, livestock, and produce. Often the only alternative to starvation was poaching game from the lord's fields, an act usually punished by blinding. Thus the peasants were the first to strike out against newly recognized sources of oppression. Their wholesale slaughter was one of the grimmest episodes of the Reformation era.

Against such a background of human inequity the drama of the Reformation took place. Yet the struggle for spiritual renewal in the church predated by many years the emergence of Protestantism as an organized movement. John Wycliffe of England, John Huss in Bohemia, and even

Savonarola in Italy had directed their attention to the spiritual darkness of the previous century in an effort to raise the aspirations and moral standards of ordinary men. Luther's own opposition to the sale of indulgences was first aroused by the sight of his townspeople flocking to purchase a release from sin not within the power of man to convey. The movement for reform finally came to a climax in Germany because that nation developed a popular resentment of central ecclesiastical authority, and because it had the political stability to resist Roman domination.

Political jealousy was deeply involved in the entire episode. Kings, secular ministers, and national sympathizers shared a displeasure at the Italian dominance of the church parliament. The councils had been ineffective in eradicating evils in religious practice, partly because monarchs used such meetings to scheme for their own advantage. The German Reformation was strengthened by an upsurge of national spirit. Luther's *Address to the Christian Nobility of the German Nation* revealed the nationalistic appeal of his theological position. Even Luther's trial reflected national pride; the Elector of Saxony refused to allow him to be summoned from German soil for examination by an Italian Curia.

Although Luther exchanged literary diatribes with Erasmus on the subject of free will, he was not entirely out of sympathy with the humanists in their efforts to revitalize the church. However, the humanist position was not compelling to the common man; it was cosmopolitan in outlook and decisively intellectual in approach. Because of a fundamental belief in the goodness and perfectability of man, humanists preferred to interpret Scripture figuratively and with a broad tolerance for all opinions. They were certainly not blind to the evils of their time. Under a cloak of satire, Erasmus loosed scathing criticism against the whole realm of religious hierarchy and practices. A common proverb of the time was, "Erasmus laid the eggs and Luther hatched the chickens." But Erasmus and his fellow humanists were deeply opposed to disrupting the process of reason and arbitration by open rebellion. Thus he served as a lonely arbiter between the decaying church and the dawning religious revolution.

The most enthusiastic supporters of Luther's cause were members of the lower nobility and the burgher class; therefore, the artistic quality of the movement was decisively conditioned by their concerns and outlook. In obvious contrast with the Roman Church, the reformed faith was not partial to the visual arts. The artist Albrecht Dürer (1471–1528) revealed a deep sympathy for the ideals of the Reformation. Nevertheless, his efforts to become an artistic spokesman for the movement went unheeded by Protestant leaders, and he remained a Roman Catholic. The Swiss reformer Ulrich Zwingli (1484–1531) went so far as to discard all visual symbols formerly used in worship—including chalices, crosses, and clerical vestments. Music was often viewed with the same negative attitude. However, under Luther and his successors Germany did produce a vast body of song that eventually blossomed into a full musical tradition.

Luther needed a style of music that would weld his followers into a strong, unified force. He had a great love for music and some skill in its performance. A few hymns have been attributed to him, including *A Mighty Fortress Is Our God*. His favorite composer was Josquin des Prez, and he admired those techniques fundamental to the international Renaissance style. Soon, the simple, sturdy German Reformation hymns called chorales received intricate polyphonic settings for both voices and instruments. Luther utilized the medieval secular song tradition still in existence within the musical repertoire of the burghers. The German middle class was generally dominant in shaping the musical style of the Reformation. Luther neither banned nor favored the use of the Latin language, and he retained Gregorian chant within the Reformed Church liturgy. For awhile, some traditional congregational hymns were sung in both Latin and German. Others were absorbed in their original musical form by simply translating the Latin text. In such a manner, *Victimae Paschali Laudes* became *Christ lag in Todesbanden* (Christ lay in the bonds of death).

Before the outbreak of the Reformation, there was in existence a large group of songs handed down from father to son and sung as folk hymns in either Latin or German. Among them, the Christmas hymns *Joseph Lieber, Joseph Mein* and *In Dulce Jubilo* remain in the modern repertoire. Secular tunes also found their way into the church liturgy, and among them were some of the most beautiful of all the chorales. The melody to *O Sacred Head Now Wounded* was derived from a frothy little love song which began, "My heart is all confounded; a tender maid is the cause." A century or more passed before such diverse elements became stabilized into the definitive form characteristic of the German chorale style. Johann Sebastian Bach, who lived two centuries after the time of Luther, provided the settings from which modern chorale literature is largely derived.

In its dominant features, the style of the chorale was typical of most Protestant music. The congregation usually sang the tune in unison, while the choir or organ provided the necessary harmonic framework. Unlike the traditional *cantus firmus* composition, in which the tenor voice carried the basic melody, the chorale often featured the melody in the highest singing voice. Instead of there being a number of independent voice parts, the chorale was more likely to have all parts moving in quite similar rhythm. In this way, all voices sang the same words at the same time, while in polyphony the voices entered at different times in an imitative plan. The form of the chorale resembled that of medieval secular song in that two or three short melodic phrases were arranged in patterns of repetition and contrast.

Outside of the congregational context, composers such as Johann Walter, Ludwig Senfl, and Benedictus Ducis began to use chorale tunes as the basis of compositions in the imitative style of the Flemish school. A vast literature of chorale preludes began to be composed for use as incidental music during the liturgical service. Thus, while allowing the composer a degree of artistic liberty, the chorale elaboration also recalled to the congregation the whole range of familiar religious associations belonging to the tune and its text. So it was that several generations of the leading musicians in Europe were nourished in the creative climate provided by Lutheran congregations.

France

The Calvinist tradition of the French Reformation provided little stimulation for the development of fine religious music. Such neglect had a deleterious effect upon the development of religious music in both western Europe and America. Even so, such significant individual items as the Doxology originated within this environment. Among the followers of John Calvin (1509–1564), the attitude toward music and the visual arts was far more restrictive than that which prevailed in Germany. Since Reformation theology was greatly indebted to St. Augustine, it naturally adopted his suspicion of music as a distraction from the essential message of the liturgy. Zwingli exhibited a truly Augustinian ambivalence in this regard. An inveterate lover of music, he nevertheless banned the singing of hymns and allowed the destruction of many fine organs in the churches of Switzerland because he could find no authority in Scripture for liturgical music. On the other hand, he was greatly impressed with the humanism of Italy and learned Greek in order to read the Bible in a critical, scholarly manner. He eventually became liberal enough to include in his concept of heaven good men of all times and faiths.

John Calvin was the first systematic philosopher of the Reformation whose major work, *The Institutes of the Christian Religion*, exerted a wide influence. His role as head of the theocracy in Geneva revealed him as a merciless servant of a merciless God who thought it his spiritual duty to restrict singing and dancing. His austere religion found its way to the people of Scotland through the preaching of John Knox (1510–1572). There the voice of the lower bourgeoisie prevailed in matters of art, as well as in church government. The long period of religious uprisings that toppled the Roman Church seemed to repress much of the original musical tendencies of the Scotch people. The *Scottish Psalter*, a late Renaissance setting of the book of Psalms, was the one lasting musical contribution to the Protestant liturgy inspired by the Calvinist movement in Scotland.

Among the lesser reformers music was often regarded as evil. John Huss (1369–1415) looked upon musicians as ungodly people, even to the extent of denying them the right to take communion. Yet he believed in the devotional value of singing. His congregation sang in unison because such a practice made all men equal in their worship. The tunes were neither recognizably secular nor liturgical in origin, but seemingly derived from a common style of folk expression. From this austere spirit Calvin shaped the character of his religious doctrine and its attendant musical expression, both of which crossed the Atlantic Ocean with the Puritans. These advocates of extreme reform used simple tunes to sing psalm texts that were transformed into rhymed stanzas by Henry Ainsworth and Thomas Ravenscroft. They nurtured in America those practices reflecting Calvin's industrious, law-conscious ethic. Their thrifty, orderly, work-centered mentality preferred restraints upon artistic innovation and thus discouraged a native American creativity in the arts.

The most enduring musical monument to the Calvinist legacy was the *Genevan Psalter*, whose texts and tunes were assembled by gifted musicians and poets. Many previous psalters contained popular songs that had been pirated and presented in rather shoddy arrangements. At one time, rollicking psalm tunes were a popular diversion of the French court. The problem of turning prose-like psalm texts into rhymed poetry with a standard number of accents for each line was crudely solved by unskilled poets. One tortured version of the Twenty-Third Psalm still preserved in modern hymnals begins, "The Lord to me a shepherd is/ Therefore want not shall I." Some secular melodies did find their way into the *Genevan Psalter* after a thorough revision by Louis Bourgeois, the musical mentor of the collection. Frequently, only phrases of a popular melody were used within the context of an otherwise unfamiliar tune. In his preface to the psalter, Calvin declared that the tunes should be equal in gravity to the psalm texts and be "proper to sing in church."

Despite Calvin's opposition to polyphony, some simple polyphonic versions of the psalter tunes were written by composers such as Louis Bourgeois and Clement Janequin. But without institutional support or broad public interest the evolution of these tunes into an art tradition never took place in France as in Germany. However, many Calvinist groups basically in sympathy with the German ideals supported a persistent musical creativity. Some descendants of the sixteenth-century Anabaptist movement migrated to America and evolved a musical life unrivaled by many European court chapels of the same period. Thus on the continent the position of music was quite variable and dependent upon the religious orientation of the people and the artistic philosophy they accepted.

England

The English Reformation followed a somewhat different course from that of either Germany or France. The initiative for reform came not so much from the common man as from the aristocracy, which found state advantage in recognizing the new faith. Henry VIII needed a male heir, but it was not politically expedient for Pope Clement VII to annul Henry's marriage to Catherine of Aragon. The papal refusal only stimulated support for the cause of the king and resentment against foreign interference in domestic affairs. The resulting political upheaval placed Henry as head of the Church of England, brought about a definition of faith and a Book of Common Prayer, and established a new creed based upon Catholic precepts. Since the quarrel over church dogma was secondary to the political implications, a closer relationship with the Roman Church was maintained in England than on the continent. Anglican and Catholic monarchs alternated frequently enough so that the people were familiar with both liturgical traditions, and musicians were

Figure 3.5a   Genevan Psalter. [New York Public Library, Lincoln Center].

able without great difficulty to adapt their material to suit either service. The polyphonic tradition never suffered the disruption it encountered in other reform movements.

The legislative acts that Henry VIII sponsored in Parliament had a noticeable effect on the course of English Reformation music. The Act of Dissolution, by which all property of the Roman Church was confiscated for royal use, led to the dispersion of cathedral choir schools. The result was an inevitable loss of technical facility in musical performance by English choirs. As a more positive influence, the Book of Common Prayer, which Henry had supervised, was the inspiration for numerous musical settings by English composers. In 1554, the new Archbishop of Canterbury, Thomas Cranmer, issued a musical setting for the Anglican service. Although it was styled after the traditional Gregorian chant, the music was altered to allow one tone to each syllable of the text. The Archbishop believed that this arrangement would prove easier to sing. The Anglican chant was given a harmonic accompaniment, and some selections were vaguely reminiscent of

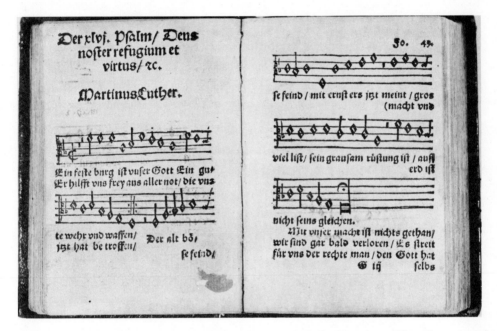

Figure 3.5b   Luther's German Psalter (*A Mighty Fortress*). Lutherhalle, Wittenberg. [Klaus G. Beyer].

both German chorale and French metrical psalmody. The musical pattern followed quite closely the ancient lection tones of the Gregorian antiphon and psalm—especially in the singing of psalms and canticles. On the whole, the music of the English church achieved a practical balance between old and new religious ideology. Among the examples of Renaissance music that have survived the centuries, Merbecke's *Booke of Common Prayer Noted* has remained in the continuous use of the Episcopal Church.

Under Henry's son, Edward VI, a period of tolerance for both Lutheranism and Calvinism reigned. And it was during this time that the English reformed church became truly Protestant. Many collections of metrical psalms were issued, and an increasing amount of polyphonic music with English texts was produced. Under Elizabeth I, English music reached a pinnacle of excellence unequaled until the early twentieth century. Public music education attained a high level, partly because of the influence of the re-established choir schools attached to the great Anglican cathedrals. The popularity of the *Plaine and Easie Introduction to Practicall Musicke*, by Thomas Morley (1577–1603), attested to the great favor music enjoyed in both religious and secular spheres and the widespread interest in musical performance.

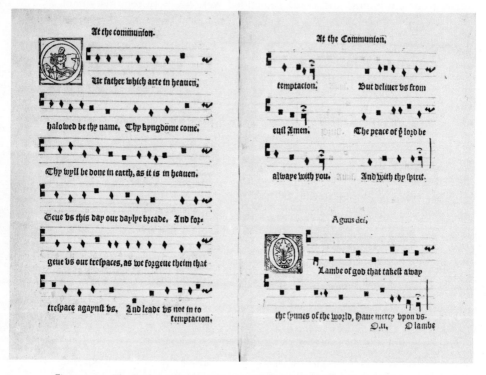

Figure 3.5c   The Booke of Common Prayer. (Music by Merbecke). British Museum. [John R. R. Freeman & Co.].

An eminent composer of the Elizabethan era, William Byrd (1543–1623), helped to create a masterpiece of Anglican musical form called the Great Service. It was a rather elaborate polyphonic setting of the texts of the *Venite, Te Deum, Benedictus Dominus Deus, Kyrie, Credo, Magnificat,* and *Nunc Dimittis*. One such Great Service extended to nearly a hundred pages. English composers were especially partial to Venetian styles of writing and used them to great effect. They originated the verse anthem, which involved a solo voice with instrumental accompaniment, a favorite device of Gabrieli. The age of Elizabeth witnessed the full flowering of a liturgical tradition, which has since served as an artistic treasury for the Protestant faith (Figure 3.5.).

SECULAR MUSIC OF THE RENAISSANCE

Choral Music

Renaissance culture was characterized by a high level of public participation in musical activities and an acceptable degree of amateur skill. As is normally the case, most evidence of the music of the lower classes has disappeared; but the extant music of the burghers and nobility reveals an unusually fine quality. As the first world hub of the Renaissance, Italy's devotion to social and cultural values was reflected in a high degree of individual self-cultivation. The humanizing amenities of music were stressed, along with the social gratuity to be gained from a graceful performance on some likely instrument. Such men as Benvenuto Cellini and Leonardo da Vinci were valued by their patrons for their musical abilities, as well as for their artistic merits. A cultivated leisure became the social aim of both merchants and courtiers; they were encouraged by that classical aura which surrounded most intellectual pursuits. Greek writings on music were given the same reverent esteem as their writings on science and philosophy. Secular music made great use of mythological imagery. Choruses of Dryads and Bacchantes enlivened plays based on stories such as Orpheus or Aeneas. The poetry of Ariosto, Tasso, Boccaccio, and Petrarch provided ample material for eloquent musical settings. Such elements of the Italian cultural style were admired and copied throughout Europe.

The style of secular choral music became in many ways indistinguishable from those general traits that characterized sacred music. The complexities of polyphony were perhaps less pronounced in secular music, and the tempo was sometimes rollicking, but artistic merit was not lacking. Indeed, the best composers of church music were also composers of excellent secular music as well. A noble patron hired a musician to write for his personal chapel services, banquets, hunts, state functions, and other occasions that might arise. Unlike previous ages, when such music only sporadically outlived the occasion for its creation, the new techniques of music printing insured wide dissemination of new compositions. In this cultural climate developed the madrigal, which was particularly dependent upon the eloquence of poetry for its musical expression, for it was the text that inseparably connected music with classical imagery and Renaissance life style. Cardinal Pietro Bembo, a Venetian nobleman and scholar, was chiefly responsible for the initiation of a poetic tradition that inspired musical settings of the highest quality. The fame of the English madrigal was somewhat less attributable to the poetry of Shakespeare, Spenser, and Marlowe than to the musical inventiveness of Byrd, Morley, and Weelkes. The *chanson,* a French counterpart to the madrigal, also reached a height of technical precision and poetic expressiveness in the works of Sermisy, Jannequin, and Certon.

The secular choral repertoire represented all varieties of musical style—from an intricate polyphony to a simple chordal sound. The form followed that of the motet and mass in using many successive imitative melodic patterns throughout the various voice parts. There was often a repetition of a section, as in the case of the "fa-la-la" chorus of the English madrigal. Attention to the portrayal of the text was the primary duty of the composer. An admirer said of Willaert, "His music is so well unified, so expressive, so appropriate, and it so wonderfully adorns the words, that I confessed not to have known what music was in all my days save for that evening. . . ." The Venetian style was particularly well suited to the development of a secular tradition because of its dramatic and highly emotional element.

A fascinating representative of the late Italian madrigal style was Gesualdo of Naples, a distinguished musician and Prince of Venosa (1560–1614). He pushed the tonal orientation or key-sense of his day to the limits of comprehensibility in order to express the meaning of texts dealing with overwhelming emotional states. By using chromatics (tones that lie outside the normal seven-note scale), Gesualdo created juxtapositions of sound emulating the twisting lines and suspended figures painted by the Venetian artist Tintoretto. Gesualdo was an eloquent representative of Mannerism in secular music.

The English madrigal was created in response to the enormous enthusiasm the Italian madrigal had stimulated. A large collection of Italian madrigals was published in an English translation under the title *Musica Transalpina,* and was soon followed by another anthology called *Italian Madrigals Englished.* The English madrigal was a product of the middle class; it lacked the status of an esoteric or noble pastime. Madrigal singing was more a popular art than a professional occupation, more a purely musical than a literary development. It was a cultural representation of the growing international power of England and reflected her efforts to relinquish the rather provincial nature of her pre-Renaissance culture. Avoiding both emotional extremity and acute polyphonic complexity, the English madrigal emphasized sheer tunefulness and a strong sense of musical form. That such pieces did not entirely avoid more sombre emotional ranges is evidenced by numerous titles such as "Weepe, Weepe, Mine Eyes," "Deepe Lamenting," or "O Care, Thou Wilt Dispatch Mee." Nevertheless, the English madrigal is generally representative of the robust optimism that pervaded the brilliant age of Elizabeth I.

In France, secular singing was stimulated by the importation of Italian arts and supported by the musical enthusiasm of the wealthy bourgeoisie. The Louvre and many famous chateaux were built under the influence of Italian architecture. This Italianism in France became particularly evident when Francis I (1494–1547) opened his palace at Fontainbleu to the Mannerists in order to encourage them to leave their imprint of worldly grace and elegance upon French culture. In this atmosphere the chanson developed as the French counterpart of the madrigal. Classical imagery, modified by colloquial language, had characterized early chanson poetry. Under the influence of Italian musicians at the royal court, the chanson adopted a more Italian pattern, but remained predominantly lyrical in effect.

The French were particularly attracted to the programmatic chanson, which rivaled even the Italian madrigal in popularity. Clement Jannequin wrote chansons such as *La Guerre* (The Battle of Mangnano), which imitated guns rattling, soldiers shouting, fanfares, and other noises of battle. Gossiping women, singing birds, bells, and animal life of all varieties appeared in this song form. While seldom approaching the harmonic richness of the Italian madrigal, it boasted great rhythmic variety and a sparkling wit.

The French were quick to exploit the new technique of printing by applying it to the musical score. Although Italians originated novel printing processes that facilitated the dissemination of new musical works, the French became the outstanding music publishers of the day. In fact, Pierre Attaignant was as famous as most of the composers whose music he published. The vast distribution of printed ballads and catches (rounds) influenced the repertoire of secular music in America. Ravenscroft's books of popular choral music called *Pammelia, Deuteromelia,* and *Melismata* were as much sung in private as the Calvinist psalter was sung in public. The texts of popular catches amply demonstrated the humorous and even ribald entertainment aspects of such music. Guests in the home were often entertained by singing or playing on a collection of instruments owned by the family. Among the homely advice found in the catch collections was this rhyme:

> He that drinks is immortal and can ne'er decay
> For wine still supplies what age wears away.
> How can he be dust that moistens his clay[1]

One of the most beautiful of all was:

> The silver swan, who living had no note
> When death approached unlocked her silent throat;
> Leaning her breast against the reedy shore,
> Thus sang her first and last, and sang no more.
> "Farewell all joys! O death, come close my eyes;
> More geese than swans now live; more fools than wise."[2]

Instrumental Music

Although the Renaissance is sometimes described as the golden age of choral music, most instruments reached a state of mechanical stability during and shortly after this period. Within a century, instrumental litera-

1 Mary C. Taylor, Margarita Windham, and Claude Simpson (eds.), *Catch That Catch Can* (Boston: E. C. Schirmer Music Co., 1945), p. 25.
2 Ibid, p. 63.

The Renaissance

106   Figure 3.6 MASACCIO. *Madonna Enthroned.* [National Gallery Photograph].

ture rivaled the quantity, although perhaps not the quality, of vocal music. The chanson proved to be highly significant in the formation of independent instrumental forms. Early compositions for Renaissance instruments relied heavily upon vocal models, and the chanson was a particularly popular pattern. The Italian *canzona alla francese* was simply an instrumental rendition of a chanson originally written for voices. The rapid scale-wise runs, trills, and other ornamentation more characteristic of the instrumental idiom gradually began to be added.

Whereas the Italians made music serve the expressive needs of the text—even to the detriment of a balanced formal design—the French maintained a very clear formal pattern that proved to be highly amenable to instrumental requirements. The chanson type of thematic identity based upon repetition and contrast provided the necessary organization for instrumental music that lacked words to indicate specific actions or states of mind. The chanson, transformed into the canzona, was adaptable to the ranges and idiosyncrasies of a wide variety of instrumental combinations. Some pieces even continued the programmatic tendencies of the vocal versions so that battles, birds, and bells were imitated to the full extent of the instrumental capacity. The canzona reached its highest perfection in the instrumental works of Gabrieli, and anticipated the development of the *concerto grosso* of the Baroque era.

Transcriptions of madrigals and chansons also formed a great portion of early lute literature. The lute was the most popular instrument of the Renaissance and was often featured in pictures by leading artists (Figure 3.6). In structure, it was somewhat like the modern guitar, and probably came into Europe from Islamic culture during the Middle Ages. A typical lute had strings tuned to six pitches, and used different methods of notation (tablature) in Italy, France, and Germany. The Italian system proved to be the most influential, and provided the basic concept of modern guitar notation. A large segment of lute literature was derived from popular dances and arranged into groups of contrasting pieces. The dances had originally been performed to lute or other instrumental accompaniment; however, the musical elements gradually began to dominate the rather simple needs of the dancers. A collection of dance movements was called a suite—a form that has had a continued significance in the modern history of music.

A suite began with two or more paired dances in contrasting tempo. The earliest dances preserved as permanent members of the suite group were the *allemande, gaillarde,* and *pavane.* The *allemande* was a simple German dance that moved in two heavy beats. It was frequently paired with a lively *gaillarde.* The *pavane* was a stately Spanish court dance. Other minor dances such as the English dompe and crampe were well described by their names. Additional movements such as the *courrente, bourré, minuet,* and *gigue* were eventually inserted in the suite and used in a variety of combinations.

Figure 3.7   *Parthenia or the Maydenhead.* (Title page of the first engraved English music for the virginal). [The Bettmann Archive].

Italy was most prominent in the building of Renaissance lute and keyboard instruments. Both the earliest and most numerous clavichords and harpsichords were made in Italy and especially in Venice. The keyboard of the clavichord was about half that of the modern piano. Its strings (paired as on the lute) were struck by a metal tangent secured to one end of a slender wooden key, which was depressed by the finger at the other end. Clavichords were small enough to be easily portable, but so delicate in tone that they were useful only for personal amusement. The harpsichord was a somewhat larger keyboard instrument that provided a number of different sound effects and could be played as part of an instrumental ensemble. The harpsichord key or "jack" operated by pushing a stiff piece of leather or a feather quill against the string in a plucking action. Upon release of the key, a piece of felt attached to the jack above the plucking mechanism dampened the string. By using several different sets of strings, the harpsichord produced a variety of timbres. In England a small harpsichord called the virginals was very popular (Figure 3.7).

As in the case of the lute, much music for these early keyboard instruments consisted of arrangements of vocal music; but the repertoire of forms soon expanded to include short dance suites, *ricercare, toccatas, fantasias,* and sets of variations. Among them, the variation was particularly significant because it has since been used in classical sonatas, symphonic movements, and as the form of independent orchestral works. English composers were fond of the variation and left such gems as William Byrd's *The Carman's Whistle* and John Bull's *The King's Hunting Jigg.* The basic principle of the variation was quite simple. A Renaissance composer would simply find a tune he liked and write it in a very plain style at the beginning of his composition. He would then proceed to write other versions of the tune by changing the rhythm, adding melodic decoration, or perhaps providing a more complex harmonic setting. The aim was to vary the tune in many interesting ways, while maintaining some basic similarity to the original. It was not unusual for a composer to use street cries of local vendors or other homely sources as the basis of rather sophisticated variations. Since the Renaissance, the form has been greatly expanded so that variations written in the nineteenth and twentieth centuries often have the most tenuous relation to the original tune.

Although they stimulated the development of some significant musical forms, keyboard instruments had the disadvantage of being difficult to tune. Throughout the Renaissance there was no international agreement on a standard pitch to serve as a point of tonal orientation. Pitch levels used for the same tone could differ even within the same city. A singer or a violinist could adjust with some ease to whatever changes in pitch level were necessary. But a harpsichordist or an organist could not retune an entire set of strings or pipes between pieces. Also, the system of mean-tone tuning then in general use allowed really accurate relationships between pitches in only a limited number of scales. Even if a musician was adept at reading music in one scale and transposing it to another as he played, the tuning of his instrument did not always allow an accurate scale at the pitch level desired.

Thus, while such composers of choral music as Gesualdo could use many semitones or chromatics outside of the basic scale without destroying the key orientation of his composition, performers on keyboard instruments were limited to a much smaller range of sounds that were accurately related. Solutions to the problem were sought by such means as experimental instruments featuring multiple keyboards, each at a different pitch level. Finally, the best alternative appeared to be the adoption of a new system of tuning, the equal-tempered system, which has since served as the prevailing practice. By distributing the pitch discrepancies normally present in the physical overtone series equally among all the pitches represented on the keyboard, twelve scales could be used with acceptable accuracy, and transitions from one to another could be accomplished with ease. Few tones on a keyboard instrument are in tune in the sense of being in a perfect vibrational ratio with any other tones; however, none of them are noticeably out of tune either.

The organ was a major beneficiary of the equally tempered system, as alterations in its pitch level were particularly time-consuming to achieve. Germany traditionally produced excellent organs and highly skilled players. German organ builders were among the first to introduce multiple keyboards, a great variety of pipe timbres, and a full pedal board. However, composition for the organ and the notation of organ music were more advanced in Italy than elsewhere. The organ Mass, in which sections of plainsong were replaced by organ music based on the Gregorian chant melody, enjoyed a great vogue in Italy and to some extent in France. The organ accumulated its literature by reference to vocal models, but concentrated on those most suitable for religious purposes. The *ricercar* was an instrumental version of the motet, just as the canzona was an instrumental version of a chanson. The famous *Buxheimer Orgelbüch* was a collection of 250 pieces mostly based upon vocal compositions. Independent forms of organ music flourished under the impetus of the Lutheran movement.

The sixteenth century was a significant period in the development of instrumental music of all types. Court records have accounted for collections of lutes, viols, harps, flutes, trumpets, drums, and bagpipes. Harpsichords were played by members of the royal families who often had them inlaid with precious stones or painted with mythological scenes. Such was the prevalence of the lute that many communities established lute schools for the instruction of children. Ensembles of eight or nine players of reed and brass instruments were formed as town bands. Played from the church tower, instrumental music was often used to signal the commencement of significant activities of the day.

The music of the Renaissance was as rich as the civilization of the great empires whose ships spanned the globe, and as varied as the scents in a Paris market. From the alehouse to the palace, from the foot-stamping country dance to the stiffest courtly *pavane,* music set the tempo for a lively and vital society tied by admiration to the classical past and by adventurous spirit to the undiscovered future. It may seem to modern students as the nymphs of Venus appeared poetically to Spenser in his "Prothalamion:"

> For sure they did not seem
> To be begot of any earthly seed,
> But rather angels, or of angels' breed;
> Yet were they bred of summer's heat, they say,
> In sweetest season, when each flower and weed
> The earth did fresh array;
> So fresh they seemed as day,
> Even as their bridal day, which was not long:
>   Sweet Thames! run softly, till I end my song.[3]

3   Edmund Spenser, *The works of Edmund Spenser* (London: Routledge, 1896), p. 473.

SUMMARY OUTLINE

RENAISSANCE CIVILIZATION

Fourteenth Century Transition
High Renaissance
Late Renaissance

GENERAL CULTURAL INFLUENCES

History: Cambrai as a cultural center; Hundred Years' War; War of the Roses; fall of Constantinople; invasion of Italy by Charles VII; trade leagues; Machiavelli's political philosophy; Roman law codes and practices revived; Council of Trent; formation of European national states.

Social Factors: origins of absolutism; mercantilism challenges feudalism; stock exchanges established; rising level of education; complex urban social climate; manners and morals in Castiglione's *The Courtier;* Sir Thomas More's *Utopia.*

Philosophy and Religion: classical humanism; Neoplatonism; Mirandola's *Oration on the Dignity of Man;* resurgence of classical literature; Erasmus as a Renaissance man; humanism in religion; Jesuit Order founded; Reformation theology.

Natural and Applied Science: Copernican theory; biology of Vesalius revived; voyages of discovery; Leonardo da Vinci's notebooks; printing; magnetic compass.

MUSICAL ATTRIBUTES

Theory: tablature notation; mean-tone tuning; transition to equal-tempered system; Morley's *Plaine and Easie Introduction to Practicall Musicke.*

Social Functions: Late Gothic spirit in works of Dufay; church opposition to an absorption of Flemish polyphonic style; music in the Counter Reformation; Protestant Reformation music.

Composers, Forms, and Works: Dufay's *Missa L'homme Armé* origin of imitative polyphony; Palestrina's *Missa Papae Marcelli; missa brevis;* Gabrieli and Venetian polychoral music; Reformation

ARTISTIC PARALLELS

Late Gothic spirit in paintings of Van Eyck.

Dürer and Reformation spirit in art. Raphael's madonnas; gentle symmetry of Roman painting; Leonardo's "Virgin of the Rocks"; Venetian painting; Mannerism with El Greco and Tintoretto.

music: chorales, metrical psalms, and Anglican chant; *Genevan Psalter;* Italian and English madrigals; *Musica Transalpina;* Jannequin's chansons; English popular music in *Pammelia.*

Instruments and Forms: harpsichord, clavichord, virginals, lute, organ, and town bands; canzona, dance suite, ricercare, toccata, and variations; *Parthenia; Buxheimer Orgelbüch.*

Poetry of Shakespeare and Spencer; Botticelli's *Birth of Venus;* The *Louvre;* French chateaux.

4
The Baroque Era

A CULTURAL PROFILE

The century and a half from the birth of opera to the death of Johann Sebastian Bach was a critical and eventful period that witnessed the emergence of the institutional and philosophical patterns characteristic of modern life. The triumph of systematic rationalism in the eighteenth century led to the use of the uncomplimentary term "baroque" to describe the effusive, irregular shapes of seventeenth-century visual arts. The word has since been adopted to apply to many other aspects of both seventeenth and eighteenth century culture. The Mannerist emphasis on the subjective vision, in which impression and experience were dominant, had served as a transitional element between Renaissance and Baroque styles. Yet an academic formalism with emphasis upon theory was a consistent factor throughout the period. The quality of the era is reminiscent of a vast series of variations upon a few centrally recognizable themes.

A basic influence on the arts of any period is the general social and historical situation in which people find themselves. The breakdown of

115

a restricted, provincial mentality begun by the crusades reached such a point by the seventeenth century that a worldwide outlook evolved from increased contact with nations outside of Europe. New modes of navigation and the discovery of a process to distill fresh water at sea made extended voyages possible. Merchants instituted a lively trade with eastern nations, which at that time were enjoying an era of prosperity under such monarchs as K'ang Hsi of China, who subsidized industry and the arts. Chinese porcelain was duplicated at the famous factory established at Meissen, Germany, and copies of Chinese paintings were widely used for decoration. Increased economic security led to a demand for delicate Venetian glasswork, intricate Göbelin tapestries, and a variety of decorative objects in wood and metal. The very techniques that made the Baroque era a golden age of handcrafts also led to the manufacturing processes that produced the industrial revolution. The mercantile capitalism developed in the Netherlands and England culminated in a commercial revolution that supported a mass market for the arts. The resulting ascendance of the middle class both numerically and in economic power became an outstanding social characteristic of the era.

The increased colonial wealth of monarchs enabled them at last to dominate the nobility and to establish dynastic national states. The monarchical image and the ideal of nationalism produced new artistic demands that developed into one of the richest streams of Baroque art. For the first time in her history, Europe was brought into contact with the whole milieu of human society from the lowliest savage to the refined dignitary of the Chinese court. This fact led to the development of a comparative view of society and a broader toleration of social differences. Next to this movement existed the censorship of the press and brutal religious oppression. The period was, indeed, a study in contrasts.

Geographical, economic, and social expansions were matched by an increase in the understanding of the physical universe. The invention of the microscope and telescope extended the range of perception, and new mathematical techniques enabled simple observation to be codified into operational systems of analysis. Scientific societies to study physics, optics, biological structure, and mathematics were founded all over Europe. Among its original members, the French Academy of Sciences included Descartes, Pascal, and Fermat. Galileo, Newton, Leibniz, Robert Boyle, and William Harvey were only a few representative figures who reformulated man's ideas of himself and his universe. But science was not reserved for an aristocracy of analysts; it was a popular hobby and a leading topic of conversation in the coffeehouses. Benjamin Franklin, with his kite, was not an oddity in his time. Some of the most humorous caricatures of eighteenth-century life show ladies and gentlemen staring into the wrong ends of telescopes, peering through magnifying glasses at a celestial sphere, or otherwise engaging in amateur scientific activity.

The discoveries of science had an immediate effect upon philosophy, religion, social theory, and the arts. The universe without Earth as its center was seen as a collection of homogeneous parts united under a system of natural law. It functioned as an efficient mechanism without divine intervention or any capricious alteration of natural circumstance. Such a view would seem to undermine the sense of human significance, but men took great pride in understanding the workings of natural law and attempting to apply it to social problems. Yet, even such a mathematical genius as Pascal (1623–1662) expressed his inner anguish at the silence of infinite space and returned to mystical revelation as his greatest comfort in a mechanistic world.

Both Descartes (1596–1650) and Galileo (1564–1642) accepted mathematics as the key to unlock the secrets of the universe, and believed that natural processes could be explained only in quantitative terms. Systematic doubt became the basic philosophical procedure, reflecting both an inquisitive scientific spirit and the effects of the religious conflicts of the period. Spinoza (1632–1677) attempted to work out a naturalistic, mechanical philosophy of the universe, combining mysticism and rationalism in one system. The greatest artists of the period achieved the same synthesis of reason and emotion in a remarkably expressive balance.

The description of the seventeenth century as the Age of Reason is based upon certain major scientific discoveries made during that period. In the following century the direct application of these discoveries to the human disciplines of psychology, politics, ethics, economics, and religion caused that period to be described as the Age of Enlightenment. Adherents of a great variety of religious and social beliefs were united by their faith in the possibility of improving human society by discovering and applying natural laws to man and his institutions. Rationalistic supernaturalism was held to be the answer to the religious fanaticism that swept Europe in the Thirty Years' War (1618–1648).

Deists, drawing from Newton's astrophysics and the rationalism of John Locke (1632–1704), postulated a God who abided by his own mechanistic laws. They proposed a religion that could operate on reason alone without any supernatural manifestations. Such leading Americans as Thomas Jefferson and Thomas Paine were advocates of this natural religion. Voltaire was so angered by the superstition and corruption of the church that he rejected both Christianity and its God, commending men to the worship of a benevolent deistic god and to the conduct of a good life. True to the violent contrasts of the era, deism was countered by a fierce craving for mystical experience resulting in a return to the infallibility of the Roman Church.

Behind the enlightened façade that the period seemingly presented was a scenic backdrop composed of conspicuous conflicts. Both society and the arts were constantly torn between the rational stream of thought established by the great scientists and philosophers and a combination of the exuberant mysticism of St. Theresa and the emotional evangelism of John Wesley. The rise of the absolute monarchs was eventually contested by the rise of the bourgeoisie, culminating in the triumph of the Third Estate in France and the parliamentary monarchy of Britain. The vast differences between upper and lower classes found at the beginning of the Baroque period were gradually absorbed by the growing economic power of a broad middle class. The growth of nationalism noted as one aspect of the Protestant Reformation became the dominant European concept of statecraft, often pitting itself against the international power of the Roman Church. Despite the efforts of deists to heal the breach, a division between the body and soul, the realm of matter and spirit was maintained whereby some elements of the human personality remained impervious to the methods of science. Within the life style of the era a persistent theme of classicism appeared independently among many contending streams of thought and culminated in a final burst of energy at the end of the Baroque period.

Within the arts a continuing conflict smoldered between the subjective, often eccentric, visions of the Mannerists and the traditions of the scholarly artists of the academies with their visual rationale based upon rules and systems. Leading seventeenth-century artists such as Bernini, Rubens, and Rembrandt revealed some Mannerist influence in their use of a cinematic view featuring oblique angles, movable planes, and loose formal arrangements. Yet the work of art no less than the physical universe was a unified vision, not simply an ensemble of interrelated parts. Details were subjected to a larger conceptual pattern in which a sweeping diagonal line or a brilliant patch of color served to organize the formal relationships. The abundant detail, the curling effusion of decoration were a revelation of the inexhaustible wealth of the artistic vision. In music also, the Renaissance formal pattern based upon interrelationships of similar independent melodies gave way to a dominant thematic unity that persisted within a wealth of tonal variation.

THE RATIONAL IMPACT ON THE ARTS

Musical thought was much influenced by scientific speculation and by such increased technical resources as made possible the famous Amati, Guarneri, and Stradivari stringed instruments. Yet from the scientists' viewpoint no less an authority than Kepler (1571–1630) believed in some mystical, musical mathematics that pervaded the universe. He thought at one time that the distances between the six known planets were related to the tonal ratios of the ancient Greek musical scale and worked out a melody

Figure 4.1   ROBERT FLUDD. *Temple of Music.* (engraving). [The Bettmann Archive].

for each planet based upon the rate of its orbit about the sun. Joseph Addison (1672–1719) revealed the same thought process in a poetic manner in his description of the universe:

> What though in solemn silence all
> Move round this dark terrestrial ball?
> What though no real voice nor sound
> Amidst the radiant orbs be found?
> In reason's ear they all rejoice,
> And utter forth a glorious voice;
> Forever singing as they shine,
> "The hand that made us is divine."[4]

The very titles of some of the major treatises in astronomy and music theory reveal a similar trend of thought. Kepler's largest work was *The Harmonies of the World*, which was followed by Robert Fludd's *The Harmonious Monochord of the World* and Mersenne's *Universal Harmony*. Fludd's *Temple of Music* related musical harmony to architectural proportions (Figure 4.1). The most significant musical theorist of the Baroque period was Jean Phillipe Rameau (1683–1764). His *Treatise on Harmony Reduced to its Natural Principles* was a fitting companion to the natural law and natural religion of the Age of Enlightenment. The further study of the overtone series, together with the emergence of the science of acoustics, provided a strong base for utilizing the physical properties of sound in a rationalization of musical practice. The harmonic peculiarities of the Mannerist composers had led to a crisis in the modal system with its polyphonic development and heralded the adoption of a tonal system posited upon vertical or chordal relationships.

Within any of the twelve possible key centers available within a one-octave range on a modern keyboard instrument, certain fundamental relationships were established among the various tones of any one key. These relationships were extended to form logical patterns of harmonic progression in both practical music making and in the writings of theorists. The focus of this logic was the sense of key center or tonal identity. The sense of tonality is dependent upon accepted patterns of relationship between chords considered close and those considered distant from the fundamental key. At first, such chordal thinking conflicted with polyphonic practice, which stressed independent melody lines. However, gradually the new chordal thinking and the old polyphonic technique achieved a rich new synthesis. Composers since the early Renaissance had used combinations of tones in chordal structures almost instinctively. However, Rameau established a rationale for vertical combinations of sound composed of intervals of thirds. He also designated a root or basic tone for each chord which would

---

4 "On the Glories of Heaven and Earth," from *The Works of Joseph Addison*, 3 vols. (New York: Harper & Brothers, 1837), II, p. 455.

identify it in any tonal arrangement. Once the system of chordal structure and progression was fully defined, it set into operation a traditional practice that has been fundamental to western music until the early twentieth century.

The Baroque period was a golden era for systematic analysis, and many of the most renowned works on musical instruction were produced for musicians and laymen alike. In 1610, Coperario, in his book *The Rules of Composition,* showed how to write in chordal combinations of sound reckoned from the bass line of a composition. The German theorist Fux even revived the style of Palestrina and codified it into a system of training for writing in the polyphonic manner. Instruction books were not limited to compositional technique; such performance manuals as John Playford's *Brief Introduction to the Skill of Musicke* became popular with amateur instrumentalists. One of the most practical and informative books on keyboard technique was *The Art of Playing the Harpsichord,* by the French composer François Couperin (1668–1733). It has remained a major source book for harpsichordists in their performance of Baroque music. Couperin advocated a modernized method of fingering using the thumb to pivot the fingers over the keyboard in swift runs; he prescribed definitive methods for performing the trills and other ornamentation that graced French music of that time. The persistent systematizing carried on in all aspects of thought extended to the development of a repertoire of musical figures used to express question and affirmation, sadness and joy, or other emotive states (then called "affections"). These musical motifs were supposed to unify a composition into a consistent expressive design similar to the way in which long diagonal lines often unified paintings. Thus, even in esthetic realms, certain consistent principles were observed because they were thought to clarify emotional intent.

THE DRAMATIC IMPACT ON THE ARTS

For all its glorification of reason, the Baroque period was enriched by a stream of mysticism that reached an apex in Spain. The bitter religious conflicts surrounding the Reformation produced a spirit of renewed fervor in that bastion of Catholicism that was simultaneously nourished by a religious revival among the Islamic peoples still living in Spain. This heightened religious awareness led both to the mystical visions of St. Theresa and the brutal oppression of the Spanish Inquisition. Perhaps nowhere else in Europe were the roots of the emotional effusion of Baroque culture more clearly revealed than in Spain during the seventeenth century. The Society of Jesus (Jesuits), founded by Ignatius Loyola, had become a leading force in the Counter Reformation and the major stimulus to Italian religious art. His *Spiritual Exercises* were an early manual of instruction on the cultivation of the religious life to be used much as the musical or astronomical treatises characteristic of society at large. The dominant esthetic of Spain was both mystical and realistic in its devotion to images of the poor and humble and in its less idealized view of the aristocracy.

As a monarch, Philip II (1527–1598) was an excellent prototype of the quality of Spanish culture. One could hardly imagine a greater contrast than that between Philip II and Louis XIV (1638–1715), who expressed the ideals of French culture. Instead of building a Versailles dedicated to the splendor of court life, Philip built an Escorial dedicated to a preparation for death and resurrection. It was a mausoleum for his father, Charles V, and was planned to include a monastery where Philip could live a cloistered life in addition to his courtly life. Its barren setting and simple architectural style represented the spare monastic temper so well expressed in the paintings of Zurbaran (1598–1663) and the music of Victoria (1540–1611). The king was fond of Venetian art and music with their rich color and dramatic impact, although he had little sympathy for the eccentricities of Mannerism. Under the later influence of Italian Baroque style, Spain developed the most flamboyant decor imaginable in religious buildings. This parallel development of an official austere monastic image and a popular effusive image exemplified once again the dichotomous nature of the era.

As a leading quality of Baroque culture, the flair for the dramatic flourished in Italy with the sensuous, colorful paintings of Titian and the music of Gabrieli. Indeed, musicians and musical instruments of Italian origin were so much in demand throughout Europe as to be a sizeable factor in the national economy. Music publishing houses founded in Venice and Bologna rivaled those of the greatest northern commercial cities, and the absence of copyright laws made musical piracy a lucrative business. Italian thinkers found formidable competition in the rational giants of France and England, but the skills of her artists and musicians were more than enough to guarantee her artistic ascendancy.

Although politically impotent and territorially dominated by Spain and Austria, Italy produced the major innovations that transformed Renaissance style into a new and powerful Baroque medium. The balance of patronage shifted from the control of the church to a domination by the rich secular courts and city states. In addition to civic and ecclesiastical patronage, the aristocratic musical societies (called "academies") supported musical activities and laid the foundation for the public concert tradition.

The history of Baroque music is usually said to have begun with a group of minor Florentine noblemen who called themselves the *Camerata*. Fundamentally a literary group, they objected to the treatment of words resulting from the Renaissance polyphonic style because the singing of different words simultaneously obscured the meaning of the text. They believed that music should strive above all to express "affections" or states of the soul such as rage, wonder, excitement, or contemplation. The key to the realization of this new expression was provided by a Roman scholar who suggested the music of the Greek theater as a model. The resulting musical form was called *monody*. Monody was the epitome of simplicity, using the free musical declamations (recitative) of a solo singer accompanied by only a few strategic chords to sustain a background flow of sound. The rhythm followed the natural accent of the words, and the melody closely matched the inflections of speech. A later Italian musician by the name of Berardi stated that in Renaissance music "harmony is master of the word," whereas in Baroque music "the word is the master of harmony."

The new style was soon adopted for all sorts of religious and secular music, but its true vocation was found in connection with the tale of Orpheus and Euridice produced in 1600 to celebrate a royal marriage. The guests witnessed not only the wedding, but also the birth of opera. Although the music was said to have made a deep impression on the audience, this early prototype of opera seems less than spectacular to modern listeners. The dominant content was a tonal declamation called recitative and carried on by the main characters. It was interspersed with passages of a more melodic quality that served as arias. With the addition of choral refrains, the composite form was useful on both a large and small scale. When the opera itself developed into a theatrical production with the splendor of orchestral ensembles and elaborate stage sets, a simpler form called a cantata was used for intimate social gatherings and for church services.

Opera was based on contrasts. The sense of dramatic contrast between singer and accompaniment, recitative and aria, soloist and chorus had its roots in Venetian polychoral music. Although solo singing had been represented by Renaissance ayres and madrigals, the new dramatic emphasis profoundly affected the form of music used to achieve a dramatic unity. In a like manner, architecture, sculpture, and painting merged to create one overwhelming effect. The theatrical nature of Baroque culture so intrinsic to the arts was enhanced by the work of such creators as Bernini, the sculptor, and Claudio Monteverdi (1567–1643), the composer.

The first genuine operatic masterpiece is generally considered to be Monteverdi's *Orfeo* (1607). The composer arrived at the new style only after a complete mastery of Renaissance polyphonic technique; he may well rank as one of the most accomplished musicians in western history. *Orfeo* was composed for the court of the Duke of Mantua, which was also graced by the presence of Tasso and Rubens. Although Monteverdi later became the director of music for St. Mark's in Venice, and even entered the priesthood, he had less interest in the composition of liturgical music than in the portrayal of human character and emotion that opera allowed.

Perhaps the most surprising thing about *Orfeo* is that the passage of centuries has done relatively little to dull its impact. It remains a masterful work in both musical and emotional aspects. The orchestra of more than three dozen instruments was unusual for that day, as was the great variety

of musical forms employed. Yet all elements were well chosen to complement the import of the drama.

The orchestral overture begins in a flurry of brasses and is followed by
a more subdued chordal section as if to reflect the wide variation in the
emotional range presented. The Spirit of Music descends from Parnas-
sus to address the audience on the power of music. The orchestral
interludes in her song make a vivid contrast between the rather spare
solo and the opulent orchestral tone. The first act celebrates the love of
Orpheus and Euridice. The second shepherd sings, "See, Orpheus, all
around you the forest and meadows laugh. Take the golden plectrum
and sing on this beautiful morning." A chorus of nymphs and shepherds joins in a gay madrigal of intricate melody and strongly accented
rhythm, both characteristic features of Baroque music.

In the second act, Euridice's nymph companion brings the news of
her death, and immediately the music becomes subdued with sudden
shifts of tonality to characterize the agony in the words. Orpheus then
sings his famous lament employing vivid word painting on the "deep
abysses" and the last farewells to earth. The chorus closes with a complex tangle of overlapping melody lines. Their constant response
beginning, "Ah, bitter sadness," has the biting rhythm of an outcry
against cruel fate.

The sinfonia for brasses, which begins Act IV, serves as a sombre
echo of their introduction to the happy first act. Orpheus stands at the
gate to the underworld where he is greeted by Hope, whose melody
soars constantly upward to a dramatic declaration of the words "Abandon all hope, ye who enter here." With a great outburst of anguish
Orpheus mourns the departure of this his last comforter. Immediately,
he is confronted by Charon, guardian of the underworld, who sings in
an ominous bass voice against a reedy accompaniment. Monteverdi
took care to indicate specific instrumental combinations he wished to
be used in a few places to heighten the dramatic effect. Detailed instructions on vocal ornamentation were given for the famous solo of
Orpheus in which he sings Charon to sleep and gains entrance to the
underworld. When sung as the composer indicated, the aria is a marvel
of intricacy.

The dark mood of the act changes as a chorus of spirits proclaim
that nothing can stand against a man's steadfast courage. Pluto, in a
kingly bass voice, ultimately pronounces his decision that Orpheus
may return with Euridice to the upper world if he does not look back
to see that she is coming. Their exit from the underworld begins with
a gay marching song, but changes into a strangely restive mood indic-
ative of Orpheus' growing doubt. How does he know she is following?
He looks back, and Euridice disappears into darkness, from whence

emerges her final song full of agonized dissonances. While Orpheus grieves, a distant voice echoes his laments. But, true to the spirit of Greek drama, Apollo descends amid a final chorus of rejoicing to take Orpheus to heaven where his sorrow may be healed. The impact of so many richly expressive moments made *Orfeo* and its successors the focus of musical concern within the bounds of a culture devoted to such imagery.

The thrust of the new musical movement originated in the interests of the aristocracy, and the church found itself in a precarious impasse between exquisite music for worship which belonged, unfortunately, to an era long past, and a new musical style so effusive as to overwhelm the religious content of the liturgy. While the older style did continue to be used widely throughout the Baroque period, a growing need to make some adaptation to the newer practices was evident. Into this breach came the Jesuits with their fervent mysticism and emphasis upon the emotional attractions of religion. Giacomo Carissimi (1605–1674), the director of a Jesuit college in Rome, set the narrative texts of the Old Testament to the dramatic recitative style for performance at special Lenten services. The music was addressed to congregations of laymen who met in the church oratorio (prayer hall) for communal observances. The word "oratorio" was eventually applied to the form of the music itself. Thus began a tradition which has produced such masterworks of western culture as Handel's *Messiah* and Bach's *Passion According to St. Matthew.* The operatic divisions of recitative, aria, and chorus were observed, but the balance was quite different. First of all, the oratorio was not intended to be staged; any action was narrated or suggested rather than acted. The lack of visual aids to the story presentation was compensated for by a narrator who sang a running commentary on the action. The chorus was used much more extensively than in opera for dramatic, narrative, or meditative purposes.

The new emotional style of music did not long remain outside the central services of the church, but gradually crept in through the oratorio and cantata to become part of the liturgy. This development was not universally admired, and some effects were undoubtedly incongrouous. Local operatic stars entertained the congregation with their fantastic technical virtuosity while instrumental groups enlivened the ritual with incidental music. However, the Jesuit aim of bringing people back into the Roman Church with renewed enthusiasm was most certainly accomplished, and their success was no less brilliant in the visual arts. *Il Gesu*, the central church of the order, was an early landmark in Baroque architecture, presenting an asymmetrical façade of undulating surfaces. All the visual arts were combined to give the illusion of endless radiant spaces opening through church ceilings. So persuasive was the style that Protestant congregations adopted it without hesitation, and German Baroque churches grew to unprecedented magnificence. The other dominant aim of the Jesuits was to restore the church to the common man in Catholic terms he could both sense and understand. Oratorios were often sung in the vernacular instead of Latin. The realistic emotionalism of such works as Bernini's *Ecstasy of St. Theresa* appealed to the senses of all classes of people. Thus, of the many themes represented in Baroque culture, enlightened reason, heightened emotion, and the rise of the common man were consistently entwined.

ARTS UNDER COURT PATRONAGE

Ironically, the era not only witnessed the rise of individualistic thinking based upon rejection of traditional rational absolutes, but also produced an equally strong assertion of political absolutes of the most ancient and despotic kind. The English philosopher Thomas Hobbes (1588–1679), one of the chief apologists for an absolute monarchy, viewed the natural state of man as one of complete anarchy driven by self-interest. Through a mutual social contract man sought to establish peace and order by the creation of government and kingship. Government was the arbiter of religion, justice, and morality; the stability of society was dependent upon an absolute monarch not responsible to the people and therefore able to keep order among them. The feeling for social reality which caused Hobbes to base his political philosophy on the premises of egotism and self-preservation was also emphasized in the art of Rembrandt, Zurbaran, and the English moralist painter Hogarth. The unity of church and state in the cultivation of a kingly image had its last historical rival in the Byzantine court of Justinian. All the theatrical quality of Jesuit religious art was transferred to the person of the king; his palace and even his portraits were dramas based upon his political self-concept. In an environment torn by religious differences and jealous political forces, absolutism seemed the only answer to the problem of social order. Even the new understanding of the universe seemed to authorize such a political structure—especially when Copernicus had described the sun as sitting on a royal throne and governing the family of stars which moved about it.

Louis XIV (1643–1715) must be named among the most outstanding of all the world's leaders who have governed under a system of absolutism. Only a man with a monumental ego and a profound sense of theater could have persisted with undiminished grandeur through a seventy-two year reign. He was, indeed, the state. About him revolved like planets the ministers of state whose most trivial decisions failed to escape the watchful eyes of the king. In his memoirs, the Duc de Saint-Simon described Louis as a person of basically modest gifts, poorly educated, and addicted to flattery. Yet he was infinitely capable of a refinement of manners and of borrowing from all the good minds with which he constantly surrounded himself. He had a remarkable sense of order and an administrative capacity to balance his equally strong craving for glory. Saint-Simon compared the era of Louis XIV to that of the Roman Emperor Augustus in its sense of opulence and security. Louis was particularly fortunate in that his aristocratic French subjects were largely dedicated to serving and pleasing him.

The court at Versailles was a prime instrument of the king's policy; it provided both insulation from Parisian mobs and an intricate system of surveillance by which he governed a restive nobility. To the arts, Louis trusted his most prized possession—his glory. Since his major artistic resources were the official academies for arts and literature, he raised the heads of these bureaus to eminent positions in the state. While exercising rare good taste, he supported the arts generously because of their propaganda value. His style preferences were decidedly classical, and he was consistently identified with Apollo, the sun god. Charles Lebrun (1619–1690) glorified Louis's self-concept as a military leader by substituting his features for those of Alexander the Great in a huge painting celebrating the conquest of Babylon. Bernini's portrait bust of Louis exalted the concept of absolutism as much as the individual it portrayed; but his plan for the reconstruction of the Louvre was rejected because of its departure from classical standards as well as its impracticality.

Louis XIV abandoned the copying of Italian artistic models, which were the rage of Europe, in order to build a new artistic concept based upon his need for a noble style removed from the confines of ordinary mortality. The paintings of Poussin (1594–1655), with their idealism and cool restraint, were direct products of a cultural philosophy conditioned by the concepts of absolutism, even though Poussin himself was repelled by the court atmosphere and lived in Rome. His opposite, Charles Lebrun, liked the circumscribed and frivolous court life and became a veritable artistic dictator as head of the academy for the arts. He was a superb decorator who combined all the arts in true Baroque fashion into interior stage sets against which Louis played his kingly role to perfection. His painting of Alexander's triumphal entry into Babylon was designed for the interior of Versailles, which demanded a heroic scale. Rubens was also well represented in the court patronage system, but his unrestrained treatment of classical subjects was not championed by the academy.

Carefully shaped to the needs of absolutism, music was dutifully regulated by the resourceful autocrat Jean-Baptiste Lully (1632–1687), who was Italian by birth and French by preference (Figure 4.2). His ideas paralleled those of the painters: discipline of materials, purity of intonation, accuracy of playing, and elegance of effect. His talent as an administrator was boundless. He founded French opera and gave it a unique style of overture. He arranged the sequence of dance movements which has since been called the "French Suite." He provided in abundance the one commodity most required by a restless, captive nobility—entertainment. He

128   combined music, story, and scenery into lavish spectacles of thinly veiled allegory which allied the king with classical heroes who were inevitably saved from disaster by the timely intervention of the gods.

The opera had a lively historic tradition upon which to draw; its theatrical techniques were derived from such contemporary dramatists as Racine and Molière. However, the preferred aristocratic form of French theater was neither music nor plays, but dance. Louis XIV was reportedly an excellent dancer and took a leading role in the court ballets, which were actually composites of dance, spoken parts, songs, and choruses set

Figure 4.2   FRANCOIS PUGET. *Reunion of Musicians and Singers—1689.* [Courtesy, Louvre, Paris, (Giraudon)].

to classical themes. Louis's guardian of state during his youth, Cardinal Mazarin, imported the Italian opera partly to divert attention from his political intrigues. The exorbitant cost of these spectacles was defrayed by public taxation, and some of the singers were beaten in the streets because of the economic oppression which they represented. French national opera expressed itself more in spectacle and staging than in music; nevertheless, such works as Lully's *Alceste* were musically significant. Lully and Molière together wrote a series of *comedie ballets* that included *Le Bourgeois Gentilhomme* with its splendid satire on aristocratic manners. When Lully finally turned to opera, the literary imagery had been well established by the classical tragedies of Corneille and Racine, with their eternal conflicts of love and glory. His great choral sections, which formed complete cantatas in themselves, were the most illustrious of Lully's musical contributions, aside from the overture which has since been used as a form independent of opera. With Lully, the French opera reached an epitome of dignity and sensuous appeal; it became a perfect vehicle for the artistic embodiment of the social ideals of absolutism.

Louis XIV established a pattern that was adopted with equally fruitful results by Frederick II of Prussia (1712–1786). Unlike Louis, Frederick was broadly educated and earned well-deserved fame as a statesman, man of letters, and patron of music. He was an accomplished flutist and a capable composer, and through his patronage the German musical tradition was founded. He personally employed German composers, theorists, instrument builders, and performers. He selected the librettos, the performers, costumes, and scenery for the operas. His own taste determined the quality of musical activities, and he needed no Lully to enhance his glory. Seldom has any art been nourished by such a rare combination of material resources and refined understanding.

Compelled by his "barracks king" father to master the arts of war and public administration, Frederick secretly managed to obtain an education in the arts through the efforts of his private tutor. He was always more at home in the French language and courtly style than in his own. He also rejected his father's Calvinism in favor of the ideals of the Enlightenment. Voltaire, who was a correspondent of long standing, regarded him as a true philosopher-king whose reign was marked by a rare respite in religious oppression. However, his reign was also marked by a pattern of ruthless political conquest which raised Prussia to the status of a world power. Although treacherous and despotic in many respects, the absolutism of Frederick II was highly enlightened in others. Universities, scientific societies, artistic academies, and theaters all experienced unprecedented productivity. Frederick himself founded and managed the Berlin opera. At the same time, the greatest artists and thinkers were still merely court attendants who performed upon his command at the hour specified; they were there to serve his artistic whim.

Frederick II was a flutist of great energy and no mean distinction. Even on campaigns, he took his flute and an accompanist with a portable harpsichord. It must have been a sad moment when in old age—with missing teeth, shortness of breath, and stiff fingers—he packed his flute and remarked, "I have lost my best friend." His compositions for flute were skillful, if not inspired, and have remained consistently in the repertoire. In his youth he championed the music of the Baroque opera and remained firmly attached to it, regarding the newer music of Haydn as a symptom of artistic decay. He was cool to instrumental music unless it included a flute part that he could play, and was visibly cold to sacred music or even polyphonic technique because of its association with the church.

Inevitably, his own narrow tastes and eventual disinterest in music led to a decline in the state of music under his patronage. The only court musician with status comparable to that of Lully was Quantz, Frederick's flute teacher who made impressive contributions to the improvement of the flute mechanism. Whole ebony tree trunks were imported so that Quantz could have good material for flute making. Despite his artistic shortsightedness, Frederick began an important tradition of national musical excellence which became a major force in western cultural history.

While both Louis XIV and Frederick II amalgamated Italian opera with native musical practices to create a truly national aristocratic style, Charles II of England (1630–1685) was so envious of Versailles that he was determined to create his own version of it. Even church music was reorganized to admit Baroque solo style into its august polyphony. The choristers were required to sing in Italian as well as English, and instrumental ensemble music was introduced into the service. His musical ideal was Lully, to whom he sent young composers to learn the lively French style.

Henry Purcell (1658–1695) succeeded in combining his native English musical style with the rhythmic precision of French dance music to become the model for generations of English composers. Until the twentieth century, his *Dido and Aeneas* was considered the one true opera in English musical history, as the English preferred musical scenes inserted in a spoken play. Attesting to the unity of church and state in England, Purcell held simultaneously the posts of organist at Westminster Abbey and the Chapel Royal, and composer to the courts of Charles II, James II, and William III.

The other great court, that of Philip IV of Spain (*d.* 1665), was graced by no musicians of subsequent note, but by the great painter Diego Velasquez (1599–1650). He produced paintings of unerring visual accuracy and formal refinement that reflected the sedate, aristocratic society he served. True to the rationalist tradition of the Baroque period, he simultaneously created intricate patterns of light and shadow in a veritable analysis of the process of vision. There was little in his work to relate him to the religious emotionalism of his contemporary Zurbaran or even the Jesuit movement. He was also removed from the immediate necessity to glorify absolutism. His reserved, rather haughty style was well suited to the temper of the Hapsburg kings.

Many petty noblemen all over Europe suffered financial ruin trying to support artistic endeavors in imitation of the illustrious courts of the leading nations. The great demand for opera at the smaller courts was served by commercialized professional companies. Nobility and merchants in Venice, Naples, Hamburg, and London jointly held subscription concerts backed by a group of shareholders. These commercial operas turned from classic aristocratic themes to tales of ambition and love, and used modernized historical characters. A comic element was also introduced, although real comic opera flourished only after the seventeenth century and used peasant or middle-class prototypes for characters. The less cultivated audience demanded plenty of activity and sheer technical display; later middle-class opera fans additionally demanded characters who reflected their own life style. *Opera buffa* (comic opera) parodied the aristocratic *opera seria* and showed the cunning of the peasant underdog in his incessant social war against the nobility.

Figure 4.3 FERDINANDO BIBIENA. Design for a stage set for a shrine of Diana. [The Metropolitan Museum of Art, Whittlesey Fund, 1950].

It is difficult to imagine the pleasure and burden that opera represented during the height of its influence. Elaborate stage sets featured costly machinery to raise and lower godlike heroes through the air (Figure 4.3). Storms, fires, and miracles were available on order from ingenious and costly stage designers. The vocal stars of these lavish productions were among the wealthiest individuals in Europe. The demand for operatic music was so strong as to cause the church, which could not tolerate women singers, to adopt a novel solution. The male castrati singers, whose high voices had been preserved by a surgical operation, were used in the papal chapel to replace the lighter voices of the choirboys. The adulation these men received for their high tones and intricate vocal technique matched that accorded a modern popular singer.

However, the position of musicians in general was rather poor; during wartime it was quite desperate. Players in private orchestras were the first to suffer from the financial disasters of their patrons. The chapel singers of Charles II wore gowns so ragged that the chapel master finally refused to let them be seen in public. The lot of a musician was precarious at best even with the most dependable patron; many hoped for better times under the more broadly based patronage of middle-class merchants.

ARTS UNDER BOURGEOIS PATRONAGE

Social philosophers in the eighteenth century were dedicated to the preservation of the rights and dignity of mankind as distinguished from the hereditary nobility. But even *they* wavered before the great masses of human beings who were economically exploited, functionally illiterate, and moved only by fear or superstition. Was it even reasonable to ask social consciousness and restraint of such people? To create artistic or literary works of biting social criticism on their behalf was one thing, but to assume the bitter and possibly fruitless struggle to change their habits and circumstances was something quite different. Philosophers preferred to concentrate on the craftsmen and shopkeepers who had some intelligence and were in a position to exercise social power if given a convincing rationale for their actions. The middle class gradually evolved an identity of its own and assumed the burdens of the great social revolutions of the late eighteenth century, which were to reshape the instruments of political control. Middle class mentality and artistic needs also shaped the art products of the period.

Music had always been bound primarily to the aristocracy of church or court, and this pattern was still the most common throughout the Baroque era. However, the burghers controlled the artistic environment of the large free cities and hired musicians through competitive examination to staff the available positions in local churches and civic organizations. Through such an arrangement the musician enjoyed a greater security. He became a lifelong part of the municipality instead of being subject to the whim of one nobleman. Also, instead of humbly requesting the patron's release, he was free to end his contract. Naturally, the possibility of bribery or outright purchase of such positions was always imminent, and the best applicants were not always chosen. Both the conduct of civic musical organizations and the choice of their musical repertoire was under the control of the city council. This group wished to create a good reputation for the city by employing the finest available musicians, but at the same time the members wanted to have their own musical tastes served.

While ordinary citizens encountered music mostly in church, university students and better informed burghers organized music clubs where they performed for one another or heard travelling virtuosi. England began the tradition of the public subscription concert open to anyone with the price of admission. Under noble patronage musicians were servants who wore the uniform of the employer and depended upon his good graces and fiscal solvency for their livelihood. Within a collective patronage musicians could organize into a union to protect both the standards of the profession and the prerogatives of its members. Social mobility was vastly increased by the possession of a remarkable talent; many musicians rose from very humble origins to become famous by their individual skill.

Musical production was largely dependent upon commissions from wealthy burghers or noblemen for occasional pieces to be used at important social events. Because these occasional patrons liked to see their commissioned works in print, a great number of such pieces were preserved for posterity. Many composers were under a continuing contract for new compositions as part of their job. Johann Sebastian Bach produced his vast collection of cantatas because of the need for new music Sunday after Sunday. Compositions could also be written on speculation and dedicated with a suitably ingratiating preface to a wealthy patron. The patron was supposed to respond with a material token of his gratitude, or, perhaps, a position within his musical establishment. The level of music education was such that patrons seemed to exert little restriction on the musical imagination. Bach did have some trouble with the less educated members of his church who did not understand the intricacies of his music and particularly resented his complex elaboration of their simple chorale singing.

The rise of bourgeois patronage was particularly characteristic of Germany, England, and Holland. As predominantly Protestant countries, their ideologies were rooted in the social egalitarian aspects of the Reformation. Holland, under the restrictive ecclesiastical dictates of a Calvinist heritage, produced no religious musical heritage to match the enduring glories of German Baroque music. Esthetic values were largely centered on the home and the growing national consciousness, while scientific and economic values were concentrated on order and security. Music was practiced somewhat informally in the home, without the necessity for a large organized system of musical production to meet the demands of a monarchical aristocracy. No lavish secular metropolitan spirit led to the founding of opera houses and public concerts prevalent in other countries. Nevertheless, municipal musicians and church organists were employed by the town council. On a more modest scale, they provided music for public observances and created a repertoire of excellent music.

Figure 4.4 JOHANNES VERMEER. *The Music Lesson.* [Courtesy, H. M. The Queen. (Photo Studios Ltd.)].

Jan Pieters Sweelinck (1562–1621), organist at the Oude Kirk in Amsterdam transmitted the music of the Venetian Mannerists to the North. Famous for his religious and secular keyboard compositions and his ability as an organ teacher, he was much sought after by German students. As a developing mechanism, the organ was largely the creation of Dutch and German mechanical genius. Builders abandoned the consistent blend of sound (representative of the Renaissance organ) in favor of a sharply differentiated collection of tone equality groups. As in Venetian music, contrasting sounds could be pitted against one another to add an expressive significance to a chorale text, or to bring out the main melody against a varying tonal background. Added technical resources and tonal flexibility were brilliantly exploited by Sweelinck and his followers in *toccatas* (touch pieces) and *fantasias,* with their rapid figures and driving rhythms.

In the visual arts Dutch domestic and civic life provided an insatiable appetite for pictures to decorate the home or to represent civic organizations. Painters catered to every social level in infinite degrees of specialization. The still life and landscape became popular and grew independent of the standard figure painting that had been the backbone of pictorial art. Vermeer's scenes of everyday life in sunlit Dutch interiors were the apotheosis of domesticity (Figure 4.4). They exemplified the quiet order and dignified decor characteristic of the Dutch social ideal. Rembrandt, on the other hand, was the artist of the human spirit in its conflicts and tragedies. His engravings on the life of Christ have the same compassionate grandeur exemplified by Bach's oratorios dealing with the crucifixion. The conditions of bourgeois patronage were as difficult for Bach as they were for Rembrandt. Knowledge of Bach's music stems from the revival of his works begun in the nineteenth century by Mendelssohn and *not* by any continuous regard for them by people of Bach's own time. Rembrandt's corporation paintings such as "The Night Watch" recorded for posterity the colorful civic groups with their sober and sometimes pompous bourgeois spirit.

Middle-class patronage, with its less than lavish financial position often preferred pictures such as etchings. (These could be produced in multiple copies.) Rembrandt raised this process to an artistic level rivaled only by Dürer, the Renaissance master.

The common man was not neglected as subject matter. The Italian painter Caravaggio (1573–1610) consistently used prototypes of ordinary men for the figures of his paintings. "The Calling of St. Matthew" was portrayed as taking place in a public tavern among the normally observed inhabitants of such a place. Chardin and Zurbaran both had a perceptive vision of the beauty to be found in kitchen utensils and ordinary vegetables for the table. The life of the common man was consistently of interest as a subject even in much aristocratic painting, but the rise of the bourgeoisie as a patron class was of more fundamental importance to the arts.

Johann Sebastian Bach (1685–1750), whose death marked the end of the Baroque era, was an enigma in his own time. He was not an innovator in the sense of initiating a new style of music, and his sons considered him hopelessly old-fashioned. He was, rather, a summary of the entire polyphonic stream of thought, achieving within a consistent personal style a complete synthesis of most of the traditional techniques and forms existent in the western world. Opera was the only form of any consequence that he never attempted. Behind Bach lay centuries of musical ancestors and the development of the musical forms into which his ideas were poured.

He was deeply rooted in the life and beliefs of the church he served, and his unerring dedication in all his compositions was *soli Deo gloria* (to God alone be glory). To him, no difference existed between elements of the sacred and those of the secular; that which glorified God also delighted the human spirit. The many strands of his art had been accumulating over the centuries. The chorales had become established in the liturgy; the rising tide of religious conflict had produced renewed religious fervor; and the Baroque recitative and aria had been amalgamated into religion as the church cantata. Through contact with Italian culture, many illustrious musical forebears such as Heinrich Schütz (1585-1672) had transmitted the major vocal and instrumental styles to the North. Frederick the Great had given major support to the growing spirit of German musical nationalism.

The most outstanding of Bach's choral compositions were the products of his long residency as the cantor of the Thomaschüle in Leipzig. The students at that institution had the responsibility of performing music for the city churches, which were conservative in their musical preferences. The municipal council members had been hoping to hire a progressive cantor oriented toward the Italian style of music; they were somewhat disappointed that the candidate of their first choice was not available and they had to settle for Bach. He was to be plagued for much of his life by the constant petty quarrels of local officials and by the assignment of such menial chores as teaching grammar to the school boys. His job was to supply music for the insatiable musical appetite of the city churches through the relentless roll of Sundays.

His basic vehicle was the cantata—a composite of introductory instrumental overture, recitative, aria, and chorale. Even his large oratorios were an expansion of the basic cantata pattern. A variant of the oratorio form was the passion—the story of the events of the crucifixion that had been read or enacted before congregations since possibly the fourth century. The two extant passion settings by Bach form a clear representation of the highest attainments in a polyphonic style.

The *Passion According to St. John* was first produced on Good Friday of 1723 or 1724. It amply illustrates the range of technique and manner of expression characteristic of Bach's style. The instrumental introduction is based upon a four-note figure that winds about beneath a sustained lyrical melody. The chorus bursts into this shimmer of sound with a firm shout of "Lord." After the initial dramatic outcry the chorus breaks into its own strands of weaving polyphony on the word "Master." Already the major stylistic factors of Baroque music have appeared—a driving rhythm, great blocks of chordal harmony, intricate polyphony, rich and constantly varied tonality, and a consistent thematic unity. Whereas Renaissance form was much like a patchwork quilt in which the theme changed to match each change of text, Baroque form is based upon a few memorable themes from which the entire piece is derived. Thus the Bach introduction is more like a textile design in which the same tiny pattern occurs over and over as the unifying force.

The choral section is followed by the recitative of the narrator, who delivers the Biblical text describing the scene in the garden of Gethsemane. As in a drama, each character has a musically defined role. The narrator, with his light tenor voice, seems to be a youthful witness to the events he describes. The role of Jesus is sung in a bass voice with a musical style conveying sorrow and great dignity. The chorus has the same ambivalent role as in a Greek drama. It can be a composite character such as the mob, a meditative unit reflecting on the meaning of events, or the congregation itself as it joins in the familiar chorale tunes interspersed throughout the oratorio.

Bach's treatment of key words or ideas is intensely revealing. When Peter hears the rooster crow and remembers the prophecy of denial, his weeping is given an eternally long, convoluted melody that falls unsteadily down the vocal range. Jesus's statement that his disciples would do battle under another leader is set to the aggressive rhythm of a French overture. The most dramatic of all the recitatives describes the rending of the veil of the temple; the whole orchestra hurtles down a long scale and trembles at the bottom to illustrate the text's allusion to the earthquake which opened the graves.

The arias are notable for their contrasting moods and tone-color combinations. They reflect the more personal pietism of the individual in contrast with the collective sentiments of the chorus. Bach generally treated the voice as another instrument within a composite of independent melodies. The alto voice with the oboe and the soprano voice with flute were combinations of which he was particularly fond. His arias follow the standard Italian form, which used a main theme, a middle section, and a return to the main theme. The choruses show a great variety of textures and forms. The response from the crowd, "Give us Barabbas," is given entirely in simultaneous chords, while the word "crucify" emerges continually from a mass of polyphony. The text which mockingly hails Jesus as King of the Jews is given a setting of vast and ironic dignity.

In the discourse concerning the division of Jesus' coat without a seam, the admonition, "Do not rend it or divide it," is set to great rhythmic hammer blows that rise to a climax of sound and trickle out once again from the culminating chords. The Baroque treatment of imitative polyphony within a unified thematic context is the basis of this fugue (literally, flight) form. The final chorus is a simple lullaby on a massive musical scale; its sombre "rest well" surges through the chorale to a final assertion of hope.

138   Figure 4.5   Cantata performance at the time of Bach showing conductor and orchestra. [The Bettmann Archive].

Bach never suffered from lack of admiration during his lifetime; his fame, however, was based upon his skill as a performer rather than his genius as a composer. As an organist at Weimar, he was repeatedly invited to inspect new organs and to give their dedication recitals. Organ students came from all over the country to be trained in his demanding technique and rigorous improvisational freedom. As a performing virtuoso he visited Frederick the Great in Potsdam and improvised on a theme given to him by that monarch. After returning home Bach transformed the little theme into a group of pieces he called *The Musical Offering.*

Bach's organ compositions form the largest proportion of works from any one master included in the modern repertoire of the instrument. The *Passacaglia and Fugue in C Minor* is one of his typical syntheses of formal design and demanding dexterity. The passacaglia as a form is simply an elaborate ground bass in which the same tune is constantly repeated, usually in the lowest voice line. Bach honors this simplicity of concept by stating his ground theme alone in the pedal pitches at the very beginning. This theme serves as the unifying motif of an extended tonal superstructure; over it is gradually stretched a musical fabric of increasing tonal complexity. As in a series of variations, each new idea enriches the constantly repeated theme by the addition of new harmonies, countermelodies, or rhythmic divisions. Finally, even the bass theme breaks into a rhythmic pattern and moves into the higher pitch ranges. The theme seems to disappear amid many light running figures and then suddenly to emerge again. As a summary statement, Bach uses most of the variants in recombination, working to a climax with a constant pattern in all the voices. The same bass theme that formed the framework of the passacaglia is then used as the subject of a complex fugue, which culminates in one massive chord that seems to shift completely out of the key. A dramatic pause follows, and then comes the solid assertion of the final cadence.

Bach's music in secular as well as religious contexts serves as a synthesis of western techniques and national variants. The *Brandenburg Concertos* were based upon a form of Italian origin called the *concerto grosso.* Antonio Vivaldi (1675–1741) established the final form of the *concerto grosso* by enlarging the parts of soloists within the context of the whole instrumental ensemble to produce a dramatic contrast of sound levels. Three movements in fast-slow-fast tempos became standard, although Bach sometimes departed from this plan. At the court of Weimar, Bach encountered much Italian music, which was then very popular with the aristocracy. He so admired the compositions of Vivaldi that he transcribed them for organ and for harpsichord so that he could study their technique carefully in the process. Bach's own works in the *concerto grosso* form were written on commission for the Margrave of Brandenburg. Bach suspected that the margrave wanted the pieces more for display than for use, so he wrote each one for a different combination of instruments and had the good sense to make a duplicate copy before he sent the works off. In contrast with the organ works and the oratorios, the concertos seem to be elegant, witty, and thoroughly sociable.

The *Fifth Brandenburg Concerto* is representative of the group, although each work is slightly different from all the others. It begins with the whole orchestra in a bold chordal assertion which returns constantly to provide a sense of formal cohesion. Out of its stern façade emerge the three soloists (harpsichord, violin, and flute) in a polyphonic interplay that merges once again with the larger group in a continuing cycle. At one memorable point the soloists conclude their section with a long series of trills shifting through adjacent tonalities and giving a vivid sensation of musical suspense, to be rescued at last by the firm chords of the orchestral theme.

In a slower tempo, the middle movement is dominated by the soloists who alternate and combine in elegant melodic conversation. The concerto concludes with a lively fugal movement patterned after the traditional dance rhythm of the gigue. The orchestra accents the heavy beats, while the soloists develop their own rippling elaborations of the fugal idea. The six *Brandenburg Concertos* have been, for many listeners, the best introduction to Bach's music, which often seems forbidding in its formal complexity.

While Bach stood at the height of the Protestant bourgeois culture of Germany, a fellow countryman found the patronage of the English middle class more to his liking. George Frederick Handel (1685–1759) was himself an international mixture of German birth, Italian musical style, and English citizenry. He had the urbane sense of the world that Bach, isolated in his obscure courts and churches, never attained. Handel was an operatic dramatist whose interests and life style made a vivid contrast with those of Bach. Nevertheless, in his own manner he reached a height of stylistic synthesis and human compassion.

Handel was interested in character portrayal even as Bach was interested in the portrayal of ideas. His efforts to transplant the emotional style of Italian opera to England were doomed to eventual failure, notwithstanding the English craving for that foreign delicacy. The aristocracy maintained what might have been a snobbish allegiance to Italian style, but, increasingly, the middle class turned to the lighter ballad opera for their entertainment. Handel recovered from the financial ruin of his Italian opera company to create a vernacular oratorio form as a substitute for grand opera. His works found a deep and responsive place in English national life, as they were entertainment on a high moral plane, glorifying the traditional English penchant for choral music. The middle-class Englishman recognized himself in the vicissitudes of Handel's Old Testament characters; nationalism was glorified at a time when it was becoming dominant in British life. The oratorios were a testament to the social climate of England and to Handel's ability to amalgamate another influence into his already complex style. German pietism, Italian sophistication, and the English bourgeois spirit all managed to mix into a conglomerate style which made a great deal of artistic sense. Handel might be compared to Franz Hals, who used deliberately broad strokes and flamboyant brush effects to achieve a sense of dramatic immediacy. Bach was more like Rembrandt, whose work revealed the careful, penetrating analyst.

Both Bach and Handel received early training in the traditional skills of the organist; Handel's first job was that of organist at the cathedral in Halle. He also wrote a *St. John Passion,* which had the same pietistic sentiments as the Bach work. However, Handel never wrote for any specific liturgical function; he was himself outside any ecclesiastical allegiance. He was much more akin to the spirit of ethical humanism of the Enlightenment. His oratorio texts, with the exception of *Messiah,* were usually written by an opera librettist, and the chorale, which was a mainstay in the oratorios of Bach, was of little interest to him. Handel was enormously adaptable, feeling equally at home within the aristocratic art societies of Italy and the Protestant middle-class patronage of England. Unlike Bach, he deliberately tried to suppress the more Germanic features of his musical style and rejected systematic intellectualism for a looser lyrical flow.

Handel presents the interesting case of a man who, caught between changing patterns of patronage, learned to adapt to the newly emerging social order. He went to England as an exponent of Italian opera, in which style he wrote forty works for aristocratic English patrons. After enduring a long series of squabbles among both singers and political factions, he found himself broken in health and in financial ruin. Yet he was able to analyze the artistic potential of the politically dominant middle class and to create works that were not simply subservient to their taste but also excellent musical craftsmanship. Handel preferred Old Testament characters for their individuality and the colorful stories that had been told about them. Esther, Susanna, Joseph, Samson, and Judas Maccabaeus all lived again in his heroic vision, swept along in a flurry of fugues and dramatic arias. One of the most delightful musical revelations awaits those listeners who first encounter the plagues in *Israel in Egypt.* With consummate skill, Handel makes his orchestra hop about like the frogs and create an impenetrable tonal gloom in the plague of darkness. His orchestral technique is well displayed in such suites as the *Water Music* and *Royal Fireworks Music.* His twelve pieces in the *concerto grosso* form are excellent in their own right.

Bach and Handel were the culminating figures of a period remarkable for its fertility of invention and range of expression. Possibly the highest achievement of the era was the rare balance of feeling and intellect observable in its greatest works. A good sense of human values permeated most of its products. Religious fanaticism and dry intellectualism were the extremes of a society generally dedicated to reason, social order, and the inherent dignity of all men. The Baroque era was, in effect, the foundation of the democratic spirit that shaped the mentality of modern man.

SUMMARY OUTLINE

BAROQUE SOCIETY

Seventeenth Century Age of Reason
Eighteenth Century Age of Enlightenment

GENERAL CULTURAL INFLUENCES

History: Absolutism with Louis XIV, Frederick II, Charles II, and Phillip IV; colonial empires; Inquisition; Thirty Years' War.

Social Factors: middle-class ascendancy; human rights versus hereditary powers; commercial revolution and mercantile capitalism; Rousseau's *Social Contract;* Thomas Hobbes and the natural state.

Philosophy and Religion: concepts of natural law; Rationalism versus emotionalism; deism; John Locke; deductive methodology of Descartes; mysticism of St. Theresa; evangelism of John Wesley; Lutheran pietism.

Natural and Applied Science: microscope and telescope; French Academy of Science; Kepler, Pascal, Fermat, Galileo, Newton; basic physical laws; ascendancy of mathematics; Spinoza's mechanical philosophy of the universe; popular scientific endeavors.

MUSICAL ATTRIBUTES

Theory: Rameau's *Treatise on Harmony Reduced to its Natural Principles;* science of acoustics; Coperario's *The Rules of Composition;* Couperin's *The Art of Playing the Harpsichord;* theory of "affections."

Social Functions: Spanish mysticism with Victoria; emotional aspects of Italian Counter Reformation; Lully as a servant of absolutism; opera for bourgeois entertainment and the subscription concert tradition; bourgeois art patronage in Holland and Germany; the English oratorio.

Composers, Forms, and Works: *Camerata* and origins of monody; *opera seria;* Monteverdi's *Orfeo;* oratorio; Lully's *Alceste* and the *comedie ballets;* Purcell's *Dido and Aeneas; opera buffa* origins;

ARTISTIC PARALLELS

Spanish mysticism of Zurbaran and the *Escorial;* emotional effects in *Il Gesu;* French classicism with Lebrun and the *Palace of Versailles;* still life, landscape, and genre scenes in painting; Hogarth's moralistic series.

Dramatic style of Bernini; *The Ecstasy of St. Theresa;* dramatists Racine and Molière; Velasquez's royal portraits; Rembrandt's "The Night Watch"; Caravagio's "The Calling of St. Matthew";

144 Sweelinck's organ works; fugue and *concerto grosso* forms; Bach's *Passion According to St. John, Musical Offering,* organ works, *Brandenburg Concertos;* Handel's *Israel in Egypt* and *Royal Fireworks Music.* bourgeois naturalism in works of Chardin and Vermeer.

5
An Age
of Classicism

THE ROCOCO TRANSITION

The last years of the reign of Louis XIV were characterized by a devout gloom and narrow-minded piety presided over by Madame de Maintenon. A marked change in the French life style occurred with the king's death in 1715. His successor, Louis XV (1715–1774), disliked the formalism of Versailles and effectively dissolved its elaborate court life by moving back to Paris. Life among the aristocracy returned to the pattern of dispersion that had been typical of society prior to the reign of Louis XIV (1643–1715), who had gathered the upper class together in one great establishment to control them. With the passage of half a century or more, the status of the aristocracy was radically altered. Previously wealth and position were based upon the ownership of land, but the most potent source of economic power was currently emerging from commercial and business enterprises.

In 1776, Adam Smith (1724–1780) published his *Wealth of Nations* in which he summarized the economic tide of his times. Fortified with a vast historical knowledge, he observed that the mechanisms holding society together were incompatible with the prevailing mercantilistic principles of

145

146 government. Relying on the controversial doctrine of natural liberty, he concluded that all business activity was regulated by the natural laws of supply, demand, and competition. If government would shed its mercantilistic regulations and leave the economy alone *(laissez-faire)*, man's self-interest, which drives him to action, would be "God's providence." With man free to do what he believed best for himself, an entire nation could become wealthy under a system of free trade and enterprise. True to Adam Smith's historical reflections, the reign of Louis XIV, under the guidance of his minister Colbert, nourished a growing affluent middle class

Figure 5.1 WATTEAU. *The Music Party.* [The Wallace Collection, London].

whose aspirations to government service were motivated by the desire to shape government policy to benefit the principle of free enterprise. Like any economic transition, adjustment to change was bound to create unpredictable social problems, which only informed government leadership could solve. Neither Louis XV nor his successor Louis XVI understood the current economic potential or problem.

During the reign of Louis XV, the position of the hereditary aristocracy continued to decline steadily. The aristocrats were constantly forced to defend their social privileges. Louis XV tried to restore the feudal nobility to positions of leadership in the government, but ignorance of governmental affairs under the domination of absolute monarchy had destroyed their capacity for administration. The business-oriented middle-class ministers had to be reinstated. The crucial rivalry between upper and middle classes deepened; the problems of the lower class intensified. Social confusion was the inevitable result of an era of political and economic transition.

The arts reflected social changes by the new role they assumed in the homes of aristocractic patrons. The main vehicle of the performing arts was the salon—a social gathering without the strict formality of the old court. There was really no court as such any longer. The only comparable group gathered at the castle of the Duchess of Maine, who presided over brilliant entertainment on a scale smaller than that of Versailles. The salon was composed of a relatively stable group of intelligent, artistic patrons representing the tastes of the nobility.

However, very often salons of rich middle-class patrons became as socially prominent as those of the aristocrats. The very setting of these gatherings was quite different from the regal grandeur of the Baroque court. Rooms were more intimate; they were decorated in pastel colors with delicate furnishings. The style of decoration called Rococo used small motifs in contrast with the dramatic effects of the large-scale Baroque images. Undulating curves and complex visual rhythms were broken into playful patterns which were easily translated into various art media. The Rococo style, however, was still typically French and aristocratic, reflecting a logical continuity from a Baroque ancestry. The underlying frivolity of the old court became dominant in the use of Rococo art for pleasure and relaxation.

Watteau, the painter of bucolic scenes, was the master artist of these courts of flirtation. His works escaped becoming sheer decoration by their more profound expression of a utopian ideal suffused with gentle melancholy. His many paintings, which feature outdoor festivities or *fêtes galantes,* exemplified the philosophical ideal of a return to nature. Retaining an urbane aristocratic manner, *The Music Party* pictures a typical bucolic scene with music lessons being given outdoors (Figure 5.1). It reflects no pretense of grandeur and attracts no mystical connotations, but simply presents a charming incident. The technique of somewhat ragged brush strokes and partially undefined figures lends itself to the less serious view of life then in vogue. The Baroque drive to control nature and reduce it to a system had resulted in geometrically planned gardens and distortions of natural vegetation. The Rococo preference for small, playful images led to the natural garden or one carefully arranged to look unplanned. At the extreme, whole rural worlds were created of haystacks, huts, and flocks of sheep so that elegantly dressed aristocrats could play pastoral games. Even artificial ruins were provided to create atmosphere.

The chief topic of art and literature was love, which was conceived as a graceful game without either deep sensuous or spiritual implications. The theatrical contrivances and the pervasive femininity of the period were synthesized particularly in the paintings of Boucher. In *The Dispatch of the Messenger* he clothed his aristocrats in the rustic dress of shepherds and invaded the countryside with their sophisticated escapades. Shimmering pools ornamented his nature scenes with a sentimental grace. His unique treatment of color and diffusion of light to create special effects anticipated the techniques of the future Impressionists. Even his supposed mythological scenes such as *The Triumph of Venus* were *fêtes galantes* with the addition of classical nudity and cosmic trappings. But his "boudoir" art with its delicate silken garments remains the most provocative revelation of the spirit and mentality of the French Rococo.

But all was not fanciful sophistication. Artists such as Jean Baptiste Greuze used events in the lives of simple village people as subjects for their paintings. Social consciousness was combined with the sentiment of a moral lesson. Although somewhat pretentious as a moralist, Greuze used realistic detail in such genre pictures as the *Broken Eggs* and *Village Bride*. He had a subtle talent for portraying behind the moist lips and bright eyes of his most virtuous women an expression of willingness to dance the gavotte if someone would only ask them. In the same vein, Jean Chardin was more direct in his interpretation of bourgeois social morality. He revered the dignity of simple things as expressed in his still life. He captured with dignity the human spirit as portrayed in *The Housekeeper*. Even Watteau pictured the ordinary existence of bourgeois characters whose human qualities were not obscured by a powdered wig.

The most characteristic musical master representing the elegant new French society was Francois Couperin (1668–1733), who, like Watteau, partook of the spirit of his time without slipping into sentimentality or sheer decoration. Both were well enough rooted in the Baroque past to have an excellent sense of formal logic. Couperin wrote a number of sturdy organ fugues along with entertaining harpsichord suites. His music was always well-bred, never straining for emotional heights or powerful effects. He created poetic miniatures to grace the ears of the salon patrons in the same way decorators planned many small, curling motifs to please the eye. Couperin was, after all, a musician of the Enlightenment who served its rational aspects along with its more emotional elements. Yet he was at home in the allegorical and mythological allusions of Rococo art and the small, delicate forms which characterized that style preference. His organ works have found a permanent place in the repertoire. The popular use of the harpsichord as a modern concert instrument brought about a significant revival of his many compositions for that instrument. The harpsichord works were usually based upon collections of old dances, such as suites and partitas, which have been known since the Renaissance.

Couperin's suites, which he called *ordres,* were given titles other than the usual dance names. Each little piece is like a small sketch or a delicate line drawing of some object, person, or idea. Some of the musical sketches seem to have no relationship to their titles, while others refer to people or events long since forgotten. *The Soul in Pain* suggests a universal human experience in a convincing musical blend of irregular rhythms and chords, which on occasion evade the logic of tonality. Even his directions to the player, in which he uses such terms as languishing, tenderly, leisurely, and majestically, convey his aim to portray the emotional effects of Bach's style in a smaller, more gentle framework. Couperin preserved polyphonic practices in a free manner; imitative motifs constituted a large part of many pieces. His forms were those of the past capable of being adapted to a less complex design. His most notable musical hallmarks were melodic delicacy and an increased use of trills and runs in decorative motifs. Like their counterparts in the visual arts, Couperin's compositions were admirably suited to the intimate social climate of the Rococo period.

THE CLASSICAL TRIUMPH

While the life style of the Rococo period under Louis XV was frivolous, lighthearted, and amoral, the reign of Louis XVI (1774–1792) coincided with a new emphasis on the classical spirit which had been evident in Baroque culture. Instead of remaining a subordinate theme in a larger stylistic pattern, Classicism became the leading current of artistic thought. The dramatists Racine, Molière, and Corneille had never deserted classical subject matter as a source of characterization, regardless of their style of representation. Poussin's radiant landscapes remained models of restraint and precision of composition, rejecting the general lavishness of his era. Archeological explorations of Pompeii and Herculaneum revealed much of the actual life of the ancient Romans whose visible remains had long since lost the attraction of novelty. Winckelmann revived scholarly interest in the art of ancient Greece, which had previously stood as a vague shadow behind the glories of Roman power. The new arts that were created in the spirit of these older models were not direct copies, but subtle reinterpretations expressed in the courtly French style. In music, interest in classical subject matter for operas had always been strong, and emphasis upon the classical ideals of systematic rationalism was apparent since the Renaissance. To call the ensuing trend "The Classical Period," simply attests to its dominance in the total cultural context and accounts for certain stylistic changes which were in great contrast with those of the Baroque period.

One of the fundamental themes dominating both the eighteenth and nineteenth centuries was that of nature. To discover the principles of natural law and uncover the secrets of the universe were the primary aims of the seventeenth-century scientific philosophers. To thinkers of the Enlightenment, natural gardens or natural societies were those which followed the dictates of reason. The Rococo period had as its motto the return to nature, which presupposed a freedom from the courtly etiquette of absolutism and a cultivation of the pastoral existence. This redefinition of the Baroque concept of nature was largely the intellectual product of Jean Jacques Rousseau (1712-1778). Unlike those who revolted only against the strictures of the monarchy, Rousseau revolted against the very structure of a civilization which he regarded as artificial and corrupting. He believed that man must approximate a primitive ideal of innocence and that society could only restore itself by reversion to the original social contract on which it had been built. His assertion that sovereigns must observe the bounds of their social usefulness became another of the accumulating preludes to revolution. Rousseau's natural man was a man of feeling rather than a rational giant. This new man prefaced the literary lyricisms of Byron and Shelley which ushered in the first great wave of the Romantic movement in England.

In contrast, Voltaire distrusted Rousseau's natural man and his freedom from the restraints of civilization. Although Voltaire agreed that laws of science and reason were applicable to man and society, he concluded through observation that man acted irrationally. His subsequent emphasis upon restraint and emotional control was fundamental to the classical spirit.

Artistic manifestations of Classicism were influenced by a paradoxical emphasis on both individualism and universality. Originality became respected as a unique endowment of a gifted man who recreated the world through his own inner vision. Recognition was given to the many aspects of mentality which could not be wholly accounted for by reason. Immanuel Kant (1724-1804) began the structure of his philosophical system with an analysis of the preconceptions of time and space, which constitute the individual frame of reference. Since the same frame of reference was shared by all mankind, then all excellent products of the creative mind must be assumed to have universal validity. Greek and Roman classical imagery, therefore, would have great relevance to the eighteenth century in exhibiting the universality of sound ideas and honest sentiments. The final break with an exclusive aristocratic tradition resulted from a firm belief that art must speak to all and be shared by all. Art must forego intellectual complexity for clarity and agreeable feeling; it must be universal in sentiment and noble in concept. The creative minds which best fulfilled these ideals became dominant figures in western culture.

Poussin's aim to portray noble and serious human action within a controlled structural unity featuring monumental simplicity and humanistic sentiment was perfectly realized in the works of the painter Jacques Louis David (1748-1825). Deserting the patronage of Louis XVI, he became the artistic voice of the French Revolution. Politically, his paintings were interpreted by revolutionists as antiroyalist allegories which promoted the virile ideals of the new order against the degenerate habits of the royal regime. Reflecting a stoic yet democratic realism, his style esthetically rejected the sweetness and grace expressed in the works of his immediate predecessors. In such works as *The Oath of the Horatii, Brutus,* and the *Battle of the Romans and Sabines,* he allowed no latitude for insipid sentimentality, but portrayed his subjects with a precision truly classical in its restraint. His portrait of *Madame Récamier* (Figure 5.2) revealed with

Figure 5.2   JACQUES-LOUIS DAVID. *Madame Recamier.* [Courtesy, Louvre, Paris. (Giraudon)].

particular force a combination of classical imagery, formal simplicity, and gentle realism. The prevailing philosophy of individual worth through noble action also inspired an awareness of human pathos which David could not ignore. He first crystallized this emotional appeal within the classical restraint of his *Death of Marat.* Such projection separated his precise style from one of emotional coolness and formal inflexibility. It labeled the art movement "neoclassical" because, in the truest classical sense, such a style reflected an age which could utilize the technique but could not capture the harmonious spirit of the ancient world.

Guided by the new classical concepts of organic unity and monumental simplicity, the formulation of a musical style can be easily observed in the case of opera. Christoph Willibald Gluck (1714-1787) was the first of many Classicists to undertake a thorough restructuring of musical form. He exemplified the predominantly German orientation of the classical movement in music which matched the classical traits in the literature of Goethe (1749-1832). Gluck matured as an opera writer in the best Italian Baroque tradition. After a visit to England, he realized that the state of serious opera was rapidly declining. An operatic conductor for sixteen years, he produced his opera *Orpheus* which initiated some of the reforms he felt necessary to secure the future existence of opera. Just as the legend of Orpheus had exemplified the birth of opera in the Baroque era, Gluck's own version of the tale heralded the rebirth of dramatic music. Two additional operas based on classical mythology completed his reformation. Gluck aimed for authenticity in the elimination of conflicting characters representing different time periods. He returned to monumental character prototypes with universal reference. The strict separation between recitative and aria was broken down in favor of a more constant flow of dramatic interrelationships between music and action. No longer could the singer extemporize added measures of ornamentations for sheer technical display; he must now pay attention to the demands of the dramatic situation. Gluck had the same basic aim as the *Camerata,* that of using music to enforce the expression of the text. He introduced the superb characterization and wonderful ensemble singing typical of comic opera into the *opera seria* or grand opera. Even stage sets and costumes were once again subordinated to the total demands of the dramatic moment; the chorus was returned to its ancient classical role in expressing the meaning of events.

Gluck's primary interest was opera, but while a student in Italy he was vitally influenced by new developments in the form and style of instrumental music. The French Rococo style had been absorbed and transformed by Italian composers. The delicate simplicity and ornate grace of Couperin's harpsichord compositions were represented in Italy in the works of Domenico Scarlatti (1685-1757). Scarlatti adopted the simple repeated structure of the French suite, but expanded the form with musical devices that offered some rather new and ultimately momentous ideas. He wrote over 500 harpsichord pieces, later called sonatas, in the prevailing two-sectional binary form. His use of contrasting themes and tonalities in these short works became a standard practice of the sonata form. Also, Scarlatti was able to combine revived polyphonic techniques with the melodically oriented operatic style in a highly original manner. Thus, certain significant elements constituting the technical equipment of Haydn and Mozart were already in evidence a generation before their time.

The musical resources of Classicism were gradually accumulating during the very time that Bach and Handel were creating the culminating works in Baroque style and other musicians were initiating the Rococo movement. Included among the leaders in the German Rococo movement were the sons of Bach, particularly Carl Philipp Emanuel, who was the court harpsichordist to Frederick the Great. The younger Bach was the leading spokesman for the German Rococo ideal which was often referred to as "sensitive style." Unlike the French movement, the German was thoroughly saturated with middle class values; it concentrated its expression of universal sentiments almost exclusively in an instrumental medium. The Baroque doctrine of affections became recast in a more delicate shape with simple, direct musical statements. Music became a projection of the ever-changing moods of the inner spirit. The consistent driving rhythm of the Baroque polyphonic style was abandoned in favor of short musical sections which altered their tempo individually in accordance with the momentary tonal feeling of the music.

Pausing for dramatic effect, sustaining a particularly crucial tone, and many other such affective devices routinely used by concert artists were first explored by leaders of this German expressive style. The abrupt contrasts between loud and soft, which marked the Baroque concerto grosso, were diffused into a wide range of gentle shadings. Some of the dramatic changes of mood which animated the new instrumental music were not pleasurable to all listeners. Frederick the Great believed that music was heading toward an early demise, and many agreed with him. To the dissenter, such a kaleidoscope of tonal colorations and emotional effects was too chaotic to sustain musical statements of much significance. Thus the tentative structural experiments of Domenico Scarlatti and the expressive explorations of Carl Philipp Emanuel Bach were well suited to correct and enhance each other. Both merged in the thinking of musicians at Mannheim, Germany, and set in motion musical events of epoch-making significance.

The elector of Mannheim was a passionate devotee of music who assembled outstanding musicians for his court orchestra. This group added technical facility and the skill of excellent ensemble playing to the existing expressive and formal properties of the emerging classical music. A contemporary writer commented upon the nuances of loudness and softness that the orchestra was able to achieve. "Its 'forte' is thunder; its 'crescendo' a waterfall; its 'diminuendo' a crystal-clear brook murmuring in the distance; its 'pianissimo' a breath of spring." The composers Johann Stamitz and George Wagenseil gradually merged the disparate elements of the symphonic tradition into a functional vehicle for musical ideas. But the final realization of the symphonic potential in design and development was achieved by Franz Joseph Haydn (1732–1809). Haydn, together with his younger contemporary Wolfgang Amadeus Mozart, developed the idiom often designated Viennese classical music because of the geographical center of its influence.

Of all the innovations that accompanied the development of the symphony, the evolution of sonata form remains a particularly significant achievement. Its principles have been applied to the whole range of solo

154   and ensemble literature from the eighteenth to the twentieth centuries. As a design the form rested on the twin principles of contrast and development. Unlike many Baroque compositions which were unified by the nearly constant presence of a single powerful idea, the classical sonata was based upon contrasting melodic materials. Often an energetic, dominating figure, the first musical idea presented was generally the main theme. After a suitable cadence or closing statement, the second theme was heard in a contrasting but closely related key. It was often lyric and flowing, a gentle counterpart to the main theme. These two themes served as the musical materials with which the composer was to deal. They were stated with suitable repetitions and extensions in the first large section of the form called the exposition. After revealing or exposing his material, the composer showed his skill at using elements of the ideas in new combinations. This section of imaginative interplay was called, appropriately, the development section. The developmental principle carried as profound an impact in its time as the polyphonic principle had conveyed 300 years earlier. The development section provided a means for both unity and variety within the same structure and offered maximum flexibility for the use of themes. The classical desire for clarity and precision of expression was thus perfectly served by such a plan.

The return of the main themes in their original presentation further served to make the composer's use of his themes clear in retrospect. This last section, called the recapitulation, was often closed by a coda (literally, tail), which brought the whole movement to an appropriately stirring finish. These few terms—*main theme, secondary theme, exposition, development, recapitulation,* and *coda*—succinctly summarize the major elements within the sonata design and facilitate discussion of the unique musical alterations in the form made by imaginative composers. The sonata principle was also applied to the overture, the solo concerto, and a wealth of solo pieces for piano, violin, and many other instruments. But the sonata as a structure represented a single movement of a composition containing a number of other movements. While the first movement almost always used the sonata design, the forms of additional movements were gradually derived from older instrumental and vocal practices. They achieved a relative stability in the works of Haydn, Mozart, and Beethoven; they continued to flourish in the romantic style of Schubert, Mendelssohn, and Brahms. The developmental idea and the variety of forms possible within a sequence of separate movements proved to be amazingly elastic and able to absorb endless extension without breaking down. Part of the sense of unity apparent in classical music may be attributed to a consistent use of the system of key relationships which were established by Jean Philippe Rameau (1683–1764). Relationships between the themes and their subsequent development were directly tied to differences in their tonalities. Such tonal distinctions were intrinsic to the very concept of development and repetition. Deviations from the tonal norms thus observed could be used for emotional effects within a controlled expressive pattern.

While the first movement utilized sonata form, the second movement of a four-movement composition was traditionally slow and featured a warm melodious quality in contrast with the more dramatic first movement. A number of different forms could be used, but quite often they were simple patterns which would not detract from the dominant melodic aspect. The form used in the aria was popular. It consisted of one distinctive musical idea broken by a middle section of complementing texture (*ABA*). When this simple pattern was extended to include repetitions of the main theme separated by a number of contrasting themes, the form became a rondo (*ABACA*). The second movement might also use the variation form or even another sonata form. The composer was never bound by demands of an inflexible design which had to be fulfilled at all costs.

The third movement was derived from the old dance suite minuet with its contrasting section called the trio. In its alternation of large and small ensembles the combination of minuet and trio was reminiscent of the function of the solo instruments within the older concerto grosso form. Beethoven changed the spirit of this once elegant dance into a brusque peasant romp which he called a scherzo (or joke, in Italian), but the dance nature of the movement remained obvious. The last movement of a classical composition most often returned to either the sonata form or the rondo pattern, and, if needed, used musical materials active and intense enough to serve as the climax of a whole symphonic epic. Such a formal design could serve only as a means of prediction; no composer would adhere to it slavishly without regard for the inherent demands of his musical ideas. However, discovering the unexpected uses that the composer makes of such basic elements is one of the most delightful listening experiences and is best served by knowing what alternatives are available.

During the mid-eighteenth century when the artistic movement called Neoclassicism began as a revival of classical technique and spirit in many of the arts, a formal musical trend called Classicism was launched. The movement became well represented by composers of impeccable crafts-manship who infused structural design with emotional significance. The Classicism of Haydn and Mozart exuded a robust optimism, a precise balance of emotion and intellect, a certain purity and nobility of feeling which made their music part of the cultural treasures of western civilization. Haydn represented the initial wave of those forces that were converging into a grand style pattern which dominated life and art for a century and still persists in various disguises. He was allied with the Baroque period in many ways. Most of his life was spent in the service of Prince Esterhazy, a leading Hungarian nobleman who aspired to imitate the courtly splendor of Versailles. As a choirboy at the Cathedral of St. Stephen in Vienna Haydn had been trained in the old polyphonic traditions, which he used eloquently with the newer instrumental concepts in his great oratorios *The Creation* and *The Seasons*. He was blessed with a highly skilled and devoted group of instrumentalists and an enthusiastic, intelligent patron. The Prince had the kindness to overlook his technical ownership of all Haydn's compositions and to allow the composer in his later life to accept commissions from publishers and patrons all over Europe. Haydn produced some of his finest works for English audiences of cosmopolitan and sophisticated tastes. Of the group of works called the *London* Symphonies, the last one, in D major (numbered 104), has often been regarded as his masterpiece in the form. It also illustrates how a composer uses an established form to achieve his own personal ends:

> Haydn was strongly attracted to slow introductions, since they served to focus the entrance of the more aggressive main theme with particular clarity. The slow beginning to Symphony 104 proceeds much as a stately funeral march, complete with violins sighing. The introductory theme appears three times. The second time it appears it has a changed tonality calculated to create an interesting disturbance in an otherwise uneventful flow. The third repetition contains an echo version, also intended to create variety. The main theme bursts forth as a graceful tune that races along busily in short phrases. The obvious repetition of the theme serves to establish a clear aural image. Hadyn was an economical genius who did not use two themes when one would do. This particular movement uses the main theme in a variable pattern instead of using a completely different second theme. Haydn's long introduction and the presentation of the basic theme constitute the exposition, which he brings to a close with a few summary chords.
>
> The development starts with a repetition of the memorable main theme, as though to remind the listener, once again, of the material he has chosen to subject to his musical manipulations. The development is based on one motif of the main theme, which would be analyzed according to a poetic rhythm as ∪∪∪∪— — (four light accents and two sustained tones). The real pleasure of listening to a development section is in following the winding pathway of an artist's imagination; it is not difficult in this case, since the same rhythmic motif is present most of the time. Like a playful musical ball, it is tossed from one section to the other through the commanding tones of the brasses and the rippling runs of the flutes. The development is like a fascinating tonal journey during which new potentials of a musical idea are constantly revealed.
>
> The recapitulation returns to the original state of the main theme, as though returning to a familiar melodic and harmonic framework. At this point, a composer with little initiative often restates the exposition with a few changes to allow for a properly flamboyant conclu-

sion. Haydn, however, seems to have found the contrast between the lyrical and the dramatic aspects of his main theme very challenging, and he includes another short developmental section to prolong the effect. The dramatic presentation becomes a coda, or ending section, which persists to the end on a highly energetic level.

The slow movement is traditionally one in which composers show their skill at warm, lyrical melody writing. It usually adopts a very simple formal pattern. In this particular symphony, the second movement seems almost as long and complex as the first. The best formal description is probably the rondo form in which the repetition of the main theme is interspersed with contrasting sections. This constant return of the main theme of the movement provides the sense of formal cohesion. The theme is the epitome of Classicism, with its feeling of leisure, its balance and symmetry, and its delicacy of projection. Yet time and again Haydn deliberately lengthens or shortens subsequent repetitions of the theme to make it unexpectedly different; he adds countermelodies beneath it, or starts recognizably and then suddenly veers off into unknown musical territory. A long flute passage seemingly destined to go nowhere suddenly emerges into a full orchestral final statement of the theme and an unexpectedly quiet coda.

The minuet and trio is the most traditional of all the movements; however, it varies the rather ordinary main theme by countermelodies and pregnant pauses. As the title indicates, the trio usually features a smaller group of instruments with a contrasting, thematic idea. In this case, the smooth scale-wise runs set the trio off from the tighter, more precise nature of the minuet theme. The ending, with its sudden pause and long trill, reflects Haydn's fondness for gentle musical humor. In the well-known instance of the *Surprise* Symphony he punctuated the gentle lyricism of one movement with a crashing chord that was reported to have dislodged wigs throughout the audience. According to those who knew him, Haydn must have been one of the best-humored, well-balanced personalities in all music history; his works seem to reflect his buoyant spirit.

The last movement of a symphony is traditionally as long and complex as the first. It is as though composers let their audiences rest a bit for two movements and then demand their total concentration for one final statement. In this last movement, Haydn chooses to deal with the dramatic contrast between themes, this being a basic principle of sonata form. His main idea starts out much like a simple nursery tune; but what interests Haydn is its rhythmic motif ∪∪— (two light accents and one sustained tone). Here, as in the first movement, he creates two aspects for his theme; one is the original childlike idea, and the other is a forceful, dramatic variant. The contrasting second theme is very distinctive and so rhapsodically lyrical that some arch-Romantic might well have written it. It is extremely effective in providing quiet sections within the highly energetic pattern dominating the movement. Again, as in the first movement, the development section of the last movement is largely based upon the rhythmic aspect of the main theme. At the climax it is adorned with soaring scale runs that heighten the sense of driving energy. Very gradually the development subsides and evolves into the main theme in the gentle guise of its first presentation, marking the recapitualation section. But Haydn's musical mind is still so full of untried possibilities of his themes that he constantly digresses into new developmental sequences. The second theme is again used as an intermediate section of rest so that he can finish the movement with a great burst of energy. The *London* Symphony, number 104, fully exemplifies the aims of Classicism with its emphasis on the warmth of human feeling within a balanced formal design. Haydn had an almost instinctive regard for the requirements of his form; yet his themes and their developments always seem free to grow without restriction.

Within Haydn's lifetime lived and died one of the most meteoric geniuses in musical history—Wolfgang Amadaeus Mozart (1756–1791). As a child prodigy he wrote six sonatas for violin and piano by the age of seven. By the age of eleven he had already written six symphonies. Even at this tender age he was famous throughout Europe for his formidable technique as a pianist, violinist, and organist. But the social structure of his time was not prepared to encompass and support such an extraordinary individual. The public found his works difficult, complex, and ponderously profound. Mozart himself declared that he was willing to write music for almost anyone, "but not the long-eared." Unfortunately, the "long-eared" constitute the great public audiences of every age.

Mozart was caught in a social situation of changing patronage patterns that brought him desperate financial hardship and contributed substantially to his untimely death. While Haydn found lifelong security as a musical servant of the Esterhazys, Mozart was never able to obtain the benefit of noble sponsors. His father often complained that all Mozart ever got for his many performances before royalty was a pile of ornate snuff boxes. As a child, Mozart obtained adulation from an admiring aristocracy. But as an adult, he found no one to assume the role of intelligent patron. He suffered for years in the service of the archbishop of Salzburg because there was literally nobody else to turn to. Finally, he left that position for an uncertain future. Commissions for comic operas, public concerts, and piano pupils brought him the few material resources he obtained. His friendship with Haydn brought him the greatest stimulus to his style, which proved to be a total synthesis of the musical currents of Europe.

Even before Mozart's time, the Rococo spirit had rejected ponderous tragedies for the witty comedies of Goldoni and Beaumarchais. *Opera seria* suffered an eclipse with the rising popularity of *opera buffa*. Salzburg, where Mozart received his first musical impressions, was thoroughly Italian in operatic taste. Audiences preferred vivid characterization and lifelike plots to the elevated sentiments of Gluck's reformed opera. Mozart was so attracted to the Italian style that, with his father's encouragement, he went to Italy during his thirteenth year and studied with Padre Martini, the most eminent music educator of the age. By the time Mozart tried his hand at opera, the *opera buffa* had adopted the more expansive formal design and choral embellishment of *opera seria*, without abandoning its purely musical impetus for the literary truth desired by Gluck. The plots of Italian operas were often implausible by realistic standards; they sprang from musical considerations, rather than from actual life situations. Music itself defined the characters and preserved their traits—even in ensembles featuring a number of participants. Above all, Mozart sought to express in opera a truth about man in the whole range of his human experience. His characters were less like Italian prototypes than actual people—comic and tragic, infinitely variable, and open to life's changing situations. He preserved the basic assertion of *opera buffa*—that middle-class people had as much sense as the nobility. In his famous aria cataloguing his master's amorous conquests, Leporello, the servant in *Don Giovanni*, shows his ability to see the man for what he is without either admiration or bitterness. The plot of *Così fan tutti* is based upon falsely idealistic views of love. The opera ends happily when the young husbands learn not to expect utter constancy of their impressionable brides, but to accept them with all their human frailties.

The *Marriage of Figaro*, which he captured within a secure artistic discipline, is one of the best revelations of Mozart's own unquenchable love of life. After reading a hundred books (by his own testimony), Mozart came across a story that appealed to him as a possible opera libretto. He chose Lorenzo da Ponte to arrange the libretto. This proved to be a task beset by the endless revisions that Mozart always found necessary. Beaumarchais' celebrated Figaro story was not only a highly popular play, but a scathing commentary on social mores. Louis XVI read the manuscript and declared it detestable because it undermined the social foundations of absolutism. But Beaumarchais had many influential political friends who arranged private productions. And at last, the king had to yield. German translations appeared almost immediately and, in turn, the German Emperor Joseph II forbade it to be produced unless certain offending sections were deleted. With thinly veiled satire, Beaumarchais bitterly attacked both the privileged classes and the morally bankrupt legal system of his time. His glorification of the common man caused Napoleon to characterize the play as "the Revolution already in action." Figaro, the leading character, was a witty, resourceful victor of many an intrigue and a veritable symbol of the rising middle class.

Mozart cared little for the political implications; unlike Beethoven, he did not aim to champion the freedom of the social underdog. He was attracted by the freshness of characterization and the human intensity that Beaumarchais had managed to develop in roles traditionally related to the old Italian *commedia dell' arte*. Beaumarchais had envisioned some musical compliment to his play, to the extent of providing songs and dances to accompany the action. For Mozart's operatic setting, da Ponte eliminated satirical social references and condensed both plot and action. The characters lost some of their underlying bitterness, and secret amorous entanglements became more objectively defined. The Countess and her servants banded together to teach the Count that he must remain loyal to his own loving wife, rather than seek the amorous favors of his servant, Susanne, who was betrothed to his steward, Figaro. When by fits and starts the plot succeeded, the Count was resigned to his fate; he joined in good-natured laughter at himself and vicariously enjoyed the foibles of men in general.

> Mozart felt no compunction to make a heroic figure of Figaro. He also complimented him with a number of equally well-developed characters. The music itself delineates their nature from the very first scene, in which Figaro methodically measures the room he and Susanna will occupy after their marriage, to see if the furniture will fit. His very practical preoccupation is countered by Susanna's vocal flurries over the hat she is trying on with girlish ebullience. The wonderfully intricate verbal profusions of "patter song" are used to bring out the devious nature of the plotting and outwitting that carries the action. The amusing duet between Susanna and the housekeeper Marcellina is polite to an extreme on the surface, while cutting asides are inserted beneath the carefree musical flow. The young page, Cherubino, is particularly well portrayed as a very young man trying to cope with new emotions toward the ladies. His aria *Non so più cosa son*, with its delicate lyricism and sudden hesitancy, particularly captures his ambivalent feelings. In stirring march tempo, Figaro describes the changes to be wrought in Cherubino from soft boy to worldly cavalier as a result of his experience in the army. Figaro's belief in his power to preserve his position by wit and daring is reflected in his refusal to take the Count's plots seriously.
>
> The Countess emerges as a person of true nobility. On the more allegorical level of *opera seria*, she might have been the symbol of moral redemption. Her aria *Porgi, amore, qualche ristoro* is almost devotional in its prayer to love to be merciful. The Count preserves a slightly pompous aspect. His commanding tones are especially well presented in Act II when he compels the Countess to open the little room where he believes Cherubino is hiding. The women's voices bubble about his stentorian tones like frightened birds. To everyone's surprise, Susanna emerges to the accompaniment of a tune with ironically grave

martial dignity. Even minor characters such as Barbarino, in her mournful aria over a lost pin, are given the full range of Mozart's powers as musician and dramatist.

The *Marriage of Figaro* gained Mozart real acclaim for the first time since his childhood. He was invited to produce it in Prague, but when he later returned to Vienna, he found that *Figaro* had been supplanted by light works of lesser composers. After the novelty of a few performances wore off, his greatest operatic masterpiece, *Don Giovanni*, was found to be too complicated for public taste. In response to such musical futility, Mozart began to sink into isolation, realizing the full force of tragedy in the death of his father and most of his children. Always an admirer of Bach, Mozart began to feel a deeper kinship with the epic grandeur of the older master. He came to a full integration of the German polyphonic tradition within his own musical thought. The commission of a requiem mass by an anonymous patron gave Mozart the opportunity to summarize much of his life's conclusions in a final musical statement. Although he did not live to complete it, the requiem was finished by a devoted student who used existing portions and the rather extensive sketches Mozart left for the remaining sections.

The beginning of a requiem mass is the prayer for eternal rest. Mozart set this first section to a sombre, pulsing rhythm from which voices rise in mounting waves. The solo voice interpolates a personal plea, and the choir ends in a soft chordal section falling as lightly upon the ear as the text's imagery of perpetual light. The *Kyrie* is set to a great fugue marked by a steep tonal cliff from the depths of which a countermelody of vast energy comes boiling out. These two ideas are combined and recombined in a dense polyphonic texture, which culminates in a dramatic Handelian pause and the final summary chords. The *Dies Irae* introduces imagery of wrath and doom, and Mozart's orchestral setting uses chords like tonal blows over shuddering figures. A poignant contrast is conveyed between the men's powerful tones of judgment and the soft pleading answers of the women's voices. The *Tuba Mirum* tells of the sound of the last trumpet ringing through earth's sepulchres; it is begun by a commanding bass voice accompanied by a trumpet solo. The subsequent quartet, which sings of the frailty of man and the power of death, is a work of rare refinement in Mozart's best operatic ensemble technique. *Rex Tremendae* continues the chordal outcries of awe at the majesty of God, and changes to mellow, soaring quietness as the chorus pleads for His mercy.

The *Recordare* signals the turning point of the whole work from moods of disturbed uneasiness and fear to recurrent patterns of radiance and reconciliation. The soloists join in a free polyphonic flow, which mixes easily with the classical symphonic style and its gentle Rococo decoration. *Confutatis* further explores the contrast between the chordal blows of the orchestra and chorus and the soft, high tones of women's voices, which perfectly fit the theme of doom and redemption. A theme of mourning, the *Lacrimosa* was written by Mozart on his deathbed. The composer joined feebly in singing the contralto part, in order to hear the vocal blend. The assurance of the promise to Abraham is set as the *Offertory* in a polyphonic weaving of rich harmonic texture, soaring ever higher in its certainty. The mood is continued through the *Hostias*, in which Mozart could well be offering his own music within the sacrifice of praise and prayer. The *Sanctus* begins with a great outcry like some cosmic proclamation and culminates in the energetic fugal exposition of the *Hosanna*. The *Benedictus* is a marvel of exquisite graciousness associated with the disposition of a minuet. The world shines with the pastoral calm of a Poussin painting. The *Agnus Dei* becomes resplendent with the peace of eternity, and recalls the prayer for eternal rest of the very beginning. The work concludes with the same music used for the *Kyrie* fugue, but now intended as a statement of jubilant triumph.

If Mozart ever imagined his *Requiem* might be used at his own funeral, his thoughts went unfulfilled. The seven people who attended his services buried him in the common grave of the poor. Not yet thirty-six years old, Mozart met his life's end in thankfulness for his inner calm and with an undiminished joy in his art. His legacy of forty symphonies and many operas, string quartets, concertos, divertimentos, and sonatas for solo instruments are imperishable gifts to mankind.

Along with Haydn and Mozart came the emerging genius of Ludwig van Beethoven (1770–1827), who was inspired by a German idealism fundamental to the cultural emphasis on natural feelings and creative liberty. In literature, this cultural emphasis was interpreted as *Sturm und Drang* (loosely translated it means storm and stress), coined from Klinger's play of that title. In retrospect, the gentle sentiments of the Rococo had been swept aside for universal sympathy with the individual struggles and aspirations of mankind so characteristic of classical tragedy. Woven into the equilibrium of this classical spirit were the embryonic threads of *Sturm und Drang*, basic to the visionary concepts of later Romantic artists.

In the works of the greatest composers, this underlying, subjective stratum of German thought served to enrich classical forms and to keep them from solidifying into an academic tradition. The greatest German literary figure, Johann Wolfgang von Goethe (1749–1832), united perfectly the persistent stream of Classicism within the ideals of the developing Romantic movement. An eminent figure in the early German Romanticism that emerged through *Sturm und Drang* was Johann Christoph Friedrich von Schiller (1759–1805) whose *Ode to Joy* was the text for the choral movement of Beethoven's Ninth Symphony. The motif of the universal brotherhood of man fulfilled by mutual, loving concern was perfectly suited to Beethoven's own philosophy of life.

The world into which Beethoven came was in ferment with the creation of new national patterns. He lived on the cutting edge of two eras and managed to make the vital transition in the social and economic position of the artist. This had eluded Mozart. The public concert organizations, which began with the *Concerts spirituel* in Paris, spread all over Europe and

Figure 5.3   MORITZ VON SCHWIND. *Beethoven.* [The Bettmann Archive].

164 created a market of voracious musical consumers. The music of the Mannheim and Venetian schools was published and played widely; the touring
virtuoso became a staple of the musical diet. The smallest towns, and many
individual churches, had their own orchestras of increasingly professional
quality. Even in America, the St. Cecilia Society was founded in Charleston
(1762).

Beethoven was the first major composer to earn a living that was
independent of specific individual patronage. His benefactor was the newly
created machinery of the large-scale middle-class concert system. This
freshly attained independence suited his gruff personality; he even refused

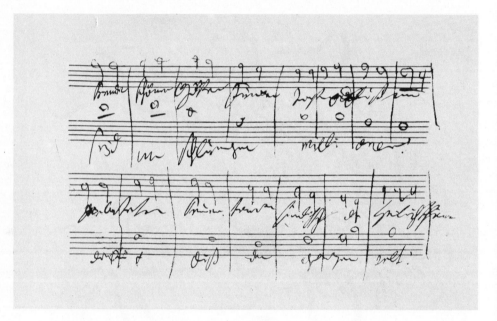

Figure 5.4 Beethoven Sketch of the "Ode to Joy." Choral section of the 9th Symphony.
[The Bettmann Archive].

to bow as Napoleon's carriage rolled through the street. Beethoven's musical
tribute to personal heroism, the *Eroica* Symphony, was not intended for
leaders in the cause of human liberty, who subsequently make themselves
dictators. Although he became a living symbol of the expectations of the
common man and the ideal of social freedom, he remained untouched by
the subjective sentimentalism of the German *Sturm und Drang*. Yet he was
very much a part of the vital imagery of its offspring—the Romantic movement. Whatever he gave to emerging Romanticism during his later years,
he still remained consecrated to the classical ideal of equilibrium. His music
exudes not the pensive nostalgia of the Romantics, but the solemn formal

grandeur of gigantic ideas which demanded expression. His concise clarity pressing ever on in a cohesive, inner logic leaves no doubt as to whether his music could have been formed in any other manner.

Beethoven the man, presented as heroic and formidable an aspect as did his music. He composed with difficulty, storming and bellowing as he forced his ideas to emerge on paper. He constantly reshaped them until they assumed the form he felt was right. His growing deafness was apparent most of his creative life; it caused him to reject social contact with its attendant embarrassment of not comprehending conversation. His music was largely a product of his own inner life; it found a rare response among people who shared his turbulent era, and reflected the comprehensive mixture of his mentality. Thus, in the Fifth Symphony, a first movement of vehement energy and precision is followed by a slow movement, the warm lyricism of which seems to embrace the whole world in brotherly affection. He raised the sonata principle of dynamic contrast to an epic balance unrivaled by any other composer. Beethoven's symphonies are, like Michelangelo's sculpture or Shakespeare's plays, monumental landmarks in the history of ideas. The economy of material, which was a hallmark of Haydn's style, became with Beethoven an almost incredible ability to suspend a vast musical structure on one pregnant motif. The familiar beginning tones of the Fifth Symphony constitute the core of such a motival development. Sometimes his themes assumed decisive personalities. In the slow movement of the Fourth Piano Concerto the orchestra takes the part of some dominating force in a dialogue with the quiet, submissive quality of the piano. Unlike his Romantic successors, Beethoven is never pessimistic. The piano, with its own melodic integrity, maintains a vibrant dignity in the face of overwhelming odds.

The Sixth Symphony, called the *Pastorale,* represents many of the characteristics of Beethoven's mentality. It is obviously a tribute to his feelings of kinship with the natural world. "I love a tree better than a man," he once stated bluntly when told that a house he was hoping to rent had no trees in the yard. He habitually composed while on his perennial woodland walks. The sketch books in which he recorded ideas reveal much about his compositional processes. The panorama of nature seemed to open his whole subjective reservoir, so that music came welling up. Yet it did not flow out freely in bursts of unrestricted lyricism; rather, it was carefully reworked to fit into a grand and intricate design. Beethoven was careful to note that his Sixth Symphony was not intended as a literal portrait of nature. It was simply dominated by a quality of being born of his experiences with the woodlands. It is not literary in the sense of having a story. Beethoven merely indicates the source of his imagery more specifically than in most other works.

The first movement, labeled "cheerful impressions awakened by arrival in the country," begins directly with the melodious image of a shepherd's pipe echoing from distant space. This is Beethoven's music at its mellowest, radiant with delight in the leisure of a long afternoon. This benign mood pervades the entire symphony. Like Haydn, Beethoven is most attracted to the rhythmic sense of his theme, which he develops through a constant shift of tonal levels. But Beethoven is no longer compelled to observe clear sectional divisions; here, one emerges from the other like a natural growth. He also deals with many significant musical ideas in the same movement so that the number of themes is increased along with their complexity. The first movement is a sonata pattern, which is not difficult to follow because of the constant return to the main idea as initially stated.

The second movement is described as a "scene by the brook" and gives a tonal suggestion of flowing water. However, the form is too complex and well-integrated to be mistaken for a literal description. By traditional symphonic standards it should be the slow movement; yet the tempo indications specify "with great movement." The accompaniment is a constantly undulating figure beneath a main theme and has a characteristic little turn that enables it to be recognized throughout a rather involved development. At the very end of the movement a long trill suggests the song of the nightingale, which is joined by a cuckoo and a chirping quail for a picturesque effect.

The third movement preserves the quality of a dance, but hardly the effete minuet of the aristocracy. Beethoven had a rough country dance in mind for his scherzo movement and even gently mimics the country bassoon player who can sound but three notes, always seemingly out of place. Instead of a subdued sound in the trio, the music bursts forth in an even more energetic dance. The main theme returns with a deep-toned rattle of strings heralding the coming storm. The "Tempest" section constitutes the most literal of all the movements. The scherzo trails off in a fugal style as though seeking shelter from the onslaught of the violence in the kettledrum and the windy scales of strings. This whole movement sounds like a great development section; terse and dramatic, it rushes about through many key centers. There is no central melodic idea—only tumult. Finally the woodwinds emerge, for all the world like the sun, and softly sound the three simple notes forming the initial motif of the last movement. Thus, Beethoven even breaks down the separation between movements. "Glad and grateful feelings after the storm" is Beethoven's description for the last movement. Its length and complexity belie its sunny disposition, and it abounds in polyphonic recasting of the main theme in long strands of melodic interplay. A very soft hymn-

like section closes the movement, foregoing the loud dramatic flourish
that traditionally closed works of such stature.

Beethoven overpowered the musicians who came after him. His symphonic summary stood as an insurmountable peak to all who aspired to compose in that form. In addition, the high tide of that advancing current of thought, which Beethoven sensed and resisted, was rapidly engulfing the mainstream of the arts. The classical restraint characteristic of eighteenth-century Enlightenment was being slowly dissolved by the passions of national revolutions. Beethoven was hailed by his successors as the man who freed music. And his works of pure instrumental music were given detailed literal meanings in keeping with the Romantic temper. His appeal to action in the *Eroica* Symphony and his universal moral grandeur in the Ninth Symphony were deeply imbedded in the struggles of Goethe's *Faust* as the Romantic prototype of man. It is a tribute to such men as Beethoven and Bach that their music is able to withstand the reinterpretations of succeeding generations and emerge triumphantly in some future age as an enduring illumination of the human spirit.

SUMMARY OUTLINE

CLASSICAL SOCIETY
Rococo Transition
Eighteenth-Century Classicism
Age of Revolution

GENERAL CULTURAL INFLUENCES
History: Court of Louis XV; reign of Louis XVI; French and American Revolutions.

Social Factors: growth of commercially based economy; *laissez-faire* policy; decline of aristocratic dominance; rivalry between upper and middle classes; social concern as dominant ideology.

Philosophy and Religion: Rousseau's "natural man"; Voltaire and the classical spirit; Kant's analysis of universal presuppositions.

MUSICAL ATTRIBUTES
Social Functions: rise of the salon; music for aristocratic entertainment; *fêtes galantes;* Couperin's continuity with the Enlightenment; dominance of classical imagery; the elector of Mannheim and Prince Esterhazy as music patrons; changing social status of musicians; Mozart as unsuccessful transitionary figure; growth of bourgeois concert organizations.

Composers, Forms, and Works: Couperin's *ordres;* Gluck's opera reforms; *Orpheus;* Scarlatti's early sonata form, its development into the four-movement symphonic pattern; German "sensitive style" in works of C.P.E. Bach; the Mannheim orchestra; Haydn's symphonies and their formal organization; Mozart as the synthesis of Classicism; *Marriage of Figaro; London* Symphonies; Beethoven's revolutionary sympathies in *Eroica* Symphony, devotion to nature in *Pastorale* Symphony, and universal moral grandeur in Ninth Symphony.

ARTISTIC PARALLELS
Arts in the service of small-scale decoration; Watteau's "The Music Party"; Boucher's "boudoir" paintings; Poussin's Classicism; discovery of Pompeii and Herculaneum; Greuze's bourgeois moralistic paintings.

Goethe and the classical movement; Beaumarchais' social satire in *Marriage of Figaro;* David as painter of the French Revolution; *Death of Marat;* spirit of *Sturm und Drang* in German literature; Goethe and Schiller.

6
The Romantic Era

THE CULTURAL IDEOLOGY

The last quarter of the eighteenth century witnessed the birth of an art style so persuasive that it established the cultural trend of the nineteenth century. Even the twentieth century felt its impact as an underlying force. Although the term "Romantic" was adopted to describe certain cultural products of the nineteenth century, it has also been ascribed to other periods of western history, such as Hellenistic Greece and Renaissance Italy. For Romanticism is fundamentally a singular attitude toward life expressed in a complexity of actions, beliefs, and ideological conflicts. Some nineteenth-century Romantics attacked reason, adopted Catholicism, became reactionaries, and adored the Middle Ages. Others defended intellectualism, avoided religion, remained liberals, and adored the Greeks. Despite individual variations, Romantics shared a common feeling about themselves and their world that made it possible for them to share a common approach to problems of artistic expression. The intellectual tradition that had nourished the Neoclassicism of eighteenth-century Enlightenment dissolved in the onrush of individual emotional freedom. Both the "sensitive style" of Carl Philipp Emanuel Bach and the later *Sturm und Drang* that infiltrated the artistic en-

169

vironment of Haydn and Mozart combined at last to blossom into a full-blown Romantic movement.

The exact elements of Romanticism have been targets of intense debate. However, some of the major characteristics have been consistently described as an emphasis on individual feeling; an escape to the remote, mysterious, and unattainable; a glorification of youthful imagination; a contempt for the discipline of tradition; and a self-esteem in national sentiment. A philosophy of life compounded of such ingredients was destined to separate the artist from his general public. But whatever capacity for self-restraint and rationality the Romantic seemingly may have lacked, he was enormously aware of the world around him.

To the Romantic, the nineteenth century embodied a paradox of revolution and reaction. In one sense, it was a revolt against the formal classical style of the eighteenth century. In another sense, it was a reaction against the extremes and excesses of revolution that touched all classes of people throughout Europe. Because of the far-reaching impact of the French Revolution, experiment, reform, and liberal doctrine became suspect to all national leaders. Desperate for security, the Metternich System (1815–1848) was initiated to restore the safe and sound political structure of the prerevolutionary past. While France's dream of national supremacy abruptly ended with the overthrow of Napoleon Bonaparte, other nations attempted to preserve national pride with a conservatism that failed to heal wounds which humanitarianism and political liberty could at least mollify. Such pioneers of the Romantic movement as Lord Byron, Delacroix, and Beethoven championed the cause of political liberty. But disillusionment with the ideals of Napoleon and Metternich disenchanted both artist and average citizen. Each in his own way reassessed personal values in terms of individual joys, sorrows, and national sentiments, rather than in terms of noble universal truths. But as national pride quickened, so did the revival of man's faith in man, religion, and country, which elevated the morals and stirred the compassions of the bourgeois class to renewed aspirations for political and social dominance.

The same disillusionment and sentiment compelled the artist to take refuge in Hegel's concept of history as an evolving process, a doctrine which was new to nineteenth-century thought. A post-Kantian idealist, Hegel (1770–1831) claimed that "each historical moment, . . . each successive generation may regard itself as the destroyer, preserver and improver of the culture which it has inherited from its predecessor." Such philosophy of change justified his view of historical development as a continuous struggle toward the freedom of mankind with tradition and stable institutions as the carriers of the culture. Since Hegel's concept of historical change claims "a brooding sense of the mutability of all things," reality could not be a thing in itself but, rather, an ideal construction of the spirit and a process of thought that emphasized the intuitive and the spiritual.

Although denied open debate by Metternich supporters in parliaments, the controversial national sentiment that resented the politically stagnant system was aired in literature. The novels of Dostoyevsky (1821–1881) expressed fervent political and social aspects of Russian nationalism. Throughout Europe a bourgeois national pride looked for a higher purpose in living through reading, reflecting, and careful social restraint. England, in particular, symbolized such national sentiment in the demeanor of Queen Victoria, whose reign made an impact on the Romantic movement with far-reaching effect. Labeled the Victorian Age (1830–1880), the era exhibited critical concern for human affairs; interest in human beings and relationships combined in an emphasis on strict morality.

Tennyson (1809–1892), the champion of Victorian morality, understood middle-class virtues and taught them through his poetry. Hawthorne's (1804–1864) preoccupation with bourgeois morality became centralized in the effect of sin on the lives of four people in *The Scarlet Letter*. Flaubert (1821–1880) flaunted the breach of middle-class values with unprecedented frankness in his portrayal of the tragic life of his heroine in *Madame Bovary*. Even painters such as Daumier (1808–1879), in his political cartoons, sensitized the public to social justice in an age that bred its own social change.

Wherever the economy permitted, the bourgeois class not only preserved the heritage of the common man, but also dominated the nineteenth century through the success of the Industrial Revolution. Machinery became an extension of hand labor. The manufacturing process improved; living conditions improved; and luxuries became necessities. The ideals of *laissez-faire*, which had been observed during the eighteenth century, were eulogized by the businessmen whose interests they served in the nineteenth century.

In stark contrast was the dark side of the Industrial Revolution. The deplorable state of the lower-class workers in society was explained simply by the bourgeoisie as the natural outcome of economic law. The novels of Dickens and the essays of Carlyle indicted the abuses of the factory system as contributors to industrial problems and social decay. In sympathy, the artist graphically portrayed the social plight of the worker to prick the conscience of the *nouveau riche.*

Utopian Socialists such as John Stuart Mill (1806–1873) believed that the solution to society's problems (which evolved from the ills of the Industrial Revolution) could be developed by the government if that government believed in the philosophy of the greatest good and happiness for the greatest number. Periodically, bourgeois benevolence softened the hostility between capital and labor; political parties dangled palliative reforms to gain the support of both groups.

According to the writings of Karl Marx (1818–1883), father of modern socialism, a deepening antagonism between capital and labor continued to grow. His philosophy of history hypothesized that the exploitation of one class by another was a common characteristic of society in every age. In modern society, the contest was between capital and labor. He believed that, in the natural course of events, the proletariat, or workers, would eventually take over the machinery of production to run it for the benefit of all.

Specific scientific aspects could not help but influence the democratic and industrial inclinations of the Victorian Age. The control of natural powers and the application of mechanical principles to industry were bound to affect both working and living conditions. Slum life and the degradation of poverty were blamed on the materialism of the new democratic spirit and the bourgeois national sentiment that supported such an economy. New concepts of biological evolution and geology altered man's intellectual outlook, religion, and mores. One remedy for the ills of society was the strict morality, realism, and didacticism of Victorian Romanticism. Another was an attitude whose disillusionment with revolutions and the Metternich System adopted escapism, melancholy, and emotional intoxication as the Romantic cure for human agonies. Since the Romantic mind was so highly individualized and subjective, those who were severely rational toward reality considered the Romantic foolish and even incomprehensible. Yet Romanticism formed the imaginative structure that became basic to the arts of the nineteenth century.

THE ARTISTIC COMPONENTS OF ROMANTICISM

The Subjective Vision

In response to the general social environment, artists experienced a sense of profound isolation within the cultural upheavals of the era and, as a consequence, turned inward for comfort and inspiration. Emphasis upon inner, personal experience represented a distinct change from the more objective attitude of Neoclassicism. Romanticism regarded man as the center of all reality; only through man's sentiments and intuitions could the real nature of the universe be known. Instead of reproducing the actual appearance of forms in the natural world, the artist sought to reveal them in the light of his own imagination. In thus penetrating an inner meaning not open to common sense, the artist became allied with the philosopher. Both stood as prophets of the Ideal within the context of the Real. The philosopher Kant (1724–1804) initiated the movement toward subjectivism in philosophy by linking certain sources of human knowledge to partly conscious mental tendencies. Intuition, revelation, and inspiration became important sources of knowledge that had a significant impact upon artistic expression. A seemingly spontaneous flow of sound became a dominant musical esthetic in contrast with the tightness and precision of neoclassical expression. Because music has little concrete reference to actual subjects

or events, philosophers throughout history have regarded music as inferior to the other arts. Yet it was just that independence from the world of concrete reality which attracted Romantic philosophers. Neitzsche placed music at the heart of the dynamic movement, which he felt to be the basic characteristic of all being. Because music occurs outside the context of a specific spatial location, Neitzsche thought its meaning could be grasped with greater immediacy and precision. In *The World as Will and Idea* Schopenhauer used much the same rationale; he placed music in direct relationship to the will itself, whereas other arts represented secondary ideas through which the will was objectified.

This emphasis on subjective phenomena opened the fantasy to artistic exploration. The dream was no longer considered to be an irrational interlude in the realization of actuality but, rather, a state of symbolic perfection at the very springs of the imagination. The German artist Henry Fuseli (1741–1825) produced such works as *The Nightmare* and *The Succubus* based on dream motifs. The great Spanish artist Francisco Goya, in his series of drawings called *Los Caprichos,* pictured animated monsters hovering over the artist in his sleep (Figure 6.1). Victor Hugo often illustrated his manuscripts with fantastic landscapes and gloomy imaginary castles. A culmination of a whole century of concentration on the subjective processes occurred in the psychoanalytical theories of Sigmund Freud.

Romanticism was pervaded by a sense of homelessness. Part of the urge toward universality of expression may be attributed to the need to feel at home in some time or place. The poet Schiller described his fellow Romantics as "exiles pining for a homeland." Artists were indeed separated from middle-class concerns that dominated the social actualities of the era. Such separation enhanced the attraction of remoteness and mystery as an artistic esthetic. The reigning self-concept was that of Faust, who became disheartened amid all his practical earthly attainments and eager to suffer the onslaughts of emotional cosmic experiences. Nor were artists reluctant to share their inner life with the world at large. Goethe's *Sorrows of Young Werther* initiated an early stream of literature with confessional overtones. All Romantic art works may not be interpreted autobiographically; nevertheless, the element of personal experience is obvious in many instances.

The sense of homelessness, of dissatisfaction with both the inner and outer environment, led many Romantics to seek to escape into another time or place. The far-off land with strange people became attractive through its very remoteness. Jules Verne imaginatively envisioned even extraterrestrial worlds. Delacroix's series of paintings based on his visit to North Africa reveal the exotic scenes that had stimulated his imagination. The fantasy of line, color, and texture in his painting *The Death of Sardanapalus* reveals both the sensuous appeal and the technical challenge that such Romantic imagery exerted upon the artist. As a young man living during the aftermath of the Napoleonic era and the rise of Metternich,

Delacroix was particularly subject to the restive, aimless melancholy that was a common malady of the time.

Escape from reality was found not only in exotic environments, but also in times that had ceased to exist. The past, with its echoes of noble deeds and forgotten sorrows, had an uncommon attraction to men at variance with their own age. Ossian, a revived Celtic hero from the third

Figure 6.2   EUGÈNE DÉLACROIX. Lithograph from *Faust: "Mephistopheles flying."*
[The Metropolitan Museum of ·Art (Rogers Fund, 1917)].

century, was the subject of a number of paintings; he inspired imitations of ancient bardic poetry such as Macpherson's *The Poems of Ossian*. The most appealing of all past periods proved to be the Middle Ages, with its evocative mixture of chivalry, mysticism, legend, and aristocratic caste. A full-scale Gothic revival in architecture was reflected in the design of such buildings as the Houses of Parliament in London. The Gothic novel became a dominant literary genre through such works as Sir Walter Scott's *Ivanhoe* and Victor Hugo's *Notre Dame de Paris*. The medieval hero, Faust, became a dominant image in all the Romantic art forms. Delacroix made seventeen lithographs for the French edition of *Faust*, and Goethe declared that the artist had "surpassed my own vision" (Figure 6.2). Hector Berlioz wrote a symphonic drama, *The Damnation of Faust*, which used separate episodes from Goethe's literary version of the Faust tale. Franz Liszt's *Faust Symphony* portrayed in three movements the characters of Faust, Gretchen, and Mephistopheles. Medieval legends, settings, and symbols were represented in Richard Wagner's operas *Tannhaüser*, *Lohengrin*, and *The Mastersingers of Nuremberg*. Part of the attraction of the Middle Ages undoubtedly lay in the fact that it was so little known and could be dealt with in imaginary fashion.

The rejection of actuality and the predominance of fantasy evolved into a concept of the "second self." Each man was regarded as having conflicting personal traits which must eternally be reconciled. The Romantic had stumbled upon the separateness and integrity of his own subconscious, which promised the fulfillment of his dreams and the answer to his aimlessness. The writer Jean Paul (1763–1825) created the literary characters Walt and Vult to represent contradictory aspects of his own personality. The composer Robert Schumann adopted similar designates for himself. Florestan was the name he gave to his fiery, enthusiastic nature, while Eusebius represented his gentle, dreamy aspect. In his imagination, Schumann gradually accumulated a number of characters who were partly abstracted from real people and disguised beneath fanciful names. For example, "F. Meritas" stood for the composer Felix Mendelssohn. Schumann created an imaginary *Davidsbündler* or League of David to oppose the musical Philistines who represented shallow bourgeois artistic values. He composed many of his piano works with reference to such characters; in the *Davidsbündler* Dances each piece is signed with the initials of one character as the imaginary composer. The duality of nature, which many artists recognized in themselves, was further extended by the alliance of genius with madness. Insanity as the logical culmination of severe subjectivism became an absorbing interest; one fortunate result of this preoccupation was an increased sympathy for victims of mental illness.

Because of their vital relationship to the inner stream of life, the experiences of love and death received a great deal of emphasis. Wagner's opera *Tristan and Isolde* effectively combined both images so that death was seen as the final perfection of love. The neoclassical view of death involved merely a quiet retiring into a world of pleasant dreams. But the Romantic clung to life and lived it too fiercely to regard death without overwhelming sadness. The major evidence of life itself was the ability to experience such deep emotions as love; therefore, love and death were bound in an intricate relationship of completion and opposition. Idealized love played a major role in Romantic imagery; it was the force that brought about the final transfiguration of the soul of man. Romeo and Juliet, Dante and Beatrice, and a vast assortment of idealized lovers pervaded Romantic works in all the arts. Nineteenth-century ballet adopted love imagery, to the exclusion of other subject matter. Death provided a dark contrast with the brighter imagery of love. The inevitable passing of life and the burden of mortality gave rise to many sorrowful expressions such as Tchaikovsky's *Pathétique* Symphony and Liszt's *Consolations*. Sergei Rachmaninov (1873–1943) created a memorable symphonic poem in which he took as his subject Arnold Böcklin's painting *Isle of the Dead*. The lonely island with its frowning cliffs and gaunt cypress trees gives a feeling of dark foreboding which was preserved in the musical setting. Walt Whitman (1819–1892) in his poem "Out of the Cradle Endlessly Rocking" eloquently summarized the terror and mystery of death:

> A word then, (for I will conquer it,)
> The word final, superior to all.
> Subtle, sent up—what is it?—I listen;
> Are you whispering it, and have been all the time,
>   you sea-waves?
> Is that it from your liquid rims and wet sands?
>
> Whereto answering, the sea,
> Delaying not, hurrying not,
> Whisper'd me through the night, and very plainly
>   before daybreak,
> Lisp'd to me the low and delicious word death,
> And again death, death, death, death,
> Hissing melodious, neither like the bird nor like my
>   arous'd child's heart,
> But edging near as privately for me rustling at my
>   feet,
> Creeping thence steadily up to my ears and laving
>   me softly all over,
> Death,death, death, death, death.[1]

The fear of death and the belief in the redeeming power of love were strongly related to mysticism and a renewed apprehension of spiritual forces

---

1 Walt Whitman, *Leaves of Grass* (Philadelphia: McKay, 1884), p. 201.

178   that evolved into the cult of the mysterious and nocturnal. Both the rising tide of philosophical Idealism and the Catholic religious revival nourished the mystical process. But despite a strong spiritual allegiance, the Romantic movement remained essentially secular. Its spirits were both demonic and

Figure 6.3 WILLIAM BLAKE. *"When The Morning Stars Sang Together,"* an engraving from the *Book of Job.* [Courtesy, The National Gallery of Art, Washington, D. C., (Rosenwald Collection)].

beautific; its expressions were far too personal and expansive in design for use in an institutional church setting. The Middle Ages provided not only exotic settings, but also a secondary stimulation to the sense of mysterious forces so prevalent in Romantic works. Religious themes, moral allegories, and fairytale symbolism were united in a heady Victorian spiritualism. William Blake (1757–1827) was a profound mystic in both his poetry and engraving. The series of prints illustrating the book of Job reveal his monumental apprehensions (Figure 6.3).

Demonic forces were celebrated in all the arts. The popularity of *Faust* as a literary framework for music was partly due to the abundance of evil spirits, which could be made theatrically effective. Carl Maria von Weber (1786–1826) in *Der Freischütz* (The Freeshooter) initiated the tradition of German Romantic opera with the Faustian tale of a man who, having sold his soul to the devil, can only be redeemed by a woman's pure love. The use of diabolical sound effects to accompany the casting of the magic bullets in the "Wolf's Glen" scene was musically unique for that time. Wagner's opera *The Flying Dutchman* was based on the legend of the haunted ship that was condemned to sail the seas forever. The famous *Danse Macabre* by Saint-Saëns and the symphonic fantasy *Night on Bald Mountain* by Mussorgsky were particularly effective essays in horror.

Such musical excursions into the realm of grisly fantasy were matched by the literary works of Edgar Allen Poe in whom the Romantic inclination toward the terrors of the supernatural reached a culmination. *The Cask of Amontillado* and *The Fall of the House of Usher* remain masterpieces in their class. However, Mendelssohn's overture to *A Midsummer Night's Dream* provided an equally strong representation of the realm of beneficent spirits. Hans Christian Andersen's collection of stories became a veritable guidebook to the land of the fairies, upon which the ballet depended heavily for many of its most ingratiating characterizations.

The spiritual imagery of Christianity was enriched by many significant musical works that reflected this renewed interest in the subconscious and the supernatural. Yet most of the compositions were not directly inspired by the liturgy of the church. Rather, they expressed general humanistic values and emphasized the composers' own inner spiritual aspirations. Franz Liszt, who wrote music to be used in the liturgical service, described his ideal of sacred music as humanitarian, "uniting on a colossal scale the theatre and the church." Hector Berlioz wrote a monumental *Requiem* and a setting of the *Te Deum*; both are compelling religious works in the most original Romantic style. Yet both are dramatic symphonies using religious texts in much the same spirit as any other poetically inspired text. One of the most enduring of all religious works from the nineteenth century, the *German Requiem,* by Johannes Brahms, uses the composer's choice of Biblical passages rather than the traditional Catholic text. The vibrant tone color and sweeping emotional range of Romanticism are fully captured in the grim death march setting of "Behold all flesh is as the grass," the joyful exultation of "Return again and come rejoicing unto Zion," and the glowing triumph of "How lovely is Thy dwelling place, O Lord of Hosts." Many works such as Mahler's *Resurrection* Symphony and Wagner's opera *Parsifal* express the fusion of art and religion basic to nineteenth-century esthetics.

Romanticism became dedicated ultimately not to any codified church practice, but to a mystical, humanistic religion of compassion drawn from the inner life of the individual. The joy of love, the terror of death, the attractions of religion, and the repulsion of mundane existence found expression in an artistic movement which glorified the subjective vision. The artist fled from the political upheavals, the economic pressures, and the moral strictures of bourgeois society into the realm of the spirit in which he hoped to sense the eternal wholeness of the universe.

The Natural World

Of all the spiritual forces that have had deep significance on the life of man, the natural world was primary in importance to Romanticism. Spirits benign and hostile flowed through images of nature; the very concept of God was deeply allied with the natural grandeur of the outdoor world. The changed view of man's relationship to the natural world illustrated a significant difference between eighteenth- and nineteenth-century patterns of thought. Neoclassicism dealt with man and nature in the same context, and more often regarded nature as human nature. Man was seen in an ideal isolation as the summary of all earthly creation, which stood in an intricately arranged hierarchical relationship to him. In his "Essay on Man," Alexander Pope expressed the neoclassical appreciation for the orderly system that was felt to undergird all creation: "All are parts of one stupendous whole / Whose body Nature is, and God the soul. . . ."[2] Pope's conception of man's unity with the universe was expressed in his "Universal Prayer":

> To Thee, whose temple is all space,
> Whose altar, earth, sea, skies!
> One chorus let all Being raise!
> All Nature's incense rise![3]

Nor did Pope seek to escape the realization of the ultimate insecurity and ambiguity of man, whom he called "The glory, jest, and riddle of the world." To read Pope's account of man in nature is to sense the glorification of reason and the laws of the universe which surpass mortal understanding.

2 Alexander Pope, "Essay on Man," *Poetical Works of Alexander Pope* (Boston: Little Brown, 1854), II, p. 47.
3 Alexander Pope, "Universal Prayer," *A Library of Poetical Literature: Alexander Pope* (New York & London: The Co-Operative Publication Society, no date), p. 222.

The Romantic sought not to understand nature as a system, but to become one with it and express the soul of nature, its atmosphere and impact. Nature was the object of mystery and reverence. To such writers as Wordsworth and Blake it was almost identifiable with God. At once inspiring and consoling, nature revealed the unseen presence of that which quenched momentarily the eternal yearnings of the Romantic spirit. In his "Lines Composed a Few Miles above Tintern Abbey" Wordsworth alludes to the mystery, the ultimate unintelligibility of nature, and projects his own feelings into his natural surroundings:

> . . . The sounding cataract
> Haunted me like a passion; the tall rock,
> The mountain, and the deep and gloomy wood,
> Their colors and their forms, were then to me
> An appetite; a feeling and a love,
> That had no need of a remoter charm,
> By thought supplied, nor any interest
> Unborrowed from the eye.[4]

Romanticism infused the very concept of nature with spiritual significance, seeing in it all that was benign and consoling. The cruel and impersonal aspects of nature were not fully realized until much later in the nineteenth century, when Darwin combined the developmental sense of history with the prevailing interest in natural phenomena to obtain a new scientific theory. The concepts of nature which nourished Romanticism began to take shape during the last phase of the Enlightenment through the belief that natural instincts of man were the source of true knowledge and right action.

The philosopher Rousseau (1712–1778) asserted that social institutions, science, and art tend to corrupt rather than elevate morals. He advocated the return to the laws of nature, which bind all men through their inner feelings of what is right. He claimed man to be innately good and to possess a free and immortal soul; his only need was to be purified of the greed and materialism inherent in social institutions. Rousseau's "noble savage" became a Romantic hero.

Another powerful influence on the rising significance of nature in nineteenth-century thought developed as a by-product of the Industrial Revolution. Centralized industries and the vast increase in urban population tended to separate most city dwellers from the open countryside. The more remote nature became from physical contact, the more it was idealized. The feeling of spiritual kinship with woods and fields served as a necessary counterbalance to the growing ugliness of urban existence. Thus, nature became the revelation of human aspiration, and Romantics abandoned themselves to it in a mystical union.

4 Wordsworth, *The Poetical Works of William Wordsworth* (New York: Houghton and Osgood, 1880), II pp. 186–191.

The rise of landscape painting was one evidence of the fervent appreciation for the natural world. In landscapes by John Constable, human figures became totally absorbed in their natural surroundings (Figure 6.4). The main vehicle of expressiveness was not human emotions, but radiant heavens and undulating curves of earth. The drama was that of wind, sun, and the changing progression of the seasons. Painters often used forms of nature as symbolic forces. In his *Horse Attacked by a Panther* and *Horse Terrified by a Storm*, Delacroix represented in the vulnerability of the animal the heroism of the human soul against the onslaughts of cruel circumstance. William

Figure 6.4   JOHN CONSTABLE. *Stoke-By-Nayland.* 1836. [Courtesy, The Art Institute of Chicago].

Turner (1775–1851) represented an extreme development by merging all natural phenomena. In his paintings *The Slave Ship* and *Rain, Steam and Speed*, the subject matter merged into a nearly unrecognizable mass of swirling light and color. In retrospect, Turner was a precursor of the later movement called Impressionism.

In music, the capturing of certain natural sounds in a musical context was a tradition of long standing. Cuckoos, hunting calls, and other naturalistic effects were used in choral and instrumental music from the time of the

Renaissance. But the new ideal connoted the very texture of feeling which infused nature. Nature was suggested or evoked, but not actually portrayed. Beethoven's *Pastorale* Symphony and Haydn's *The Creation* and *The Seasons* formed the spiritual background for the musical realization of nature. Von Weber's overture to *Der Freischütz* became famous for its eloquent portrayal of the profound peace of deep woods. Mendelssohn's overture called *Fingal's Cave* was another memorable nature image. Wagner's long orchestral interlude in *Parsifal* known as the "Meadow Music" expressed the shimmering landscape of the Good Friday scene. The ideal of Romanticism was the merging of man and the natural environment. The disharmony in man was attributed to his preference for shaping his life in accordance with such institutions as religion and state in order to meet artificial standards. Wagner believed that only when man "recognizes the essence of Nature as his very own" will he attain true knowledge.

Artist and Society

The political and economic revolutions removed artists from their traditional roles in society; artists began to look upon their separation from mass concerns as the ideal situation for the free, creative individual. They gradually assumed the obligations of world improvement and strove to formulate the dynamics of a new society. A rash of artistic and cultural manifestos decried current conditions and reformulated public cultural philosophy. However, they were ignored, as the aristocracy was no longer the major source of artistic patronage, and the middle class was not sufficiently educated or responsive enough to fill the role of patron. In forming his imaginary League of David, Robert Schumann had in mind the eventual ideological defeat of the bourgeois artistic Philistine whose values were so mundane and materialistic that art had no meaning for him. The artist, who saw the presence of the Ideal within the Real, was the seer of the new age. The heroism with which the artist endowed himself could be his only response to a situation in which he was free to express his own inner life while feeling deeply menaced by society at large.

The Romantic hero was a prototype with certain relatively stable characteristics, of which a predominant factor was youth. The idea of youth as more perceptive and generally superior to age was new in the world. Youth represented a triumph over traditional suppressions; it was symbolic of spiritual progress and emotional freedom. Byron was a particularly effective representation of the hero who pressed his moral claims as an individual against conventional social demands. The Byronic hero could additionally be identified with the popular image of the medieval knight and with the confessional literature that stemmed from acute consciousness of the subjective self. Byron was the real Don Juan of his poem; Berlioz was the real hero of the *Symphonie Fantastique*; Richard Strauss and his family were the

184   subjects of the *Domestic* Symphony. In his portrait of Chopin, Delacroix
captured with great finesse the fires of genius which consumed the youthful
hero (Figure 6.5).

Another aspect of the artist as hero was portrayed by the virtuoso performer who thrilled audiences with a display of technical skill and emotional
intensity. The preferred arena for such bravura feats was the salon—an

Figure 6.5   EUGÈNE DÉLACROIX. *Portrait of Chopin.* [Courtesy, Louvre, Paris. (Giraudon)].

aristocratic association providing a sympathetic audience for writers, artists, and musicians. Middle-class audiences sponsored a public concert system which provided material rewards and public adulation for those who could brave the rigors of constant travel and serve that level of musical taste.

A more clearly creative artistic force was the circle of serious students who gathered about a central master of some art form. The constantly increasing demands on performance skill soon eliminated the amateur from active participation. The drive toward virtuoso performance began with the violinist Nicolò Paganini, whose skill was so great that he was accused of sorcery. Because of their craving for anything novel the bourgeois were captivated immediately. But the best musicians also were impressed by Paganini's command of both the technical and expressive resources of the violin. Pianists began to transfer many of his achievements into the piano medium. The result was a sudden conquest of the vast tonal possibilities of the keyboard. Sarasate, Ysaye, Joachim, Kreisler, and Stern are representative of a long series of distinguished violinists descended from the Paganini tradition. Beginning with Liszt and Chopin, a brilliant group of virtuoso pianists include Busoni, Tausig, Hofmann, Paderewski, Schnabel, and Rubinstein.

The art of conducting changed from little more than beating time and correcting obvious flaws in pitch and rhythm to a detailed interpretation of the musical score. Liszt's pupil Hans von Bülow established the tradition of interpreting symphonic music of the past through a careful dissection of form and style. He was followed by such eminent conductors as Gustav Mahler and Arturo Toscanini, both of whom were admired for their superb musical discipline and the amazing precision of their orchestras. Other conductors added the element of pure showmanship which helped to establish the musical ensemble as a fashionable bourgeois enterprise. The role of the virtuoso with its emphasis upon the heroic prototype of the Romantic artist exerted a powerful influence upon the imagination of nineteenth-century audiences. It also provided an excellent source of caricature based upon personal foibles of these eccentric individualists (Figure 6.6, 6.7, 6.8, 6.9).

Nationalism

One of the most significant cultural movements that began with the revolutionary wars was the rise of national consciousness. The feeling for and interest in the native heritage greatly enriched the artistic imagery of Romanticism, and provided a distinct contrast with the more universal imagery of Neoclassicism. As Russia, the Scandanavian countries, and America emerged from their isolation into an international exchange of ideas, each adopted the style and imagery of Romanticism. Composers outside the mainstream of German Romanticism sought to maintain a balance between the international style of expression and the unique imagery of their own people.

Figure 6.6   *Wagner Conducting.* Cartoon by SPY. [New York Public Library].

The political ideal of the nineteenth century was the federation of territories and resources into great alliances. The Congress of Vienna and the Congress of Aix-la-Chapelle assembled to realize a reorganization of European society. Groups such as the Society for the Rights of Man pressed for the economic betterment of the lower working class. This Romantic humanism sustained great dreams for a new society which collapsed in the two world wars of the twentieth century.

In his many theoretical writings, Wagner consistently allied his work as a composer with his social ideology. In *Art and Revolution* he expressed the view that art should represent the whole community; it should be free of commercial pressures and accessible to all. He referred to Greek society as an example of the dominance of public consciousness in the arts. His great concern was for art as religion rather than distraction. Wagner all but deified "the Folk" who, he believed, were motivated by their sense of common identity; he bitterly opposed the bourgeois politicians who were motivated only by egotistic and materialistic needs. But Wagner, the angry idealist, actually knew nothing about "the Folk." He merely assumed that their values and artistic needs were identical with his. Of all his works, *The Mastersingers of Nuremberg* came closest to being a national social drama. In a plot that pitted knight against burgher, the hero, Hans Sachs, used his natural artistic inspiration to triumph over the musical Philistines of the medieval guild.

Some nineteenth-century composers achieved a deep rapport with their countrymen through their artistic embodiment of shared cultural backgrounds or political sympathies. The composer Giuseppe Verdi (1813–1901) felt that the true expression of the Italian musical genius was opera. He also believed in the stream of lyrical opera founded by Monteverdi and wrote almost entirely outside of the Wagnerian ideology. Verdi was ardently patriotic and an outspoken advocate of national unification. The letters of his name were adopted as an abbreviation of the phrase *Vittorio Emmanuele Re D'Italia.* Verdi was truly the artistic voice of "the Folk" and was dependent upon them spiritually as well as materially.

In Russia, Michael Glinka (1804–1857) first recognized in the liturgical chant and folk music the true sources for Russian national music. His opera, *A Life for the Tsar,* furnished the first impetus to the development of an independent national tradition. Because of the lack of conservatory training, the principle Russian nationalist composers such as Borodin, Mussorgsky, and Rimsky-Korsakov did not receive thorough indoctrination in the German Romantic style. Although less equipped to write music with technical precision, they were better prepared to incorporate musical tendencies far removed from the European mainstream. The masterpiece of Russian musical nationalism was the opera *Boris Godunov,* by Modest Mussorgsky (1839–1881). His text and music arose from the inflections of natural speech; his melodies were rooted in the idiom of folk song. He drew upon ancient modal

188   scales and harmonic progressions foreign to traditional western principles. But not all Russians believed in nationalism as an artistic force. Peter Ilyich Tchaikovsky (1840–1893) remained firmly attached to the tradition of Mendelssohn and the French Romantic composers.

The national pattern was emerging not only in music, but also in literature and the visual arts. The artist as hero and social reformer was eloquently represented by Tolstoy and Dostoevsky. Ibsen, Burns, and Dickens captured the essential qualities of their peoples within works having an international appeal. In America, James Whistler, Winslow Homer, and Thomas Eakins initiated a trend of American visual art, which was destined to influence twentieth-century movements.

The artistic products of Romanticism were enormously varied and richly emotional. Even with the twentieth century, western civilization continued to be caught in their assertions of individuality, the sense of loneliness, and the worship of youth. Romanticism existed as an external variable of the human spirit; yet its developmental history during the nineteenth century was a provocative incident in the growth and decay of a recurrent ideology during a specific era. The transition from the early lyricism of the Schubert songs to the flamboyant expressionism of the late symphonic poems and music dramas reveals graphically the intricate ideology of Romanticism as it operated within the technical possibilities and expressive potential of the art of music.

THE MUSICAL DEVELOPMENT

German Lied

A flowering of lyric poetry nourished the lyric spirit of the Romantic movement. Indeed, literature of all varieties deeply influenced the development of both technical and ideational resources in music. The very term "Romantic" was derived from the medieval romance, a tale of heroic persons and events written in one of the Romance (vernacular) languages. In addition to such connotations as the remote, mystic past residing in the word, the term carried overtones of the individual and his inner developmental experiences. The Romantic in the nineteenth century saw everything in terms of his own emotions; he even conceived the natural world as a reflection of his artistic imagination. In both literature and music the most characteristic expression of the emotional viewpoint took the form of lyricism.

German Romanticism was born amid a flurry of literary programs and manifestos. Hegel (1770–1831) saw the embodiment of the whole movement in the intensely musical language of both Johann Paul Friedrich Richter, also known as Jean Paul (1763–1825), and Friedrich von Hardenberg, also known as Novalis (1772–1801). Writers often regarded music as the most complete of all the arts because it fully embodied the poetic ideal. The philosopher Rousseau believed that in the original state of mankind music, speech, and poetry were one. Nietzsche thought the origins of tragedy to lie in the artist's musical need to convey his feelings beyond the power of words. The early and highly influential Romantic writer Wilhelm Heinrich Wackenroder valued music above all the arts for its ability to deliver thought and feeling above the realm of earthly existence. Even Goethe once declared that Mozart should have written *Faust*. The capacity of music to intensify images expressed in words was fully exploited as the century progressed.

One of the most distinctive developments in nineteenth-century music was the rise of a large body of songs, partly in response to an increased amount of poetry. The eighteenth-century melodrama, which used spoken words over orchestral accompaniment, was not comparable to the complete partnership of words and music which characterized the German *Lied*. The true creator of the *Lied* was Franz Schubert (1797–1828), whose spontaneous grasp of the emotional essence of poetry in a musical framework has never been surpassed. Not only did he have excellent texts supplied by his Viennese friends, but also the Romantic movement in literature had made available the translated masterpieces of Petrarch, Dante, and Shakespeare. Schubert shared the life span of Beethoven and, like his contemporary, managed to blend both Classic and Romantic qualities into music of rare balance and spontaneity. He was rooted in the tradition of Monteverdi and Gluck in his subservience to the requirements of the poem. But for the first time, the accompaniment played a significant role not only in capturing the impact of the poem but also in highlighting the dramatic tone color intrinsic to Romantic composition. Schubert's song style seldom varied from the regular pattern of repeated musical verses; yet he did not hesitate to create the most unpredictable extensions when the text demanded such treatment. As sensitive as any Italian to the particular qualities of the human voice, he molded his music to the natural phases of stress and breathing. Because of the perfect interrelationship of vocal line, text, and accompaniment, his songs achieved a quality of unprecedented and timeless beauty.

Schubert was a Romantic in his fusion of separate lyrical settings into whole sequences or song cycles by means of recurrent musical motifs in the accompaniment. Beethoven had used unifying devices such as literal repetition in his song cycle *To the Distant Beloved*, which appeared in 1816. Schubert's two great cycles bring the element of psychological unity to a lyric perfection that was envied and copied by later composers. A great many Romantic art works were autobiographical in some sense. Some critics identified the young miller of the song cycle *Die Schöne Müllerin* (The Fair Maid of the Mill) as a portrait of the youthful Schubert. Its very gloomy sequel, *Winterreise* (The Winter Journey), was also reminiscent of the life of this thorough-going Bohemian. Prophetically enough, Schubert began *Die*

Schöne Müllerin in a hospital while recuperating from an illness that recurred throughout his lifetime. Although the story ends unhappily, the music breathes a boundless joy in the natural world and in the very capacity to feel deeply:

> The miller, whose testimony relates the story, is a typical Romantic combination of youth and the urge to roam. Significantly, the tale unfolds not so much in terms of objective description as in terms of intimate confession of what lies in the mind and heart. The brook is the thread of unity, and its restlessness is reflected in the rippling piano accompaniment. In the first song, "Wandering", even the mill wheel and the grinding stones described in the text seem to join the constant movement. The unity of the cycle depends upon the brook motif and consistent poetic images, so that the whole work is like one song with many individual inflections. The brook pattern is first lost in the sixth song, "The Question," in which the miller ponders his love for his employer's daughter and speculates on her probable response. The song "Impatience" is an excellent example of the impetuous quality of love in which the miller feels that the wind, flowers, and stars reflect his emotional state. The tremulous accompaniment is especially helpful to the poetic imagery. An effective contrast is attained with the next song and its simple, somewhat formal address to the miller-maid. It is much like a folk song in the repetition of certain phrases.
>
> "The Hunter" marks the pivot of the song cycle with the introduction of a rival who competes for the affections of the miller-maid. With an inner anguish the miller describes the loss of his loved one to his rival. The song is sung to a piano accompaniment, which provides an emotional undertone for a text that reflects little agony in itself. The green symbol of the hunter haunts the miller in two notable songs that explain his attraction and repulsion for the color. With a touch of irony, the miller ends his sorrows forever in the brook, and "The Brook's Lullaby" murmers a final consolation, poignantly mixed with a hunting-horn motif.

Toward the end of his life, Schubert reflects a mood of bitter despair in the song cycle *The Winter Journey*. The text heightens the musical mood through imagery that evokes the desolation of nature.

> The hero of this cycle is not the young miller who is new to life's cruelty, but someone haunted by a betrayed love and spent moments of joy and still too young to die. The story of his love and his rejection is told only in fleeting images amid the howl of winds and the pain of a desolate journey. The musical setting seems much more dominated by the poetry, which demands specific tonal effects and digressions for

the sake of poetic expression. The type of rolling accompaniment that bubbled along with the brook in *The Fair Maid of the Mill* is now evocative of cold wind. "The Lime Tree" is reminiscent of the halcyon days of the young miller, with its clear sectional form and gentle flow that evolve dramatically into soaring winds, and a sudden return to quieter expression in an artful accompanimental feat. The unity of *The Winter Journey* relies on recurrent poetic images and a pervasive mood, rather than repeated musical materials. In "Frozen Tears" the accompaniment has a persistent rhythmic pattern; one isolated note heightens the sense of constantly falling tears. In "A Backward Glance" the same rhythm of one isolated note seems to make the snow glisten with cruel fire. Yet each accompaniment pattern has its reciprocal gentle version to be used with the reminiscence that breaks the texture and carries the thread of the story. In "Last Hope" sporadic tones emerge from the tonal landscape to evoke the image of the few remaining colored leaves that tumble on the trees. The final song, "The Organ Grinder," is a surprising element. Here, at the very last moment, is another living being—mysterious, rejected even by the dogs that howl about him. The wanderer is absorbed by his monotonous tune and becomes the organ grinder's companion. The song seems to pose the question: Has he found a sympathetic friend, or, perhaps death?

Certainly, whatever sorrow lay in Schubert's own heart found immediate rapport with the poetry of Wilhelm Müller, whose works were used for both song cycles. Schubert, like Mozart, lived a pitifully short life in constant struggle against poverty and illness. He had the same bottomless well of musical ideas and wrote one piece after another in a seemingly spontaneous abandon. One of his teachers is reported to have remarked: "I can teach him nothing; he had learned everything from the good Lord God himself."

Most Romantic composers wrote songs patterned after the German *Lied,* and Robert Schumann (1810–1856) became the immediate successor to Schubert in that medium. He was primarily a pianist; therefore, the piano accompaniment was prominent in his songs. It often shared the melody line with the voice, and at times added extended sections entirely without the voice. One of Schumann's song cycles *Dichterliebe* (A Poet's Love) is particularly noteworthy in that the accompaniment almost outgrows the framework of the song by becoming elaborate, stormy, or going to great lengths to depict isolated images of the text. The choice of Heinrich Heine's poems was significant because the poet himself emphasized the musical aspects of his words. The imagery of these poems is the confessional mixture of rhapsodic joy and pessimistic resignation used so well by Schubert. Schumann depended on the dominant motif of love in its varying aspects to unite the cycle. The unity is less obvious in the Schumann cycles, and a greater em-

192   Figure 6.7   *Brahms Conducting.* From a drawing by PROF. W. VON BECKERATH. [The Bettmann
           Archive].

phasis is placed upon a constantly changing panorama of moods and images so typical of the restless tide of high Romanticism.

Schubert also served as a model for Johannes Brahms (1833–1897), whose similar mixture of Classic and Romantic tendencies rejected the impulsive, often chaotic character typical of Romantic songwriting. Like Schubert, he preferred to write in some freely realized verse form. The great beauty of individual songs generally overshadowed such collections as his *Magelone* cycle. The accompaniments are rarely the pictorial sort, but they are wonderfully varied and intricate. They seem to stand on their own apart from the vocal line. A most noticeable distinction is the rich harmonic idiom, which uses many chords not directly related to the main key of the song. These chords impart to the listener an alternation of wandering and rest, which continually infuses the musical flow. The song "How I Wandered in the Night" displays the use of very high and low registers of the piano for tonal effects. The balance of formal simplicity with a highly sophisticated musical realization is typical of the songs of Brahms. From the spare recitative of "Autumn Song" to the ebullient tapestry of sound and soaring melody of "Spring Song," he creates a feeling tone as wide as that of Schubert. A rhythmic idea sometimes serves to unify a song such as the gentle rocking rhythm of "On the Lake." From his little boat the singer rejoices in the shimmering world reflected in the water.

Gustav Mahler (1860–1911) has been called a post-Romantic composer because he lived after the main thrust of the Romantic movement. Nevertheless, he drew his techniques and imagery from Romanticism. He was best known as a conductor and composer of symphonies. His *Song of the Earth* embodies the rich culmination of the German *Lied* and the growing resources of the nineteenth-century symphony orchestra. Both the style and actual melodic content of his songs often appeared in his symphonies. This symphonic framework was not new with Mahler. Beethoven had introduced the use of solo voices and a chorus in the last movement of his Ninth Symphony. Many other composers throughout the nineteenth century used the innovation in their symphonies. Mahler's work is simply an outstanding example of this common Romantic practice:

> The six songs comprising the cycle *Song of the Earth* were written for tenor and contralto. The text was derived from verses written by an eighth-century Chinese poet and later translated into German under the title *The Chinese Flute*. The musical composition evolved to a size that was decidely more symphonic than song-like, and Mahler called it a "Symphony of Songs." Yet, with the exception of the last movement, which features a long orchestral development of theme upon theme in a dense texture, the form retains a typical song pattern by using a number of variable repetitions of a main theme, a digression, and a return to the main theme (an ABA pattern). A work of his last years,

the *Song of the Earth* exhibits in a very different tonal language that weariness and melancholy which suffuses Schubert's *The Winter Journey*. It has moments of fragile delicacy and ringing drama in a tonal kaleidoscope of ever-changing colors. The tonal coloration and shading with which the piano traditionally underscores the text is given to the incomparably more diverse resources of full orchestra. One example of a unifying device that Mahler uses to give the great, sprawling work a sense of shape is the horn call that begins "The Drinking Song of Earthly Woe." It is heard again in the interludes between the vocal sections, as a melody, and as a vague rhythmic motif. In addition, it might serve as a symbolic call of death. Highly notable is the tone color of the strings as they heighten the sweetness of forgetfulness to be found in golden goblets. The excursion returns constantly to the line, "Dark is life and death."

"The Lonely One in Autumn" is as delicate in sound as a Chinese painting of misty mountains in muted colors. It reflects the typical late-Romantic wandering of tonality, the loss of certain key sense, and the feeling of suspension in glowing sound colors. Even the voice has an unworldly quality amid such surroundings. The nineteenth century was not an era given to formal polyphonic techniques; however, a free interweaving of voice with oboe and strings was both technically adroit and emotionally effective.

Were the *Song of the Earth* to be considered as a symphony, the second song would serve well as the slow movement. The following three songs would have to be considered together as a group of third movements, for they are somewhat dance-like in character. "Of Youth" has a folk quality with some rhythmic drive. The poem gives an idyllic view of a Chinese home with garden, pool, and friends who are talking. The music deliberately introduces the Chinese pentatonic scale in order to heighten the imagery of the Orient. The vocal part seems to flow over the colorful orchestration as though the singer is distant and only dreaming of the happy scene. "Of Beauty" is a gentle dance that uses orchestral interludes suggesting a chase. This song has much of the transparent quality of "The Lonely One in Autumn." The orchestra underlines specific images of the text (such as the girl glancing through swirls of strings at her admirer). "The Drunkard in Spring" has a general quality of joviality, complete with twitters of spring birds, but an underlying nostalgia occasionally creeps through in a surge of strings.

"The Farewell" is made all the more dramatic by the preceding buoyant song. It begins with deep tones evocative of the sudden descent of something frightening. The spare texture of flute, voice, and a persistent low drone heightens the effect of utter loneliness. This very long movement is based upon successive repetitions of the main theme in an extended series of verses broken by a long orchestral development just before the last verse of text. The final verse is begun in a particularly effective manner by using the main theme in a low register. From this point Mahler drives toward a rhapsodic ending that gradually flowers to fit the theme of the soul's illumination and absorption into some vast, living cosmos. One of the most eloquent statements of the visionary aspects of Romanticism is to be found in Mahler's setting of the last lines of the poem:

I journey toward my native land, my home;
I will roam no more in foreign places;
My heart is calm and waits its hour.
The dear earth blossoms everywhere and turns
    green again.
Everywhere and always distant spaces grow
    bright and blue,
Forever . . . forever. . . .

Piano Music

One of the most significant musical aspects of the nineteenth century was the development of the piano and a vast increase in the quantity of music literature written for that instrument. The piano developed over a long period of time and became a primary vehicle for the poetic imagery of Romanticism. Among the keyboard instruments, the harpsichord had been the most popular for home and concert use throughout the Baroque period. However, the new musical esthetic of the Mannheim orchestra, with its subtle shadings of dynamics and tone color, impelled instrument builders to invent a keyboard instrument capable of similar subtleties. In 1709, an Italian named Bartolomeo Cristofori first assembled the escapement device and back-catch mechanism, which are basic to the inner workings of the modern piano. J. S. Bach played a similar instrument made by the German organ builder Gottfried Silbermann.

By the time of Mozart, the delicate, weak-toned piano had, by virtue of incessant tinkering, developed into a strong, reliable mechanism that could be comfortably heard in a medium-sized room. Its tone was still comparatively dull beside that of the many-hued harpsichord. It proved difficult to play, partly because of mechanical sluggishness and partly because it opened a whole new range of unprecedented technical possibilities. Tone, color, degrees of loudness, and a wide span of sound duration were all under the control of one player. The difficulty was in learning how to manage these many elements at once, while simultaneously reproducing the pitches and rhythms indicated in the musical score. Mozart dazzled audiences all over Europe with his skillful use of these variables in a musical style that was both technically exciting and emotionally satisfying. By the dawn of the nineteenth century, the piano became the most popular instrument in Europe. Both instrument builders and music publishers were kept busy meeting the demands of a large middle class with "aristocratic" taste and the money to indulge it.

Both Haydn and Mozart wrote extensive collections of works for piano. They adapted a short version of the form and sequence of movements basic to the structure of the symphony. Although these pieces (referred to previously as sonatas) were admirably suited to the capacities of accomplished amateur pianists, many of them continue to challenge the skills of the best professional performers. Some sonatas of Beethoven stand like rugged mountains, which any pianist could spend a lifetime struggling to surmount and never feel that he had entirely conquered. The Beethoven sonatas attained a fusion of technical grandeur and emotional expressiveness characteristic of the best Romantic works. But Beethoven gave to his works an intricate and cohesive form—an element that many extended compositions of the nineteenth century lacked. The demonic energy, the flowing lyricism, and the intellectual grasp of formal problems that identify his nine symphonies are present to a significant degree in the piano sonatas. The fact that the piano sonatas were written over much of Beethoven's lifetime makes them invaluable for the study of the composer's development. The first three sonatas, which he dedicated to Haydn, are firmly entrenched in the classical tradition, while the late sonatas amply reflect the experiments in form, tone color, and polyphony, leading Beethoven to the realm of Romanticism.

The piano was used both as a solo instrument and as a dominant instrument within an orchestral ensemble. Again, the form was a shorter (three-movement) version of the symphony. When written for a piano-orchestra combination or in concerto form, the thematic material was shared in a relatively balanced way by soloist and orchestra, and the pianist was given an opportunity to exhibit his technical prowess in a brilliant cadenza just before the coda. In Mozart's time, the cadenza was usually improvised by the performer, allowing him to exhibit inventiveness along with a sheer dexterity. During his lifetime, Mozart wrote twenty-three large concertos that he played with local orchestras on his tours of Europe. Beethoven's five concertos, which were written relatively early in his career for his own concert use, managed to exploit the full capacities of the solo instrument. With his concertos, Beethoven approached the Romantic sense of struggle and resignation without the world-weary desolation of Schubert's *The Winter Journey*. In much of the best music of Romantic inclination there seems to be a direct but unexplainable reference to universal human qualities. The restrained struggle of the piano to hold its own amid overwhelming orchestral forces can be so easily related to the inner struggles within the listener, while the piano's melodic outbursts seem to constitute a victory by which the concerto achieves a final equilibrium.

The literary orientation of early Romanticism in Germany influenced the form and style of piano music in the same way it influenced the German *Lied.* The piano became the vehicle of the composer's most intimate poetic longings. The short song-like form served as a favored mode of expression. The treatment of harmony, tone color, and singing melody distinguished the style of Romanticism from that found in the precise thematic development and contrasting textures of the classical sonata. A Romantic dependence upon sudden inspiration led to the attempt to capture fleeting thoughts in small designs that recorded the main impulses of the idea without exploring its developmental consequences. Schubert's *Moments Musicals* were early examples of the style. They were joined by overwhelming numbers of amateur "parlor pieces" before the century ended. Such short works of unified mood became immensely popular, partly because they made more demands upon the imagination than the technical capacity of the performer. The naive tone painting common to some Renaissance and Baroque keyboard music was continued in the very popular battle or storm pieces filled with connotations of roaring cannon and lashing wind. Such leading composers as Beethoven contributed to this genre. However, a more restrained use of the literary or poetic idea generally prevailed.

Schumann was close to the literary world through his activities as editor of the *New Journal of Music* published in Leipzig. A story or visual image strongly influenced his piano works. Individual pieces were sometimes linked together in a form resembling the song cycle; the descriptive titles often exhibited some unifying image. Many were suffused to a high degree with Schumann's personal associations. For example, the *Carnaval* is subtitled "Miniature Scenes on Four Notes." The letter names of the four notes spell the name of a small town in Bohemia where a woman friend lived. In addition to Schumann's more stereotyped musical portraits of Pierrot, Harlequin, and Colombine, he also alluded to contemporaries such as Paganini and Chopin. He included references to the forms of the old dance suites in several waltzes and a promenade. Miscellaneous images such as butterflies and memories completed the range of imagery. If a unifying factor is to be ascertained, it is not to be found in a story but in a consistent musical personality which pervades each piece. Schumann's *Scenes from Childhood* evokes for adults the days of the rocking horse, games of catch, and dreaming by the fireside. The *Album for the Young* features equally charming pieces suited to the skills of young piano students. They are not intended to form the kind of psychological whole that Schubert achieved in *The Winter Journey.* Several pieces from the various collections are song-like not because of their simple sectional form, but because the melody might be sung.

The influence of literary ideals upon music is illustrated in the typically Romantic title *Songs Without Words* that Mendelssohn (1809–1847) gave to a collection of forty-eight short pieces. True to his more classical turn of mind, he did not wish to portray any literal, extramusical image. The names given to the separate pieces were largely supplied by publishers.

Along with Schumann and Mendelssohn came the pianistic giants of the century who fused poetic impulses with a formidable technical facility. They raised the skill of playing the piano to the status of a great art. To some degree, twentieth-century concert pianists draw upon the discoveries made by Chopin and Liszt in their explorations of the tonal capabilities of the piano.

Frédéric Chopin (1810–1849) was one of the most original, inventive geniuses within the Romantic movement. Having rejected the main implications of Classicism, he retained only those formal outlines amenable to his way of thinking. Although he admired the works of Mozart, he approached the emotional range of the Beethoven sonatas and drew heavily from the lyrical style of piano music currently in vogue. The result of this mixture of influences was entirely his own product. Although his three piano sonatas adhered to the classical structure, his ballades were extended compositions in a freely constructed form. He adopted the nocturne for shorter, more reflective pieces, and the étude for short studies involving one or two distinctive musical motifs. The preludes were inspired by his admiration for Bach's *Well-Tempered Clavier*. Chopin was not too interested in the literal images which attracted other Romantic composers. He sometimes indicated a general image by titles such as the *Berceuse* (Lullaby) and those works that followed well-known dance rhythms such as the waltz and mazurka. The titles of many pieces denoted nothing more than their form; nevertheless, the music gives the impression of profound poetic statement. The études are individual studies of some specific technical difficulty; yet, unlike the thousands of finger exercises that have been written to discipline piano technique, Chopin's études are exemplary artistic creations. As small tonal images, their compelling quality has attracted many descriptive names that the composer did not give them. He did not ordinarily call attention to specific personal associations in his music; however, the "Revolutionary Étude" in C minor may be one possible exception, since it was a musical response to the news of the fall of Warsaw to the Russians in 1831.

With Franz Liszt (1811–1886) the fruits and follies of the Romantic movement were combined into one meteoric personality that transfixed concert audiences of Europe. Although he was one of the most successful concert performers in history, Liszt yearned above all to be a first-rank composer. Whether or not he succeeded in this ambition has been a matter for debate; however, he showered his piano music with a technical display that came close to rivaling anything the orchestra could do. He was the master of the transcription, which is a piece originally written for orchestra and translated into keyboard music. In concert he often played paraphrases of Beethoven symphonies and Wagnerian operas. His colleagues sometimes complained that the performance of their music included much that was not written in the score. His style was based on the pianistic techniques

of Chopin and infused with the poetic imagery of Schumann. The *Years*
of Pilgrimage are musical sketches of his life in Switzerland and Italy; they
were composed almost as a private diary for himself and his closest friends.
In order to clarify the meaning of the piece "Obermann Valley," he included
a long selection from the novel that inspired it. The novel's hero, Obermann,
is a man with highly introspective tendencies, and Liszt's music seems
almost to give voice to his persistent question: "What am I?"

Figure 6.8   Two caricatures of Franz Liszt. Anonymous. [The Bettmann Archives].

The various transformations through which the main theme passes
can be related to states of Obermann's mind, which reaches a state of
joyous affirmation toward the end. Yet the final measures return to the
gloomy tones of the theme in its original form. Perhaps there really was
a valley that brought Obermann's plight to Liszt's thoughts; however, the
Years of Pilgrimage recorded his mental occupations along with his physical
locations. The more flamboyant element of this consummate showman is
represented by the *Twelve Études*. Their subtitle, *Of Transcendental Execution*,
graphically describes the technical training necessary to negotiate their

complexities. These works are longer than the Chopin études and are involved with more than one technical problem. Yet even in this form Liszt had some definite images in mind and provided titles for most of the études such as "Landscape," "Wild Hunt," and "Snow-whirls."

Symphonic Program Music

No assessment of musical development in the nineteenth century would be complete without considering one of the most Romantic of forms—the symphonic tone poem. As the name implies, a literal story or image ("program") is used as a framework for the music. The symphonic poem is a long, complex orchestral version of the kind of imagery used by Schumann and Liszt in their piano pieces. Usually, the composer was satisfied to capture the mood or general impression of the character or incident he had in mind; however, he sometimes included extremely realistic detail such as the bells and cannon in Tchaikovsky's *1812 Overture*.

So pervasive was the programmatic ideal that many works called symphonies were thinly disguised musical descriptions without the requisite formal machinery that holds a symphony together. Their musical success depended upon imagery that would unfold within the listener's mind, rather than upon the composer's use of the formal and structural devices of sonata form. The vast increase in orchestral resources and the new techniques of writing music for tone color greatly enhanced the descriptive power of the Romantic symphony.

Program music began within the context of the symphonic form, and some of its basic materials appeared early in the nineteenth century. Composers themselves considered Beethoven's *Pastorale* Symphony as their foundation. The Schubert *Unfinished* Symphony was called the first truly Romantic symphony because of its emphasis upon tone color, harmonic variety, and expanded classical form. Yet the work has not attracted programmatic interpretations. Felix Mendelssohn had a powerful descriptive style which was particularly adept at capturing landscapes. His *Italian* and *Scotch* Symphonies reflected his impressions of these locales in typically Romantic style; yet his formal design showed a consistently classical shape. Even with all its fairyland quality, his *Midsummer Night's Dream* Overture is conceived in classical sonata form. His contemporary, the arch-Romanticist Richard Wagner, regarded Mendelssohn's *Fingal Cave* Overture (*The Hebrides* Overture) as a masterful landscape painting. Mendelssohn had visited the cave on the island of Saffa off the coast of Scotland. He created an effective musical portrayal of its vast echoing chamber where the waves rushed in and out; yet the swelling seas inspired a finely wrought development section of the sonata form. In this sense, the overture is not a prelude to something else, as in the case of the opera overture, but, rather, it is an independent composition complete in itself.

The literary implications of the foregoing works are pale in comparison with the works of that master of programmatic genre, Hector Berlioz
(1803–1869). His *Symphonie Fantastique* exhibits a remarkable combination
of symphonic form and programmatic content. To some extent, the work

Figure 6.9 *Berlioz conducting his super orchestra employing a cannon in the tympany section.* Cartoon by GRANVILLE, 1846. [The Bettmann Archive].

was autobiographical, since it reflected the composer's agonized romance with an English actress. However, the subtitle "Episode in the Life of an Artist" was mistakenly construed to mean that the music contained some complex personal confession. The symphony is saturated with images gleaned from such literary sources as Goethe's *Faust* and De Quincey's *Confessions of an English Opium Eater.* Berlioz thought consistently in both musical and literary terms. He furnished a detailed description of all the actions and personifications implied in his music to be used in the event that the work was staged. For concerts alone, Berlioz regarded the title of each movement as commentary enough. His own term for combined musical form and literary content was "instrumental drama." This he amply illustrated in his *Symphonie Fantastique.* However he may have infused the form with new allusions, Berlioz's music remained firmly within the spirit of the symphony. But traditional movements, such as the slow movement and the minuet and trio, which were usually presented with the least complexity of form, stimulated his most ingenious musical expressions. To describe the situation he portrays in his *Symphonie Fantastique*, Berlioz appropriated the function of the preface:

> In the depths of amorous despair, a young musician of morbid sensibility and ardent imagination poisons himself with opium. Not strong enough to kill him, the narcotic plunges him into a deep sleep during which strange visions induce sensations and recollections that take the form of musical thoughts and images. His beloved becomes a melody like a fixed idea, which he hears everywhere.

The music begins:

> A long introduction is purposely vague to evoke the "sickness of soul, the vague despair" in Berlioz's description of his musical hero. The nostalgic horn solo over sustained bass tones forms one of the few complete musical ideas. The main theme of the exposition is the *idée fixe*, the fixed idea or recurrent melody which personifies his beloved; it is repeated in various guises throughout the entire work. Also called a leitmotif, such recurrent melody had been used frequently in opera to recall dramatic situations important to the plot. Berlioz used this device to unify his long symphonic work and to give it a specific tone color as the symbol of a personality. The fixed idea soon became the most significant of all Romantic devices employed to replace the exposition-development-recapitulation principle of unity. The *idée fixe* of the beloved soars through the violins and encounters an agitated response from the orchestra, which pictures "the volcanic passion with which she suddenly inspired him."
> While the main theme weaves subtly through the dense tonal

texture, the development continues the mood of anguish and culminates in a series of rising and falling scales. After a dramatic silence, the main theme appears as a more complex statement of its original presentation and glides in high tones over the chaos of a second development. In a quiet, resonant tonal setting, the movement ends with a nostalgic recall of the beloved's theme evoking "his return to tenderness, his religious consolation."

The second movement, "A Ball," begins with an ominous rustle of strings that resolves into a lilting waltz. It is a gay period piece in which the theme of the beloved gradually becomes mixed with the rhythm and movement of the dance; she is whirled away in a rush of orchestral exuberance. Plucked strings, harp, and very high overtones create the great mixture of tone colors that add to the sense of whirling vibrancy. A final quiet recall of the main theme is followed by a brilliant swirl of sound.

The third movement, "Scenes in the Country," begins with a shepherd's tune played by the English horn echoed in the distance (offstage) by an oboe. The gentle stirring of trees is pictured by a rustle of trembling strings. This represents a sudden calm of spirit enjoyed by the hero. Yet the image of the beloved intrudes with her persistent melody. The strange combination of its pure tones against a great turmoil in the deeper ranges of string tones is at once wonderfully evocative of a joy of love and an anguish of dark foreboding. Much of the effect is gained by mixing the personification of the beauty of nature in the shepherd's tune, the beloved in the *idée fixe*, and the hero in the rich turmoil of low tones. Using only the English horn against a drum roll, the last few measures of the movement summarize both the solitude amid the sound of thunder and the symbolic evocation of a state of mind.

The "March to the Scaffold" reveals Berlioz's mastery of the pictorial resources of tone color. His unrestrained use of strident sounds, unusual pitches, and peculiar instrumental combinations was something genuinely new in the history of orchestral writing. The high register of the bassoon, the low and blatant sound of tubas, the roar of the drums, and the shake of the tambourine were employed without hesitation in this grotesque picture of the grim procession. In his nightmare, the hero, having killed his beloved, is witnessing his own death procession. The two main ideas, the one in plucked strings and the other in a brilliant fanfare of brasses, carry most of the formal construction in their continual alternation. A last reminiscence of the *idée fixe* is broken by a great chord, which is graphically evocative of the axe descending; the three pizzicato notes that follow could be nothing but the falling of a head. A last brilliant fanfare pictures the crowd's response.

The final movement, "Dream of the Witches' Sabbath," is another essay on the power of instrumental portrayal; the strings cluck, chuckle demoniacally, and groan in a tonal evocation of a witches' dance. The clarinet begins a mocking caricature of the *idée fixe*, which joins the tonal orgy. At the height of complexity a tolling bell is combined with the melody of the *Dies Irae* from the traditional Roman Catholic requiem mass; both are interspersed with snatches of the witches' dance. A spectral version of the dance, all in trills, leads to a resounding climax.

Berlioz managed to deal successfully with programmatic content within the sequence of movements and the design restrictions of the traditional symphonic form. However, other composers felt that program music required certain internal demands that could not be met by traditional patterns. Franz Liszt was the first to use the literary image to shape a symphonic work more like an overture than a four-movement symphony and to use the *idée fixe* or leitmotif as the sole unifying factor in this context. Liszt was not content with the fixed idea as a simple melodic recurrence. He expanded the principle used by Berlioz to disguise the melody of the beloved as a grotesque parody in the witches' dance. Liszt's process of melodic restatement, which he called "the transformation of themes," allowed him to build a lengthy composition from a rather simple basic motif by using it in many different ways. He was attracted to literary interpretations in music, but not to the same extent that such implications inspired Berlioz. Liszt never attempted concrete description through unfolding actions; his attention centered more on problems of form than on description. Moreover, the nature of the fundamental musical idea in its various transformations was determined to a large extent by the structure and movement sequence of the whole composition.

Liszt was searching for a new sense of formal logic along with a medium that would allow a full range of emotional color. Of all his symphonic poems, *Les Préludes* is the one most often played on concert programs. It was originally intended to serve as an overture to an unpublished choral work from which its themes were derived. In deciding to make the overture an independent work, Liszt wished also to supply some program that would describe the mood connotation of the piece. He eventually found that Lamartine's poem *Les Préludes* would fit his needs and placed a short quotation at the beginning of the orchestral score: "What is our life but a series of preludes to that unknown song of which the first solemn note is sounded by death?"

Les Préludes is divided into four large sections, each of which has a short descriptive title. The first, "Spring and Love," is preceded by an introduction which forms a constant swell of sound culminating in a fanfare. This resonant brass fanfare is used again to close the whole work and to give an additional sense of unity. The introduction is based on the first four tones of the main theme, which is heard in its entirety in a passage scored almost exclusively for strings. The movement is centered on this theme with a contrasting idea in the brasses and is culminated in a quiet restatement of the fixed idea. The second section, "Tempests of Life," introduces the theme in a transformation of great energy sweeping up from the cellos. The original intervals are not always recognizable; only the jagged shape of the first four notes is consistently present. The rhythmic fanfare of the introduction reappears and subsides into a last moan of strings. The third section, "Consolations of Nature," returns to the original form of the fixed idea. Previously used melodies are given new tone color settings and are provided with winding countermelodies in a polyphonic interplay. In a combined presentation, the last section, "Struggle and Victory," collects the most memorable themes played by the brass instruments in the introduction and first section. The plan of alternating moods and final full orchestral coda is common to a great many pieces and could be given dozens of equally convincing descriptions.

The post-Romantic composer Richard Strauss (1864–1949) carried the emphasis on descriptive power and visible imagery to a synthesis of technical perfection. He was the eager recipient of the accumulated knowledge of effects of tone color and dynamics. A virtuoso performer, he used the full resources of the symphony orchestra as his instrument. He was also adept at portraying the realistic detail that Berlioz introduced in his "March to the Scaffold." *Don Juan,* with its vivid description of scenes, and *Till Eulenspiegel,* with its comic antics, are representative of Strauss's blend of detailed realism and consummate orchestral technique. Amenable to Nietzsche's doctrine of the superman, his personal philosophy was the background for *Thus Spake Zarathustra.* Although this work does not represent a tonal system of philosophy, neither does it reflect the realism so characteristic of his many other works such as the opera *Salome.* However, many of his works feature heroes who are closely patterned after Nietzsche's prototype. Strauss himself declared that *Thus Spake Zarathustra* dealt with the various phases of the human race in its development toward the idea of the superman. The title is that of Nietzsche's long poem. An excerpt telling of the great prophet's descent into the world is a preface to the orchestral score. The symphonic work is divided into a number of episodes; each episode is furnished with a title from the poem. Some sections are musically evident, while others are apparent only by written indications on the score.

Using Liszt's plan of thematic identity, Strauss built the entire work on very few recurrent motifs. But unlike Liszt, these themes do not transform themselves with great variety. The basic motif, the "world-riddle" theme, which is announced by the trumpets in the opening measures, appears in a multitude of contexts, but always in its original configuration. After a brilliant climax punctuated by the resonant peal of an organ, the "Dwellers in the Back World" are pictured. They are seekers of truth through religion and are symbolized in the Gregorian hymn "I Believe in One God." "Of the Great Yearning" and "Of Joys and Passions" form a long turbulent section full of the kind of complexity which, by the sheer multiplicity of sound, seems to defy analysis. The division of instrumental sections into even smaller units gives an increased sense of harmonic richness and spatial dimension. At one point, the first violin section alone has eight different parts which are played at once. The episode entitled "Of Science" is in fugal form and uses for its theme the "world-riddle" motif expanded to include all twelve tones of the chromatic scale. It ends with the same crashing flourish employed in the introduction. As a delightful contrast, the "Dance Song " features a waltz that is as flowing and sweet-tempered as that of the ball scene in the Berlioz symphony. The "Night Song" returns to a wild chaotic mood that is climaxed by twelve strokes of a bell. The lullaby in the "Song of the Night Wanderer" diffuses into the pure high triads of the strings, which are pitted against the final statement of the "world-riddle" theme in the basses.

Strauss was the last of the giants in a musical language rich with personal associations and symbolic overtones. His style was enormously complex and reflected a transcendent orchestral competence. He was a composer who was thoroughly in command of his technical resources and unrestrained by traditional forms. In him, Romanticism reached its end in a burst of autumnal color.

The Music Drama

The literary image and lyric spirit, which were born in Schubert's songs and nourished by Berlioz's dramatic symphonies and Liszt's symphonic poems, culminated in the music dramas of Richard Wagner (1813–1883). Composer, writer, and prophet, Wagner exerted a critical influence on the course of nineteenth-century thought. In his music dramas one of the fundamental ideals of Romanticism was realized—the principle of universality and the fusion of all the arts. The urge for a union of the various artistic media was expressed in the early stages of the German Romantic movement. In some sense, the inclusion of realistic detail in program music was an attempt to adopt the descriptive powers of the painter. Novelists began to depict their characters with the penetrating accuracy of a portrait painter. Painters, in turn, were greatly attracted to literary themes; Delacroix, for example, used the works of Dante, Shakespeare, Byron, and Goethe as sources of inspiration. But in the total effect, Delacroix wished his paints to express something that was not only literal but also as personal and evocative as music. For Nietzsche, lyric poetry was a realization of music in images and concepts. Writers such as Goethe, Hoffmann, Stifter, and Mörike also painted and composed. Architecture was sometimes referred to as "frozen music." Indeed, all arts became increasingly definable in terms of one another. And Richard Wagner stood at the apogee of this way of thinking so intrinsic to the Romantic movement.

Wagner became entangled briefly in the political manifestations of Romanticism. He believed that the course of German uprising against the monarchy in 1849 would lead to an artistic millenium. While in political exile, he wrote many of his theories for shaping a concept of music to fit the needs of the emerging new society. The *Artwork of the Future* revealed the first envisionment of Wagner's final goals; his succeeding essays realized the components of his union of drama and music. Even though his earliest works such as *Forbidden Love* and *Rienzi* repeated the musical clichés of predecessors, their intent to glorify the unrestrained life of the senses fully represented Wagner's lifelong preoccupation. The lack of a German national tradition in opera may have afforded him a freedom of innovation not enjoyed by a French or Italian opera composer. Works such as *The Flying Dutchman, Tannhäuser,* and *Lohengrin* revealed a gradual development away from the Italian type of opera and an accumulation of themes and theatrical techniques forming the basis for his greatest music dramas. The years he spent in exile (1848–1852) afforded a period of reflection and formulation of ways to realize the true requirements of dramatic music. With a rare burst of candor, he confessed in a letter to Liszt that separately his musical, poetic, philosophical, and directorial talents were not great; that he could achieve memorable works of art only when he combined these several talents.

Wagner had an uncanny ability to absorb and transcend the vast multitude of social, political, historical, and artistic ideas circulating within the intellectual circles. He adopted and rejected these ideas as his fancy and artistic requirements demanded; he gave permanent allegiance to nothing but himself. Ardent disciples such as Nietzsche, who saw in Wagner an incarnation of the spirit of the Dionysian Greek drama, were eventually embittered when they realized that neither philosophy nor ideals exerted any claim upon Wagner unless they served his theatrical purposes. The mission of his art was to communicate and interpret emotions, not philosophical concepts. The central concern of all his works dealt with man as a sensual being; and he regarded drama as a process of realizing deeds and personalities. The dominant consideration was the poetic aim; in theory, everything else existed to serve it. The chorus must disappear from the opera unless it has more to contribute than its sound quality and visual enhancement.

Wagner resolved that only the characters essential to the action must appear. The lyrical Mozartean aria must be replaced with a better compromise between poetry and music; the spoken vowel must be dissolved into a musical tone to produce a tone-speech. The orchestra must contribute an embodiment of the unspeakable emotional forces generated by the drama through its enhancement of the physical gestures of the actors, the recall of past feelings, and the foreboding of emotional states to come. The "merely musical" form of traditional opera, with its set sections of recitative, aria, duet, and finale, must be transcended by some new, binding principle of form. To embody the poetic idea as a program within independent instrumental music was not enough; the poetic content must be communicated immediately and visibly to achieve an all-emcompassing emotional effect. The orchestra must assume the same role as that of the ancient Greek chorus; it must be intimately connected with and yet distinctly apart from the stage action.

Wagner's theories contained the same reverence for the poetic ideal that was basic to the thought of Gluck and Monteverdi. Yet it remained for Wagner, the musician, to put his theories into practice. Since music is consistently the dominant factor, the music dramas themselves exposed the irony of his position. Wagner revealed himself not as the supreme dramatist, but as the supreme symphonist. His musical father was Beethoven, whose Ninth Symphony was regarded by Wagner as the foundation for his own work. Wagner's problem was to find the new form that would allow him to set sail on those musical seas discovered by Beethoven. For him, as for many other Romantics, the guidepost was the poetic idea. Wagner confessed that he was unable to function well as a composer without a definite subject or image to stir his musical thought and direct the course of its development. In this respect, the poetic idea can be seen as a limiting factor. Wagner cautioned against creating musical effects for their own sake; there must always be a dramatic cause or necessity for such materials. "Never leave a key so long as what you have to say can still be said in it," the master of harmonic complexity counseled his students. The complexity was saved for those moments of intricate emotional entanglement dictated by the drama. The freedom Wagner found lay in the fact that given a sufficient dramatic necessity any musical effect could be employed. He then cautioned, "But to try to apply what is thus made possible to the symphony itself must necessarily lead to the complete ruin of the latter."

For the writer of symphonic poems and music drama the use of a poetic idea opened new possibilities of instrumental effects without the risk of becoming incomprehensible to the listener. Here, the relationship of Wagner to his poetic and musical materials is not clear. Other composers wrote in symphonic and vocal combinations; as noted earlier, Berlioz even made provision for the *Symphonie Fantastique* to be staged. But the music drama was distinctively different from all other combinations of music, poetic idea, and staging. It was classified as opera; yet its main resources were drawn from the symphonic medium.

Wagnerian scholars have made the observation that Wagner did not actually write music to fit the form or poetic connotations of his previously written text. Rather, the text was a concrete projection of his already conceived musical idea. His ideal was to create a stream of unending and emotionally effective musical fabric whose texture, color, and pattern could be made definite through words. In *Opera and Drama* (1850–1851) Wagner explained his preference for myth as the poetic vehicle of the music drama. He felt it had an eternal symbolic truth that expressed the experiences of mankind from his beginning to the advent of that new society for which Wagner yearned. Myth did not speak of the "purely human" in terms of an appeal to reason as it did in neoclassical drama; rather, it spoke of the "purely human" in terms of the senses. For Wagner, myth was an "emotionalization of the intellect"; it appealed directly to the feelings. Apart from such theory, the use of myth enabled Wagner to alter details and infuse his own personal emotional experiences into the plot to a degree not possible with the poetic ideas that could be derived from history, well-known personalities, and current events.

The new, binding principle of form for which Wagner searched was obtained through the development of the leitmotif. His debt to Liszt for ways of expanding and transforming the leitmotif was acknowledged only to the extent that Wagner ever acknowledged any debt. In his early operas, Wagner had typically carried certain significant themes from one scene to another. But these themes simply occurred with the entrance of a character, some bit of action, and certain significant words. As mere labels, they did not change with the nature of the character or situation in a genuine transformation. They also bore evidence of an origin in vocal rather than instrumental style. Such were the characteristics of leitmotifs used in *The Flying Dutchman, Tannhäuser*, and *Lohengrin*.

The period of exile, which gave Wagner the opportunity to formulate his theoretical writings, produced a change in the composer's concept of the leitmotif and its potential for dramatic expression. Collectively called *The Ring of the Nibelungs*, the subsequent group of four operas was unified by leitmotifs with the quality of instrumental themes. The long lines and terminal rhymes of previous texts were exchanged for shorter statements that were more representative of natural speech.

Particularly in operas involving a great deal of stage action, the leitmotif provided the link between visual and musical events. The leitmotif is generally brief. Although it may consist of an entire melody, such as that of the Rhine-maidens, it is sometimes simply the successive tones of a chord in a memorable rhythmic framework or a striking harmonic progression. It is given a distinctive tone color and impressed upon the listener by its repetition. The leitmotif is varied according to the emotional needs of the drama. It can be combined with motifs that represent other characters and events to give a dense polyphonic texture. The tone color or harmony can be changed; a melodic extension may be added. Still the heir of Beethoven, Wagner adopted a brief, pliable musical motif to achieve the dense complexity of the symphonic development within the longer, more psychologically involved machinery of the music drama.

To some extent, the characters, the action, the symbols, even the leitmotifs, reflected Wagner's personal experiences and life style. A typical Romantic, he regarded himself as one who was eternally evolving toward some high goal. His visions of a new emergent society and his concept of organic unity in art were conditioned by evolutionary theory. The music drama was to deal exclusively with emotion that was continuously in the process of becoming. His many autobiographical studies charted the path of his evolution as an artist. According to some scholars, the characters in his operas reflect symbolically the experiences through which Wagner passed. A most obvious case is that of the critic Edward Hanslick, who was satirized in the character of Beckmesser in *The Mastersingers of Nuremberg*. Yet once he objectified his malice, Wagner treated the character as the necessities of the drama required, not as his hatred dictated. *Tristan and Isolde* was inspired by his relationship with Mathilde Wesendonck and conditioned by an initial encounter with Schopenhauer's doctrine of renunciation. In a more symbolic vein, the character Wotan could have been Wagner as the dreamer—the slave to moral conventions, who is doomed to find only a dream-maid. Siegfried emerged as the youthful reincarnation, the natural man freed from the bondage of convention. He was the "Fearless One" of Wotan's dreams.

Wagner himself left voluminous writings on the intricate philosophical meanings buried in his works. They are so redolent with the Romantic sentimentality then in vogue that it is difficult to know how seriously to consider them. The music dramas continue to live on their great artistic merits alone; they were emotionally effective without a minute cataloguing of leitmotifs and symbolizing of events.

Wagner regarded *Tristan and Isolde* as his "most fullblooded musical conception." In it his theories and techniques seem to be most fully realized. The coincidence of music and action is excellently balanced; the simplest plot is used as the vehicle for the deepest emotional intensity. The leitmotifs that form the musical texture achieve a continuous mingling flow while they remain true to the poetic intentions. Inspired by Liszt's opulent chromaticism, Wagner's enriched harmonic vocabulary became fully coherent in the dramatic setting of *Tristan and Isolde*. Wagner skirted so close to the edges of the key system of tonal harmony that subsequent works drew back from the chasm. Indeed, *Tristan and Isolde* is recognized as the starting point from which the revolutionary tonal systems of the twentieth century evolved. Finally, despite mythological, philosophical, and symbolic overtones, the work became decisively musical in concept. It is music of such intricacy that only an overwhelming emotion within a poetic idea could have justified it.

Wagner wrote in a letter to Liszt in December 1854: "Because I have never tasted the true bliss of love, I shall raise a monument to that most beautiful of all dreams wherein from beginning to end this love may for once drink to its fill." In the Germanic and Anglo-Norman Tristan romances he found the perfect vehicle for his purpose. The complex plot with two heroines of the same name had to be stripped to a skeleton to deliver a dramatic impact. Wagner took only the essentials: the young hero Tristan, who is wounded when he kills a despot; Isolde, who heals him before she knows he is her uncle's murderer; the love potion that substitutes for the poison with which Isolde hopes to avenge the murder; Isolde's husband, King Mark, who discovers the lovers and forces Tristan to flee; and the death of the lovers—Tristan, who dies of wounds, and Isolde, who dies of a broken heart.

The three acts focus specifically on the love potion, discovery, and death. The two lovers become symbolic embodiments of the power of love and its superior claim over social honor and morality. Once freed by the potion, love is allied with the power of fate to fulfill its decrees even to the grave. Tristan's anguished endurance and inexhaustible longing represent the more passive aspect of love. The active force is personified in Isolde, who offers the potion, deals with King Mark, and voyages to the dying Tristan. The opera centers on the subjective relationships and assigns the narrative to the secondary characters of Kurvenal and Brangäne. These two confidants serve as intermediaries between the exterior world of people and events and the inner world of the lovers. The mundane requirements of this exterior world create such barriers to love's fulfillment that the only remaining course is to eliminate the barriers through death. In his program notes Wagner justifies his naming the death scene "Transfiguration": "Life divides the loves of Tristan and Isolde, but death, removing all barriers, glorifies them. To the dead Tristan the dying Isolde brings blessed consummation, eternal union endless, boundless, free and indissoluble."

In his theoretical writings, Wagner had posited the abandonment of poetic rhyme, which he regarded as the product of reason rather than emotion. When reinforced by devices of assonance and alliteration, the vowel sound is the primary conveyor of emotional meaning. The association of words with the same primal feeling should substitute for the artifices of rhyme. Not only did he advocate abandoning the device of rhyme, but also that of conventional meters. The natural rhythm of the rise and fall of speech accent should become the musical rhythm without any predetermined number of accents in the line. The final text should not be determined by the requirements of either poetic or musical form, but by the emotional progression of the subject matter. In *The Ring of the Nibelungs* Wagner followed his theories consistently; in *Tristan and Isolde* he broke with them time and again and declared: "In writing it I completely forgot all theory." The text is peppered with very short ejaculations that dart between the characters. Even the lyric intensity of Isolde's final song is captured in short phrases with rhymed ends. The voice parts themselves are so absorbed in the strands of orchestral texture that, for concert purposes, Wagner did not oppose the use of the "Love-Death" section without singers. He advised Nietzsche on one occasion: "Take your glasses off! You must hear nothing but the orchestra." Voice combinations were chosen in order to display contrasting tone colors. Brangäne's rich contralto added the color needed for the "Night Scene," and the higher soprano tones of Isolde suited the closing idea of transformation. Sound for the sake of its sheer sensuous appeal is an important factor in the total effect.

The germ of the musical form emerged with the songs that Wagner wrote to poems by Mathilde Wesendonck. The "Night Scene" and other significant musical motifs of *Tristan and Isolde* were subsequently derived from those songs. Thus, in its general form, the opera began to take the shape of freely elaborated songs with orchestral transitions between them. He provided no long stretches of scenic musical painting to match the "Magic Fire Scene" or the "Ride of the Valkyres." The leitmotifs were constantly in action; they moved the inner drama along even when the exterior stage action was at a minimum. From *Tristan and Isolde* alone, almost four dozen leitmotifs have been catalogued, labeled, and traced through the various changes which underline their emotional significance.

> The prelude begins with the theme of infinite and unfulfilled longing, which can find its completion only in death. Much of the opera's poetic meaning is captured in the soaring and falling of the melody, the unresolved suspensions of the harmony, and the eloquent silence which separates the phrases. Of all the memorable themes in the opera, the initial theme of longing is the most significant. It reappears time and again in each act. In the scene between Isolde and Brangäne the theme is a background to the details of the story that opens with a ship bound for Cornwald, where Isolde is to marry King Mark. The brilliant sea motif of the interludes sung by the sailors and the narrator, Kurvenal, break the anguished scene between the women. Tristan is announced by Kurvenal and his motif is played by the horns.

Tristan's theme is a sustained tone that grows constantly louder and ends in a short flourish. He is persuaded to drink a death potion because it is the only honorable penance for the murder of Isolde's uncle. Isolde shares the drink to quench her unfulfilled desire for Tristan. There is a moment of utter silence; then the orchestra reveals the outcome with the theme of longing from the prelude music.

Although very little happens on stage, the second act is the high point of the opera in many respects. It is a summer night; a burning torch lights Isolde's chamber. The prelude is agitated with faint references to the longing theme and a memorable horn call section, which identifies a departing group of hunters. Particular attention is given to the torch as a symbol of light holding back the love that waits in the darkness. Narrator Brangäne fears that the light of reason will be extinguished by emotion. The orchestral turmoil leading to Isolde's extinguishing the flame supports her suspicions. In the very long love scene that follows, Tristan appears as the image of light. The themes of night, love, and death become intertwined in a rich density of polyphony. A contrast to the first agitated section, a second long episode follows based on the "Peace of Love" motif. The orchestra exerts its most ingratiating effects and extends the emotional range of the scene in a veritable soliloquy on the "Peace of Love" theme.

The parting song is based on the second most important motif in the entire opera—the "Love-Death" theme. Built on constantly ascending tonal levels, the melody seems to summarize not only the musical ideas of the act, but also the two fundamental ideas of the opera. Even at the height of the love scene, much of the text deals with death as the only means to prolong such a relationship. The second distinct division of the scene is dominated by King Mark after his discovery of the lovers. The sorrow and emotional anguish of his words are accented with rich tones of his bass voice and a clarinet in a very low range that plays the motif of his sadness. In one memorable instance his question, "What is the cause of all my grief?" is answered by the theme of longing in the orchestra. The act ends with the wounding of Tristan by Melot and a final plaintive statement of King Mark's theme.

The third act begins with a prelude composed of the motifs of solitude and the pain of death. Attended by Kurvenal, Tristan lies dying at his childhood home. They await the arrival of Isolde. This long section of relative inactivity is filled with foreboding and frustration in the anticipation of a sudden rush of emotions with Isolde's arrival and Tristan's death in her arms. The rest of the act is devoted to Isolde's transfiguration through the "Love-Death" theme. With one final call of the theme of longing, the orchestra literally absorbs the lovers in a great tissue of glowing sound.

Tristan and Isolde became a symbol for Romanticism itself. It was a culmination of artistic technique and vital images, which lay at the heart of the movement. In a letter to Mathilde Wesendonck, Wagner explained: "To me Tristan is and remains a wonder! I shall never be able to understand how I could have written anything like it."

Richard Wagner was in many respects the summary figure of his age. His music dramas exemplified the Romantic belief in the union of the arts, in the primacy of the emotional life, and in the efficacy of the spiritual realm. His very life style exhibited the restless nature of Romanticism in its quest for all-encompassing love, expressive freedom, and the life of the senses. Composers of succeeding ages could choose to accept or reject his example, but none could ignore his pervasive influence on the evolution of the art of music.

THE ROMANTIC ERA
Age of Revolution and Reaction
The Victorian Era

GENERAL CULTURAL INFLUENCES

History: Revolutions of 1815 to 1848; political liberty and national identity; defeat of Napoleon.

Social Factors: emotional freedom versus the intellectual tradition; industrial revolution and bourgeois dominance; growth of factory system; social liberalism and political conservatism; Victorian morality.

Philosophy and Religion: Hegel and historical change; Marx and dialectical materialism; Utilitarianism; Kant and subjectivism; resurgence of Roman Catholicism; Nietzsche's nationalism; Schopenhauer's *The World as Will and Idea.*

ROMANTIC THEME: THE SUBJECTIVE VISION

MUSICAL ATTRIBUTES	ARTISTIC PARALLELS
Berlioz's dream imagery in the *Symphonie Fantastique;* escapism in Berlioz's *Damnation of Faust;* medievalism in Wagner's *Tannhäuser.*	Dream images in Fuseli's "The Nightmare" and Goya's "Los Caprichos"; escapism in Jules Verne's science fiction and Delacroix's African scenes; medievalism in Scott's *Ivanhoe* and Gothic revival architecture.
Crisis in self-identity: Schumann's League of David; love and death imagery in Wagner's *Tristan and Isolde* and Tchaikovsky's *Romeo and Juliet;* metaphysical imagery in Wagner's *The Flying Dutchman;* Saint-Saëns's *Danse Macabre;* Mussorgsky's *A Night on Bald Mountain.*	"Second self" concepts in Jean Paul's characters Walt and Vult; love and death imagery in Whitman's "Out of the Cradle Endlessly Rocking"; Bocklin's *Isle of the Dead;* metaphysical imagery in Goethe's *Faust,* Poe's *Fall of the House of Usher,* and Blake's Biblical engravings.

ROMANTIC THEME: THE NATURAL WORLD

Beethoven's *Pastorale* Symphony; Mendelssohn's *Fingal's Cave* Overture; Wagner's "Meadow Music" from *Parsifal.*	Wordsworth's "Tintern Abbey"; Constable's "Hampstead Heath"; Turner's "The Slave Ship"; Rousseau's concept of the "noble savage."

ROMANTIC THEME: THE ARTIST AS HERO

MUSICAL ATTRIBUTES

Berlioz's *Symphonie Fantastique;* Strauss's *Domestic* Symphony; rise of the virtuoso tradition with Paganini, Liszt, and Chopin.

ARTISTIC PARALLELS

Byron's *Don Juan;* Daumier's political cartoons; Flaubert's challenge of middle-class values in *Madame Bovary;* Dickens as a critic of the industrial revolution.

ROMANTIC THEME: NATIONALISM

Wagner's *Art and Revolution;* Mussorgsky's *Boris Godunov;* the nationalist composers Verdi, Grieg, Glinka, and Borodin.

Nationalist writers Ibsen, Burns, and Dickins; Dostoevski and Russian nationalism; nationalist painters Homer, Eakins, and Whistler.

STYLISTIC DEVELOPMENTS

COMPOSERS, FORMS, AND WORKS

German *Lied* with Schubert's *Die Schöne Müllerin* and *Winterreise;* Mahler's *Song of the Earth.*

German *Lieder* poets Müller and Heine.

Piano literature with Beethoven's sonatas and concertos; Chopin's ballades, nocturnes, and études; Liszt's *Years of Pilgrimage.*

Influence of the literary ideal on the form and content of piano music.

Romantic symphonists Schubert, Mendelssohn, and Brahms.

Programmatic symphonists: Liszt, *Les Preludes;* and Strauss, *Thus Spake Zarathustra.*

Lamartine's poem *Les Preludes;* Nietzsche's literary version of *Thus Spake Zarathustra;* Mythology in *The Poems of Ossian;* Wagner's adoption of Schopenhauer's doctrine of renunciation.

Music Drama: its leitmotif technique and mythological subject matter; Wagner's *The Ring of the Nibelungs* and *Tristan and Isolde.*

7
The Era Of Impressionism

ROMANTICISM IN TRANSITION

Nineteenth-century French musicians shared the general European enthusiasm for the Wagnerian music dramas and journeyed to Bayreuth to experience the almost mystical attraction that surrounded their production in that festival center built especially for their performance. A French musical journal, the *Revue Wagnérienne,* reported in great detail upon many aspects of Wagner's musical attainments. Particularly since the dominant vehicle of French Romanticism was painting, many composers were content to adopt Wagner's musical techniques and ideals as their own. However, the general movement toward nationalism in the arts provided an opportunity for a new flowering of French musical expression within an international framework. Such composers as César Franck and Gabriel Fauré created lasting works within an expanding tradition of French Romanticism. The creative power of French musical thought, which they revived, eventually evolved into a style called Impressionism.

César Franck (1822–1890) belonged to the French tradition of Classicism and remained opposed to Romantic extremes of expression. His religious and nationalistic idealism gradually infused a technique basically derived from Wagner. Subtle detail and elegant nuance appeared as the primary French characteristics in his works. Independence from German musical resources was gained very slowly, and one of the significant influences was the Franco-Prussian War (1870–1871). The defeat of France and the subsequent necessity for a revival of national spirit was partly responsible for the formation of the National Society of Music. The financial limitations of the society conditioned their emphasis on instrumental music, rather than on the more costly music drama. Although less ardent in its nationalism than musical associations in Russia and Bohemia, the National Society of Music formulated the manner in which French musical life was to develop in the future. As president of the organization, Franck has been regarded by some historians as the founder of the modern movement in French music.

The National Society of Music was hardly the official public institution that its name implies. Indeed, the Second Empire was apathetic to serious development of native music and was under the spell of imported German and Italian opera. Not many orchestras existed before 1870; the few chamber music societies were virtually closed to newcomers. With his small band of students and disciples, Franck set about to change these musical conditions. He taught respect for classical forms, high technical standards, and expressive individualism. The first concert of the society was held in the concert hall where Chopin had often played. To the great mass of French music lovers, the event went unnoticed; however, composers themselves were inspired by the proximity of excellent performers and a small but sympathetic audience for their works.

For years, the National Society of Music functioned as the radical arm of new music, but interest in music of the past and broader international developments eventually caused it to become more conservative. Some members seceded to form a new society with radical ideals. This society was called the Independent Musical Society. The first president was Gabriel Fauré (1845–1924), who rejected even more of the Germanic elements of Romanticism and emphasized song and chamber music as the truly French strongholds. His criteria for music in the French spirit included formal clarity, emotional restraint, and a definable national personality. Through students such as Maurice Ravel and Georges Enesco, his influence reached well into the twentieth century. His own compositions were influenced by the work of the *Schola Cantorum,* which studied church music of the past and revived the rich stream of medieval polyphony through which France first gained musical ascendancy in western culture. True to his vision of national music, Fauré avoided the large orchestral forms in favor of songs, piano music, and chamber music. He rejected any aim of programmatic description or metaphysical symbolism; his great purity of thought has been described as "Hellenic" in its Classicism.

While French nationalism was rising, German Romanticism was disintegrating into various derivative styles. The excesses of late Romanticism were eloquently summarized in the music and life of Alexander Scriabin (1871–1915), whose erratic, eclectic style remains unclassifiable. He was a classmate of Rachmaninoff, but did not share the traditional Romantic lyricism that suffused the latter's *Isle of the Dead* or the memorable piano concertos. Scriabin's dominant musical characteristic was his preference for complex harmony, which often necessitated the restructuring of common chords into new patterns of intervals. His break with traditional tonal restrictions was as radical as that represented by the prelude to *Tristan and Isolde;* his melodies often wandered about in an effusive, sprawling manner. His unsettled life style and his intense, unchurchly mysticism were typically Romantic. He was addicted to exoticism and had a life ambition to compose a ritual Mystery to be performed by thousands of worshippers in celebration of the dematerialization of the world. He longed to develop an ultimate synthesis of all the arts into an expression of mystic rapture. He coveted the image of the revolutionist and found the French impressionistic techniques compatible with his esthetic and technical requirements for that role.

Scriabin was fascinated with the opposing forces of his personality; he believed ultimately in mystical inspiration as the source of his work. A man of adventurous and theosophical mentality, Scriabin was a major influence in Russia; also, his contribution helped to bridge the gap between the music of the Romantic movement and that of the twentieth century.

ASPECTS OF REALISM

On the whole, Realism may be viewed as the concentrated development of a single aspect of Romantic thought. In part, it was a deliberate cultivation of art on a small, human scale in contrast with the grandiose heroism of the Romantic movement. Realism proved to be somewhat less fruitful as a musical representation than as a literary or painting style. In addition, it was a trend of some inconsistency, which involved several competing viewpoints.

For the sake of philosophical clarification, the term "Realism" must be distinguished from the term "Naturalism," since both denote separate systems originating at different times. However, in the realm of the arts the separation is both difficult and misleading. The Naturalism springing from the philosopher Rousseau and his doctrine of the return to social simplicity has a limited representation in music. Mussorgsky has been regarded as a Naturalist because of his deliberate rejection of the techniques and social significance of German Romanticism in favor of the folksongs and chants of his native land. He was largely untaught and dependent upon his musical instincts rather than an academic tradition. By using the imagery of his own imagination and environment Mussorgsky vindicated

220   Rousseau's belief in the inherent creative freedom of man. His counterpart in painting was Henri Rousseau (1844–1910) who started to paint late in life without any systematic training. His magnificent failure to imitate the current academic tradition revealed him as a folk artist of great imagination.

    A more widespread aspect of Realism centered on the presentation of actual life situations in contrast with the Romantic devotion to exotic places and situations. The essence of such Realism consisted of placing the individual in a matter-of-fact perspective. Truth gained ascendance over beauty

Figure 7.1 GUSTAVE COURBET. *Bonjour, Monsieur Courbet.* [Courtesy, Musée Fabre, Montpelier (Giraudon)].

as the leading esthetic ideal. Gustave Courbet (1819–1877) captured much of the spirit of Realism in his painting *"Bonjour, Monsieur Courbet"* (Figure 7.1) in which he pictured himself with his painting gear upon his back. The swirling colors of Romanticism and the graceful poses of neoclassicism were replaced by three ordinary-looking men and a landscape composed of a few small bushes, a dog, and a farm wagon. The Byronic hero was exchanged for a portrayal of the "heroism of modern life." The heroes of *The*

Stone Breakers were a man too-old and a child too-young for their heavy work. Artists of this style rejected the escapist aspects of Romanticism and acquired a devotion to actuality. Courbet relied only on that which he could see and experience directly; visual truth was the dominant consideration of his life. Many artists became deliberate or unwitting social commentators who revealed the injustices of the time. From Goya's painting *The Third of May* to Daumier's political cartoons there was a constant preoccupation with the theme of man's inhumanity to man.

Realism was both artistically and politically revolutionary. Art critics decried the lack of idealism and the choice of "degrading" subject matter. Political leaders quickly sensed that the movement toward social realism was symptomatic of the growing power of the peasant and constituted a radical protest against prevailing society. Thus, by speaking hard truths about a world dominated by bourgeois concepts, artists and writers alienated themselves from the economic support of the middle class. Only such a work as Flaubert's *Madame Bovary*, with its added scandalous attraction, could draw attention sufficiently to assure public dissemination on a large scale. In fact, the sensational success of *Madame Bovary* helped to turn the tide of public opinion. Yet for many years the university and the academy remained closed to Realism both in principle and in practice. Courbet resorted to setting up a competing art show in a tent after his paintings were refused for official exhibition.

In addition to a realism centered about social conditions, a realism of method was evident in many works of the late nineteenth century. Zola's commitment to scientific determinism produced in him a desire to probe society with methods appropriate to scientific dissection. Although Flaubert agreed that art had reached a stage in which it could blend with scientific objectives, Zola was ready to subject literature to the experimental method and support his status as an artist by his reliability as a scientist. Zola's procedure was based on systematic and minute observation; he wished to be remembered as the first man to portray humanity as it really was. To him, the number of buttons on a dress worn by a minor character was a factor not to be disregarded.

In music, several aspects of Realism were evident. In addition to the Naturalism of Mussorgsky, there was Strauss's realism of particulars. In his program music Strauss desired to establish a direct relationship with daily life and to sharpen the descriptive powers of the orchestra. The wind machine and imitations of bleating sheep that he introduced in *Don Quixote* were an ultimate summary of the naive tone painting of the Renaissance. Realism proved to be as theatrically effective as Romanticism; but in the words of one critic, Richard Strauss (1864-1949), sometimes gave it the guise of primitive eroticism "with the impudence of a guttersnipe." Strauss preferred to use impersonal associations for operatic purposes in order to establish the objectivity he felt necessary to dramatic Realism. For his requirements, the tales of *Salome* and *Elektra* proved invaluable, and the version of *Salome* by Oscar Wilde offered the added attraction of sensationalism. The range of Strauss's descriptive power is exemplified in the contrasting death scenes of *Till Eulenspiegel* and *Salome.*

> Till, the eternal prankster, carries on his merry, disjointed leitmotif until the very end. The fateful dirge representing social justice gradually transforms his loping rhythm into a march to the gallows. His melody wriggles valiantly within the overwhelming force of the full orchestra. As the drum roll signals the execution, Till cries out in clarinet squeals, only to be answered by the unyielding mutters of low wind instruments and laments of muted strings.
>
> Salome's death is portrayed in such a manner as to display her monstrous aberration. The extremely rapid declamation of text and the low, peristent rumble in the orchestra give a sense of impending madness, which is even more clearly implied in her serenade to the decapitated head of John the Baptist. The brasses flutter and drums tremble at Herod's declarations of fear; the soaring lyricism of Salome's final solo culminates in a chord of dissonant violence. The musical language may belong technically to the realm of *Tristan and Isolde,* but the macabre detail and masterful orchestral effects belong to the mind of Strauss alone.

In the works of Puccini (1858–1924), bourgeois Realism became an overwhelming success in Italy. *La Bohème* was praised by Debussy as a true portrait of life in the artistic hovels of many a large city. Yet the musical technique was firmly rooted in the Italian lyrical spirit of Verdi, which undoubtedly contributed to public acceptance of somewhat ordinary characters as replacements for aristocratic Romantic heroes. His opera *Tosca* rivaled *Salome* and *Elektra* in its melodramatic sadism, while remaining within the bounds of traditional theatrical devices. The same feminine torment pervaded *Madame Butterfly* and *Turandot,* both of which exploited oriental melodies and sonorities for added colorful effects. For Puccini, this cult of the orient was entirely in keeping with the spirit of Romantic exoticism. For Debussy, however, oriental musical materials served as a means of expanding musical practices themselves. The vagabond characters of the opera *La Bohème* were used not as symbols of social revolution but as exotic elements within a familiar social context. Thus, Puccini's Italian operatic Realism called "verism" emphasized a truth to life considerably closer to actual existence than that reflected by the symbolic heroes of the Wagnerian music drama or by the sensational effects of Strauss's *Salome.*

IMPRESSIONISM

Among the various alternatives to Romanticism that arose in the late nineteenth century, Impressionism proved to be the most influential. In both ideology and methodology the movement was partly derived from Romanticism and Realism; yet it promulgated some of the revolutionary changes that eventually characterized twentieth-century music. In some respects, Impressionism was as contradictory and complex as Romanticism, and its various qualities were not shared to the same degree throughout the arts. The term "Impressionism" was derived from art (specifically from Monet's painting called "Impression—Sunrise") and subsequently used to denote other artistic products of the time. All the arts were decisively influenced by scientific consciousness. Painters were fascinated by the physics of light; novelists by social sciences; poets and musicians by the inner world newly discovered by psychology. The greatest point of divergence proved to be the essential objectivity represented by some art forms in contrast with the deliberate subjectivity cultivated by others.

Impressionism arose first in the visual arts as a means to explore scientifically the true appearance of the world. Artists abandoned indoor studios to study the light and color of the world under naturally prevailing lighting conditions. Claude Monet (1840–1926) even established his studio in a boat. An impressionistic definition of art considered the subject as seen through and within its natural environment. Thus Monet painted a series of works based upon the lily pond in his yard; individual paintings recorded minute changes in light intensity and weather conditions. Painters soon discovered that in actual practice, objects are not perceived by the eye in great detail. They turned to fragmentation of images and omitted details not fundamental to the apprehension of light, color, and general configuration. They also rejected the story or anecdote typical of much Romantic painting and, indeed, almost everything that lay outside the actual optical experience. In its insistence upon the primacy of artistic principles, rather than exterior thematic demands, Impressionism founded the basic attitude of twentieth-century art. In response to the advent of the camera, painting was forced to find new forms of visual expression and a new role in society.

The deliberate reduction of the visual experience to its bare essentials was both a continuation of the attitude of Realism and a restriction of art to elements and purposes that have no counterparts in the normally experienced world. In breaking the last ties with both Idealism and the world of ordinary appearances, Impressionism lost its connection with the vision of the common man. People felt they were being made fun of and responded with outrage. Impressionist painters had even more difficulty than the Realists in establishing their point of view and creating an understanding audience for their works. Yet their art was founded upon the most significant imagery of the modern world—the urban environment. Turner's train fantasy in "Rain, Steam and Speed" was followed by Monet's study of the "Old St. Lazare Station" (Figure 7.2). The human drama of arrival and departure was completely submerged by a studious rendering of the atmosphere of smoke and sunlight caught between the bulging form of the engine and the sharp angle of the station roof. The matter-of-fact situation typical of Realism became an abstract study in blue and green.

Impressionism in art aimed to formulate new means of visual apprehension. A significant discovery was that reality is composed of constant flux; thus forms in movement became a dominant pictorial subject. Edouard Manet (1832–1883), in his lithograph *Races at Longchamp,* captured the fragmentary movements of racing horses in the typical abbreviated style of

Figure 7.2 CLAUDE MONET. *Old S. Lazare Station, Paris.* [Courtesy, The Art Institute of Chicago].

Impressionism (Figure 7.3). The sense of action captured in the very momentum of its passing pervaded all the arts and formed a decided contrast with the monumental organic unity of Romantic masterpieces. Henri Bergson (1859–1941) established a philosophical framework for this pervasive sense of change. His stress upon the uniqueness of the moment found amplification both in painting and poetry. The devotion to single well-shaped, intensely evocative images was one of the unifying features of most late nineteenth-century art forms.

Impressionism in literature reached its highest development in the works of the symbolist poets; yet the initial impetus of Symbolism was somewhat different from that of the impressionist painters. The symbolist poets were searching for a psychic reality in the tradition of Freud (1856–1939). Their discoveries deeply influenced the later modern movement called Surrealism. Baudelaire (1821–1867) was regarded as the initiator of Symbolism because he reconciled the new mystic spirit of the subconscious with the older Romantic estheticism. The concept of the arts as self-sufficient entities not dependent upon exterior reality was first made explicit in painting. Later, the concept became characteristic of both poetry and music. "Art for art's sake" became not only the leading esthetic point of view but also a veritable life style. Poets did not find the reality of Zola or Courbet nearly so compelling as the artful illusion. Poetic Impressionism, or Symbolism, carried Romantic Idealism to its ultimate conclusion by replacing practical life with

Figure 7.3 EDOUARD MANET. *"The Race at Longchamp."* Lithograph, 1864. [Boston Museum of Fine Arts].

life of the spirit. Some poets and musicians who supported the art style lived in almost monastic seclusion; they were known to only a small circle of friends.

Symbolism was a conscious rebellion against practical and restricted bourgeois existence. It retained the vague Romantic sense of weariness with the world. The Symbolists searched for a sense of reality in forms of expression which held open a wide range of subconscious associations. The poignant style of Rimbaud's works made him famous as a very young man. He later became a wandering Bohemian with a purposeless existence, and died never believing that his poems had any universal value.

In some respects the Symbolists represented emerging modern attitudes. They were devoted to the urban environment and were more likely to extol nature in the form of a public park than as a forest wilderness. They were greatly influenced by the philosophy of change; thus, their aim was to capture the fleeting experiences easily lost in the flux of daily existence. Fundamentally, they depended upon sense data and sometimes extracted the connotative aspects of the pure sound of words from their contextual meaning. Mallarmé (1842–1898) described his art as "a labyrinth illuminated by flowers." Sometimes he was deliberately obscure in his choice of words in order to provoke unconscious related associations in the mind of the reader. Needless to say, bourgeois readers were as impatient with his demands as they were with the new visual orientation required by the painters. Color and nuance had replaced the conventional statement of painting; sheer beauty of sound had replaced the traditional linguistic structure of poetry. The world was no longer described but rather evoked.

A leading Symbolist, Paul Verlaine (1844–1896), rejected reason as basic to poetry and exalted the evidence of sight and inner feelings. His poetry was highly visual and produced an atmosphere as powerful as that of the painters. His poem "The White Moon" is a particularly fine example of the almost tactile quality of his style:

> The white moon
> Shines through the woods;
> From each branch
> There comes a voice
> Under the green bough . . .
>
> O Beloved.
>
> The deep mirror
> Of the pond reflects
> The silhouette
> Of the dark willow
> Where the wind weeps . . .
>
> Our time to dream has come.
>
> A vast and tender
> Calm
> Seems to descend
> From the firmament
> Of iridescent stars . . .
>
> Exquisite hour.[1]

1 Translated from the French by the authors.

In music, Impressionism was a movement of international scope that produced a small number of genuine masterpieces and a horde of colorful, ingratiating additions to the instrumental repertoire. The central composer was Claude Debussy (1862–1918), in whose mind certain fundamental esthetic aims and concrete techniques achieved a functional synthesis. As in the case of the symbolist poets, Debussy owed a great deal of his imagery and part of his technique to Romanticism. Of his artistic philosophy he declared, "I am an old romantic who has thrown the worries of success out the window." In his youth, he shared the general enthusiasm for Wagner and made several trips to hear the music dramas at Bayreuth. He shared the realm of illusions preferred by the poets and made it the dominant theme of his compositions. A critical review of his orchestral poem *Nocturnes* summarized the spirit of musical Impressionism as "pure music, conceived beyond the limits of reality, in the world of dreams, amidst the ever-moving architecture that God builds with the mists, the marvelous creations of the impalpable realms. . . ."

Debussy retained some significant traits from the Romantic movement; among them was the predominance of the melodic element. His profound literary orientation inspired a close association with the symbolist poets. They were admirably suited to fill his need for a librettist "Who will only hint at things and will thus enable me to insert my dreams into his. . . ." Reciprocally, Mallarmé was delighted with Debussy's setting of his poem *The Afternoon of a Faun.* Upon hearing the music for the first time, he reportedly remarked: "I didn't expect anything like that. This music evokes the emotion of my poem and fixes the background much more vividly than color could have done."

The influence of the Romantic salon was represented in Debussy's life by the literary salon held by Mallarmé. The active association of artists from various disciplines kept alive the Romantic ideal of unity in the arts. Medievalism appeared in Debussy's *The Martyrdom of St. Sebastian* and in the use of Gregorian chant for its rhythmic flexibility. Nature, particularly water, was a primary source of imagery. Such works as the symphonic poem *La Mer* and the piano selections "Reflections in the Water" and "Gardens in the Rain" attest to his power of evocation.

Debussy's sense of national pride partly led him away from the broad stream of Romanticism. He never claimed as Wagner did to speak either to or for "the Folk." He realized that his music would appeal to a limited audience and humorously advocated founding a "Society of Musical Esotericism." Nevertheless, he emphasized a musical subtlety and nuance which he felt to be specifically French and signed himself proudly *Musicien Français.* He felt distinctly burdened by the whole tradition of western music, and yet too well-rooted in it to free himself.

Debussy was greatly aided in the creation of his own musical esthetic by the anti-Wagnerian ideals of Russian nationalists such as Mussorgsky.

The Russians wanted to abandon the symbolic heroes and to restore the impetus of action and expression to the singers instead of the orchestra. They regarded the leitmotif as a mechanically imposed label and advocated developing additional themes as the action demanded. Debussy was much influenced by the Russian ideal of an opera which was integrated simply by a series of loosely related scenes.

A secondary influence that diverted Debussy from the dominant Romanticism of his time was his encounter with the Javanese orchestra (gamelan) at the Paris World Exhibition of 1889. He was captivated by their seemingly natural expressive skill and delicacy of sound, which contrasted with the overwhelming emotionalism of Wagner. He ultimately found in the harpsichord music of Couperin and Rameau the basis for a French national style to match the distinct national quality represented in both Javanese and Russian music. Thus, armed with such powerful defenses, Debussy set out against the musical current of his time to create a new musical esthetic.

In some respects, Debussy may be considered the founder of twentieth-century music. He lived much of his life in the atmosphere of the twentieth century, with its economic prosperity, artistic freedom, and social turbulence. The bourgeois market for the arts was forming with its accouterments of publishers, managers, and unions of performing musicians. A new universality of musical style was served by rapid communication; compositional rights were better protected by copyright laws. The music festival pattern begun at Bayreuth expanded everywhere; the increased pace of musical events was halted only by the World War I. An avid interest in nonwestern societies and the arts of ancient men began to develop among psychologists and anthropologists. Debussy was particularly modern in his use of nonwestern music in a manner that did not do violence to its spirit. Despite his nationalism, he was not a devotee of French folksong. He confined its use to isolated connotative effects.

Debussy disliked to be called an Impressionist and declared he was trying to create realities. He sought no musical parallel to Impressionism in painting and admired the American painter Whistler more than the French exponents of the movement. However, both Debussy and the painters found significant motifs in the eastern arts. The Japanese print particularly provided a contrary esthetic through which to counter the pervasive European painting tradition. Debussy used wedges of tone color in the same deliberate manner that artists used individually distinguishable strokes of the brush. His dominant tool was that of tone color used for sensuous appeal rather than for emotional effect.

In adopting the sensuous imagery of the symbolist poets, Debussy was consciously striving to develop musical equivalents for their verbal techniques. His interest in the sheer quality of sound led him to utilize such divergent resources as the five-tone (pentatonic) scale of Asia, the sonorities of the gamelan, and the intense chromaticism of *Tristan and Isolde*. He nearly destroyed the traditional harmonic system by adding on occasion the scale built completely of whole-tone intervals. The effect erased all sense of key center. Debussy's many daring innovations emerged from an ideological mixture of the spirit of Impressionism in painting, the techniques of the symbolist poets, and the tonal resources of nonwestern musical systems.

Part of Debussy's modern quality was his ability to absorb diversity. His freedom from ingrained habits of musical thought was gained through the Gregorian chant, the Renaissance polyphony, Javanese music, and American ragtime. His occasional rejection of the western tonal system led eventually to the development of the theoretical structures of the twentieth century. He also prefaced modern Neoclassicism by using the old suite forms and adapting the sonata form to his own style in his only string quartet. He greatly advanced the pianistic techniques developed by Chopin and Liszt by using extreme gradations of loud and soft, vast ranges of pitch, and orchestral effects of overlapping sonorities. In summary, the essence of his style included a primary allegiance to melody and tone color; a use of harmony for subtle coloristic emphasis rather than traditional progression; a new shape based upon asymmetrical units; a retention of the improvisatory style of Romantic music; and the creation of a supple rhythmic flow without repetitive accentuation.

Debussy's opera *Pelléas and Mélisande* was an eloquent realization of a musical style fundamentally opposed to that of the Wagnerian music dramas. Wagner and Debussy were supreme exemplars of their respective musical spheres. Their individual solutions to common musical and dramatic problems served to clarify the essential differences between them.

> *Pelléas and Mélisande* was planned in accordance with Russian operatic ideals, in the sense that no consistent stream of dramatic action is evident. The many scenes were intended to provide musical cohesion in themselves. The prelude alone gives an accurate impression of the difference between Debussy's opera and *Tristan and Isolde*. Its indefinite tonality is infinitely delicate and wistful. No intricately combined leitmotifs are used, but, rather, a few significant melodies suspended in a glitter of orchestral tone color. The initial scene between Golaud and the lost Mélisande reveals the almost speaking quality of the vocal style in which the music follows the rhythm and pitch of the natural inflection. The orchestra adds poignancy and emotional tone to the encounters on stage, but the singers carry the main impetus. The listener may be entirely unaware of repeated themes; however, the effect of unity by similar stylistic devices creates a possible substitute. The music gives the impression of constant variation within a well-defined range of tone color, and the many orchestral interludes serve as expressive transitions from scene to scene. These interludes are

often short tone poems in themselves. The last words of scene two, "It is dark here in the garden! And what forests there are around the palace," are followed by a lyrical portrait of the summer night. The prelude to Act II initiates the setting of the fountain in the park by animated music to fit the shifting patterns of water.

The relationships of the characters are also handled with great delicacy. The story is much like that of Tristan, in that the young bride of an older royal personage falls in love with his younger brother. However, in the details of plot and manner of presentation the operas are quite different. The symbol of the love potion, the imagery of light and darkness, and love and death are replaced by a new symbolic range. Some are isolated symbols such as the lost wedding ring, tossed playfully into the fountain. The dominant theme is that of guilt and innocence which underlies scenes that would otherwise have little relationship to the opera as a whole. The scene of the child Yniold and his encounter with a herd of sheep is irrelevant except for the obvious relationship to the imagery of innocence. The orchestra, with its sheep bell and vague rustling movement, underscores the brief interlude.

The last and most intense of the love scenes serves as an interesting contrast to the "Night Scene" of *Tristan and Isolde*. The element of innocent play is still pervasive; both Golaud and the audience cannot be sure of what is taking place. Unlike the passionate outbursts of Wagner's lovers, Pelléas hears Mélisande avow her love in a voice "that has passed over the sea in spring." Particularly dramatic is the sudden expressive shift that occurs when Mélisande sings, "There is someone behind us." The pure tonal translucence of Pelléas's love song breaks into a throb of drums and a rush of dark, reedy tone colors.

Mélisande's death scene is possibly the finest section of the opera; it offers a decided contrast to the scene of Isolde's death. The leading symbol is that of the setting sun, the light of which falls into the room through a tall, open window. Mélisande's vocal lines are embellished by nearly transparent orchestral colors, and other characters are given contrasting darker hues. The real drama takes place in the minds of the living. Golaud must know if the love of his wife and his brother was guilty or innocent. Mélisande's assertions of innocence are so clouded by her delirium that he cannot be certain of their accuracy. He will go to his grave tormented by the question of guilt and the consequences of his anger. Mélisande sees her newborn child with little sense of recognition, murmuring "She is tiny . . . She will weep too . . . I pity her." The old king Arkël cautions Golaud, "We must not disturb her . . . The soul needs silence . . . but the sadness of all that we see." A distant chime symbolizes her death, and the orchestra fades, as luminescent as the final rays of sun.

Although *Pelléas and Mélisande* was a masterpiece in its style, Impressionism was more centered upon purely instrumental music. In this latter category, the *Prelude to the Afternoon of a Faun*, written in 1894, has long maintained a significant position. Debussy described the intentions of the composition in a note attached to the score: "It evokes the successive echoes of the Faun's desires and dreams on a hot afternoon." Mallarmé's poem provided a perfect vehicle for Debussy's tonal splendors. The poet conveys the nature of the faun and his setting through a language rich in connotation:

> Inert, all is burning in the tawny hour
> Without noticing that all art flees
> The plenitude of marriage wished by him who seeks the *A:*
> Then will I awaken to the first ardour,
> Pure and alone, beneath an ancient flow of light,
> One among the lilies in my simplicity.

The final lines convey the elegant langour of the musical setting:

> . . . the spirit
> Of empty words and my heavy body
> Succumb at last to the proud noon silence.
> I must sleep now, forgetful of blasphemy,
> Lying as I please on the parched sand,
> Opening my mouth to the wine-swelling sun!
>
> Farewell, lovers; I seek the shade in which you mingle.[2]

Debussy's aim was not to create an actual setting of the poem, just as he disclaimed any "wave by wave" description of the sea in *La Mer*. Rather, he presents the vague reverie of a faun who, upon waking, cannot be sure whether he has experienced or only dreamed about finding two nymphs asleep. Debussy said of the music that it was "what remained of the dream in the recesses of the flute."

The work begins with a flute solo broken by sudden splashes of orchestral color and the tonal waterfall of a harp. The flute theme, which forms the melodic basis of the composition, continues within constantly shifting harmony. The mood is that created by delicate, surging lyricism. A modified and more rapid version of the main theme is played by the clarinet as a reedy answer to the first section. A middle section of great vigor features an intricate movement of buried melodic fragments coursing about in a dense texture. The main theme, in all its simplicity, emerges against a simple harp accompaniment and persists in many tone color disguises until the end. The

2   Translated from the French by the authors.

Prelude to the Afternoon of a Faun was Debussy's first purely orchestral composition, which has come to characterize the very essence of Impressionism.

The French music critic Pierre Lalo eloquently summarized the essence of Debussy's musical contributions in an article for *Le Temps* in March of 1907: "All that is precious and admirable in Debussy's art—all that makes his a profound originality—is a new sensitivity, a sensitivity marvelously intense and delicate, a sensitivity toward nature, which lets him evoke the soul of things without any descriptive anxiety."

POST-IMPRESSIONISM

Debussy attracted a flock of followers both in France and abroad. Some were content to reproduce the obvious musical clichés of the surface of Impressionism. Others followed the pattern established by Debussy in his late works in which he attempted to recover a sense of formal design. The tonal, coloristic sheen of musical Impressionism and its parallel in the visual arts had threatened to create products that were nothing more than a kaleidoscope of sonic or visual stimuli. Debussy and his younger contemporaries developed free forms with certain recognizable principles of cohesion; the études for piano fully exemplify such principles. Although the études have descriptive titles and the pervasive mood typical of Impressionism, they were influenced by Chopin's pianistic style and designed around formal and technical problems.

A most prominent successor to Debussy was Maurice Ravel (1875–1937), who came to musical maturity about 1910. Thereafter, he was torn between the ideals of Impressionism and the emerging movements of the twentieth century. In many respects, he remained part of the older pattern, particularly in his predilection for fantasy and imaginative creations in preference to images of the real world. He ventured far into the new harmonic developments that Debussy had opened for exploration, and his late works contained evidence of the use of two distinct tonalities at once (bitonality). In his devotion to simplicity, clarity and purity of form he prefaced contemporary neoclassicism. Ravel always professed great admiration for Debussy, but asserted that he was taking another musical path. He was equally influenced by his friendship with Stravinsky and Schönberg, who were fully representative of the twentieth century. The popularity of the *Bolero* and the *Daphnis and Chloë* suites have tended to overshadow his other more significant compositions.

The influence of musical Impressionism was felt both in France and abroad for many years. The traditional system of harmony further stretched to encompass divergent elements. The modality of Gregorian chant, the tonality of Bach, or even the use of two or more tonalities at once were no longer exclusive choices but merely related aspects of the same musical language. The choice of tonal resources for a given segment of music was dependent upon expressive needs alone, rather than upon the necessities of a system. In Spain, Manuel de Falla's "symphonic impressions" such as *Nights in the Gardens of Spain* combined the musical devices and esthetics of Impressionism with an unmistakable Spanish style of expression. Charles Martin Loeffler (1861–1935) served as the bridge between French and American Impressionism. The same role in Italy was filled by Alfredo Casella. The works of Frederick Delius, Ernest Bloch, and Ottorino Respighi sounded the last musical echoes of Impressionism.

Like music, painting took the same turn from the beguiling world of iridescent color to a recovery of form. Cezanne (1839–1906) continued to paint from nature, but, above all, sought a sense of order and design. He wished "to make of Impressionism something solid and durable, like the art of the museums." Nor would he hesitate to distort the actual proportions of his subjects in order to achieve that perfection of interrelatedness he desired. His radical simplification and systematic esthetic allied him to twentieth-century Abstraction.

Van Gogh (1853–1890) used the ragged brush strokes of Impressionism to produce an art without overtones of the vague, shadow world of escapism. His brilliant swirls of color and portrayals of the agony of real life have established him as an ancestor of twentieth-century Expressionism.

Gauguin's (1848–1903) works were the last fruit of the Romantic distrust for civilization. In his use of art style of the South Pacific he may be regarded as the initial figure in modern primitivism. In painting, as in music, the eclectic nature of the Post-Impressionist period was its predominant characteristic. Actually, no central movement existed at all, but, rather, a series of relatively parallel activities without any generally acknowledged common aim. Such a condition continued to exist in the twentieth century. The artistic problems became increasingly apparent, but the solutions were no less diverse. Debussy, his fellow Impressionists in painting, and the symbolist poets were of fundamental significance to the development of modern arts. Through them the whole complex mentality of Romanticism found a fitting summary and, under the pressure of social circumstance and artistic need, became gradually transformed into those broad channels which nourished the arts of the twentieth century.

SUMMARY OUTLINE

POST-ROMANTIC SOCIETY

The Edwardian Age

The Modern World

GENERAL CULTURAL INFLUENCES

History: the Franco-Prussian War.

Social Factors: revival of French nationalism; economic prosperity; bourgeois support of the arts; dominance of social realism as an attitude; international laws and communications systems established.

Philosophy and Religion: Bergson and the philosophy of change; continued influence of Rousseau's Naturalism; religious idealism mixed with political sympathies.

Science: impact of the camera on visual arts; modern color theory based on works of Helmholz.

MUSICAL ATTRIBUTES

Theory: breakdown of Rameau's harmonic system; adoption of nonwestern elements; influence of Javanese *gamelan;* use of whole-tone and pentatonic scales, bitonality, and polytonality.

Social Functions: expression of French nationalism in music; Fauré's Independent Musical Society; bourgeois Realism in Puccini's *La Bohème;* Strauss's realism of particulars in *Don Quixote;*

Mussorgsky's Naturalism; Impressionism as an anti-Wagnerian esthetic; continuity of mystical inspiration concepts in works of Scriabin.

Composers, Forms, and Works: Franck's organ works; Fauré's songs and chamber music; Scriabin's piano sonatas; Strauss's *Salome* and *Elektra;* Impressionism in Debussy's *Pelléas and Mélisande, The Afternoon of a Faun,* and *Nocturnes;*

Post-Impressionism in Debussy's études; recovery of formal structure; Ravel's *Daphnis and Chloë;* da Falla's *Nights in the Gardens of Spain.*

ARTISTIC PARALLELS

Visual revolution toward two-dimensional forms; influence of Japanese prints on western art practices; study of atmospheric effects upon subject matter; theories of sight and new techniques of color mixtures.

The literary salon as a vehicle of artists, writers, and musicians; Realism; truth vs. beauty in Courbet's "The Stone Breakers" and Goya's "The Third of May;" "Madame Bovary" as the victory of social realism; Zola's scientific determinism; Naturalism of painter Henri Rousseau.

Impressionism in Monet's "Old St. Lazare Station" and Manet's "Races at Longchamp"; Symbolist poets Mallarmé and Verlaine;

Post-impressionism in Cezanne's paintings; Van Gogh's expressionism; Gauguin's primitivism.

8
The Twentieth Century

MASS CULTURE AND THE ARTS

The twentieth century, with its revolutionary changes in both the style and content of western civilization, has not yet advanced far enough to allow a positive statement of its most significant tendencies. To be purposeful, therefore, only a few intersections in the complex web of movements comprising modern culture have been examined. To be practical, this inevitably limited view must omit many important coexistent cultural ideologies. Those artistic movements selected have been considered in contexts that are not intended to be fixed categories. A great deal of the art of the century belongs to several streams of thought. Among the many possible ideologies, the impact from relatively new concepts in such fields as psychology and technology in particular may be traced in almost every art movement. Although the variety of art media and their products seems to preclude unifying observations, specific characteristic principles peculiar to the century can be isolated as an expedient cultural rationale. Because so many art movements prevail at the same time, a chronological account of their development is much less significant than a consideration of certain basic themes which have molded their artistic environment. By both accepting and rejecting these influences, the arts of the twentieth century reflect the attitudes of all

235

men caught up in the shifting intellectual and social patterns of their time.

With the end of the Franco-Prussian War (1871) that apparently concluded the Victorian Age, the ensuing era proceeded with a dual concern for the victors and victims of modern society. Compassion for the peaks and nadirs of change that characterize the forward movement of any era became tantamount to world survival. The increased pace of the Industrial Revolution invited a technological repercussion which ushered in almost immediately an Electronic Age. Industry not only steadily gained in superceding agriculture as the main source of livelihood but also determined the cultural environment of the urban industrial centers.

In the early years of the twentieth century, the eminent economist John Maynard Keynes (1883–1946) predicted an unprecedented production capacity of the individual worker. With the advances made not only in technology, but also in medicine to extend man's life span and make existence safer, an increase in world population was predestined. Those years between 1871 and 1914, commonly referred to as the Edwardian Age or *la belle epoque,* were characterized by widespread material affluence secured through the efforts of the influential middle class. This bourgeois group completely dominated the political and industrial machinery responsible for mass production, instant communication, and rapid transportation symbolized by the housing project, radio, and automobile respectively. But convenience produced its own inconvenience; every privilege that identified a better way of life for the many induced an obligation that the growing affluent society of the Edwardian Age found no time fulfill in the madcap race to reap the rewards of the machine age.

The internal conflict between labor and management widened from the union movement to active socialist parties; their economic ideology rejected the private charitable contributions of the prevailing economy as a solution to social justice. The lack of serious social legislation was paralleled by a series of international diplomatic crises, which stimulated armament production and a search for international security alliances. Ironically, a colonialism perpetuated by the inevitable need for capital and raw materials to maintain the economic revolutions induced an imperialistic competition for world survival.

The nationalism that precipitated the European wars of the nineteenth century culminated in the chauvinistic liberation wars of the twentieth. Despite the necessity of international agreements, national independence continued to dominate the ideology of many emerging nations. The affluent appearance of increased industrialization, booming trade, and riches from colonialism supported the Edwardian philosophy that society had become too refined to indulge in anything so grim as war. But, inevitably, the social refinements of Europe's last age of splendor faced the undermining conflicts on the battlefield of the First World War.

The allies who fought to make the world safe for democracy won the war. They accepted their victory as a mandate to renew the democratic struggle toward a brighter future. By the 1940 decade population trebled; by the 1960 decade the factory worker's production capacity was five times that of the worker who lived during the time of the American Civil War. Capitalism, with its intricate systems of investments and controlling interests, flourished. In the meantime, the worldwide economic depression of 1929 dealt a mortal blow to the business class that had become a dominant force in cultural life after World War I. Bankruptcies, unemployment, and dwindling foreign trade strengthened military control of government in Japan, helped Hitler and the Nazis rise to power in Germany, and encouraged Italy's Fascist element to indulge an imperialistic ambition. Such a resurgence of totalitarian ideology reminded the democratic governments of the basic conflicts that the First World War had failed to resolve. But the capitalistic wheels of reform rolled too slowly to alleviate social and economic discrepancies which totalitarian philosophy sought to eliminate through revolution.

When the attempt to cultivate international relationships through the League of Nations failed to sustain world peace, the technology of the democratic nations was again adjusted to accommodate a second world war. This total, global and most costly war of the world's history was fought not just to make the world safe for democracy but for the survival of democracy itself. Democracy survived; but the war suspended some fundamental liberties that failed to be regained because of the secrecy and restrictions of an ensuing cold war. Although the old order of the glittering goodwill of a chauvinistic, self-sufficient economy was swept away by two wars, the vistas of convenience and diversion first promised by the democratic freedom of the Edwardian Age climbed to even more affluent heights by the 1960 decade.

In such a milieu, the search for newer methods of artistic expression grew more intense as the cultural climate gradually acknowledged the need to strike a balance between the despairs and hopes of both the artist and his public. Through the individual pattern of his acceptance and rejection of certain broad cultural imperatives, the twentieth-century artist has revealed the many images of his society. Whether or not society's many revelations reflect a meeting of minds between artist and public has become second in importance to the revelations themselves. Totalitarian societies link their artistic demands to traditional practices. Free societies encourage a search for new means to realize such traditional values. Ironically, democratic materialism, which has often alienated the artist from mundane social reality, has provided him with a larger, more responsive audience. Industrial wealth and its accouterments have made it possible for great masses of people to achieve an adequate income. Education and the leisure time that is necessary to explore fine books, good music, and beautiful paintings are readily available. Thus, twentieth-century arts have no alternative but to become involved with mass thinking and participation by means of mass production and mass media.

ARTISTIC EXPRESSIONS OF MASS CULTURE

In the last third of the twentieth century, the cultural atmosphere continues to be conditioned largely by mass processes. In retrospect, critics of the era have maintained that the inevitable result of such a mass culture is mass mediocrity. Mass cultural participation breeds a wider range of artistic tastes which obscures the standards of excellence maintained by the traditional circle of the elite few. In rebuttal, apologists of the mass esthetic process have been equally vehement in pointing out certain excellent results of mass participation in the arts. Standards of performance in all the arts have risen to a new level of technical perfection, and the wide circulation of inexpensive recordings has created a large and increasingly discriminating audience. Systems of mass communications have made it possible for millions of people to see and hear experts in all fields of artistic and intellectual endeavor. Audiences for the performing arts have been both consistently large and attentive. Museum and art gallery attendance has risen each year, and the acceptance of new and somewhat radical innovations has grown to a degree unprecedented in the world's history. The cultural centers of Europe have relinquished their traditional leadership in recognition of American esthetic excellence. New York has become the undisputed world capital of the visual arts, and can match other world capitals in almost every field of artistic endeavor. Modern dance and architecture have been largely American-inspired movements which have flourished in the dynamic freedom of the democratic system. From an overall view, both critic and apologist agree that something new has engulfed the arts of the western world. A true mass culture based upon the broadest social diversity is providing for people of every class or economic status complete access to significant intellectual products.

The victory of the artistic "vernacular" has been achieved through technological and social innovations so vast as to provoke concomitant esthetic dilemmas and blessings. In America, the traditional preference has been for the useful rather than the beautiful; this attitude has contributed to the historic gulf between the American artist and the general public. Many artists had to become expatriates in order to gain their due recognition and the monetary and moral support not available at home. In past societies, patronage was the natural duty of aristocratic individuals and established institutions. However, in a society dominated by mass consumer tastes, the artist has found himself in an economically untenable position because of a lack of suitable substitutes for the system of individual patronage.

The mass communications media do not merely provide the means for selective encounters with the arts, but actually serve as arbiters of public taste. Indeed, they have to some degree reshaped the very modes of perception through a progressive bombardment of all the senses. The perceptual structure created by mass media is impatient with a leisurely use of time; music, which exists in time, has to be constantly condensed to gain the most sensory impact in the shortest period of time. Schubert's symphonies, described by a fellow Romantic as being "of heavenly length," seem today to be intolerably protracted. The preference is for symphonies in one movement or opera-oratorios (such as Stravinsky's *Oedipus Rex*) that are complete on one long-playing record. The esthetic of total involvement enacted in theatrical "happenings" has reduced the appreciation for arts which explore in detail single modes of perception. Still, one fruitful outcome of the sense of involvement has been a development of amateur musicians with a taste for the bittersweet tang of folk music.

The mass production of such media as musical instruments has had a fundamental impact upon the economy of musical culture. Almost everyone can own at least a record player, and such electronic devices as the ersatz organ have displaced the piano in many middle-class homes. One instrument succeeds another in waves of popularity, and each brings its own style of music literature and esthetic contribution. In a consumer society, the only reliable factors are both the rapid rate of production and wide dispersion of the means of musical production and reproduction. If the level of production and consumption were considered alone, the state of music would seem riotously healthy. However, critics of modern culture point out that a vital difference exists between music and mere sound stimuli. The means of mass communication are sometimes used not for enlightenment or even pleasure, but merely to fill the gaps in otherwise blank aural spaces. The listener is constantly conditioned by sound patterns typical of a hundred years ago. This comforting devotion to the familiar contributes to the evident cultural lag that places eminent musical craftsmen years in advance of even the most adventurous popular musical practices. Such an enigma can be noted in many eras of western culture.

In any period, the work of a Galileo, a Kant, or an Einstein would be far in advance of the thought patterns of most members of society. Once the cultural lag is reduced to historical significance, the artistic practices remain formidable contenders in challenging the innovations of the future. As in the case of the arts, the forces of a past era are constantly interacting with the more modern aspects of civilization. Mass communications media often use modern technology to deal with ideas and techniques of the past. Through the reinforcement of instant communication, a twentieth-century cultural lag begins its out-of-phase cycle.

To a large degree, composers are indebted to the individualism permitted in a democratic society and stimulated by the lack of restraint imposed upon their search for new ways of expressing their ideas. But, in spite of the vast twentieth-century public audience that potentially waits to absorb a variety of artistic products, the inevitable gap between the artists' musical innovations and the less revolutionary practices popularized by the mass media and supported by middle-class taste sometimes makes it difficult for the composers to earn a living.

Society at large has never provided adequate artistic support; within the existing social framework the more perceptive affluent class is unable to assume the entire financial burden. Into this breach has stepped the university, the foundation, and an occasional benefactor. Such largess has its price, although many artists are quite willing to pay it. The university demands that the composer teach, even to the detriment of his creative activities. Reluctant to donate to a visionary project, the foundation prefers to support an already operable enterprise. Even the most tolerant benefactor has his preferences, which must be served. However, resources are available for most artists who are persistent enough to press their claims and believe in the value of their work.

The various unions of performers and technicians have had a profound effect upon cultural life. The more predictable employment pattern and higher income secured by these organizations have contributed greatly to the well-being of performing artists. On the other hand, their activities have so increased the cost of rehearsals that the composer finds it difficult to secure an adequate performance for his demanding new compositions. Unions have often blocked innovations in technical resources and prevented the student from gaining experience by working with professional performers. "Live" music has become so expensive that dance or theatrical groups are forced to use tape recordings or records. Composers themselves have turned to the tape recorder and the tone synthesizer as the ultimate solutions to such problems.

Mass media and a mass taste have exerted a vital effect upon all the twentieth-century arts. Poetry has become a rather specialized concern, and fiction above the level of the magazine serial and best seller is distinctly less popular than non-fiction. The often-decried decline of reading as a dominant pastime is also allied with the absorption of knowledge through aural and visual sources concurrently. The university presses have become the major organs through which new young writers become known. Such writers as Hemingway, Faulkner, and Fitzgerald have been recognized by much of the mass audience through adaptations of their works for such mass media as the movies and television.

The leading art styles have also been popularized through adaptations of their principles in advertising. Many highly skillful artists have found it possible to combine their interest in personal expression and technical innovation with occasional assignments from advertising agencies. However, among the visual arts, the impact of mass taste is possibly most apparent in architecture. The architects of the middle-class are the tract developers who are still largely caught within the waves of nineteenth-century stylistic revivals. A long-outmoded esthetic based on the farm house with its related plot of land is still being inefficiently applied to the demands of urban life.

The cultural lag is particularly notable in the case of the urban environment. Before 1910, Frank Lloyd Wright conceived the basic principles of the interrelationships of form and function, the building and the landscape. Yet cities are still largely failing to adapt to new imperatives of design and are in danger of succumbing to their built-in structural inadequacies. Despite the dangers evolving from lack of environmental planning, multitudes of people are better housed than ever before and able to distinguish both good and poor designs in all price ranges.

The Social Critic

Twentieth-century arts have been major avenues for expressing the impact of mass culture on the individual. One characteristic feature has been their often pessimistic view of man within society.

The opera *Wozzeck,* by Alban Berg, is particularly graphic in its portrayal of a man caught in a sophisticated organization that affronts his dignity, assaults his body, and leaves him a mental wreck. The military establishment is accused of a pitiless skill that caused a political scandal after a performance of the work in Prague. The army psychiatrist is interested in the common soldier Wozzeck only as a scientific case-history through which some notoriety is possible; he exclaims on one occasion: "Oh my theory, my fame! I shall be immortal." The relationship of poverty to the process of individual destruction is underscored by Marie: "Ah, we poor people . . . I cannot much longer endure it." Virtue is regarded as a luxury of the prosperous middle class; Wozzeck's child cannot be particular about such niceties as legitimacy.

The music is as effective as a nineteenth-century tone poem in delineating the characters and the general mood of despair. In Act I, the Captain is given complex vocal patterns that cover a wide tonal range; the sounds connote the image of a strange, erratic man who loves the flamboyance of military life. In a dead monotone, Wozzeck responds with "Jawohl, Herr Hauptmann." The manner of vocalization combines speaking and singing, and uses tones indicated on the score only as relative pitches. Some passages are actually spoken, and others are sung in an almost Romantic lyricism. The very structure of the work is a shifting montage of human encounters that range in moods from festive dancing to murderous madness. Yet the focus remains the barbaric way in which society drives one man to criminal insanity.

Some characteristics of the opera are drawn from the traits of late Romanticism. In Act III, Marie's soliloquy and Wozzeck's reflective memories about their life together are given a Romantic nostalgia with the rich, lyrical timbre of stringed instruments. The instrumental interlude that closes the act contains the entwined melodies and chromatic complexity reminiscent of Wagner along with the slow rise and fall of volume so characteristic of his style. A dramatic incongruity is captured in the clear, young voice of Marie's child, who is doomed, despite his innocence, to suffer the final revenge of respectable society.

Many realistic orchestral effects heighten the mood and action. The basically atonal idiom (written in no apparent key center or tonality) is perfectly suited to reflect the irrational state of Wozzeck's mind. However, snatches of popular German tunes written in traditional tonalities appear in such scenes as that of Marie's fliratation with the drum major. When Marie slams the window during a verbal battle with a neighbor, the impact is heard throughout the orchestra. The murder scene is suspended musically over the constant tone *B*, which rises to a terrifying climax as Marie is killed. The tone returns once more to emphasize the full horror of the initial impact. When Wozzeck returns to the pond and drowns, the orchestra produces a mass of tones slithering up and down the strings like the water rushing over poor drowned Wozzeck.

In general, the opera creates a powerful image of man menaced by society. It first emerged from the era after World War I, which produced a similar despair in Eliot's *The Wasteland* and in German expressionist painting.

One of the prevalent themes of twentieth-century art is the sense of estrangement, of human isolation. Although the feeling is attributed to the vast impersonality of contemporary society, even in the nineteenth century it was a major element of Degas' "Absinthe Drinker" and Manet's portrait of the bar maid at the "Folies Bergère." Toulouse-Lautrec turned scenes of gay café life into portraits of human misery. The artist Ben Shahn (1898–1969) is typical of many twentieth-century artists who have felt an urgent need to comment on social and moral conditions through images that can be understood by a mass audience. The disadvantage of such a practice is that the works may become merely topical, with little interest, other than the memory of some specific event of public concern. Shahn's "The Passion of Sacco and Vanzetti" is such a painting. However, his "Miners' Wives" communicates the feeling of poverty, despair, and isolation without benefit of title or some specific event (Figure 8.1). Picasso's "Guernica" is, perhaps, the most famous twentieth-century painting in the social protest tradition. Created to protest the senseless bombing of a Spanish town by the Nazis, its visual terms are so striking and so full of formal

Figure 8.1 BEN SHAHN. *Miners' Wives.* 1948. [Courtesy, Philadelphia Museum of Art Collection].

interest that the painting has assumed the status of a universal outcry against man's inhumanity to man.

Even in images that concentrate on formal structure without an obvious social or moral aspect, a hint of commentary on the feelings of the individual among the masses may be evident. The American sculptor Joel Brody has produced a large group of pieces showing figures of men and women sharing the same environmental space. But they are featureless and seem to be unaware of each other's presence. Their very surfaces seem deliberately old and worn. They sit or stand transfixed, looking past unseen walls. Louise Bourgeois's group of wooden forms called "One and Others" is not even related to human figures. Yet their dense crowding within a limited space suggests mankind pressed together in a suffocating proximity.

The theme of man against the massiveness of society has been dominant in the theater. Berthold Brecht's character Gayly Gay in *A Man's a Man* is a satirical but strangely unnerving parallel to Wozzeck. The type of play related to the Theater of the Absurd is sometimes labeled an "anti-play." Such works as Ionesco's *Bald Soprano* capitalize on a lack of individuality in characters, to the extent of sometimes providing them with no names. They lack a correspondence between dialogue and action, and confuse reality with hallucination. The major theme of estrangement involves people who have lived together all their lives but act as though they had never met. Much verbiage and little communication are reflected in dialogues of clichés and stereotyped phrases that serve as parodies on the lack of depth of most conversations. The Theater of the Absurd reflects an essentially tragic view of human existence. The underlying fear that no man really has the power to decide his fate stems from his feeling overwhelmed by an over organized world.

The Social Apologist

Although a dominant tendency among twentieth-century artists is to remain aloof or to condemn mass cultural processes, the apologist poses an important exception to this viewpoint. Composers in the Soviet Union have served the purposes of the national ideology without greatly compromising their artistic aims. The musical medium with its less concrete subject matter has had, in this respect, a distinct advantage. Nevertheless, painters, sculptors, and writers have not been so successful in exploring new artistic techniques while remaining within the good graces of the communist elite.

A leading Russian composer of the century, Sergei Prokofiev (1891-1953), served the national cause with consummate skill and some degree of personal satisfaction. He agreed that the composer and all other artists had a primary duty to serve the people. "He must beautify human life and defend it. He must be a citizen first and foremost, so that his art may consciously extol human life and lead man to a radiant future.

Such, as I see it, is the immutable goal of art." A student of the nine-teenth-century composer Rimsky-Korsakov, he achieved a mastery of the orchestral techniques of Romanticism.

Since Debussy, Stravinsky, and Schönberg were well known in his country by 1920, he was not insulated from contact with his contemporaries outside Russia. Prokofiev himself concertized successfully as a pianist throughout Europe and America. During the early phase of the communist revolution, he came to resent the artistic restrictions imposed upon his homeland and so left it for sixteen years. He later returned voluntarily and achieved a satisfactory measure of success among the Russian people.

Prokofiev was able to avoid producing music simply for propaganda use. Dunayevsky and Dzerzhinsky were the leaders of the social-realist stream who depended heavily upon popular songs and nineteenth-century operetta styles to achieve their desired results. The many influential com-posers of political slogans set to simple march melodies persuaded the Cen-tral Committee to brand as "Formalists" the few Soviet composers who had achieved a well-deserved international status. The accused apologized, attached a literary-political explanation to succeeding compositions, and survived the incident. Prokofiev was indebted to his country for much of his basic imagery. He based *The Sythian Suite* upon Russian history; his orchestral work, *The Steel Leap*, glorified the industrialization of the country.

As a group, the Russian composers have been the least experimental among first-rank composers of the twentieth century. Prokofiev himself declared that the form of the sonata contained all the structural elements he found necessary for his music. Lenin had loved the music of Beethoven and insisted on the continuity of classical style, which was achieved ele-gantly by Prokofiev in his *Classical* Symphony. A lyrical melody and a delicate formal balance are combined with unexpected variation in the harmony to produce a classical impression in a mildly modern harmonic idiom. The brilliant, sardonic, and highly rhythmic style of his early works tempered even the most Romantic scores, such as the ballet music for *Romeo and Juliet*. His work ranges from the epic scale of the opera *War and Peace* to the humorous fantasy of *Peter and the Wolf*, and includes even a touch of American "blues" style in the slow movement of the seventh piano sonata.

Dmitri Shostakovich (1906–   ) belongs to a slightly later group of Russian composers who have had less contact with the West. After the success of his first symphony, he was able to gain access to music that had been forbidden in the national conservatory. By 1934, his opera *Lady Macbeth of Mzensk* revealed too close a stylistic relationship to *Wozzeck* for official taste; he was censured for it by the official newspaper *Pravda*. Like Prokofiev, he accepted the criticism without protest and attached to his Seventh Symphony a program describing the heroism of the Russian people during the battle of Leningrad. Again, in 1948, a congress dominated by popular commercial writers condemned his works as being too "formalistic" and not enough in touch with the masses. Composers are fortunate in that they can often escape such criticism by providing a supposed literary meaning to all but the most experimental compositions and thereby remain within the accepted political limits. The average listener fails to note that the music would as easily illustrate any number of literal ideas. However, many gifted Russian composers who have honestly accepted their roles as spokesmen for a mass social process have contributed notable works

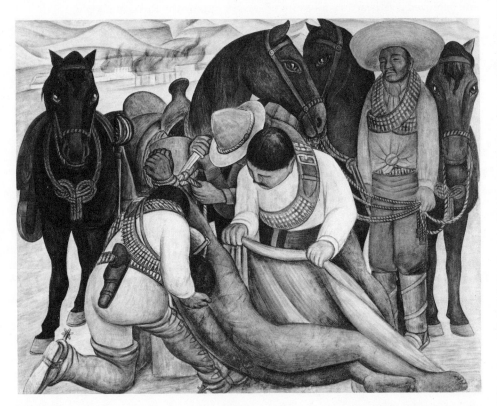

Figure 8.2 DIEGO RIVERA. *Liberation of the Peon*. Fresco, 1931. [Courtesy, Philadelphia Museum of Art Collection].

to the repertoire of twentieth-century music. The extreme individualism supported throughout much of the West has not proved to be the only worthwhile pattern of artistic life. The Association of Artists of the Revolution, which was formed in 1922, eliminated the experimental spirit that had just begun to flower in Russia; the dominant art style became a social realism descended from Courbet and his emphasis on the heroism of modern life. However, the pictorial glorification of the tractor driver and the collective farm worker have not proved to be any more artistically decadent than the politically inspired statuary in most American public parks.

In Mexico, the artists Rivera, Orozco, and Sequieras have been widely recognized as spokesmen for nationalism. Rivera's family was firmly imbedded in national revolutions in both Spain and Mexico. At the age of fourteen, he led a student revolt against the politically appointed director of the *Belles Artes* Academy. Deeply sympathetic toward the Soviet revolution, he painted a portrait of Lenin as part of a fresco in Rockefeller Center. The Rockefellers dismissed him and destroyed the picture. In a fresco for the Mexican Ministry of Education, Rivera took revenge by featuring a vicious caricature of Rockefeller, Morgan, and Ford at a champagne party admiring their financial success on an endless ticker tape. As an educator, Rivera, through strong and simple pictorial images, taught illiterate Mexican peasants the history of their land and the meaning of the agrarian reformation.

"The Liberation of the Peon" (Figure 8.2) is typical of the subject matter and human concern found in his best work. He found his artistic needs filled by a traditional technique called fresco, just as Prokofiev found his musical needs served by the sonata form. Rivera's visual forms are large, simple images reminiscent of the works of Giotto; they have the additional colorful appeal of native peasant designs. Part of the reward of the agrarian reform in Mexico was the freeing of artists and composers from the European academic conservatory tradition. Artistically speaking, they found their true language only by discovering the folk heritage of their people. Thus, a complex pattern of man in relationship to twentieth-century society emerges. The artist is seemingly nourished by the same cultural patterns he simultaneously fears will, by their very massiveness, overwhelm and crush his individuality.

THE IMPACT OF TECHNOLOGY

Patterns of Affirmation

In the twentieth century, with its concentration of industrialization in large urban centers, the focus of the arts shifted largely to the imagery of city life previously cultivated by the Impressionists. Emphasis on the dynamism of modern life and the glorification of the urban landscape constituted a period devoted to the "romance of the machine." Much of the music of the 1920 decade has failed to persist with great vigor in the orchestral repertoire; however, its singular reflection of the thinking of that period makes it worthy of mention. The Swiss composer Arthur Honegger (1892–1955) created a rather sensational glorification of the locomotive in

248   his symphonic poem *Pacific 231*. Although it was not a completely literal train portrait, he intended the piece to evoke the dynamic drive of "three hundred tons hurling itself through the night at one hundred miles an hour." Beginning with a ghostly mixture of very high and very low sounds, the piece slowly gathers a rhythmic momentum that becomes a complex tangle of sounds and then drops suddenly to a wind-like effect. A gradual increase in intensity brings the music to a climax of churning rhythms spanned by a lyrical trumpet melody. Suddenly, the momentum is lost in a long, grinding finale. A completely opposite musical description of a train is represented by Villa-Lobos's *The Little Train of the Caipira*. The eminent Brazillian composer connotes the image of a delightful little machine that a child might ride around a park. It chugs on for several musical miles through jungles of native-sounding tunes. Finally, it grinds to a screeching halt evoked by very high harmonics; a last, backfire resounds through the percussion section.

The Mexican composer Carlos Chavez (1899–   ) wrote a ballet-symphony called *HP* (Horsepower), which he described as "a symphony of sounds around us, a revue of our times." The American George Antheil (1900–1959) composed *Ballet Mécanique,* in which he pictured the "brutal, hard-boiled, super-athletic, non-sentimental" period after the 1918 armistice. He disclaimed the actual description of machinery as found in Mossolov's *Iron Foundry*. Rather, his ballet was to be a mechanistic dance of life, a tribute to mechanical beauty and a warning of the danger of machine-dominated society. He described the feeling of the piece as "streamlined, cold as interplanetary space, but also often hot as a furnace."

The American composer John Alden Carpenter (1876–1951) sought the noise of riveting machines and the cacophany of urban life for his score to the ballet *Skyscrapers*. As described in his written preface, the composition reflected the many rhythms and sounds of American life in all its aspects. For the performance of such music, the resources of the normal orchestra were expanded to include a variety of motorized sound mechanisms. One of the foremost experimentalists of the century, Edgard Varése (1885–1965), wrote *Ionization* for percussion instruments and two sirens. Without stating any program or literal image, the composer creates a powerful musical evocation of the atmosphere of the city, with its rapid pace and implied incidents of disaster interpreted by the wailing sirens. With the growing invasion of such sound creations, composers began to have some difficulty defending themselves when asked, "But is it music?" Varése preferred to call his compositions "organized sound", in order to express his concept of music as both an art and a science. The same question was being asked about the art style called Futurism. The Futurists were intrigued by the process of movement and the forces of energy. Duchamp's paintings of a nude descending the staircase are a graphic portrayal of the arresting of vision reminiscent of a time-exposure photograph. Duchamp disclaimed his work as a painting in any traditional sense, and considered its basic principles as concerns of geometry and mathematics equally. To him, the painting expressed simply "organized kinetic elements" in the movement of time and space. Such redefinitions became symptoms of twentieth-century departures from the accepted artistic philosophies of the past.

The belief in the machine as a thing of power and beauty was widely shared throughout the arts. Oscar Wilde (1854–1900) expressed his view that the Chicago waterworks, with its great revolving wheels, was the most beautifully rhythmic thing he had ever seen. He found in American machines a perfect union of strength and beauty. Carl Sandburg (1878–1967) was greatly inspired by the excitement and dynamism of city life. His "Portrait of a Motorcar" is a classic in the romance of the machine:

> It's a lean car . . . a long-legged dog of a
>   car . . . a gray-ghost eagle car.
> The feet of it eat the dirt of a road . . . the
>   wings of it eat the hills.
> Danny the driver dreams of it when he sees women in
>   red skirts and red sox in his sleep.
> It is in Danny's life and runs in the blood of
>   him . . . a lean gray-ghost car.[1]

"Subway," "Nocturne in a Deserted Brickyard," and "Prayers of Steel" articulate other feelings he had about the expressive power at the heart of the technological revolution.

In the visual arts, the image of the machine has been an intriguing motif since the advent of Turner's train in "Rain, Steam and Speed." Charles Sheeler's "American Landscape" (Figure 8.3) reveals the compelling structural clarity inherent in a large industrial complex. The industrial image was a popular motif among Russian artists before the advent of Soviet Realism.

Fernand Leger (1881–1955) was perhaps the most outstanding of the many artists who adopted images of the machine age as a basic point of visual orientation. Fascinated with mechanized warfare during World War I, he described the singular effect of guns shining in the sunlight: "During war men and things are seen in all their intensity." His postwar paintings continually featured machine parts in contrasting solid and flat shapes. The city, with its cumulative impact of flashing electric signs, comprised a long series of paintings. Even Leger's human figures were often contructed of interrelated shapes like their machine counterparts. Yet he disclaimed

---

1 From *Cornhuskers* by Carl Sandburg. Copyright 1918 by Holt, Rinehart and Winston, Inc. Copyright 1946 by Carl Sandburg. Reprinted by permission of Holt, Rinehart and Winston Inc.

250 any effort to copy the machine in an exact sense, but wished rather to invent images of it. The aim of his work was to produce a beautiful art object, just as the aim of *Pacific 231* was to provide an exciting musical experience. Leger's interest in commonplace objects, as exhibited in "Still Life with Lamps" and "The Siphon," has been revived on a massive scale in Pop Art. However, Leger did not entirely overlook the less desirable aspects of mechanization; to him, the piles of broken-down farm machinery symbolized the ruthless waste of the American consumer society.

Patterns of Rejection

Many creative artists of the twentieth century have not shared an appreciation for the power and beauty of the machine. Some have fiercely rejected the growing tendency toward mechanization as a destructive pattern leading ultimately to the dehumanization of man. In *1984*, George Orwell (1903–1950) presents the frightening picture of a society dominated to its very thought processes by a power structure based upon mechanized pro-

Figure 8.3 CHARLES SHEELER. *American Landscape.* 1930. [The Museum of Modern Art, New York].

paganda. Among the poets of the next generation, Philip Lamantia, in his "Terror Conduction," creates chains of images based upon menacing machines and faceless crowds that pass like "mechanical toys." Allen Ginsberg, in *Howl II*, calls the whole threatening complexity of modern culture "Moloch, whose mind is pure machinery . . . whose soul is electricity and banks." Sherwood Anderson (1876–1941), deeply puzzled by the machine's role in the destruction of traditional values, wondered how man could resist their cold efficiency. "They are too complex and beautiful for me. My manhood cannot stand up against them yet." The same environment of war that stimulated in Leger an interest in mechanical forms was envisioned by Stephen Spender as death by machines in his poem, "Two Armies." The machine as the dealer of destruction seems to be the real enemy rather than the men of opposing armies.

> Deep in the winter plain, two armies
> Dig their machinery, to destroy each other.
> Men freeze and hunger, no one is given leave
> On either side, except the dead, and wounded.
> These have their leave; while new battalions wait
> On time at last to bring them violent peace.
>   .   .   .
> When the machines are stilled, a common suffering
> Whitens the air with breath and makes both one
> As though these enemies slept in each other's arms . . . [2]

Some twentieth-century artists living in a society impatient with their modes of expression released their despair in the short-lived movement called Dada. The very nonsense name connoted a revulsion for all the genteel values of society with its mechanized sophistication. Dada was, in some respects, a great practical joke staged in the tradition of "happenings." On one occasion, a performance featured five people dancing in stovepipes, a sonata played on typewriters, and three poets simultaneously reading their works. The Dadists were in revolt against a world which had wrecked itself upon the misery of the First World War. Accordingly, their art rejected all conventional standards which comprised the esthetic foundations of western culture. A small core of positive meaning was nurtured by Duchamp and Picabia in their opposition to the increasingly ominous role the machines were assuming in human life. Picabia's "Daughter Born Without a Mother" is pictured as a mechanized construction, and Duchamp's "The Bride" is not the warm human companion the title indicates, but a cold, metallic monster. Frequent allusions are made to people becoming machines and machines turning into people.

2   Reprinted by permission of Faber and Faber Ltd. and Random House. The extract from "Two Armies" by Stephen Spender from *Collected Poems 1928-1935*. Copyright 1942 by Stephen Spender.

Many other creative individuals revolted against the machine age by initiating a movement to revive qualities of mind and art which exalt the intrinsic humanity of man. Such values have been found repeatedly throughout western culture in the form of Classicism, and it was to this stream of thought that many disillusioned individuals turned. Undoubtedly, some element of escapism was involved; yet at its best twentieth-century Neoclassicism was a reassertion of those typically human qualities of reason and formal dignity. It did not aim to copy the musical mannerisms or artistic images of any particular style period, but to revive certain enduring principles which had been obscured during the Romantic period.

The trend toward recovery of formal values had begun with the late works of Debussy and the paintings of Cézanne. In music pictorial effects, psychological overtones, and massive emotional evocations were eliminated in favor of a lean, spare design, which existed simply for its formal appeal. Neoclassicism represented a period of recovery after the excesses of the nihilism of Dada. The most ardent spokesman for the neoclassicist position has consistently been Igor Stravinsky (1882–   ). His statement that music is powerless to express anything outside itself reveals a significant assumption of the movement. The composer is once again considered a craftsman, rather than a semimystical figure. His concern is the material and skills of the profession; any idiom useful to their development is quite legitimate. Stravinsky's compositions thus represent a wide range of styles including a piano rag, the opera-oratorio *Oedipus Rex*, and the barbaric post-Romantic ballet *The Rite of Spring*. Stravinsky demands that the listener forego his daydreams and concentrate on the actual tonal configurations in order to receive genuine pleasure. Yet, despite this somewhat ascetic orientation, Stravinsky creates music that has profoundly expressive qualities. Also, despite his stated preference for music unrelated to any extramusical context, some of his best works have been written for the ballet or for use in conjunction with a text.

The *Symphony of Psalms* is one of the masterpieces of Stravinsky's neoclassical period. Although it is not so severely stylized as other compositions in that genre, the original inspiration was neither religious nor liturgical, but, rather, the urge to create a large work with polyphonic complexity. The psalms proved to be particularly well adapted to this musical ideal. The use of Latin was intended to achieve a sense of separation from the mundane world of associations that are mediated by a vernacular language; the choice also reflects the neoclassical orientation toward timeless, monumental forms. One of the most revealing contrasts between the Romantic and the modern spirit may be noted in the differences between the *Symphony of Psalms* and Brahms's *German Requiem*. The former is spare, masculine, and somewhat reserved in spirit, while the latter is lyric, rhapsodic, and richly emotional. The dominant feature of the *German Requiem* is soaring melody entwined in rich strands of counterpoint. The most compelling aspect of the Stravinsky work lies in its serene austerity and monumental design.

As a stylized composition, the *Symphony of Psalms* is perhaps most reminiscent of the late medieval period of the Paris motets. Most of the main themes proceed by narrow intervals typical of Gregorian chant, and even the rhythmic setting of *Laudate Dominum* maintains a chant-like flavor. The radiant clarity and pristine solemnity has the timeless appeal found in the music of Palestrina. The three continuous movements utilize portions of Psalms 38 and 39, and all of Psalm 150. In the first movement, the psalm of penitence is given long strands of choral sound suspended over an accompaniment of constantly running figures and abrupt chordal punctuations. A particularly interesting contrast is maintained between the slowly swelling voices and the rapid movement and quick tonal blows of the instrumental parts. The second movement is planned as a double fugue, which is begun by a single oboe and joined by other solo instruments in turn. After an unusually extended instrumental introduction, the voices enter with a new theme also delivered by fugal devices in a rich polyphonic web of sound. In various rhythmic disguises this basic thematic material constitutes the whole movement.

The third movement is perhaps the most impressive of all. It opens with a quietly intoned *alleluia,* and the tonal preface to the movement is summarized in a great chord on the word *Dominum.* With a gradual accumulation of rhythmic momentum and tonal excitement, the praises proceed toward a final brilliant climax. The last section of the movement is a very long coda built almost entirely upon a constantly repeated figure heard best in the soprano voices. This persistent ostinato gathers increasing psychological drive and certain ponderous inevitability as it swells to the dimension of a universal force. But true to a neoclassical preference for simplicity and restraint, Stravinsky ends the work in a quiet repetition of the initial *alleluia.* The *Symphony of Psalms* reveals much of the ingenious technique and wealth of ideas which mark its composer as one of the giants of the twentieth century.

Neoclassicism in music has an excellent counterpart in one period of the work of the artist Picasso (1881–   ). Both Stravinsky and Picasso have ultimately developed their creative processes in movements other than Neoclassicism, the former within the twelve-tone system, and the latter in abstraction. Yet Neoclassicism remains the common spiritual source to which both return at intervals for fresh inspiration. For Picasso, the initial development of classical imagery constituted a return to a system of discipline after the mannerisms and distortions of Cubism. Like Stravinsky, Picasso had no special style period from which he drew his form or tech-

254   Figure 8.4 PABLO PICASSO. From etchings of *Lysistrata: Kinesias and Myrrhine with a Child.*
[Courtesy, The Baltimore Museum of Art].

niques. Some of his classic heads seem directly inspired by Greco-Roman sculpture. The ponderous giantesses are more akin to the colossal figures of Michelangelo. The delicate line drawings are more reminiscent of the nineteenth-century works of Ingres. In the same manner, Stravinsky adapted his ballet *Pulcinella* from music by the eighteenth-century composer Pergolesi. The polyphonic wizardry of Bach is apparent in the *Octet* for wind instruments. The subject matter and imagery of ancient Greece were sources for the ballets *Apollon Musagetes* and *Orpheus.* Picasso's etchings of 1934 for a new version of Aristophanes's *Lysistrata* show the delicate calligraphy and the classical subjects typical of one aspect of his Neoclassicism (Figure 8.4).

The twentieth century has witnessed the full gamut of attitudes in reaction to mechanization and the fear of dehumanization. One of the last to develop was the satiric approach. Perhaps the humorous implications of being able to cause a case of mechanical indigestion merely by folding or stapling a punchcard have finally dawned upon modern society. The idea of poking fun at mechanical contraptions is not entirely a mid-century innovation; in 1920, the composer Darius Milhaud set to ironically lyrical music "A Catalogue of Agricultural Implements," complete with the prices. The determined optimism of Pop Art, with its extroverted, unabashed use of the means of mass production was born in the spirit of Leger. It has the same ridiculous elements as Dada. For example, Claes Oldenburg's oversized pair of trousers and a carefully arranged black plastic belt bought at a store hang over a clothes hanger. The label of this art objects reads "Giant Blue Pants." Pop Art examines the incongruities of the gap between art and life in order to come to acceptable terms with life as it is lived. The final triumph of the artistic vernacular is celebrated in the production of art which is meant to be as expendable as a paper cup. It is an impersonal art, just as twentieth-century society appears largely impersonal and apparently unmoved by public and private disasters. Whatever "art" exists in a stack of Brillo boxes, or a stuffed cloth typewriter hanging limply in its vinyl sheath, indicates a willingness to live in the mechanical, mass-production environment without regret for a lost past or fear of a grim, dehumanized future.

THE IMPACT OF SCIENCE

Patterns of Affirmation

The sweeping ideological changes that came about early in the twentieth century, radically altering even the sense of space and time, were destined to have a profound effect upon arts which use these modes of perception. New systems in mathematics gradually replaced Euclidian geometry, and Einstein's view of the universe widened that of Newton. Discoveries in the mathematical and physical sciences have precipitated a vast change in human perspective. New interpretations of the universe and man's relationship to it have shown how truly insignificant man may be as one among many entities in the evolution of life forms. The absence of ultimate conclusions even in the once-firm belief in cause and effect has created a new regard for the power of uncertainty in the natural world. The idea of universal scientific laws has been largely abandoned in dealing with fundamentals of matter. The belief in both the physical and spiritual significance and the ultimate progress of man has suffered a heavy blow.

As though in sympathetic response to the scientific revolution, the system of tonal organization codified by Rameau in the eighteenth century began to crumble before the vast technological and artistic demands of the twentieth century. Already in the music of Wagner with its wandering transitions from key to key, and that of Debussy with its wholesale use of exotic scales, the established system of harmonic relations was surpassed. Such constructs as Scriabin's "mystic chord," built-in intervals of fourths, and the upsurge of interest in medieval modes and scales used in folk music, were symptoms of the need for a more inclusive tonal vocabulary. The need was not for a complete lack of compositional norm, but for the development of a positive system of tonal relations to augment an equally positive but limited system. One notable attempt to expand the available tonal resources was made by dividing scales into smaller interval distances than those on available keyboard or wind instruments. But the use of such microtones within the traditional scale system, as practiced by American composers Hans Barth, Harry Partch, and the Mexican composer Carrillo, was not the final answer for which other composers were searching. Arnold Schönberg (1874–1951) conceived the basic principles of a new system of musical procedure known variously as twelve-tone, dodecaphonic, and serial music. He preferred to be called a constructor rather than a composer, and the stated aim of his system was comprehensibility.

The twelve-tone system was one answer to the search for a unifying principle; this was obtained by constructing all the musical material of a given composition from a basic series of pitches called a tone row. Each of the twelve tones in the octave of the western scale was used in this row without emphasis on any particular tone. This lack of orientation around a tonal center toward which other pitches eventually resolved thoroughly destroyed the traditional key relationships and established a complete freedom of progression among all the pitches of the tuning system. The sense of structure was provided by the organization of materials drawn exclusively from the tone row upon which the piece is built. Actually, such limitations are not stringent, since by mathematical calculation 479,001,600 different rows are made possible by rearranging the twelve available tones. Also the row is not used mechanically with one note of the row succeeding another in endless repetition. All of the newly developed rhythmic resources of the century are fully utilized. The row can be used backwards, upside down, on many different pitch levels, or distributed among various instrumental sound qualities. The listener is not expected to be able to sing the row after hearing the piece; he is only to be aware of a unifying idea obtained by the repetition of memorable interval relationships and thus, sometimes, motifs. In this sense, the row provides the same effect as a Wagnerian leitmotif; both fulfill the need for a perpetual variation of materials.

Schönberg's original system has been expanded by his followers to include a calculated control of rhythm, harmony, and tone quality. This total serialization has been especially useful to composers using the electronic medium in which the problem of organization is particularly acute.

As the originator of one of the most revolutionary musical concepts of the century, Schönberg experienced all the bitterness of having his contribution virtually ignored by the general public. His greatest satisfaction lay in students such as Alban Berg (1885–1935) and Anton von Webern (1883–1945), who maintained a lifelong devotion to him as a man and to his system of thought. Having matured under the spell of Wagner, he was never wholly removed from the traditional compositional practices of his time. His early string sextet, *Transfigured Night,* is a testimonial to the late Romantic style. Toward the end of his life he achieved a synthesis of the twelve-tone system and nineteenth-century musical traditions in his Piano Concerto. Schönberg's emphasis on the intellectually abstract nature of music was closely akin to Stravinsky's neoclassical ideals. Some years after the death of Schönberg, Stravinsky began using the twelve-tone system, and has produced such notable works as the *Canticum Sacrum* and the ballet *Agon* in that idiom.

The enumerated characteristics of twelve-tone music set it apart as a distinctive listening experience. Because there is no limitation as to the pitch level at which any tone in a row must be sounded, there are often gigantic leaps between pitches which the voice could not negotiate. Traditional distinctions between consonant and dissonant sounds are eliminated; all tonal combinations are equally acceptable depending on their musical context. The experience of change is graphically illustrated in the constant flux and endless variation of twelve-tone music. The repetition of themes, which provides a sense of formal progression in a conventional musical structure, is almost entirely absent. Repetitive, machine-like rhythms so characteristic of popular music are seldom in evidence. As with the neoclassical music of Stravinsky, Schönberg's idiom is predominantly polyphonic, although chordal patterns and melody with accompaniment patterns do regularly occur. Not infrequently, conventional forms are used. For all its complex harmonic and melodic texture, Berg's *Wozzeck* is composed of a long series of traditional forms, including the suite and sonata.

Twelve-tone technique unites two elements of thought which the visual arts separate into the styles of Abstraction and Expressionism. The rational aspect of the technique is akin to the principles of abstraction in the visual arts. Webern's compositional style has often been referred to as a musical counterpart of the pointillist technique used by the nineteenth-century artist Seurat. In its reduction to absolute essentials and its purity of execution, Webern's music also resembles the structured paintings of Mondrian with their sparse intersecting lines and primary colors. Only the absolute, nonobjective essentials are present in the works of both men. Both styles closely resemble architecture, which uses clear undecorated geometric shapes and undisguised construction methods and material. All these works represent the logic and sense of order that the Greeks equated with universal harmony.

As in the case of Abstract Expressionism in art, the subjective element of the twelve-tone system is its obvious alliance with Expressionism. Schönberg's statement that the greatest goal of the artist is to express himself is typical of the expressionist position. Music exists, in this viewpoint, not to portray literally some episode or objective reality, but, rather, the inner experiences of mankind through such reality. Music should give artistic shape to inner and often subconscious ideas; it should not try to capture impressions made upon the senses from without. It does not aim to imitate what nature presents to the eyes and ears.

The extramusical inspiration for the emotional content of twelve-tone music came originally from the paintings of Kandinsky, Kokoschka, and Klee, and the poetry of Stefan George, Richard Dehmel, and Georg Trakl. During one short period of his life, Schönberg had a great desire to paint in the expressionistic style and produced enough works to have an exhibition. The major impact of the style came from the condensation of feeling into a high-pitched emotional tension; in this respect the style was a strong link with the Romanticism of the past. The Romantic love for the grotesque and macabre may be directly translated into some manifestations of Expressionism, as illustrated by *Wozzeck.* The basic motivation behind the search for a new system of musical organization was the need for more powerful means of communicating emotion.

For the listener, one of the more easily comprehended examples of music with a high expressionistic content is Webern's *Six Pieces for Orchestra.* Written in 1910, before the composer adopted a thoroughgoing twelve-tone technique, these short selections illustrate the composer's intellectual and emotional synthesis, which was particularly amenable to the twelve-tone system. They are suffused with the same sense of impending disaster which characterized the expressionistic paintings reflecting the social anxiety and economic hardship surrounding the era of the First World War.

In comparison with the Romantic symphony or tone poem, each

of the *Six Pieces for Orchestra* is extremely brief, but exhibits an individual pungency that grows with repeated listening. The first is a study in contrasting textures, which seem almost impressionistic in the variety of sound effects. Yet, the melodic line soars in lyric reverie above the chaos in the strings. The general affective sense of most atonal music—the endless wandering through a kaleidoscope of sound—is particularly apparent. The sense of search, of partial disorientation, is an underlying factor in many twentieth-century works throughout the arts. The second piece begins with ominous sounds in the basses, mocking responses from brass instruments, and erratic rhythmic pulsations. The movement is full of suspense, gradual increases in tension, and a sudden chilling climax. The third piece forms a contrast with the second and features ethereal sounds high in the instrumental registers. Solo instruments seem to echo from vast spaces, and the celeste drops a last tonal rainbow.

The fourth piece begins with a clock-like chime and a pervasively despondent mood. A high whistling tone emerges, and a constantly pulsating gong marks the passage of time. There is a clear sectional change with a flute imposed over a chorus of low brasses. Suddenly, a blast of horns, chaotic rhythms, a roar of percussion, and silence leave the impression of a grim conclusion to some mysterious sequence of events. The fifth piece begins with shuddering strings and a long series of lyric melodies, which resemble a constant overlapping of vague sighs. The ending is strangely indeterminate, consisting only of a very low rumble combined with very high pitches. The last piece is conceived more melodically, with instrumental lines overlapping in a polyphonic interplay. Each solo statement is punctuated with short bursts of sound from other instruments much as a chorus functions in a Greek tragedy.

The expressionistic style exemplified by the *Six Pieces for Orchestra* has a wide and affective emotional range. It includes both the personal associations of the artist or composer and the universal experiences of mankind. The union of Expressionism and the twelve-tone system has provided the most significant musical movement during the first half of the twentieth century. Like similar revolutionary concepts in science, the synthesis has established a new framework within which to organize and to perceive the art of music.

Among the visual arts, the need for a new system of thought was evident by the time of Manet. He responded by rejecting the traditional concept of the canvas as a surface through which to perceive a three-dimensional reality. Manet returned to the ancient view of a painting as a flat surface and art as an autonomous problem of design. Cézanne reduced the concept of forms in space to the shapes of cone, cylinder, and sphere. Matisse introduced an economy of line similar to the studied simplicity of oriental painting. A pattern of thorough simplification and detailed analysis of visual forms was established which led to the development of Cubism. With Cubism, the dictum that the medium is the message is particularly true, for the chief interest of artists who work in this style is the visual medium itself. Yet the subject matter is not limited to the objective world alone but embraces the artists' own thought processes as they interact with the materials of the craft. Picasso, Kandinsky, Schönberg, Stravinsky, Eliot, and Pound all eventually reduced their inner experiences to an expressive form which encompassed both the demands of structure and a quality of feeling. In Cubism, the emphasis upon order, simplification, and a multiplicity of views which merge in new space relations is somewhat mirrored in the twelve-tone system and its manipulation of the tone row. The fragmentary perceptual experience mediated by the qualities of atonality and Cubism is captured particularly well in Webern's *Six Pieces for Orchestra.*

Even though Picasso himself defined Cubism as a process which concentrated primarily on forms, he disclaimed any purely scientific or experimental motives, declaring that a painting had an expressive life of its own. Both Picasso and Braque insisted on stressing the intuitive element of inner feeling which they believed dictated their systematic analysis of visual experience. When creative individuals representing many disciplines came together in Paris during the period between 1910 and 1925, the result was a general sharing of many stylistic innovations among all the arts. Picasso's series of studies for the painting "Les Demoiselles d'Avignon" showed a gradual abandoning of scenic elements and realistic figures and a growing emphasis upon the planes and contours of the forms themselves. The artist found the widely shared motif of Primitivism derived from African sculpture was well suited to express the quality of life characteristic of these women. The process of construction used by the cubist Juan Gris was to plan the structure and then to impose the subject matter. In a later phase of Cubism even the subject matter was not adapted from the objective world but was created entirely by the imagination of the artist. Except for the retention of geometrical clarity, the underlying purpose of this phase of Cubism merged perceptably with the aims of Expressionism. In their essentials both Cubism and the twelve-tone system represent a search for clarity and the solidity of new relationships amid the destruction of an old order of thought.

The Experimental Method

Composers have always experimented in some sense with the materials of their craft. Even Haydn reportedly said, "I experimented, but the Prince was always pleased." However, experimentation carried on in the twentieth century is somewhat more controlled and not always dedicated to a practical end; it is patterned after the same impersonal process typically carried on in scientific studies. The experimental method, while highly fruitful in scientific endeavor, has been less consistent in producing artistic results. Particularly in the realm of experimental studies it is often difficult to distinguish significant innovations from artistic departures calculated only to gain sensational publicity. Experimentation as such does not always imply some process entirely removed from a traditional musical context. Béla Bartók (1881–1945) was a leading experimentalist who remained well within western conventions. As an example of the experimental method, his children's pieces, called *Mikrokosmos* (The Little World), systematically explore the expressive potential of a single interval or rhythm. They are experiments in simplification, much as Mondrian's structured, nonobjective, cubistic paintings are experiments within a limitation of straight horizontal and vertical lines using only primary colors. Experiments do not always succeed in the arts any more than in the sciences; Picasso's "Les Demoiselles d'Avignon" remains an unfinished project because of conflicting style patterns that refused to blend. However, even Leonardo da Vinci had failures with his novel ideas on new oil substitutes for his pigments.

In addition to experiments in compositional practice, very often experiments modify or extend performance techniques. Béla Bartók's Fourth String Quartet is a veritable thesis in what can be done with four stringed instruments. Bartók was greatly influenced by folk music of his native Hungary and the mannerisms of folk musicians which were not part of the performance techniques of art music. Much of his admiration for the expressive exuberance and performance style of folk music is exhibited in the Fourth Quartet.

It begins with a series of chords made deliberately harsh by pulling the bow sharply into the strings. The very lyrical second theme is produced by sliding the fingers up and down the strings in wailing streams of sound. The second movement is played at an extremely fast tempo on muted strings so that the texture resembles an argument among ghosts. The third movement is more traditional in the use of tone color and harmony for the main effect, but it includes sharp chordal punctuations and a violin which sounds like a chirping bug. The fourth movement is a stunning dance performed entirely on plucked strings. The middle section of the movement is particularly interesting in its use of a rhythmic guitar-like strumming of the strings. The last movement has an unusual accentual pattern and a series of dissonant chords which punctuate the rhythm like great handclaps.

No consideration of experimentation is complete without mention of the American composer Charles Ives (1874-1954). One of the most astonishingly original innovators in western musical history, he employed multiple rhythms, two key systems used simultaneously, and even a twelve-tone concept he called "tone roads." Completely unrecognized by circumspect New England society, he continued to write music he never heard played. He systematically examined and often eliminated such ingrained western musical traditions as bar lines, meter signatures, and symmetrical phrasing. Ives's style was an uneven composite of folk and hymn tunes, Impressionism, and intense dissonance; it was the product of an indominable experimental spirit and a steadfast courage.

The mainstream of twentieth-century experimentation for the most part centers on the development of new tonal media, and particularly upon the use of electronic tone generators and tape recording. Composers are especially attracted to the idea of having their work in a permanent form, which is not subject to the vicissitudes of public performance. The electronic media furnish a new means of gaining ascendacy in a musical world long ruled by the performing artist. A number of attitudes underlie the increasing concentration upon electronic music. One is the desire to eliminate private feelings in favor of a completely objective style. For example, Edgard Varèse (1885–1965) stated his wish to express the imagery of an urban machine age and consider sound as a pure abstraction without traditional cultural associations. In such a viewpoint the role of the composer merges with that of the scientist, and successful composers of electronic music do indeed have strong backgrounds in science and mathematics. Yet, in the realm of feeling or mood content, the evocative quality of music produced by an electronic tone generator is strongly surrealistic and is popular as background music for science fiction productions. In such a spirit, *Le Marteau Sans Maitre* (The Hammer without a Master), by Pierre Boulez, uses the hallucinatory images of the poet Reńe Char. Although the piece is for conventional performance rather than electronic generators, it illustrates the link between traditional practices and emerging experimental sonic systems.

The first center for the production of electronic music was established shortly after 1950 in Cologne, Germany. It was shortly followed by a French research center, Radiodiffusion Francaise, and the American center at Columbia University. The French center developed *musique concrète*—a system of recording and modifying sounds gathered mainly from the urban environment. Transformations of traditional instrumental sounds, along with the tones produced by an oscillator, have all been added to the basic repertoire of sounds to be used alone, in various combinations, or even in conjunction with an instrumental ensemble. The most pressing problem for the electronic media is that of organizing the almost limitless resources of tonal range, quality, loudness, and spacing into a coherent musical experience. In this matter, the twelve-tone system has proved invaluable by providing a means for controlling all these elements in a total serialization. The German composer Stockhausen (1928–   ) has drawn from Webern's ideal of absolutely pure music exhibiting an ultimate degree of rational control that also provides the possibility of limitless variation. With the establishment of such fundamental esthetic ideals and the concurrent development of the means for their artistic transformation, the electronic movement continues to gather momentum.

A whole range of problems must be solved in order to utilize effectively each advancement made in such musical production. The traditional musical score would naturally be inadequate; to indicate the multitude of new tonal variables, charts, graphs and other useful devices from the sciences have been appropriated. Each succeeding electronic score tends to be both more detailed and more precise than its predecessors. For example, the score for Stockhausen's second electronic study is divided into three parts. The upper part contains geometrical shapes indicating pitch and timbre; the lower has a series of triangles indicating volume in decibels, and the middle indicates the duration of the sounds in terms of centimeters of tape. The score is in actuality a work sheet used to program the computer, which then produces the sounds and records them on tape. The process of composing in an electronic medium is in every respect as painstaking a task as that of traditional composition. It is additionally beset by an almost limitless choice of possibilities from which some limitations must be selected.

Iannis Xenakis, one of the younger electronic composers, has a degree in mathematics and has constructed a new organizational system based upon mathematical probability. He views even the twelve-tone system as part of the defunct world of scales, chords, and melodies. Additionally, such a system seems to him too complex to be identified with ease and understood formally in an electronic medium. Xenakis prefers to think of music as consisting of small clouds of tonal indeterminacy, which the composer must shape into forms that appeal to both mind and emotion. Since these tonal clusters are largely unpredictable, the best method of regulating them is by means of statistical probability. The very existence of such new theories for the formulation of musical experiences attests to the profound impact the electronic media have made upon the very thought processes of western culture.

In addition to its status as a factor of aural perception, music exists as an attribute of time. Thus, durational experiments in music are as logical as tonal experiments. Stockhausen's *Zeitmasse* (Tempo) for five woodwinds is based on a new concept of rhythm. The tempo is chosen in relation to the breathing capacity of the player, who must perform all of a given group of pitches in one breath. The shortest notes in the group are played as fast as that player can manage. A very flexible system of relative rhythm is thus established within a constant system of note values. Pierre Boulez eliminates the steady pulsing of regular meter familiar to jazz enthusiasts in favor of a supple rhythm that has no compulsive accent. He accordingly seats the players who perform his orchestral work *Doubles* in order to bring the tones to the ears of listeners without the usual distortion created by distance from the performing group. Electronic media are dependent upon the alterations of time produced by manipulating the normal time span of sounds into highly condensed or lengthened variants. Also, music that is improvised by more than one person (aleatory music) has the problem of temporal coordination to a high degree. Good performances under such conditions result from great sensitivity to the activity of other players and to the logical necessities of the musical materials.

Music also exists partly in space; in a limited sense, the popular stereophonic sound is an experiment in the spatial elements of tone. Henry Brant (1913–   ) is a foremost experimenter in the directional distribution of music. By dividing performers into groups gathered in separate locations and giving each group different rhythms, tempos, and harmony, he may obtain a great sonic variety. In the same manner, the Brussels World's Fair featured a fantasy of light, color, and sound created by Varèse and the architect Le Corbusier in order to celebrate the electronic age. The resulting *Poem Electronique* was played in distributed sounds over some 400 loudspeakers adjusted to create an almost physical sense of spatial dimension. Experiments have even been designed to enhance the visual element of a musical performance. In Mauricio Kagel's *Match*, a contest between two cellists is refereed by a percussionist. The musical score consists simply of stage instructions, according to which the performers display their technique, shout at each other, or merely sit, quietly dozing. The percussionist engages in some futile exercises on his collection of instruments and, finally, blows a whistle to end it all. Despite some possibly ridiculous aspects, the experimental urge is deeply rooted in the texture of twentieth-century life and is basic to the methods by which much knowledge is acquired. Indeed, some of the vast number of experimental enterprises have already opened the way toward even newer realms of artistic realization.

As a primary feature of the visual arts of the twentieth century, experimentation has resulted in art objects which alter the sense of visual perception. The movement called Op Art unites experimental psychology with basic design. Its primary subject matter is neither the exterior world nor the inner vision, but, rather, the act of seeing. The debt owed to scientific theories of perception is reflected in many titles of Op Art paintings: "Physichromie Number 116," "Optical Variations," "Kinetic Structure," and "Black Moving Planes XIX" (Figure 8.5). Many paintings exhibit a close relationship to mechanical patterns or scientific diagrams. A pioneer experimentalist, Josef Albers, based his paintings on the inter-action of colors placed in a relationship bounded by simple forms. His art represents a systematic exploration of the interaction of color and vision. The eye is often stimulated to provide a complimentary after-image, to soften hard edges, and to experience a rhythmic recurrence of luminous shapes. His black and white paintings often deal with optical illusion and employ small geometric units known in science as periodic

Figure 8.5   JEAN PIERRE VASARELY-YVARAL. *Acceleration No. 19, Series B.* [Courtesy, The Museum of Modern Art, New York].

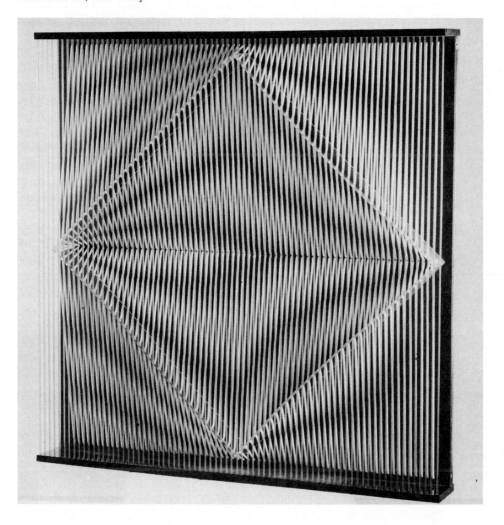

structures. The persistently repeated lines seem to transmit a sense of movement on a static surface. Albers's engravings on plastic use interrelated geometric shapes, which seem alternately to recede and advance.

At the extreme of visual perception, Minimal Art seemingly presents nothing more than a plain monochromatic surface. Only a penetrating study reveals the almost nonexistent planes of contrasting hue lying just under that surface. Minimal Art is based upon an esthetic of pure contemplation, which is as well controlled as an electronic score. Both leave nothing to chance and invade the limits of perception. In its more objective, experimental aspects even Psychedelic Art may be regarded as a study of perceptual overloading. It sometimes aims not merely to connote sensory derangement but to create its very conditions. The visual arts thus seem to be torn between the pure, rational traditions of science and the unstructured conditions of the emotional and sensory life.

Like music, the visual arts have been subjected to radical alterations of space. The sculptor Calder (1898–) creates mobiles that define their own constantly varying spatial dimensions as they move. The sculptor Henry Moore (1898–) uses the holes in his figures to create a heightened impression of the thickness and texture of his construct. Nicholas Schoffer creates kinetic machine sculpture that reflects patterns of projected light. Because these patterns are infinitely variable, Schoffer believes he has added the element of time to an art which has always existed only in space. The mixture of musician and scientist found in electronic music has a parallel in Nam June Paik, who is both artist and television technician and produces his works by electrical impulses projected upon a color television screen.

The controlled heightening of one aspect of an art to explore its particular influence has been realized in literature as well. The French poet Mallarmé (1842–1898) was interested, above all, in the sound of words, or what he described as their "music." In his late works, Mallarmé also experimented with the expressive potential of the typographical arrangement of words. In his poem "Un Coup de Dés" (1898) the words are so arranged on the page as to express visually his train of thought. Each dominant theme appears in a constrasting type size surrounded by close modifiers of its meaning, and the work makes its impact as a visual unit rather than as a line-by-line sequence.

Ezra Pound (1885–), in his Cantos, used a mixture of languages to emphasize the untranslatable mystery of poetic meaning. His Chinese ideograms, with their pictorial origins, presented ideas as images rather than as verbal abstractions. Poets such as Gertrude Stein (1874–1946) experimented with the elements of sound, as in her famous line "a rose is a rose is a rose." Many others have sprung from the spirit of Mallarmé. The poetry of e. e. cummings (1894–1962) reflects his training as an artist because of a reliance on visual effect for the perception of meaning. An example from the series "No Thanks" cannot be read aloud, as the very way in which it is seen upon the page captures the image and sudden, erratic movement of the grasshopper it describes.

<pre>
                    r-p-o-p-h-e-s-s-a-g-r
              who
      a)s w(e loo)k
      upnowgath
              PPEGORHRASS
                              eringint(o-
      aThe):1
              eA
                 !p:
  S   a
                      (r
      rIvInG   .gRrEaPsPhOs)
                                    to
      rea(be)rran(com)gi(e)ngly
      ,grasshopper;   3
</pre>

Patterns of Rejection

In the wake of increased knowledge of the world and an increased emphasis upon experimental and scientific thought in the arts, there has evolved an attitude generally termed antiintellectualism. Some artistic representatives of this attitude seem to reject the mind altogether, in opposition to the overwhelming emphasis in modern culture upon either intellectual or materialistic values. However, representatives of a more moderate approach assert simply that man is largely at the mercy of irrational forces in himself and the universe. They do not deny rational processes, but simply distrust the existence of reason as a dominating force in human affairs. In his book *African Genesis*, Robert Ardry conceives the mind as free only in the sense that it witnesses the continual battle of instincts going on inside all men. The antiintellectual attitude looks upon the doctrine of the perfectability of man as at least questionable.

Scattered evidences of antiintellectualism may be found in a number of art media. The primitivism in John Steinbeck's *The Grapes of Wrath*, Stravinsky's *Rite of Spring*, and Picasso's "Les Demoiselles d'Avignon" is a prime example of rational resentment. Thomas Hardy's scientific determinism and Theodore Dreiser's definition of man as a "chemism" reflect a negation of intellectual infallability. The last lines of the poem by Robinson Jeffers, called "Apology for Bad Dreams," exhibit in another way the essence of the ideology:

> I have seen these ways of God: I know of no reason
> For fire and change and torture and the old returnings.
> He being sufficient might be still. I think they admit
>   no reason; they are the ways of my love.
> Unmeasured power, incredible passion, enormous craft:
>   no thought apparent but burns darkly
> Smothered with its own smoke in the human brain-vault:
>   no thought outside: a certain measure in phenomena:
> The fountains of the boiling stars, the flowers on the
>   foreland, the ever-returning roses of dawn.[4]

As a less intense manifestation of antiintellectualism, the concept of indeterminacy has led to a growing emphasis upon chance as part of the artistic process. The attraction of sheer coincidence has been strong in modern art; it was early exemplified in the nihilism of Dada. Dada theory was that the world is essentially irrational and that art is part of the cult of the absurd. The theory has supported a number of practices such as the use of found or ready-made materials in virtually every conceivable natural or manufactured form. The construction by Duchamp, entitled "Why Not Sneeze, Rose Selavy?" consisted of a small bird cage filled with marble blocks, wood, a thermometer, and a cuttlebone. Picasso's head of a bull made with the combination of a bicycle seat and handle bars was a clever visual pun of the same derivation. Kurt Schwitters took the collage technique of Picasso and Braque a step further in his "trash pictures"—combinations of wood, wire, paper, buttons, and anything else he found suitable to create a balanced design (Figure 8.6). While the nihilism of the Dadaist movement passed with time, the attraction of chance as a possible element in a more profound art persisted.

Action painting, which utilizes the direction and force of paint hitting the canvas, has more control than its appearance might indicate; yet the process includes a high degree of chance. Jackson Pollock (1912–1956) spoke of his work in this medium as the exertion of his will over potentially wild forces. He also admitted losing control occasionally and producing a mess rather than the delicately brilliant screen of color that he intended. The Pop Art movement has firmly embedded change in the mainstream of its development; such artists as Jasper Johns have insisted that even mundane objects can assume a relationship that is esthetically rewarding to contemplate. The partly theatrical, partly artistic "happening" is another product of a penchant for the unplanned.

---

4 Copyright 1925 and renewed 1953 by Robinson Jeffers. Reprinted from *The Selected Poetry of Robinson Jeffers* by permission of Random House.

Figure 8.6   KURT SCHWITTERS. *Syng Ring of a Poet.* [Lords Gallery, London].

The Art of Assemblage exhibition held in 1961 at the Museum of Modern Art summarized a long standing fascination of sculptors for the manufactured commercialism of the environment. Some mechanical assemblages featured electric motors that enabled their collection of hardware and springs to move about. Jean Tinguely calls his sculpture "antimachines" because they are constantly on the verge of a breakdown. In a flight of rare insight and a touch of horror, his assemblage, called "Homage to New York," was designed to destroy itself upon being set into motion. Like American society, it carried on an internal mechanical warfare but refused to fall apart. Tinguely does not design his assemblages to be efficient, but to be surprising; even he is not quite sure what they might do.

Perhaps the leading exponent of music based on chance is John Cage (1912–   ), who has conducted a number of performances with the dancer and choreographer Merce Cunningham. One of their joint endeavors featured a dance to the accompaniment of radios switching rapidly from one station to another, interspersed by recorded excerpts of music, news broadcasts, and reception interference noises. The underlying assertion, that art can be created by chance mixtures of noise, silence, and movement, is one evidence of the great distance between contemporary esthetics and that of the past. The work of John Cage is in diametrical opposition to the ideal of total control of elements as provided by the twelve-tone system. One of his compositions for piano directs the performer to drop the pages of the score and to play the compositions in the random order in which the pages are picked up. At the esthetic extreme, total chance may be used by obtaining the shape of a melody line from accidental imperfections in a sheet of paper and the durations of tones from coin throws. As long as the quality of indeterminacy continues to be particularly basic to twentieth-century life chance as an esthetic element may well persist as an artistic description of the age.

THE EXPLORATION OF THE MIND

One of the most significant influences upon modern arts has come from new concepts of the mind introduced by Freud and Jung. Virtually all the arts have been caught to some degree in this stream of thought which has pervaded such disparate styles as Cubism, Expressionism, and Neoclassicism. The work of Freud summarized the subjectivism intrinsic to Romanticism. Modern subjectivity was rooted in the artistic philosophy of Impressionists and Symbolists before the turn of the century. To them, the work of art was the symbol of their own inner life and emotions. Their fundamental dependance upon intuition or subconscious guidance in the creative process has been strongly maintained. Moreover, artists synthesized their visual representation of personal symbols and associations into universal archetypes. The archetype is a broadly shared symbol that represents an emotional state or a physical and mental reality. Such generally recognized symbolic meanings have been adopted as a major resource for communication in the visual arts. Perhaps the clearest statement of the impact of the analysis of consciousness upon the arts can be found in the movement called Surrealism. Its fundamental aim is to open the realm of the imagination and reveal the psychic life hidden under a practical, objective mental façade. The very term "Surrealism" implies a unity of dream and actuality within a deeper realm of awareness. However, it is not synonymous with irrationality, as the intent is an objective exploration of the contents of the unconscious in order to develop additional levels of perception. Since awareness of the undirected mechanisms of mentality is most acute in the dream state, many products of the surrealist style resemble dreams. To express such disembodied meaning the artist resorts to a personal iconography of visual symbols which he believes will be recognizable to the viewer simply because human beings tend to share similar unconscious associations.

The realm of the unconscious has been explored in various ways in most arts. The surrealist painter Salvador Dali (1904–   ) believes his role is to portray the inner world as faithfully and in as precise detail as the Late Gothic painters portrayed the exterior world. Kandinsky retained a formal impression in his Abstract Expressionist work, but rejected the necessity of copying any forms of reality literally. Even Picasso in his Cubist period transformed actually perceived objects into the forms of his artistic imagery. Giorgio de Chirico (1888–   ) based many of his early pictures upon the agony of his own mental disturbances, and Marc Chagall (1887–   ) memorialized forever the piquant delights of his Russian childhood. The Spaniard Joan Miró (1893–   ) represents the fullest development of a nonobjective Surrealism dedicated to an unorthodox world of imaginary creatures painted in vibrant primary colors.

Of all those who have benefited from the surrealist philosophy, Paul Klee (1879–1940) was perhaps the most articulate about his intentions and the dominant interests that formed his style. He was constantly aware of the objective world and never wholly abandoned observed reality for a realm of subjective pictorial symbols. His *Pedagogical Sketchbook* often refers to biological and mathematical propositions that are used to explain artistic ideas; yet he uses the principles in an intuitive, almost metaphysical manner. Klee conceived pure line as the main key to the subconscious, unpremeditated responses that attracted him as an artist. He was especially interested in the art of children because it is spontaneous and unaffected by social convention. He believed the art of the mentally deranged revealed universal elementary human imaginative processes. Yet to his own art, based on geometric abstraction and childlike images, he added a complex and personal symbolic range (Figure 8.7). An almost mystical meaning may often be sensed in addition to the rather simple surface presentation of his forms. His works sometimes resemble psychological puzzles, and the titles are extremely important in revealing a secondary level of meaning.

Although they represent different aspects of twentieth-century thought, Klee was perhaps best exemplified in music by Bartók, whose *Mikrokosmos* pieces deal in a highly sophisticated manner with the imagery

Figure 8.7   PAUL KLEE. *Bird-Drama*, 93. 1920. [Courtesy, Solomon R. Guggenheim Museum].

of childhood. Like Klee, Bartók was a composite of the most formal and abstract propensities which he coupled with the imaginative freshness characteristic of children. He also maintained an objective, almost scientific frame of reference and studied variant versions of folk songs with the particularity of a scholar. Even Klee's use of symbolic meanings concealed beneath an innocent exterior had some parallel in Bartók's works such as *Bluebeard's Castle, The Wooden Prince,* and *The Miraculous Mandarin.* All use a fairy tale as the basic framework. However in *Bluebeard's Castle,* the tormented Bluebeard, his imprisoned wives, and the mysterious doors represent much more intense psychological complexities than the simple fairy tale structure might indicate.

Surrealism is not a description easily applied to music without an accompanying text; yet it can be more than a literary convention. Even a neoclassical work such as Prokofiev's *Classical* Symphony resembles in one sense the type of Surrealism practiced by Dali. Although the basic style is traditional, unexpected alterations occur either in the tonal system or in overlapping visual images that give the resulting works a slightly dream-quality effect. Erik Satie (1866–1925) was the most notable early composer of music in a surrealistic vein, but his effects were dependent largely upon stage action or the incongruence of his titles. *Three Pieces in the Shape of a Pear* and *Three Flabby Preludes for a Dog* are the titles for two sets of skillful but not highly erratic pieces for piano. His ballet *Parade* features such puzzling activity as a Chinese gentlemen finding an egg in his pigtail, eating it, and having it appear again in the toe of his shoe. He subsequently spits fire and burns himself. The music simply intensifies the quality of the characters and action. It is scored for a conventional dance band, although Satie yearned to include a battery of noise makers such as compressed air, sirens, typewriters, and a propeller.

Such direct alliances with the spirit of Surrealism that can be found in music are best exemplified by the expressionist element in atonal music. Schönberg's *Erwartung* (Expectation)—a monodrama in one act—has been described as the first Freudian music drama. It consists entirely of an interior monologue, which antedates the use of this literary device in Joyce's *Ulysses*. The only stage action is the entrance and exit of the solitary character.

> The plot is slowly formed by the memory associations of a frightened woman who stands on the edge of a forest that symbolizes her psychological morass. She is searching for a man within those woods, and finally gathers the courage to go in among the trees. As the scenes unfold the woman sinks deeper into her trauma and links the woods with the garden in which she remembers the man. The listeners gradually become aware that the motivating force behind the entire sequence of events is the woman's guilt. The audience is in the position of a psychiatrist listening to a ghastly tale of jealousy and revenge. At last, the woman stumbles over the man's body and speaks irrationally to him while the orchestra concludes the work with an ominous rumble of strings.
>
> The music is perfectly related to the erratic kaleidoscope of emotional states represented in the stage action. *Erwartung* introduced a range of vocalization from actual speech to pure song. This later gave *Wozzeck* much of its expressive power. The orchestration is composed of a feast of tonal textures from the dream-like soarings of the strings and celeste to shattering dissonance and violent rhythmic turmoil. The sense of form is particularly noticeable in the repeated bass patterns (ostinato), which hold some long sections together. *Erwartung* is the nearest musical exemplar of "stream-of-consciousness" writing.

Schönberg's *Pierrot Lunaire* is based on poems by Albert Giraud, unified only by a focus on certain stable images. Pierrot, the traditional lover, is moonstruck and, therefore, his growing madness, the white flowers, the pale of sickness, the Madonna as a feminine symbol, and his own doomed love are all eventually symbolized by the moon. Secondary themes of night, death, violence, and displacement additionally overlap in increasingly illogical associations. His *Die Glücklich Hand* (The Golden Touch) is full of symbolic autobiographical references. The main character is Schönberg, in the same way that Dedalus is James Joyce. He is tempted by Woman, who symbolizes success. But she is stolen by a composer of popular tunes. Life becomes a cycle of ecstasy and grief in the grip of the monster, symbolic of his ego.

The music is united with every utterance and action on stage through complex tonal symbols that are functionally akin to the Wagnerian leitmotif. There are even directions in the score for lighting effects to heighten the psychological impact of the drama. A great deal of the music of Schönberg, Berg, and Webern uses a text that serves to make certain symbolic meanings more explicit. They greatly preferred the works of the symbolist poets because of the rich images of the subjective life. The poet Stefan George reflected his apprehension of the cultural decay of Germany amid the prosperity of the Bismarck regime in a poem set to music by Webern:

> Escape on gentle wings
> intoxicating ideas,
> so there will be less regret for your flight.
> Watch this whirl of light-blond mystic powers
> and frenzied fervor unfold—without being charmed.
> So that not sweet rapture will envelop you
> with new sorrow.
> Let quiet mourning fill this spring.[5]

The principle aim of all art styles based upon the contents and manipulations of the mind is to free the imagination from the demands of premeditated or reflective logic. Nowhere is this aim better fulfilled than in the improvisational practices of jazz. The basic form of jazz is a simple pattern made of a few chords, a pervasive four-beat rhythm, and a singable tune. This very simplicity is responsible for its widespread popularity; nor has it proved unattractive to more select audiences who have found an intellectual dimension in the jazz vocabulary. The jazz idiom represents a vast divergence of performance practices ranging from the elementary emotional expression of rock and roll to the imaginative subtlety of cool jazz styles. The written score remains only a skeletal representation of what actually transpires, since jazz is primarily a performer's art in which the creator and executor are one. The process of improvisation gives an immediacy to the resulting musical expression seldom heard in more traditional musical styles. The improvised cadenza in Liszt's second *Hungarian Rhapsody* and

---

5 Werner Striedieck trans. *Stefan George Werke* (2 vols.) (Düsseldorf and Munich: Verlag Helmut Küpper vormals Georg Bondi, 1969).

the continuing tradition of improvisation among organists represent the last frontiers of a once vital musical practice. With the impact of the scientific study of the mind, spontaneous products of mental operations have again become respected elements in the artistic mainstream.

Traditional musical notation systems cannot accurately convey the swing of a beat, unorthodox rhythms, brass smears, the distortion of blues tonality, and the throb of syncopation. But fortunately the advent of the tape recorder has been a boon to the preservation of such sounds. Whether the form is a blues lament, a ballad that swings, or rock and roll, it is the artist's spontaneous combination of manipulative skill and musical vocabulary which gives jazz a permanent status among the arts. What may seem like tonal chaos to the impatient ear is this virtuosic talent for shaking off the basic stereotype of the musical framework by subtle alteration of musical components.

Jazz was born of historically dissimilar ingredients, including the European scale mixed with an African pentatonic modal pattern, and producing half-flatted tones on some pitches. A traditional dance rhythm, along with the basic four-beat group, became infused with the unexpected thuds of the African drummer, producing a lilting, syncopated rhythm. The result is a music in which movement and unrest are characteristic features. Many legendary figures helped to form variants of the jazz vocabulary. The early Dixieland beginnings and the Big Band era were summary points of the style. Dizzie Gillespie exploited simple onomatopoetic rhythms basic to the bop sound. Charlie Parker included the simultaneous use of several tonalities to vary the somewhat dull harmonic repetitions that comprised the repeated bass figures of such styles as boogie woogie.

Louis Armstrong was one of the first to paraphrase the original melody with subtle tonal and rhythmic distortions and give emphasis to the individual soloist as distinct from the effect of the total group. Duke Ellington added the resources of a big band, recovering something remotely akin to the *concerto grosso* and giving a richer tonal color to the dialogue between soloist and ensemble. Group improvisation in jazz depends upon the ability of each player to develop his individual manner of varying the basic melodic-harmonic framework without conflicting with the concurrent expressions of others. A regular protocol is observed in yielding dominant solo positions, while preserving a consistent sound texture. Gerry Mulligan was followed by Dave Brubeck in the development of the "cool" approach, which incorporated polyphonic practices and transformed the percussive beat into a more subtly pervasive structural element.

Jazz also reflects the influence of fundamental cultural characteristics which have pervaded all the arts. Exotic sound effects have been cultivated by the use of nonwestern instruments patterned after Afro-Cuban and Afro-Brazilian practices. Gourd rattles, bongo drums, and marimbas are used along with the dance rhythms of South America and the West Indies.

American West Coast jazz has included various scale devices and instrumental sounds reminiscent of Oriental, Arabic, and Hindu music. Soul jazz has returned to the religious roots of the style in a more openly expressed emotional manner in contrast with the intellectual emphasis of cool jazz. Third Stream jazz has attempted to utilize techniques from concert music and to combine jazz groups within the context of the traditional orchestral ensemble. Dave Brubeck's *Dialogues* for jazz combo and orchestra represent an experimental interchange between two rather distinctive musical esthetics. Jazz has also found a place within the liturgy of the institutional church where it has been used in an attempt to correlate worship practices with modern modes of expression.

Regardless of the particular brand of jazz he practices, each artist follows his own intuitive path. In some groups, no formal limits are defined; each man plays to the dictates of his own inner logic. The performer is confronted by a vast range of possibilities, and his success is determined by the originality of his selection and his ability to realize the fullest potential of his musical material.

The combination of momentary inspiration with great technical proficiency has had a growing influence outside the jazz medium. Stockhausen, Morton Feldman, and Earle Brown represent a number of composers who have tried to restore improvisational freedom to the concert pianist. They have given him scores that have only the raw materials of a composition contained in a few phrases and written in no particular order. The performer plays these snatches in whatever combination his fancy dictates, expanding upon their implications for a limited number of repetitions. In the visual arts, Kandinsky created paintings he called improvisations because they were largely spontaneous and expressed some inner impulse. Those works he called compositions were products of careful revision in which consciousness of purpose played the leading role. Improvisation has never been a lost practice in the theater from the era of the Greek dithyramb through the *Commedia dell 'Arte* to the silent film. However, modern interest in the imaginative contents of the mind has given the art of improvisation a new status in the general culture.

TRADITIONALISM

Even in the most changeable eras, when experimentation and novelty seem to run rampant, there are composers who do not wish to escape the claims of traditional musical practices. Nor are these people minor figures who simply lack the imagination to adapt to new circumstances. Composers who combine twentieth-century style with traditional forms and skills serve as a valuable force of stability in a society caught between the extremes of exhausted Romanticism and visionary experimental projects. These composers most readily find an audience willing to listen without demanding consistently familiar aural experiences or overwhelming sensory stimulation. Composers who support the social realist ideology and those devoted to the neoclassical movement might also be considered among the forces of stability. In addition, composers representing many national traditions have contributed significantly to the traditional continuity in twentieth-century culture.

One of the most illustrious musical minds was possessed by the Englishman Ralph Vaughan Williams (1872–1958), who was quite content to remain outside the radical movements led by Schönberg, Stravinsky, and the electronic experimentalists. He maintained a remarkable tenacity to his own ways of thinking and to English historical styles. He completely opposed the scientific definition of music as organized sound patterns. He also rejected a too literary or programmatic approach. For him, music existed to communicate a moral, spiritual, or emotional experience deeply felt and convincingly formulated. He believed that the love of one's country, its language, customs, and religion were necessary to any nation's health and artistic well-being. His own love of England was reflected in such diverse works as *Five Tudor Portraits*, an opera, *The Pilgrim's Progress*, film music for *Scott of the Antarctic*, and *A Thanksgiving for Victory* broadcast on the occasion of the German surrender in World War II. He collected virtually a thesaurus of the finest hymn tunes in the western world for his edition of the *English Hymnal*, and thus heralded an international revival of interest in the historic styles of religious music. The hymnal particularly reflected his love for the folk heritage of his nation and coincided with an international movement for recording and comparing the indigenous songs of many peoples. He meant his music to reflect the whole life of the community and saw no reason for originality just for originality's sake. He committed the composer to finding the exact means necessary to his expressive task, even if those means have been used many times before.

The *London* Symphony written in 1920 is illustrative of Vaughan Williams's technical facility and his use of the musical idioms of his nation. Originally conceived as a tone poem, the work reveals the difficulty involved in adapting folk materials to the requirements of a long and complex symphonic form. The very beginning retains much of the feeling of a tone poem with its image of London fog gradually lifting over a sea of strings. Through the gentle ebb of tones, the chimes of Big Ben are heard from the harp and clarinets. Then, in a great surge of sound, the whole city seems to come to life with a bold fanfare of brass instruments. A procession of energetic themes follow; yet the form retains the protracted development characteristic of Romanticism. The gentle tonal swells are both familiar and awesome echoes of a past era. The introduction is climaxed by a series of parallel chords full of dramatic suspense, from which emerges a musical texture as dense and full of movement as the traffic on a London street. The depth of sonority evokes great canyons of sound range, while the complex underlying polyphony is carried upon a tide of lyricism reminiscent of Brahms. A martial flourish in the brasses introduces a gay folk tune that evolves into a brass band style of presentation. The composer follows the traditional sonata form and repeats the dramatic sliding chords heard at the end of the introduction to mark the beginning of the development section.

The development is a vast tapestry of themes overlapping and moving through many tonal centers. In an unusual textural break, a solo cello and harp initiate a warm, lyrical section of rare intimacy as a contrast with the full orchestral sound of the rest of the movement. From this nucleus, Vaughan Williams weaves the main theme into long, plaintive strands of tonal fabric. Again, the great chordal slides announce the recapitulation, which is somewhat condensed in order to develop the ideas further in a polyphonic section. The long brilliant coda completes the movement, which ends with the familiar brass fanfare used continuously to separate the sections.

The next movement is slow in the traditional pattern of symphonic second movements. It features a poignant folksong treated with a blend of archaic mode and Romantic orchestral style. An excellent example of Vaughan Williams's ability to give the simplest tune a monumental depth and radiance, the movement does not overwhelm its homely origin. Even when the music builds to a great sweep of orchestral sound, the pungent archaisms add a quality foreign to the Romantic chromaticisms of the nineteenth century.

The third movement begins with a flourish of trills and boils along in a rollicking scherzo composed of a number of tune fragments as though heard while passing through the London streets at night. The rhythmic impulse of the main theme is passed about in a patter of instrumental voices that descend to the bottom of the orchestral tonal range. Suddenly, a rush of windy sound, for all the world like a harmonica, wavers about in an off-key tune, forming a humorous sectional break before the return of the persistent rhythm of the main theme. There is a lapse into a quiet mood, and the movement trails off indecisively.

The last movement is again in traditional sonata form and is built upon one main theme used in various guises. It begins with a great surge of surprisingly dissonant sounds out of which emerges the stately main theme. This memorable tune is a veritable marching panorama of English life clothed in a noble rhythmic dignity. Long scale runs in the strings lead it up to increasingly higher levels of intensity. The development section concentrates almost entirely upon the rhythmic motif constantly repeated in different instrumental colors and tonalities; the recapitulation adds a new lyrical sweep and a dramatic restatement in the low brasses. A final climax is punctuated by a brilliant percussive stroke, and the whole edifice of sound seems to run slowly down. The soft chimes of Big Ben begin a long coda, which seemingly goes backward in effect until London sinks away in a deep tonal mist. The *London* Symphony is a vast love song to a people and the values that have sustained them through the centuries.

England can claim perhaps as many illustrious musicians in the twentieth century as she could during the High Renaissance. They include Gustav Holst, Benjamin Britten, Sir Edward Elgar, Frederick Delius, Sir William Walton, and Michael Tippett. America can present a long list of major and minor figures engaged in every sort of musical movement. Beginning with the great experimentalist Charles Ives, such men as Aaron Copland, Roy Harris, Douglas Moore, Walter Piston, William Schuman, Virgil Thomson, Samuel Barber, George Gershwin, Leonard Bernstein, Roger Sessions, and Elliott Carter have become internationally known.

Born in Brooklyn as the son of a Russian-Jewish immigrant, Aaron Copland grew to share Vaughan Williams's aim of reflecting the cultural consciousness of his parents' adopted homeland. As a writer, teacher, conductor, and performer he found the nation willing to support his endeavors; he in turn made progress in gaining acceptance for new music through performances in concerts and festivals. He adopted American idioms of jazz and cowboy tunes as easily as Vaughan Williams adopted the English folk song. Music for him became a compound of everything man is, reflected in his feelings, perception, and imagination. Copland has produced some singularly austere and complex music, but has steadily grown toward an idiom well related to a fundamental American heritage in all its variety. The film score for *Our Town*, the ballet scores for *Billy the Kid, Rodeo,* and *Appalachian Spring,* an opera *The Tender Land,* and *A Lincoln Portrait* all draw from the experience and imagery of the American people. He has the rare musical stability that enables him to draw even on twelve-tone techniques without overshadowing his unique style.

Among his most popular works is the modern tone poem "*El Salón México*," which he described as a musical souvenir of his trip to Mexico. It is a tourist piece based on themes connected in his mind with a popular dance hall in Mexico City called Salón México. No attempt is made to reflect the deep historical aspects of the nation; it is simply an honest reflection of the composer's own aural experiences. The piece captures not simply the tunes, but the impression of the dance and the spirit of the people there. However, the tunes themselves are not Americanized popular songs but are taken from scholarly collections of folk tunes.

The introduction, with its flourish of cymbals and strongly accented rhythms, subsides into a trumpet theme ornamented by one grandiose trill. It soars over a sluggish and slightly off-key accompaniment. All of the themes chosen were planned to alternate this langorous singing quality with a bright, rhythmically accented motif. The form is held together more by this contrast in spirit than by extensive literal repetition. The second important theme has a low reedy sound with rhythmic halts and spurts also set in a quiet, nocturnal mood. A short transition to the bright, lyrical version of that same tune forms a contrast in its use of the same thematic material. The development section that follows is highly rhythmic and exceedingly dense in texture with tunes against tunes punctuated by the rhythmic motto of the introduction. The development is interrupted quite suddenly by a clarinet soliloquy sounding a langorous variation of the second theme. After a transition, the section builds to a brilliant tune, climaxed by a long-memorable clarinet slide. It is full of cross-accents and rhythmic patterns moving against or in distortion of the main metric pulse. It concludes with a tune characterized by a drum crash and a moment of silence. The recapitulation is a slow variation on the theme of the introduction. Previously heard tunes are presented in new arrangements that are interspersed with a constant influx of new themes. The entire piece concludes with an exhibit of the sort of brilliant tonal audacity so characteristic of Mexican brass ensembles.

The nationalism so common to Romanticism became a more stable tool of inspiration in the hands of composers whose emphasis on twentieth-century techniques relies upon their native musical heritages. Bartók filled his music with the folk melodies and rhythms of Hungary; his *Hungarian Peasant Songs* and *Romanian Dances* are an interesting contrast with the *Hungarian Dances* of Franz Liszt. Bartók recorded and studied the songs of the people in the places where they lived, whereas Liszt merely borrowed tunes from gypsy entertainers and turned them into grandiose technical displays. Bartók was content to leave the elements of the folk music largely unaltered; he simply used his skill to arrange them into expressive combinations. His rhythmic genius drew heavily from the accentual impulses of Hungarian dances and refined them into an extremely sophisticated form. Bartók ranged widely, from the almost atonal melody that begins the *Music for String Instruments, Percussion, and Celeste* to the tonal opulence of the *Concerto for Orchestra.* With his vast technical facility, he reconciled almost all the dominant movements of the twentieth century, while remaining within a national heritage and a formal tradition.

Heitor Villa-Lobos (1887–1959) rose to be the leading composer of South America. He employed much of his Brazilian cultural heritage in his works. Perhaps his greatest contribution was the series of music texts he wrote for the public school system. Like Bartók, he refused to make the Brazilian idiom conform to European traditional forms or styles but let it exhibit its own somewhat improvisational patterns. His *Bachianas Brasileiras* series represents the stylistic mixture of his thought. These pieces are dedicated to the spirit of Bach, and yet are replete with the imagery and tonal resources of Brazil. Carlos Chavez (1899–   ) has been the leading composer of Mexico. He revolted against the European conservatory tradition in which all artists were trained. He revived interest in the musical instruments of the Aztec and Mayan peoples and amalgamated these ancient elements into his ballet *The Four Suns.* In his *Sinfonia India,* Indian drums and various ancient rattles and cymbals were included in the standard orchestra. Both Villa-Lobos and Chavez were never insulated from international developments in music and the arts; they were simply able to absorb such influences without loss of their own cultural impetus.

Forces of stability have been quite evident in other twentieth-century art forms. Some major poets such as Frost, Auden, and Dylan Thomas are decidedly rooted either in forms or styles of expression related to the previous century. The poetry of Dylan Thomas is spiritually identified with the soaring lyricism of the Welsh bard; yet the tone of voice is distincly modern. Frost's much quoted poems, "After Apple Picking" and "Stopping by Woods on a Snowy Evening," seem to be reminiscent of another time;

Figure 8.8 EDWARD HOPPER. *Early Sunday Morning.* 1930. [Courtesy, Collection of Whitney Museum of American Art, New York].

yet they express a lack of fulfillment and an uncertainty about existence not so acutely experienced in the Victorian period. In painting, artists who use a traditional realism are decidedly an undercurrent in a culture dominated by Abstraction and Expressionism. Yet they have solid technical foundations and highly expressive styles, which are not likely to be submerged in the final analysis of the era. In his realistic pictures of the American scene, Edward Hopper (1882–   ) captures the transcendent loneliness, the eerie stillness of the city amid its sunlit serenity. His *Early Sunday Morning* (Figure 8.8) might well serve as a visual counterpart to Copland's *Quiet City*. It has the vague nostalgia of a small town street, coupled with a strong geometrical precision and clear, penetrating colors. This is not the Romantic landscape with man reconciled in the bosom of nature, but the landscape made by man in all its ugliness and strange beauty. Charles Burchfield (1893–   ) pictures his native Ohio with a combination of love and the ruthless realism of a Romantic who rejects man-made ugliness. The strong, solid images of the Realists do not necessarily have a specific message to convey. They simply reflect a determination to speak of the condition of the human community in ways that can be understood without being outworn remnants of another era.

The texture of the twentieth-century artistic environment is extremely complex in the variety of stylistic trends which coexist in the same era. The whole range of man's capacity to absorb and unify artistic possibilities is represented within a state of almost compulsive change. Yet a fundamental dependence relies upon certain psychic and formal devices from the past. In all the aspects of the new world culture, the arts are an assertion, a reflection, and even a denial of their time.

SUMMARY OUTLINE

TWENTIETH-CENTURY SOCIETY

The Mechanical Age
The Atomic Age
The Electronic Age
The Age of Anxiety

GENERAL CULTURAL INFLUENCES

History: totalitarian ideology and Imperialism; World Wars I and II; League of Nations and United Nations; economic depression of 1929; rise of modern socialism; international wars of liberation; cold wars; Korean and Vietnamese conflicts.

Social Factors: democratic materialism; union movement; cultural lag; Keynesian economics; cold war secrecy and restrictions; radical individualism; American class warfare; changing familial structure and relationships; international cultural adaptations.

Philosophy and Religion: modern Existentialism in Sartre and Tillich; Logical Positivism; American Pragmatism; "death of God" theology; neo-orthodoxy; "demythologization" of Bible.

Science: as a dominant influence through Freudian psychology and Darwinian evolutionary theories; scientific archeology; golden age of mechanical inventions; atomic energy; Einstein's time-space continuum; electronics as science and industry.

MODERN CULTURAL CHARACTERISTICS: THE IMPACT OF MASS CULTURE

MUSICAL ATTRIBUTES

Man against society in Berg's *Wozzeck*

Prokofiev as social apologist in *War and Peace* and *Classical* Symphony.

ARTISTIC PARALLELS

Estrangement in Eliot's "The Wasteland"; Picasso's "Guernica" as protest painting; Rivera as social apologist in "The Liberation of the Peon."

THE IMPACT OF TECHNOLOGY: THE MACHINE AGE

Honegger's *Pacific 231;* Chavez's *HP;* Varèse's *Ionization;* Carpenter's *Sky-scrapers;* Antheil's *Ballet Mécanique.*

Futurism with Duchamp's "Nude Descending the Staircase"; Sandburg's "Portrait of a Motorcar"; Sheeler's "American Landscape."

THE IMPACT OF TECHNOLOGY: FEAR OF DEHUMANIZATION

Neoclassicism and the recovery of values in Stravinsky's *Oedipus Rex, Apollon Musagetes,* and *Symphony of Psalms.*

Neoclassicism in Picasso's "Lysistrata" etchings.

rejection of the machine in Orwell's "1984," Spenders "Two Armies," and Duchamp's "The Bride."

MODERN CULTURAL CHARACTERISTICS:
THE IMPACT OF SCIENCE

MUSICAL ATTRIBUTES

Schönberg's twelve-tone system; Webern's *Six Pieces for Orchestra;* development of electronic media.

ARTISTIC PARALLELS

Mondrian's analytical simplifications; Picasso's cubist phase in "Les Demoiselles d' Avignon."

THE EXPERIMENTAL METHOD

Bartók's *Mikrokosmos,* Ives's *Three Places in New England;* Stockhausen's electronic experimentation; Brant's use of tones in space; Xenakis's probability theory.

Op Art; Albers's color theories in "Homage to the Square," spatial concepts in Calder's mobiles; Pound's "Cantos;" e. e. cummings's visual poetry.

ANTIINTELLECTUALISM

Primitivism in Stravinsky's *The Rite of Spring;* chance music in John Cage's *Indeterminacy.*

Primitivism in Steinbeck's *Grapes of Wrath;* chance art in Pollock's action painting; Theater of the Absurd.

EXPLORATION OF THE MIND

Surrealism in Bartók's *Bluebeard's Castle;* Schönberg's *Erwartung* and *Pierrot Lunaire;* jazz improvisation.

Surrealism with Dali and de Chirico; Chagall's "Memories" series; Miró.

TRADITIONALISM

Vaughan Williams's *London* Symphony; *Five Tudor Portraits;* Copland's *El Salón México;* Bartók's *Hungarian Peasant Songs;* Villa-Lobos's *Bachianas Brasileiras;* Chavez's *Sinfonia India.*

Dylan Thomas's bardic lyricism; Frost's "After Apple Picking"; traditional realism in Hopper's "Early Sunday Morning."

Bibliography

The works listed have been found particularly helpful in the preparation of this book and are recommended for more detailed study in the various disciplines represented. Additional information may be obtained in individual biographies not listed here.

GENERAL WORKS

Apel, Willi. *Harvard Dictionary of Music.* Cambridge, Mass.: Harvard University Press, 1944.

Barnes, Harry E. *Intellectual and Cultural History of the Western World.* 3 vols. New York: Dover Publications, Inc., 1965.

Bauer, Marion. *Music Through the Ages.* New York: G. P. Putnam's Sons, 1946.

Brinton, Crane. *Ideas and Men.* Englewood Cliffs, N. J.: Prentice-Hall, Inc., 1950.

Cannon, Beekman, Alvin Johnson, and William Waite. *The Art of Music.* New York: Thomas Y. Crowell, 1960.

Chailley, Jaques. *40,000 Years of Music.* trans. by Rollo Myers. London: Macdonald, 1964.

286   Dorian, Frederick. *The History of Music in Performance.* 2d ed. New York: W. W. Norton, 1966.

Epperson, Gordon. *The Musical Symbol.* Ames, Iowa: Iowa State University Press, 1967.

Ewen, David. *Great Composers, 1300–1900.* New York: H. W. Wilson Co., 1966.

Ferguson, Donald. *A History of Musical Thought.* New York: Appleton-Century-Crofts, 1938.

Fleming, William. *Arts and Ideas.* 3d ed. New York: Holt, Rinehart and Winston, Inc., 1968.

Garvie, Peter, ed. *Music and Western Man.* London: Dent, 1958.

Geiringer, Karl. *Musical Instruments.* trans. by Bernard Miall. London: George Allen, 1949.

Gombrich, E. H. *The Story of Art.* 11th ed. New York: Phaidon, 1967.

Grout, Donald Jay. *A History of Western Music.* New York: W. W. Norton, 1960.

Hauser, Arnold. *The Social History of Art.* 2 vols. New York: Alfred Knopf, 1951.

Janson, H. W. *History of Art.* Englewood Cliffs, N. J.: Prentice-Hall, Inc., 1963.

Knobler, Nathan. *The Visual Dialogue.* New York: Holt, Rinehart and Winston, 1966.

Lang, Paul Henry. *Music in Western Civilization.* New York: W. W. Norton, 1941.

Lang, Paul Henry, and Otto Bettman. *A Pictorial History of Music.* New York: W. W. Norton, 1960.

Leichtentritt, Hugo. *Music, History and Ideas.* Cambridge, Mass.: Harvard University Press, 1958.

Morgenstern, Sam, ed. *Composers on Music.* New York: Pantheon, 1956.

Sachs, Curt. *The History of Musical Instruments.* New York: W. W. Norton, 1940.

van Loon, Hendrik Willem. *The Arts.* New York: Simon and Schuster, 1937.

Bibliography by Periods

MUSIC IN THE ANCIENT WORLD

Beckwith, John. *The Art of Constantinople.* London: Phaidon, 1961.

Byron, Robert. *The Byzantine Achievement.* New York: Russell and Russell, Inc., 1964.

Diehl, Charles. *Byzantium: Greatness and Decline.* trans. by Naomi Walford. New Jersey: Rutgers University Press, 1957.

Downey, Glanville. *Constantinople in the Age of Justinian.* Norman, Oklahoma: University of Oklahoma Press, 1960.

Engel, Carl. *The Music of the Most Ancient Nations.* London: The New Temple Press, 1929.

Hadas, Moses. *Imperial Rome.* Great Ages of Man series. New York: Time-Life, Inc., 1965.

Mathew, Gervase. *Byzantine Aesthetics.* New York: Viking Press, 1963.

Nettl, Bruno. *Music in Primitive Culture.* Cambridge, Mass.: Harvard University Press, 1956.

Reese, Gustave. *Music in the Middle Ages.* New York: W. W. Norton, 1940.

Robertson, Alec, and Denis Stevens, eds. *The Pelican History of Music,* vol. 1. Baltimore, Md.: Penguin Books, 1960.

Sachs, Curt. *The Rise of Music in the Ancient World.* New York: W. W. Norton, 1943.

288   Säve-Söderbergh, Torgny. *Pharoahs and Mortals.* London: Robert Hale, Ltd., 1961.

Wellesz, Egon. *A History of Byzantine Music and Hymnography.* 2d ed. Oxford: Clarendon Press, 1961.

Werner, Eric. *The Sacred Bridge.* New York: Columbia University Press, 1960.

MIDDLE AGES AND RENAISSANCE

Burckhardt, Jacob. *Civilization of the Renaissance in Italy.* New York: Washington Square Press, 1958.

Harmon, Alec and Anthony Milner. *Late Renaissance and Baroque Music.* London: Barrie and Rockliff, 1959.

Meyer, Ernest H. *English Chamber Music.* London: Lawrence and Wishart, 1946.

Pattison, Bruce. *Music and Poetry of the English Renaissance.* London: Methuen, 1948.

Reese, Gustave. *Music in the Middle Ages.* New York: W. W. Norton, 1940.

_____. *Music in the Renaissance.* New York: W. W. Norton, 1959.

THE BAROQUE ERA

Blitzer, Charles. *Age of Kings,* Great Ages of Man series. New York: Time–Life, Inc., 1967.

Bukofzer, Manfred E. *Music in the Baroque Era.* New York: W. W. Norton, 1947.

Gay, Peter. *Age of Enlightenment,* Great Ages of Man series. New York: Time–Life, Inc., 1966.

Gramont, Sanche de. *The Age of Magnificence* (Memoirs of the Duc de Saint-Simon). New York: Capricorn Books, 1964.

Helm, Ernest Eugene. *Music at the Court of Frederick the Great.* Norman, Oklahoma: University of Oklahoma Press, 1960

CLASSICISM AND ROMANTICISM

Courthion, Pierre. *Romanticism.* trans. by Stuart Gilbert. Cleveland, Ohio: World Publishing Co., 1961.

Einstein, Alfred. *Music in the Romantic Era.* New York: W. W. Norton, 1947.

Gilman, Lawrence. *Nature in Music.* 2d ed. New York: Books for Libraries
Press, 1966.
Locke, Arthur Ware. *Music and the Romantic Movement in France.* New York:
E. P. Dutton, 1920.
Pleasants, Henry, ed. *The Musical World of Robert Schumann.* New York:
St. Martin's Press, 1965.

IMPRESSIONISM AND THE TWENTIETH CENTURY

Austin, William W. *Music in the Twentieth Century.* New York: W. W. Norton,
1966.
Bauer, Marion. *Twentieth Century Music.* New York: G. P. Putnam's Sons,
1947.
Collaer, Paul. *A History of Modern Music.* trans. by Sally Abeles. New York:
World Publishing Co., 1961.
Cornell, Kenneth. *The Post-Symbolist Period.* New Haven, Conn.: Yale Univer-
sity Press, 1958.
Goodrich, Lloyd and John I. H. Bauer. *American Art of Our Century.* New
York: Frederick A. Praeger, Inc., 1961.
Hall, James B., and Barry Ulanov. *Modern Culture and the Arts.* New York:
McGraw-Hill Book Co., 1967.
Hansen, Peter S. *An Introduction to Twentieth Century Music.* Boston: Allyn
and Bacon, Inc., 1961.
Lippard, Lucy R. *Pop Art.* New York: Frederick A. Praeger, Inc., 1966.
Machlis, Joseph. *Introduction to Contemporary Music.* New York: W. W.
Norton, 1961.
McMullen, Roy. "Music, Painting, and Sculpture," *The Great Ideas Today.*
Chicago: Encyclopedia Britannica, Inc., William Benton, Publisher,
1967.
Read, Herbert. *A Concise History of Modern Painting.* London: Jarrold and
Sons, 1959.
Schwartz, Elliot, and Barney Childs. *Contemporary Composers on Contemporary
Music.* New York: Holt, Rinehart and Winston, Inc., 1967.
Seroff, Victor I. *Debussy: Musician of France.* New York: G. P. Putnam's Sons,
1956.
Slonimsky, Nicholas. *Music Since 1900.* 3d. rev. ed. New York: Coleman-
Ross, 1949.
Symons, Arthur. *The Symbolist Movement in Literature.* New York: E. P.
Dutton and Co., Inc. 1958.
Ulanov, Barry. *A History of Jazz in America.* New York: The Viking Press,
Inc., 1952.

COLLECTIONS

History of Music in Sound (10-vol. set). RCA Victor LM 6057. Commentary
     booklets published by Oxford University Press.
Masterpieces of Music Before 1750 (3-record set). Haydn Society Records 9040.
     Commentary book by Carl Parrish and John Ohl published by W.
     W. Norton.
Ten Centuries of Music (10-record set). Archive Records.
A Treasury of Early Music (4-record set). Haydn Society Records 9103.
     Commentary book by Carl Parrish published by W. W. Norton.

SPECIFIC WORKS LISTED BY CHAPTERS

The recommended recordings are listed in the order in which they
appear within each chapter. Those works which are specifically mentioned
or analyzed in the text are marked by an asterisk (*). Other musical forms
or specific works also readily available are included under the relevant
form or composer.

CHAPTER 1: THE ANCIENT WORLD

Much material for this section is included under the general works.
See also listings under primitive, ancient, and nonwestern peoples and
under Folkways Recordings. Byzantine Music is often found listed as Russian Liturgical Music or Russian Orthodox Choral Music. For Jewish music
see listings under Synagogue Music.

CHAPTER 2: MIDDLE AGES

For Gregorian Chant see that subject listing, or look for Collections:
Choral section in the record catalogue.
Machaut: *Mass of Notre Dame*, Ballades, Rondeau, Virelais.
The Play of Daniel
The Play of Herod

CHAPTER 3: RENAISSANCE

Dufay: *Missa L'Homme Armé*
Josquin des Pres: Masses, Motets, Instrumental pieces
Gabrieli: Canzoni for Brass Choirs

Sacrae Symphonae

Palestrina: *Missa Papae Marcelli, Missa Brevis, Magnificat*
Reformation Music: see the Liturgical Service (Episcopal)
Samuel Scheidt: organ works
Walther: chorale preludes
Byrd: *Magnificat*, Madrigals, Motets, Anthems
Gesualdo: *Italian Madrigals
Morley: *Elizabethan Madrigals, Ayres, Harpsichord pieces
Jannequin: *Chansons
Bull: Keyboard Music

CHAPTER 4: BAROQUE

Rameau: *Pièces de Clavicin*
Monteverdi: *Orfeo, The Return of Ulysses*, Madrigals
Lully: *Bourgeois Gentilhomme, The Triumph of Love*
Frederick II (The Great): *Sonatas for Flute*
Purcell: *Dido and Aeneas, The Fairy Queen*, Anthems, Suites for Harpsichord
Sweelinck: Organ Music, Psalms
J. S. Bach: *Passion According to St. John,* *Musical Offering, Well Tempered Clavier,
   *Passacaglia and Fugue in C Minor, *Brandenburg Concerto #5*, Cantatas
   (especially Nos. 1, 4, 80, and 106).
Vivaldi: Concerti for Orchestra (*The Four Seasons*) Motets, *Magnificat*.
Handel: *Messiah, *Water Music, *Royal Fireworks Music, *Israel in Egypt,
   Judas Maccabaeus.*

CHAPTER 5: CLASSICAL ERA

Couperin: *L'Art de Toucher le Clavicin, Concerts Royaux, Lamentations of Jeremiah*
Gluck: *Orfeo ed Euridice, Iphigénie en Aulide*
Scarlatti: *Harpsichord Sonatas
Haydn: *Symphony #104*, also Nos. 94 ("Surprise"), 101 ("Clock"), and
   103 ("Drumroll"), *The Creation*

Mozart: *Marriage of Figaro, *Don Giovanni, *Requiem, Serenade in G (*Eine Kleine Nachtmusik*), Sonatas for Piano, Symphonies, particularly No. 35 ("Haffner"), and No. 41 ("Jupiter").

Beethoven: Symphonies, especially *No. 6 ("Pastorale") No. 3 ("Eroica") and No. 9 ("Choral"). String Quartets, Piano Sonatas, especially No. 8 ("Pathétique") No. 14 ("Moonlight"), No. 21 ("Waldstein"), and No. 29 ("Hammerklavier"), Missa Solemis.

CHAPTER 6: ROMANTICISM

Schubert: String Quartets, particularly No. 14 ("Death and the Maiden"), Quintet in A ("Trout"), *Die Schöne Müllerin, *Winterreise, Symphonies, particularly No. 8 ("Unfinished") and No. 9 ("The Great").

Mahler: *Songs of the Earth, Nine Symphonies.

Schumann: *Carnaval, *Scenes from Childhood, Symphony No. 1 ("Spring") and No. 4 ("Rhenish").

Chopin: *Etudes, Ballades, Mazurkas, Scherzos.

Berlioz: *Symphonie Fantastique, Childhood of Christ. Requiem.

Liszt: *Les Preludes, *Transcendental Etudes, Piano Concertos, Hungarian Rhapsodies.

Strauss: *Also Sprach Zarathustra, *Salome, *Till Eulenspiegel, Death and Transfiguration, Don Juan.

Wagner: *Tristan and Isolde, The Ring of the Nibelungs, The Flying Dutchman, Tannhäuser, The Mastersingsers of Nuremberg.

CHAPTER 7: IMPRESSIONISM

Franck: Organ Music, Symphony in D, Symphonic Variations for Piano and Orchestra.

Fauré: Requiem, Songs.

Debussy: *Pelléas and Mélisande, *Prelude to the Afternoon of a Faun, Images for Orchestra, *La Mer.

Ravel: *Daphnis and Chloé, Rhapsodie Espagnol, La Valse.

CHAPTER 8: TWENTIETH CENTURY

Berg: *Wozzeck, Lulu, Lyric Suite.

Prokofiev: *Classical Symphony in D, Romeo and Juliet.

Honegger: *Pacific 231, King David.

Villa-Lobos: *Bachianas Brasilierás (No. 5 particularly).

Chavez: Toccata for Percussion, Sinfonia India

Varèse: *Ionization, Octandre.*

Stravinsky: *Symphony of Psalms, Pulcinella, Octet for Wind Instruments, Canticum Sacrum, Firebird Suite, The Rite of Spring.*

Schönberg: *Pierrot Lunaire, *Erwartung, Verklärte Nacht.*

Webern: *Five Pieces for Orchestra,* *Six Pieces for Orchestra.*

Bartok: *Music for Strings, Percussion, and Celeste,* *Quartets (particularly No. 4), *Mikrokosmos, Concerto for Orchestra.*

Jazz by Ellington, Parker, and Brubeck.

Stockhausen: *No. 5 Zeitmasse, Gesang der Junglinge, Mikrophonie II.*

Cage: *Amores* (for prepared piano and percussion), *Indeterminacy.*

Vaughan Williams: *Symphony No. 2* ("London"), *Symphony No. 1* ("Sea"), *Fantasia on a Theme by Tallis.*

Copland: *Appalachian Spring, *El Salón México, Symphony No. 3.*

Name Index

A

Addison, Joseph, 120
Akhnaton, 7
Albers, Joseph, 265
Ambrose of Milan, 46
Apollo, 13,16
Aristotle, 15, 17, 64, 82
Aristoxenus, 10

B

Bach, C. P. E., 153
Bach, J. S., 133, 135–140
Bartôk, Béla, 261, 272, 280
Baudelaire, Charles, 225
Beethoven, Ludwig van, 162–167, 196
Berg, Alban, 241
Berlioz, Hector, 179, 201

Blake, William, 179
Boethius, 45
Brahms, Johannes, 179, 193, 252
Byrd, William, 102

C

Cage, John, 270
Calvin, John, 98
Carissimi, Giacomo, 125
Chardin, Jean, 148
Charlemagne, Emperor, 47, 54
Charles II of England, 130
Chopin, Frédéric, 198
Constable, John, 182
Copland, Aaron, 279
Couperin, François, 121, 148
Courbet, Gustave, 220
cummings, e. e., 267

Subject Index